An Indispensable Man

A Novel
by
Bob Ford

Copyright 2005 by Bob Ford

ISBN   0-976-6524 – 0-4

Correspondence should be addressed to:

Bob Ford
29 Woodberry Ln.
Nantucket, MA 02554

To
Bonnie, of course
and to
Marvel Sebert - Bay Village High
School
She taught me the joy
of putting words on paper.

1
Vocational Adjustment

That management had misspelled Angus Waddington's name on his retirement watch was disappointing, but not surprising. It was, in fact, a kind of left-handed tribute to his corporate longevity and his determination to remain virtually invisible so that he might slip through the years totally unnoticed by the gods of employee downsizing. During his son's formative years, he had tried to impart his personal philosophy for survival in school: "Don't sit in the front row or the back row. Those are the people who get noticed by the teacher. Sit somewhere in the middle, off to the side where they really can't see you. Blend in. Avoid eye contact. Don't volunteer. The only time you should raise your hand is when you can't wait for the bathroom break." And then when Preston got his first job, Angus offered this: "Keep a low profile, son. Keep your head down. Don't spend too much time in one place. Remember, it's hard to hit a moving target. If you think there's chance you might screw something up, pass the buck. Always be ready to pin the blame-tail on somebody else."

Several years after his retirement, Angus had an epiphany that he felt compelled to share with his son whose employment with the Car Company had begun to look tenuous, if not terminal. "In addition to all the advice I've given you about keeping a low profile, there's one more thing you need to know,"

Angus began, "if you want to survive in the corporate world, you've got to find a way to make yourself indispensable."

"Keep a low profile and make myself indispensable? In a company with over two thousand employees. How do I do that?"

His father smiled. "I wish I had an answer, but I'm afraid, my boy, that's something you have to figure out for yourself."

Preston Waddington did figure it out for himself, but it wasn't easy. The process began the day he felt *her* presence outside his office cubical. When he turned around and looked up, he saw an intensely thin, boney-looking woman dressed in a white blazer, with a small insignia on her breast pocket that he could not read. She wore a white skirt, white stockings, white shoes, and her hair was white, not grey white, but silky white. Even her skin had an albino-like whiteness to it.

She smiled down at him with suspect benevolence. "My name is Felicity Truehart, and I'd like to have you pick up all your personal belongings and follow me."

She continued smiling at him, but he did not find her smile the kind of smile one would expect of someone who was about to sit down for a pleasant chat. What was it with her smile? It didn't look real. It was almost as if she'd been the victim of a bad face-lift that deadened the nerves around her mouth and left her with a ridiculous grin permanently plastered over her teeth. She repeated her instructions, "I'd like to have you pick up all your personal belongings and follow me."

"Why?" Preston asked blankly.

"That will be made clear to you in a few moments," the woman in white said.

She held out her hand in the same way she might have offered it to a small child before crossing a busy street. He stared at her fingers. They were as boney, white, and as unappetizing as the rest of her. Preston tacitly declined the offer.

"Please, just come with me, and we'll do our best to make this as painless as possible."

Painless did she say? Why are we talking about pain? He wondered.

"I'm waiting, Mr. Waddington." Her voice was now laced with impatience.

Sonnavabitch! I'm being canned. That's what this is all about. They're firing me. His stomach dropped somewhere just above his shoe tops, leaving a hollow place in his mid-section for panic to run rampant.

"We are on a schedule, Mr. Waddington." There was urgency in her voice.

"They operate like a swat team," he'd been told by a neighbor who'd been the victim of downsizing at his plastics company. "Their tactic is to sneak onto an office floor, target the victims, and then surprise 'em, strip 'em, and slip 'em out fast, before they can do any damage or alert other employees to what's going down."

"Please, just your personal things," she repeated.

The woman is a broken record, Preston thought.

"We'll take care of the rest."

7

"I've been fired, right?"

"Let's just say that you have been ..." She paused as if intent on finding the right term. She found one. "Vocationally Adjusted."

"Which is another way of saying I've been fired," Preston responded, making no attempt to suppress his obvious disdain for the euphemism.

"We would like you to think of this experience as being given the opportunity to reset your career horizon." The plastic surgeon's mistake remained fixed in place.

"Is there any reason the word 'fired' seems to be missing from your vocabulary?"

"It's not a pretty word," she said.

"It's not a pretty act, either" Preston retorted.

"Now, Mr. Waddington," she said, avoiding eye contact and addressing herself to a point high above his head as though she expected her words to rise, then cascade over him like a warm shower, "the first rule of successful career redirection is to adopt a positive mental attitude."

Screw a positive mental attitude. Preston was angry. What had he done to deserve this? Was this just some random act that he had fallen victim to? Or was there someone upstairs that had it in for him? He took a deep breath and stared at the desk that had been his office home for over four years. He picked up his briefcase, the picture of his wife and young daughter, a couple of books, and then glanced around to see if there was anything else he should be taking with him.

"*Just* the personal items," Felicity Truehart reminded him in a voice that did little to mask the authority she was prepared to exercise. "Try and think of this as an old door closing, and that I'm here to help you open a new door in your life."

The thought of having to face his wife with the news of his firing weighed heavily on him. The fact that he would be without a paycheck was bad enough, but first he had to endure the humiliation of having to walk past all his fellow employees knowing that they knew he was being carted off to Outplacementville.

As he left his cubicle, he felt like one of those criminals he'd seen on the television news being led off to the police station. The *perp walk*. Only they always seemed to be carrying raincoats that they used to hide their faces. But he didn't have a raincoat. There was no cover, no way to hide his face. He would have to bear the full shame of having been selected for Vocational Adjustment. Barely a dozen steps out of his office, he realized that he didn't need a raincoat.

As Preston looked out over the sea of cubicles, he saw dozens of Felicity Truehart clones, both male and female, each delivering a personalized and smiling *coup de grace*. At least he was not alone. Blood was everywhere. It was now evident that his selection had been just the luck, the bad luck, of the downsizing draw.

The elevator carrying Felicity Truehart and Preston sank to the lowest floor in the building. To the best of his recollection, he had never ventured into the sub-basement. The woman in white was talking at Preston. Not *with* him. *At* him. He was doing his best to ignore the litany of little reassurances and simple platitudes presumably programmed into her training to help facilitate the acceptance and adjustment phase. He wanted her to stop talking. No, he wanted God to strike her dumb. And if God wouldn't accommodate him, he was prepared to take matters into his own hands. If management had intended that he direct his anger toward her, and not toward them, they were succeeding.

The elevator released them into a long, dimly lit passageway that looked foreign and strange to Preston. For a moment, he was convinced that somehow they had passed out of the building altogether. At the end of the hall, he saw double doors begin to open, slowly, filling the corridor with a bright, white light. A man appeared, silhouetted in the doorway.

Felicity Truehart stopped and moved aside, gesturing for him to continue. "I will rejoin you later," she said. Her voice was hushed, as though they had entered a funeral chapel.

As Preston approached, the man in the doorway spoke to him in the same genteel tone and manner as the woman in white. Clearly, their training involved some type of procedural cloning. "My name is Bob, and I'm here to help you through this."

"Bob? Just Bob?" Preston expected him to have a more imposing name.

"Just Bob," Bob affirmed.

Preston was immediately struck by how big Bob was. He had been handed off to what appeared to be a bar bouncer turned outplacement specialist.

Preston imagined that he could, and possibly would, use his size to deal conclusively with any of those being Vocationally Adjusted who might decide to rebel or express their displeasure in some aggressive manner. Preston could not make out Bob's facial features as he was still silhouetted by the bright white light behind him. He could, however, see that Bob's head was large, and that there had been a long interval since his last visit to a barber. Preston found himself involuntarily amused that this large, faceless, hairy man was the angel assigned to escort him to the way station of unemployment. He was wrong. The Angel Bob simply pointed him into a large room filled with chairs and an assemblage of employees who had suffered the same fate as he.

It was an Ellis Island of despondent rejects. A grey cloud of humiliation hung heavy in the room. Preston noticed that a few of the people were openly voicing their anger, two were crying, and several others stared blankly at the floor. He found a seat, leaned back, and stared at the ceiling, wishing that somewhere in the acoustic tiles, he might find some answers. What now? What would he do? He had to have a paycheck. He had a mortgage, car payments, a three-year-old daughter with an asthmatic condition, and his wife was expecting their second child in less than two months. Maybe there would be severance pay, but how long would it last? To the next job?

An hour passed. Two hours. Preston looked up every time another unfortunate arrived. It wasn't long until all the chairs were filled. Those who straggled in last were resigned to sitting on the floor or holding up a wall. More time passed and he wondered why someone hadn't appeared to talk to them. Where were Felicity Truehart and the Angel Bob? Was he supposed to sign something? Meet with an outplacement specialist? Leave?

At first, he wasn't sure what it was that had been placed on his shoulder. But a quick glance revealed the pressure had come from one of Angel Bob's enormous paws. His other handheld out a folded piece of paper.

"It seems you will not be going on with us. Another time, perhaps, but not today." The Angel Bob sounded as if he regretted having to disappoint him. "You've been called back." He handed him the message. "It appears Mr. Axel McPherson has other plans for you."

***

McPherson, a VP who was Preston's boss, had brought him back from the brink. Apparently, Human Resources ,in their frenzy to reduce the headcount, had never seen Axel's memo promoting Preston to sales training manager and had, inadvertently, included him in the carnage.

At first, Preston was just happy to have survived the purge. He felt reasonably secure knowing that his job was protected under Axel's VP umbrella. But as more employees from various departments found themselves meeting with clones of Felicity Truehart and the Angel Bob, and as it became clear that no one's job was totally secure, Preston decided he had to find some way to protect himself. He made up his mind to take his father's advice and create an aspect of his job that was so important, so indispensable to the company as to make him immune to layoffs, budget cuts, or the caprice of some bean counter. An idea began to form and take shape in his mind ... *a plan* was born. It rolled out in front of his eyes like a red carpet bearing weekly paychecks leading all the way to retirement. And, hopefully, maybe even to a promotion. Maybe several promotions. An unobstructed route to the executive floor. *Yes! Yes! Yes! That's it!*

To implement his plan, Preston got his name inserted on the distribution list for the manufacturing division's daily production standards compliance reports. Each day, the foremen on the several production lines would record endless columns of figures and production details that would numb the faculties and stifle the discernment of even the most fanatical production manager. In truth, ninety-five percent of the information in these reports was unnecessary. Like many things in corporations, the reports had long since become part of the daily fabric. Preston organized the minutiae and numbers, reformatted the reports, and added pages of commentary which only restated in words that which was immediately apparent in the numbers. The result of his effort was a several hundred-page document that he titled the *Company Eyes Only* report. Soon, management referred to it simply as the *CEO*.

Preston was sure that someone would see the CEO for what it was and a clone of Felicity

Truehart would knock at his cubicle and send him to outplacementville. Months passed and no knock came. He continued to look for ways to enhance his report.

He decided it would add impact if he had a large rubber stamp made with red ink that read: *"Private Information---Approved Distribution List Only."* Soon to be included on the *CEO* distribution list, became a status symbol that the chosen managers who could point to their copy of the CEO as one more testament to their importance. So highly regarded was his publication that upper management moved him up four floors, gave him an office with a door, a raise and assigned him a secretary.

As time went by and no one questioned what he was doing, or why, or even who had authorized the publication, he began to add reports and documents from other departments - marketing, sales, finance. Within less than two years, virtually everyone in the company assumed that copies of all documents and reports, whatever the subject, should be sent to Preston.

Once all the information was in Preston's hands, he would sort and sift and evaluate for inclusion. His monthly reports were masterpieces of dull reading. He worked hard to be sure that it would be literally impossible for any of those on the distribution list to read more than the first page without having their eyes glaze over. Unlike most people who create reports, Preston's goal was not to inspire praise for the content, but to create awe at the poundage. He understood that the larger the document, the greater its perceived importance, but the lower its actual readership. The last thing he wanted was for someone to read, *really* read, the *CEO* for fear they might begin to ask questions: "Do we really need this?" or "Aren't we wasting a lot of paper duplicating reports we already have? Should the company be wasting its time on this?" Yes, a perceptive reader could have well been his undoing. But the odds were against that ever happening. One thing Preston had learned during his years with the corporation: The company was long on egos, but short on perceptive readers.

During the third year of the *CEO*'s publication, he conceived a *truly* brilliant idea. He decided to add a summary page to the front of the report. It proved to be a masterstroke. As he explained to his father during a visit to Sun City, "You're an executive and a report crosses your desk. What's the one thing you'd really like to see in that summary?"

"That the company is making money."

"That's secondary. What you really want to see is ... *your name*. But only if it's associated with something positive, praiseworthy, or even heroic. When people see their names praised in a report, they feel good about themselves and more importantly, they feel good about the person who put their name there in the first place."

That was the essence and brilliance of his summary page. Preston never found fault, never criticized, never questioned production decisions or noted declines in productivity or sales. He made sure his reports praised, lauded, commended, complemented, and extolled leadership. He created high profile heroes of dozens of men, if not in the eyes of their underlings who knew better, at least in the summary pages of his report.

His success with the CEO aside, he nevertheless lived in fear that his bogus publication would be exposed. One day, the company president, Charles Fair came to him with a complement and a suggestion. He loved the *Company Eyes Only*. "But wouldn't it be an even better publication if each monthly report contained a note, a quote, and a pithy bit of industry insight from the president?"

Talk about validating the weekly report and assuring its longevity. Preston was more than happy to accommodate him. The *Fair Opinion* from the company's president became a featured segment in *Company Eyes Only*. The president's sycophants loved it. And, Preston was told, so did members of the board of directors. Charlie decided to move Preston up to the executive floor and give him a raise and VP title. Charlie also made a point at one of his quarterly management meeting to declare that the CEO report was an *indispensable* component of inner company communications. And by inference, so was its creator.

There was only one problem: He was doing both his job as sales training manager and *CEO* publisher too well. He had, in the eyes of upper management, become exactly what he had aspired to become - *indispensable*. For that reason, no one wanted to see him promoted. He was simply too valuable, too *indispensable* where he was. All his hard work had done nothing more than to leave him stranded in the same job for almost fifteen years. He was like the mountain climber who chooses the wrong route to the summit and finds himself on a ledge with but two options: hang on or jump off.

2.
How It All Began

The showroom floor that morning at Jack Poor Motors in Greenwich, Connecticut, was deader than roadkill until *she* walked in.

"My God," one salesman blurted impulsively as his feet fell off his desk. "She right out of a Victoria Secret's catalogue.!"

If not her twin, a reasonable facsimile. She was what one might expect to encounter in a <u>Victoria's Secret</u> catalogue: leggy, five-nine to five-ten, balanced confidently atop five-inch spiked heels. She had long ashen blond hair that fell with a planned carelessness over twin orbs that rose invitingly above the top of her low-cut mini blouse. The blouse itself looked as if the blouse-maker had run out of fabric at about her belly button. Her short, white leather skirt had all the inherent properties of shrink wrap. This was not the type of customer any of the five salesmen on the floor ever expected to see in their showroom. Down the street at the Beemer or Benz dealerships, maybe. But not here.

"Who's up, is it?" *(Translation: Car salesmen's parlance for whose turn is it to wait on a customer.)* The question came from a salesman on the opposite side of the sales floor as he sprang from his chair and adjusted his tie.

"Fuck whose up it is," Spud Korman, the ales said. "She's mine."

Barely noticed as she paraded her package of

pulchritude across the showroom in the direction of a Verite 300 sports coupe was Alfie Swenson, a fiftyish, slightly balding man who trailed slightly behind her like a dog out for its morning walk. He stood a good four inches shorter than his tower of delight and wore the apparel and jewelry adornments of a man on the downhill side of a mid-life crisis, making a last stab at reaffirming his virility. His beige cashmere sport coat, the open-collar blue shirt with just a hint of chest hair showing, the heavy gold-plated chains around his neck, the gold Rolex on his wrist, and Bruno Magli shoes suggested that he could more than afford the eye-candy at his side. It also spoke loudly to what she saw in him.

"Welcome to Jack Poor Motors," Korman said, extending his hand to Alfie, but taking advantage of the opportunity to let his eyes accept the invitation offered by the woman's attire. "My name is Spud Korman. What can I do for you today?"

"I'm Florence," the woman volunteered in a high-pitched, baby doll-like voice. She held out her hand to Korman. "We're here to buy a car."

"I knew right away you weren't here to buy a boat," he joked. She gave him an uncomprehending and confused look. Alfie, who got the joke, didn't laugh. *Oops*, Spud thought. *Not good. Sales train just jumped the track. Get it back, quick.* "Well, what might I show you today?"

Alfie, who had the nervous impatience of a dog in heat, spoke rapidly and intently. "I'd like to buy that Verite 300." Alfie pointed to the silver sports car sitting in the middle of the showroom floor. "That one. Right there. As it sits. And I want to drive it outta here in the next thirty minutes."

Jack Poor *the* Jack Poor whose name was splashed all over the exterior and interior of the dealership–had been on his way down to the floor to harangue his sales force for the lack of sales activity. Gravity had not been kind to Jack Poor. In his fifties it had pulled what were once broad shoulders and a trim waist into something that more resembled a pear. The part in his black hair had widened from a thin line to a six-inch barren landing strip. He attempted to cover it by letting his hair grow long on the left side of his head and then combing it over to the right. To keep the comb-over in place, he used a heavy jell that left his head looking as if he'd stood too close to a lube job. By the time he was sixty, his face like his body, had drifted south, with fat filling his jowls like saddlebags. His mustache was scruffy as though his razor had malfunctioned for the last several days. Now, at sixty-seven, he looked every bit the satirical treatment one might expect from a cartoonist drawing the classic nail-their-shoes-to-the-floor-and-squeeze-the-weasels-for-every-nickel-they've-got car dealer.

The moment Jack spotted Florence, he decided to exercise his privilege as the owner and opt for a closer look at this marvelous specimen of womanhood. He would not have been surprised to see staple holes in her mid-section, which he was delighted to find available for viewing. This was indeed a two-trick pony.

"I'm Jack Poor, *the* Jack Poor," he said, holding out his hand to Alfie. "Welcome to my dealership and you are ...?"

"My name is Alfie Swenson." Before Alfie could complete introducing himself, Jack turned to give his attention to Florence and Swenson ended up offering his name to the back of Jack's suitcoat.

"We'd like that silver car, there," she said, pointing to the Verite 300. "I just love it. It's really me. Don't you think so, Alfie?"

Alfie might have thought so, but his expression was not unlike that of a man suffering an attack of acid reflux. Looking around, he could see one salesman after another seeming to find a pressing reason to come onto the floor and busy himself near the Verite. He obviously did not appreciate having Florence the object of these gawkers. His annoyance showed when he barked, "Look, if you're going to let me buy this car, say so. If not, we'll take a walk."

"Mr. ... Mr. ... Mr. ...?" Jack was begging for his name.

"It's *still* Alfie Swenson," he said, obviously irritated that Jack had forgotten his name in the space of fifteen seconds.

Jack put his arm on Alfie's shoulder and turned on the charm. After all, while enjoying the landscape of a delectable woman was nectar for the imagination, a man with a checkbook was manna for the bottom line. "Mr. Swenson, I assure you that we're here to sell cars and from where I stand, this car has your name written all over it. We're having a hell of a time keeping these in stock, and I hate to give up a display car." There were fifteen more like it outside, but Jack was sure Alfie hadn't noticed. "But we're here to serve our customers. If this is the car you want, it's yours."

"Then, do it. How long is this going to take?"

Nothing like a man in heat looking to buy a car, Jack thought. *His brain is in his pants and my hand is in his wallet. He won't know what the hell he's buying. One nice payday on the way.*

"Well, Mr. Swenson, I'm sure Mr. Korman here can have the papers ready for you to sign in just a few minutes. Are you interested in looking at our finance package? We've got some very attractive rates."

"You take credit cards, right?" Alfie asked.

"Of course," Jack replied. "Credit cards are as good as cash." He smiled. And he might have added, but did not, better than a check which would have to be certified and leave little room for Korman to load the deal with extras.

"I'd like to try it on," Florence giggled, approaching the Verite's passenger side door.

If ever a woman had the ability to make getting into a car look X-rated, she was that woman. One of the salesmen quickly stepped up to the car to open the door for her. But instead of opening it and stepping back toward the rear of the car, he stood in front of the door, pulling it to him and stepping backward toward the front of the car. Still holding the door, he positioned himself so that he had an unobstructed view of the car seat. As Florence sat down, she swung first one leg and then the other inside which, for an extended moment, caused her short dress to open, giving the salesman a clear view all the way up her thighs to the frilly white triangle that passed for her underwear. It was an old salesman's trick called a "beaver shoot," and the salesmen at Jack Poor Motors were all expert marksmen when it came to beavers.

Korman pulled Jack aside and said, "Defiantly a spot delivery." *(Translation: The customer buys and takes delivery of the car on the spot.)*

"This guy is so hot to get in her pants, he's gonna pay any price we give him," Jack Poor said. "Bang him for a full sticker. No discount. Then bump him with every goddamn thing we can add to the invoice. An extended warranty, rust protection, fabric protection, paint protection, the whole nine yards."

Korman invited Alfie and Florence to sit down at his desk. Jack Poor, who normally would have excused himself and let his salesman conclude the deal, found it convenient to take up a position that afforded a view down Florence's front.

It was not often that a lay down *(Translation: A customer ready to pay the full sticker price without asking for a discount or bothering to negotiate the price.)* walked into the showroom. Especially Jack Poor's showroom. Korman maintained a steady stream of obsequious what-a-great-deal-I'm-giving-you-because-I-really-like-you persiflage, all the while adding up the numbers and tacking on every option and warranty coverage he could think of. Spud Korman could have been talking to stone.

"Whatever, whatever! Let's get this done," Alfie kept saying. "Here's my credit card. Where do I sign?"

As Korman hurried to fill out the order, Florence popped up and circled the car, caressing it in the most suggestive manner. When Florence returned to Alfie's side, she purred, "I get to drive it a lot, right?"

"Anytime you want. In fact, you can take it home every night, if you like."

"What will the others in the office say?"

"It's my car. I'm the boss. So, it's none of their damn business."

"Ooooh, Alfie," she purred. "You're the best boss I've ever had." She supplemented her appreciation by casually rubbing her right breast on his arm and whispering in his ear what appeared, to the onlookers, as a salacious secret. Alfie's carnal reward was fully primed.

"I can drive it off the floor, right? I mean, like right now?" Alfie's impatience was bordering on the comical.

"Right," Korman replied, doing his best not to laugh at the scene being played out across his desk.

"What do I do about license plates?"

"We can put our dealer plates on until you get it registered."

"Good. Do it."

"George!" Korman called to one of the salesmen. "Put dealer plates on this Verite."

Alfie signed the credit card chit without even looking at the total. It could have been for double the amount, but at that moment, he didn't appear to care. Once the plates were on, Swenson and Florence got into the car.

"Would you like me to explain the controls and some of the features?" Korman asked.

"Some other time."

"If you drive it around back, we'll fill it up with gas."

"I'll get it later."

Two salesmen pushed back the large sliding glass doors that were installed so that display cars could be easily driven on and off the showroom floor. Alfie started the sport coupe and drove it through the open doors, down the driveway and into the street. The entire transaction had been completed in twenty-three minutes. A record for Jack Poor Motors. The salesmen who had been witness to the transaction were useless, at least more useless than normal, for the next three hours as they entertained each other with their individual recounting and imitations of what they had witnessed.

***

The Verite 300 left Greenwich on I-95, took the ramp to I-287, and headed toward Tarrytown, New York, on the Hudson River. When Alfie got to Tarrytown, he left 287, and took Route 9 north along the Hudson River. Destination? Two days of *coitus noninterruptus* at the plush Hudson Resort and Spa lay ahead. The road was lightly traveled and the swelling in his trousers seemed to have a correlating effect on the pressure he was putting on the gas pedal. He never saw the cop with the radar sitting off to the side. The road began to wind and Swenson, who envisioned himself as an unrequited Mario Andretti, decided to impress Florence with his driving skills.

The road felt good. The car felt good. Suddenly he felt her unzip his fly. The blond head descended slowly into his lap. The road signs indicated a curve ahead and announced that 25mph was the appropriate speed. The Verite 300 was doing at least sixty.

***

It was after five o'clock when Jack Poor walked out of his dealership. He was about to get in his car when a flatbed trailer pulled into the dealership carrying a Verite 300 that looked as if it had been run over by a truck.

"What's this?" Jack asked the driver.

"This, I think," the driver nodded in the direction of the Verite, "is one sorry looking hunk of metal. We didn't know what to do with it. Cops said since the car had your dealer plates on it, we should bring it here."

Jack immediately recognized it as the car Alfie Swenson and Florence had driven off the floor not six hours before. "Where's the owner? And the bimbo? When he left here, he was with one great looking piece of tail."

"And he still is. They're both on a slab in a morgue somewhere."

"They're dead?" he asked, genuinely shocked.

The driver shrugged and nodded.

"Jesus! How'd it happen?"

"It was pretty much self-inflicted. According to the cops, they were chasing this guy up Route 9 north of Tarrytown. He had this car flyin.' Fifty-five, sixty maybe. And considering they found him with his Johnson hangin' out and her head in his lap, he was flyin' in more ways than one. What got 'em was the sucker curve."

"Sucker curve?" Jack asked.

"Yeah. That's what they call a descending radius curve."

"Which is …?"

"A curve that tends to turn in on itself. At high speeds it can be tricky to negotiate. 'Specially if you got some broad's mouth on your dick. The cop chasin' 'em said it looked like the rear end spun out and then WHAP! The car wrapped itself around a big fucking oak tree. Considering his mind was in his lap, he probably never knew what hit him."

"I wonder if he had a family?"

"We know he had a wife. However, I'm sure it won't be a big surprise to learn she wasn't the woman in the car. They tracked Mrs. Swenson down using the address on his driver's license."

Jack shook his head as a thought crossed his mind, "Can you imagine what she said when they told her Swenson died while getting a BJ?"

"They didn't tell her and probably never will."

"Yeah?"

"One of the cops told me they were going to omit that detail from their final report. They said there was no need to make things worse for the wife. Her husband's dead. He was with another woman. That's painful enough. The full truth of what happened sure as hell isn't going to make her feel any better. Y'know what I mean?"

Jack nodded to indicate that he did know what the flatbed driver meant, then told him where to put the wreck. He shook his head slowly as he thought about how lucky he'd been that Swenson had put the car on his credit card. "Damn," he said aloud to no one but himself, "if Swenson had opted for the finance package, I'd be holdin' the bag right now. It would have taken me months to get paid."

3
Meeting Truth in Verite

The headline in the newspaper clipping read:

Local Man and Unidentified Woman
Meet "Truth" in "Verite 300"

"I wonder how long it took some smart-ass writer to come up with this clever little play on words?" Charlie Fair was not happy. This was not the kind of news article that the President and CEO of the company that manufactured the Verite 300 Sports Coupe wanted to find staring up at him from his desk the first thing in the morning. He looked up at his secretary, Emma Rae–she preferred administrative assistant–and asked, "Where did this come from, the <u>Detroit Free Press</u>?"

"No, it came from someplace in New York. I think it says where in the article."

"Yeah, it does." Charlie went back to reading, "May 15, Westchester, NY. Adolf Swenson ..." he started to laugh. "Adolf? Now there's a name you don't hear much anymore. Talk about parents giving their kid a handicap." He began again, "Adolf Swenson, the 54-year-old president of a swimming pool company, and an as yet to be identified woman, were killed last night on Route 9 north of Tarrytown when their Verite 300 careened out of control during a high-speed police chase." Charlie looked up at Emma Rae. "Ten to one the woman wasn't his wife."

"No bet," she chuckled.

Charlie took a moment to savor the visage on the other side of the desk. Central casting would never have picked her to play an administrative assistant, but then central casting had not selected her for this job. He had. Emma Rae had originally been hired to work in the legal department as a secretary. Apparently, whoever had hired here–and it was most certainly a male from the Human Resources department–had been so bedazzled by her physical assets that he overlooked the fact that she had virtually no computer experience. In truth, she could barely type.

"She just can't seem to figure it out," was the way the woman who supervised the secretaries put it. "It takes her forever to get anything done."

One day during lunch with Harvey Nichols, the company's chief legal counsel, the conversation drifted around to Emma Rae. Harvey regaled Charlie with stories of Emma Rae's singled-handed destruction of the department's productivity. Apparently, in addition to her lack of computer skills, she was creating departmental gridlock. Her desk was near the water cooler. Frequently, during the day, entire cadres of young men would arrive like parched desert travelers, stopping by an oasis for refreshment, and create such congestion that getting from one side of the department to the other was nearly impossible. The more Charlie heard about this siren, the more determined he was to steer his ship in her direction. Immediately after lunch, he found himself with a pressing need to visit the company's legal department. Two days later, to relieve the gridlock,

Charlie moved her to the executive floor just outside his office.

Charlie innately understood that Emma Rae was fully aware of her bankable libidinous assets. Like rich women who keep their jewelry under lock and key when not on display, she unveiled the full measure of her physical opulence only when the occasion warranted. The occasion was warranted whenever Charlie found himself in the mood for a little recreational sex. Her routine was always the same, but Charlie never tired of it. She would say something about it being too warm in his office and slowly unbutton and remove a suit jacket, or sweater, revealing a provocative tank top that held her breasts up like ripe melons lolling in the sun. Her "inner-office uniform," as Charlie called it, was, to say the least, distracting, and not just to him. Once, when he found himself in the middle of a difficult negotiation with some union officials, he called her into the meeting wearing her "inner-office uniform," ostensibly to serve coffee. By the time she left, no one could remember what they'd been negotiating and, more to the point, it didn't seem to matter.

Charlie turned his attention back to the article. "Sources confirm that Mr. Swenson had purchased the Verite 300 at Jack Poor Motors in Greenwich, CT, just hours before. Police say they first noticed the Verite turning off the Cross-Westchester Parkway at better than 70 miles an hour. They gave chase as Mr. Swenson sped north on the narrow two-lane Route 9, going well over the speed limit. Police say that when Swenson entered the curve, clearly marked for 25 MPH, they clocked him at sixty-two miles-per-hour. One of the officers reported that while the wheels were turned sharply to the left, the rear end of the car seemed to break free just before it skidded and slammed into a tree.

"Mrs. Swenson, who was not with Mr. Swenson at the time of the accident, announced, through her lawyer, that she believes the crash was caused by a design flaw in the rear suspension system having to do with an improper geometric offset between the stabilizer bar and the torsion action in the struts."

Charlie reacted as though he had just been notified of an IRS audit. "What the hell is she talking about?" He thumped the article with his fist. "It's gibberish." He continued to read, "Mrs. Swenson said that she is considering suing Jack Poor Motors and the Verite manufacturer." Charlie read the rest of the Swenson article in silence. When he finished he said, "Where does this shit-for-brains reporter get off asking if the Verite could be another Ford Pinto disaster waiting to happen?" To even bring up the specter of exploding Pinto fuel tanks in the same article brought Charlie's adrenalin to the near overload level. "Good God, has this woman no appreciation for the laws of physics? Her husband is bombing into a twenty-five-mile-an-hour curve at sixty miles-per-hour, spins out, and it's our fault?" Charlie laid the article down on his desk and stared at it for a long moment. Finally, showing just the slightest degree of concern, he looked up at Emma Rae and said, "Tell Harry Spar to drop by this afternoon. I think maybe he should take a closer look at this. I want to be sure this is no more than just some ambulance chaser thinking we'll pay him off to avoid negative publicity. Let's just say that if he ..." He stopped in mid-sentence, as though his train of thought had suddenly been derailed.

It was almost three years ago back when the Verite 300 was still just a prototype and he'd been confronted with the fact that, in order to price the Verite under the competition, they were going to have to take some costs out of the car. No way was he going to eliminate any of the sporty interior amenities that shouted, *Sports Car!* to prospective buyers. Things like body-molded bucket seats, a big knob on the shifter, a racy instrument panel, and a sports steering wheel - the sexy stuff that customers could see and feel. That meant, the only place to reduce cost was in those places the customers couldn't see and couldn't feel, specifically in the chassis, under the hood, and the suspension. The suspension! What was it that he had ordered engineering to eliminate from the suspension? There was something. But what? There was no way he was going to remember at that moment. Not while confronted with this phenomenal paradigm of pulchritude leaning over his desk. He finished his original thought. "Let's just say, if the lawyer and Mrs. Adolf Hitler Swenson think they can put the squeeze on me," he added a touch of bravado for emphasis, "they're going to find that nobody ... and I mean nobody, can screw Charlie Fair."

Immediately Emma Rae responded with a

tantalizing smile that said, "Right, only *I* screw Charlie Fair."

4
What's This bout a Lawsuit?

Preston Waddington called it the Perk'n Charlie puppet show. Perkins Byrd, Chairman of the Board, pulled the strings and Charlie Fair danced as directed. Once every three months, the Executive Committee of The Board of Directors and all the managers in marketing and sales, which included Waddington as the manager of sales training, were asked to come to the executive conference room to hear Charlie's quarterly state-of-the-company report.

Charlie stood behind a podium at the front of the room and began the meeting, as always, by obsequiously thanking each member of the Executive Committee for his support and counsel. "Before I get to the sales figures, I want to bring you up to date on the Le Vent." *(Translation, 'The Wind' and pronounced Lay v'haun with much nasal resonance.)* "It's in full production; we'll have more than enough units ready for shipping immediately after the dealer meeting. The dealer council has had a chance to view the car and drive it at our test track. I'm happy to report that, to a man, they are enthusiastic. They *love* the car."

As Charlie's presentation wandered into self-serving hyperbole, laced with numeric minutiae, eyes began to glaze over and the attention of most of the managers began to drift off to distant places. There was not a great deal of respect in the room for Charlie. Most of the managers resented the fact that his corporate success was due almost entirely to his relationship with Perkins Byrd–a relationship that he unabashedly exploited at every opportunity. Although, as of late, there had been some suggestions that, due to the poor performance of the company, Charlie was treading on shaky ground so far as Perkins was concerned.

Waddington was not among those who resented Charlie. While others hung derisive labels on him, Waddington saw him as simply lucky. Lucky to have married the boss's daughter. Lucky to have been blessed with regal good looks, self-assurance, and a deep sense of personal worth. Lucky to have a name that sounded like it belonged to a successful man. Charles Dunwood Fair. Charles Dunnnnnwood Fair. It had substance, a resonance. It reeked of authority and confidence. To Waddington, it was the kind of name one would expect a CEO to have. It was the kind of name that always appeared on patrons' lists next to significant dollar gifts. Yes, the name Charles Dunwood Fair evoked the image of position and money.

And then there was his name, Preston Olivier Waddington. *(Olivier, as in Laurence Olivier.)* Considering how little he had accomplished in his life, he decided that Preston Olivier Waddington was akin to hanging a Tiffany sign on a Wal-Mart. His first name he felt was cumbersome and, frankly, a little prissy.

Once, when he asked his mother, who was French, about his name, she told him that while she was carrying him, she'd read several books on the power of self-fulfilling prophecies. She had come to the conclusion that if she gave her first-born son a name that sounded important, he just might one day *become* important. Waddington learned that it was only over the strenuous, but futile, objections of his father that his mother hung the name Preston Olivier on her slightly jaundiced, six-pound four-ounce son.

"It is my fervent hope," his mother frequently told her friends, "that with a name like Preston Olivier, my son will somehow be able to avoid the paycheck-to-paycheck existence that has been the lot of his father."

Sadly, Waddington saw his mother pass to her reward having done little in his life to help her realize the dream of seeing her son ascend to a prominence worthy of his name.

If ever the word "nondescript" described a man, Waddington felt he was that man. When he looked at himself in the mirror, what he saw was the definition of medium—medium build, medium height, medium weight, medium brown hair, medium features. He had long ago accepted that he looked like everybody, and he looked like nobody. "A kind face," he had heard it said, "but a forgettable face." Often people would be drawn to him and ask, "Aren't you so and so?" He never was. "Don't I know you from somewhere?" They never did.

Waddington concluded that, had he pursued a life of crime, he could have walked into a bank without a mask, come face-to-face with the tellers, left with bags of money, and the victims would have been hard-pressed to give the police a useful description other than "he was sort of medium."

During his formative years, his father often tried to impart his personal philosophy on his son. "Keep a low profile," his father had told him the day he left for his first year at the Teaneck, New Jersey, grade school. "They can't pin-the-tail on the blame-donkey if they can't see you. Don't sit in the front row or the back row. Those are the people who get noticed by the teacher. Sit somewhere in the middle, off to the side where they really can't see you. Blend in. Avoid eye contact. Don't volunteer. The only time you should raise your hand is when you can't wait for the bathroom break. Keep a low profile. That's the key to survival. If they can't find you, they can't hurt you." Not surprisingly, Waddington's father was proud that he'd managed to slip through his career mostly unnoticed. His only real disappointment was when he discovered they'd misspelled his name on his retirement watch.

In truth, Waddington harbored ambitions that more nearly reflected his mother's hopes. Unlike his father, he did not want to slip through his career unnoticed. He wanted to be successful at something. He didn't have to be the president of a company. Vice-president would suffice. He wanted a job where he would be recognized, where he could rise above the crowd, where there was little chance his name would be misspelled on his retirement watch.

That he worked for an automotive manufacturer in Detroit was purely the result of circumstance. He had been married only a month and found himself facing all the expenses of a newlywed. The ad in the paper said the car company was looking for people in their sales training department. He'd always liked cars. He liked the excitement of the automotive industry and the people in Human Resources convinced him that his career potential was limitless. "All those offices with mahogany doors on the top floor have to be filled by someone; why not you?" the interviewer had asked. Yes, why not?

Well, one reason why not was because of what he'd seen in the company parking lot less than a year ago. It wasn't so much the fact that Charlie Fair and his *administrative assistant* were making love, it was *where* and *in what* they were doing it that startled Waddington and involuntarily brought him to a stop. In the company parking lot? In the front seat of a Verite 300? The company parking lot was clearly inappropriate. But in the company's newest sports car? That was patently impossible. Or so Waddington would have assumed. But there were Charlie and Emma Rae proving him wrong. If only Emma Rae had not glanced up at the moment. But she did and she recognized him before he could dart away.

Emma Rae was convinced that Waddington was the only one who knew about her affair with Charlie. In truth, everyone knew, yet she saved her verbal vitriol for Waddington alone. "I will see your ass out of here one day," or "You're just a voyeuristic shit," or some other similar endearment was how she greeted him on those occasions when

39

they found themselves in unavoidably close proximity. It would be hard to imagine the President and CEO promoting a man who had witnessed his performance in the parking lot.

Waddington chuckled inwardly at the memory of that afternoon. *How absolutely perfect*, he thought, *how intrinsically appropriate it was that Charlie had chosen a Verite 300 for his early afternoon tryst*. It was as if he had decided to personally demonstrate one of the heretofore-unrecognized benefits of the eight-way adjustable Verite 300 seats.

The Verite 300 was to Charlie Fair what the Mustang had been to Lee Iacocca when he was at Ford. It was "his baby." It was the car that he believed would carry him to automotive immortality. Like Iacocca, he not only wanted to be thought of as a great car man, but as the father of an automotive concept that changed the course of his company. Prior to the Verite 300, the company's model line was prime fodder for late night comedians. And for Waddington, creating meaningful sales training for their cars, was a nightmare.

He wrote the programs and then gave them to his four sales trainers. It took enormous creativity, and a little self-delusion on the part of the trainers, to present a positive selling story on the company's model line. Except for the Verite, the line-up was an automotive embarrassment.

First, there was the four-door Defiant that defied description, raison d'etre, and salability. It made no pretense at performance. It had the weight of a hearse and drove like one. The Cadence was the full-sized car. By full-sized, they meant it could swallow six oversized people, all their luggage, and still have room in the trunk for their walkers and wheelchairs. With its endless front hood and half-moon rear windows, it looked like the type of car that blue-haired ladies and Sanza-belted gentlemen might buy for cruising around Sun City. Waddington frankly found it embarrassing when he was asked, on behalf of the company, to accept an award from the Senior Citizen's Alliance for the Cadence as the most accommodating car for "challenged" senior citizens.

Finally, there was the Road Warrior SUV, which never managed to finish higher than seventh in the voting for Four-Wheeler of the Year. It was described by one of its critics as a Warrior in search of a Sport, a Utility, and legitimacy as a Vehicle. Survival of the company dictated   no, demanded - a new approach to design. Charlie understood that need perfectly. He had been fully supportive of the board's decision to fire half of the design department and tap the reservoir of imaginative automotive designers in Irvine, California, who had proven they could create a truly good-looking sports coupe. They had done exactly that with the Verite.

Waddington was well aware that in Charlie's case, as in Iacocca's with the Mustang, there were those who claimed the Verite 300 was already in its clay model form months before he saw it. Charlie, on the other hand, dismissed his detractors' assertions by claiming that he alone had fertilized the egg that spawned the car. In truth, it was probably more accurate to say that he had adopted the Verite rather than fathered it.

Whatever the actual facts, Charlie went to some length to allay any questions about paternity and to assure that he would be given his due when automotive historians wrote about the Verite. He instructed the VP of Marketing to have their ad agency create an advertising campaign that would forever bind him to the Verite 300, much in the same way that the late Tom Purdue was linked to his chickens. Further, Charlie made sure Waddington included a mention of his role as the Verite creator in all the sales training materials.

In a very short time, Charlie Fair was appearing on the TVs of America's homes with his Verite. "This is my car and I built it for you," was the way he began the commercial. They were thinking about reworking Iacocca's famous Chrysler K-Car tag line, "If you can find a better car, buy it." It was dropped when Waddington's boss, Axel McPherson, VP of Sales, argued that potential customers might do exactly that.

While there was some question as to how many cars were sold because of Charlie's role in the commercial, there was no question in Waddington's mind but that Charlie did help create a strong, GQ image for the company. He also succeeded in getting the attention of female viewers. For Charlie Fair was more than fair, he was beautiful. His brown hair was streaked with blond as though the sun–actually a discreet hair stylist–had selected choice strands to favor. His face had the ruddy look of an avid outdoorsman, and his piercing blue eyes had the power to inspire flights of orgasmic fantasy in certain women.

Waddington had heard it said that the women who knew Charlie, both socially and in a more biblical sense, would, when asked, never suggest that he was just handsome; *gorgeous* was the more frequently heard description. And carnal philanthropist that he was, he seldom denied any worthy female the pleasure of his pleasure. It was not uncommon to have a new initiate into Charlie's coterie wonder how he ever ended up with *her,* meaning his wife, Olivia. It was an easy question to answer, of course. She, the *her,* was Perkins Byrd's daughter. To Waddington's knowledge, he had never met or even seen Olivia Byrd Fair. She was reported to be a low-profile person, which, considering to whom she was married, was understandable. How she had put up with Charlie's ego and his blatant philandering was a mystery he assumed he would never have an opportunity, or even the inclination, to solve.

***

Charlie pressed a button on the podium and a slide, titled "Monthly Sales Results," popped up on the screen behind him. "I'm happy to report," he began directing his commentary to Perkins Byrd, "that our total sales have increased by 1.2 percent over the previous month. We are over the hump." He punctuated his announcement by jabbing at the air with his fist. "The market is turning in our favor, and we're about to see a sustained period of growth. To me, these figures confirm that our marketing strategies are working and that we are well on the way to a sustained period of profitability."

Waddington was frankly not all that surprised to see Perkins begin to frown and scowl as Charlie laid on the hyperbole. Nor did it surprise him when Charlie's well-tuned antenna picked up the lack of favorable return signals from his father-in-law. Immediately, Charlie deferred to him by asking if he'd like to make a comment.

Perkins Byrd's six-foot-four frame dominated the room. He had large features, accented by his reddish, rosaceous complexion, which contrasted sharply with his snow-white hair, trimmed close in military style. He leaned forward and glared up at Charlie. Perkins Byrd, Chairman of the Board and Chairman of Executive Committee, indeed wanted to make a comment.

"If you think," he exploded, "we're going to believe this phony-baloney song and dance you've given us that a 1.2% monthly increase indicates a turnaround, you're singing the wrong tune and off-key at that. This increase of yours is a fart in a windstorm. Our dealers are sitting on a one-hundred-and-twenty-day supply of cars. If memory serves me correctly," he said, drawing out every word, and icing each with sarcasm, "a forty-five-day supply of cars on their lots is considered the norm. I'm getting calls from dealers who tell me that their dealerships couldn't be emptier if the goddamn health department had put a quarantine notice on their front doors. What are we doing to help those guys? All we're doing is burying those poor bastards in iron. Bottom line? They ain't happy, Charlie." He jabbed his finger at his son-in-law. "What is today?" He looked at the date window on his watch. "May 21st. In less than three months we're going to have all of our dealers flying into Detroit for the dealer meeting. Unless we can get those inventories under control, someone had better call whatever hotel we've rented and have them double their fire insurance. Those sonsabitches are likely to burn the place down with us in it. So, Charlie, maybe you'd like to tell us what the hell you're going to do to help them move all those cars off their lots?"

Waddington could see that Charlie was visibly shaken. Perspiration beaded up on his forehead and he rolled his neck from one side to the other, like a fighter trying to slip punches. Clearly, he hadn't expected to be attacked by his father-in-law. The room fell silent, expectant. Perkins looked like a man prepared to wait for as long as it took to get an answer. Everyone's eyes were on Charlie, waiting to hear how he would respond.

Waddington likened Charlie to the glory-hungry football player who keeps the ball anytime he sees an opportunity to run for a touchdown. But at that moment, Charlie appeared more like the option quarterback who realizes that if he hangs onto the ball, he is going to get buried by a three-hundred-pound lineman. So, Charlie did what any man with a finely honed sense of self-preservation and pain-avoidance would have done—he handed off the ball. "I'm going to ask Axel McPherson to address that question. As VP of Sales, I think it only fair that he be given a chance to defend his department's performance."

Waddington glanced over at his boss, fully expecting Axel to tell Charlie to perform an anatomically impossible act. Much to his surprise, Axel only smiled, leaned down to pick up his briefcase, stood up, and walked up to the podium.

As Axel approached, Charlie began to slowly back away. The expression on his face seemed to say, if you guys think you need to throw someone under the bus, I'll be happy to provide you with a body. But it's not going to be mine. Charlie took a seat next to Perkins. "Axel, why don't you tell us how you plan to reduce these bloated dealer inventories?"

Axel was a squat, burly man with an ex-Marine type confidence that dominated any space he happened to invade. Waddington, who regarded his boss as the only legitimate car man in the company, would not have been surprised to see him fall down, fumble, or throw a long incomplete pass. Axel didn't. He had a plan and he was fully prepared to tell them about it. Which he did. It made a great deal of sense, and everyone bought it. A couple of the board members even applauded.

Recognizing that Axel had scored a touchdown, Charlie immediately decided to get back into the game. Within less than five minutes, he had let it be known to several committee members, in privately whispered asides, that he should be given at least some of the credit for helping Axel formulate his sales strategy.

"Well," Charlie said, looking to escape before Perkins could inflict any more damage, "I think that about does it."

"Not quite," Perkins said abruptly. "There's one more thing." He moved forward in his chair and held up a newspaper clipping. It was the article from the Westchester paper, reporting on Adolf Swenson and the unnamed woman's accident in the Verite.

"Axel, have you seen this?"

"What is it?" Axel asked.

He handed Axel the clipping. "It's a story from a Westchester, New York, newspaper about some guy and a woman who were killed when their Verite 300 ran off the road. It says the wife plans to sue the dealer and us. Charlie gave it to me this morning." Perkins paused and looked first at Axel who was reading the clipping and then turned to Charlie. "Should we be concerned?" There was an edge in his tone.

Seeking to regain some favor in Perkins' eyes, Charlie answered authoritatively. "Our response should be that you don't take a twenty-five-mile-per-hour curve at sixty. Clearly, the driver was at fault. But you know as well as I do that, when somebody thinks they can make a manufacturer responsible for their fuck-up, they'll try."

Perkins turned to Popper Poppenhaus, the VP of Marketing. "Have you seen the article, Popper?"

"I have," he said.

"What's your take? Are we going to see a lawsuit here?" Perkins asked.

"Hard to say. There are a number of things we don't know," Popper began. "Like, who was the 'unnamed woman' in the car? If it was his sister, that's one thing. If it was a girlfriend, then maybe Mrs. Swenson won't want to expose all the family's dirty laundry. Maybe. Then there's the question of the lawyer's intent. What's his game? If he's one of those fuckin' liberal lawyers that love to stick it to corporations, then chances are we're gonna hear from him. On the other hand, if this guy is just some schmuck ambulance chaser, he may think he can get us to settle out of court to avoid the negative publicity. We wouldn't be the first company that some sleaze-bag lawyer has tried to blackmail into protecting their corporate image. They know it's a hell of a lot cheaper for companies like us to buy them off than to rebuild a reputation that's been chewed up in the newspapers and cable channels."

Axel nodded his agreement. "Back in the nineties, Mercedes elected to settle what many considered a bogus claim on the S-Class just to avoid the potential fallout of a public trial. It cost them a ton, but they felt it was worth it to protect their brand image."

Perkins Byrd nodded and leaned back in this chair. "Has anyone talked to our Greenwich dealer to see what he knows? What's his name?"

"Jack Poor," Axel offered.

"Not yet," Charlie said. "I just saw the article yesterday. Let me add a third possibility to what Popper has suggested. I predict that once the lawyer looks into the cause of the accident–I mean the guy was violating the laws of physics and the speeding laws of New York State–he's going to lose interest. He hasn't got a case. However, if he gets the idea we're worried that a suit, even a bogus one, could hurt our reputation, the bastard will come at us. My suggestion is to sit tight and let him make the first move. Frankly, I don't think we have anything to worry about."

Waddington saw a frown arrive on Perkins' face as he leaned forward, resting his chin on his hands. He took it as a sure sign the Chairman was not convinced by Charlie's contention that they didn't "have anything to worry about." "Maybe we don't, then again maybe we do. Either way, I'd like to know sooner than later." He looked around the room to be sure he had everyone's attention. "Let me tell you what concerns me. It's no secret to any of you that this company is in trouble. Without a major infusion of cash, we're out of business. That's why, as you all know, we're doing our best to finalize the deal to sell fifty-one percent of the company to the French Consortium. Right now, we're at a very delicate point in our negotiations. If the truth be known, and I don't want what I'm tell you to go beyond this room, it wouldn't take much to scare off the French. That's why this is not a good time for bad press, noisy lawyers, or angry widows looking for a payday. Let's say, for example, that it turns out this Swenson fellow was having an affair and that maybe he was a prominent member of the community or, God forbid, a politician. If Geraldo or Drudge got onto the story, they'd be all over it, and the Verite 300 would be center stage. The Frogs would sprout wings, and this company would be history. That's why I want to know all the details, if there *are* any details, beyond what we've learned from this news story." Perkins measured his words, sending a clear message to every man in the room, "I don't want to get blind-sided. And that, in my opinion, Charlie, is something to worry about."

Charlie jumped quickly to this own defense. "When I said we didn't have anything to worry about, I meant we shouldn't *appear* to have anything to worry about. I mean, for the reasons you just mentioned, I thought it best that we keep a low profile on this."

"Here's what I want to happen," Perkins said. "First, someone's got to talk to Jack Poor. See what, if anything, he knows that we don't know. Axel, can you do that for me?"

Axel nodded. "I could, but I don't think you want me talkin' to him. If Jack gets a call from me, and I ask about the accident, he'll start asking me questions about what corporate thinks. He'll want to know whether we're going to help defend him if Mrs. Swenson sues. No matter what I tell him, he's going to start worrying that we might bail out on him. Trust me, when Jack worries, he gets pissed off. When he gets pissed off, he becomes a loose cannon. I know Jack and you don't want that. Not if you want to keep a lid on this."

"Are you saying we shouldn't talk to him?"

"No, I'm saying *I* shouldn't talk to him. Let's have Pres do it. Jack Poor is his father-in-law. He could just casually bring up the subject next time he talks to him like it was some sort of afterthought."

Waddington adjusted himself uncomfortably in his chair. His relationship to Jack Poor was not something he brandished about in the company. Mainly, because he didn't like Jack Poor very much.

Axel leaned over to Waddington. "I don't mean to put you on the spot Pres, but I think Jack will read a lot less into you asking him about the accident than if I were to bring it up. Do you agree?"

Waddington saw no immediate alternative but to nod his agreement. "Sure," he said in a tentative voice.

"Axel's right," Perkins said turning to Waddington. "It's better for you to talk with Poor. Here's the way I suggest you handle this. Next time you're on the phone to Poor, and I'd hope the next time will be no later than tomorrow morning, begin with some small talk. Make it sound like you're calling on family business or whatever it is that you normally talk about when you call."

Actually, there was nothing Waddington and Jack Poor normally talked about. Ever. Their relationship had always been perfunctory and distant. On those occasions when Waddington traveled to Greenwich with his wife for family functions, the two men would acknowledge one another, exchange a few empty observations, usually about the weather or the car business, and then behave like two grey ships passing in the night. Finding a reason for making a phone call out-of-the-blue to his father-in-law was going to take some creative thinking.

Perkins continued, "Then, after you've had a nice little chat about whatever you decide to chat about, tell him you saw a copy of the news story. Make it sound like you're only half interested, like asking about the weather. Whatever you do, don't tell him where you saw it. As far as you're concerned, nobody here in corporate has even heard about it. Understand?"

Waddington understood, but he had a question. "Wouldn't it make sense to fly Jack in here for a meeting, find out what he knows and then plan some sort of strategy *if* and *when* Mrs. Swanson decides to go through with the suit? I don't understand why we have to be so circumspect with him."

"A fair question," Perkins said. "I'm sure we may get to that point, sooner rather than later, if we hear from her lawyer. But right now, I don't want to stir the pot. I don't anyone beyond this room to know, including Jack Poor, that we are even aware of the accident. I'm asking you to trust my judgment on this and make the call for us, okay?"

"Okay." Waddington wasn't about to argue with Perkins Byrd.

"If I were a betting man, and maybe I am," Charlie said, "I'd bet this won't amount to anything. Odds are that Mrs. Swenson and her lawyer will just fade away."

"If you're looking for a good bet, Charlie, I'll give you one," Axel offered.

"Yeah, what's that?"

"You can bet that Mrs. Swanson isn't going to add her name to our list of satisfied customers."

5
Shred Everything

Well after six on Friday, Charlie looked up from his desk as Harry Spar walked into his office. Harry had the title of Personal Assistant to the President, which, as everyone in the company knew, meant that he was Charlie's designated spy, presidential errand boy and, when necessary, the "Hatchet" Man." Charlie got right to the point. "Harry, anything on that Verite article I gave you the other day?"

"I checked with legal this morning, and they've heard nothing from Mrs. Swenson, or her lawyer. Frankly, I don't think we will. This looks cut-and-dried to me. When you're doing sixty in a twenty-five mile an hour curve ..." he shrugged. "Sorry, Mrs. Swenson, you're SOL. Case closed."

Charlie listened intently and said nothing for almost a minute after Harry finished. "I think," he said slowly, "that you might want to keep an eye on this. No matter how bogus their claim, we don't need any negative publicity right now. It could send the French running for cover, to say nothing of what it could do to Verite sales. As soon as they file suit, if they actually do, I want to hear about it."

"I'll stay on it," Spar promised.

Again, Charlie became reflective. "There's something else that's been on my mind lately. I've concluded that it might be in the company's best interest to reduce the amount of paper we keep on file." A sheepish smile crossed his face. "We really should make it a point to have our people go through their files from time to time and toss out the extraneous, unimportant stuff. I'd like for you to set the example."

Harry appeared to have no idea where his boss was going with this.

"As I recall, we conducted some performance tests on the Verite 300, cornering tests, lateral acceleration, things like that, both before and after I ..." Charlie quickly corrected himself, "... after *the company* authorized engineering to redesign the rear suspension. If I remember correctly, the proving grounds then retested the Verite with the new suspension and, well ... let's just say the results were not quite what we might have hoped for. Now, the documentation for those performance tests are on file, probably out at the proving grounds and in engineering. Correct me if I'm wrong, but aren't those the only departments authorized to have those reports?"

"Exactly," Spar replied. "Test information is always confidential. All copies are numbered and signed for."

Charlie nodded, signifying that this was his understanding as well. He eased himself out of his chair, walked around to the front of his desk, draped a leg over the corner, and looked down at Harry Spar. He liked to be in a dominant position when he was giving orders. "Why don't you launch our paper reduction initiative at the proving grounds and in the engineering department?" Charlie folded his hands and put them on his knee.

"I would suggest that you begin with all the paper relating to the Verite tests." He bent down so that his head was very close to Harry's. "I presume you get my drift?"

Harry nodded obsequiously.

"One more thing. I would hope that you will take special care to be sure that anything with my name on it, or my initials, gets *reduced* as well." Charlie stood up and made his way over to the window that looked out on the urban wasteland that stretched between downtown Detroit and the Grosse Pointe town line. "We need to start thinking more progressively. The company doesn't need all the irrelevant paper clogging up our files. Agree?"

"Absolutely," Harry responded.

"You might also want to check the computer files. If we're going to eliminate paper, we probably should free up some hard drive space as well. I'd hate to see us waste hard drive space."

"And once I have completed my paper reduction assignment, I am to ..."

He had phrased it as an open statement, waiting for his boss to finish it.

"Shred everything."

6
Butt Buster

"Puff, puff, puff, wheeezz, puff. You're *not* talking business on Saturday, are you?" Muffy Waddington asked acerbically as she bent into her Butt Buster Home Toning Machine.

Waddington hung up the phone in the alcove off the kitchen. "I was talking to Jack."

"Jack?"

"Your father."

"My father? You were talking to my father? What did he want?"

"I called him."

"You called him?" Wheeezzz, puff, puff, aaarrgg. "Why? You never call him." Puff, puff, puff.

"I wanted to ask him something about an accident with one of his Verite 300s."

"My father was in an accident?" Muffy stopped busting, but only long enough to hear Waddington's reply.

"No, one of his cars was in an accident."

"And?"

"And he might be getting sued."

"Sued? My father might be getting sued? Mummy will kill him."

"If she does, that will be one less thing for him to worry about."

"You're not funny." And with that, Muffy lost interest in her father's problems.

Jack Poor's only daughter's body folded,

unfolded, and then pivoted to one side and then the other as though she were an unwilling hostage trying to free herself from the Velcro straps that secured her to the Butt Buster. It was a complex and formidable-looking contraption that in former times might have passed for a torture device.

Puff, puff. "Shit!" Puff, puff. She worked the intricate series of pulleys and counterweights, busting a butt upon which there really wasn't all that much to bust. "Oh, I hate this." She leaned back and stared at the ceiling. "This is utter torture!"

"So why do you do it?" Waddington began to search the refrigerator for something to serve as breakfast.

"Oh, Christ, Pres. Have you looked at the lard on my ass lately?"

"Muffy, if you had any less fat on your behind, you'd cut right through the upholstery every time you sat down. You're not fat!"

"And you're not funny." She rolled her eyes, signifying that it was futile to argue with him.

This "I'm too fat" "You're *not* fat," discussion, if one could call it that, took place at least three times a week. Muffy was definitely not the person that the guy in the T-shirt and shorts was yelling at through the TV. She didn't need a Butt Buster, or Thigh Thinner, or Hips Helper, or Tummy Tucker, or any of the other anatomical annihilators that UPS periodically dropped at their door.

"You know, Muffy, they're looking for someone to become this year's anorexia poster girl.

Maybe you should apply."

For a moment she said nothing, letting the pressure build before, like a volcano, she erupted and then spewed her ire on him. "Preston, you are an asshole. You are a sonofabitch, and I will make you pay for that remark. You are going to pay, believe me. You can go to the bank on that, you shit!" She said nothing for several minutes until she had regained some of her composure. "May I remind you of the Babe Palely axiom that, 'No woman can ever be too thin or have too many shoes.'"

"I think her quote was, 'too rich or too thin.'"

"That's even better," she spat back.

"Oh, thank God," Waddington got up to leave the room. "You're not suffering anorexia *nervosa* after all, just *axiom absurdum*."

The first time Waddington saw Muffy, he was twenty-three-years old, on his hands and knees, scooping wet coffee grounds into a paper cup with a plastic spoon. It was only his second day as a salesman at Jack Poor Motors, and he had accidentally knocked over the coffee pot in the break room, spilling the soggy grounds and sending shards of Pyrex into every corner. Unable to find a broom and dustpan, he had resorted to the cup and a plastic spoon. He felt ridiculous and hoped to have the mess cleaned up before anyone discovered him. He happened to glance up, and there she was, staring at him.

Muffy was dressed in what he later came to call her I'm-marching-in-a-protest-clothes. She wore a long sack-like, recycled cotton dress with a braided rope wrapped around her waist. On her feet were large platform, walking sandals, secured with wide Naugahyde straps. To show her symbiotic relation with nature, she had woven flowering herbs in her hair, giving her the look of a garden gone to seed. Waddington noticed that she wore no make-up and let her hair fall naturally where it might, encumbered though it was with all the herbs. Her natural state seemed only to validate her innate beauty. He could not help but notice how her ample, firm breasts refused to be denied acknowledgment as they pressed against her Mother Hubbard attire. In her limpid blue eyes, he sensed the hint of a latent sexuality lying in wait, like a hungry jungle animal ready to spring on its prey.

Years afterward, she would tell people, usually in front of Waddington, that she had stopped into her father's dealership to use the bathroom during a protest march against the unethical treatment of whatever was on her protest menu that week. In retrospect, she could not explain what it was about Waddington that had stirred her passion as she looked at him on his hands and knees, spooning coffee grounds into the paper cup. "Something snapped," was the way she put it. He was an empty vessel needing to be filled. A paint-by-the numbers canvas looking for someone to apply the color. She began their relationship with a lie. "I'm looking to buy a car. Can you help me?"

Waddington, having yet to make a sale for Jack Poor Motors, brightened immediately and stood up extending his hand to the wondrously unkempt, but very an attractive woman with the herb garden sprouting from her head. "Please excuse the mess, I'm a little new at this." He gestured feebly at the coffee maker. "My name is Preston Waddington. Welcome to Jack Poor Motors. What did you have in mind?"

"A test drive," she said intently, her eyes searching his for some sign of mutual chemistry. "It doesn't matter what car; I just want a test drive."

The test drive didn't last long. They parked in front of his rented room and spent the next two days mostly in his bed where she drained him of his essential fluids.

Waddington was well aware that no salesman at Jack Poor Motors was permitted to demo a customer for more than fifteen minutes. Two days was certainly over the limit. He knew that meant the end of his career as a car salesman. But he was so totally consumed by his passion for this insatiable woman, he didn't care. He had been dazzled, overwhelmed by the female whirling dervish that claimed his every waking hour. No woman had ever been so enamored of him. It was uncharted territory. To be wanted, to be desired, to be treated as a virtual sex machine was truly a heady experience. He was like a man on a concupiscent binge, lost in a delirium of euphoria that clouded his vision and impaired his judgment.

On the afternoon of the second day, as he lay on his bed, his physical resources depleted, his energies drained, too weak to register much concern over the loss of his job, Muffy revealed who and what she was.

Muffy, her real name was Margaret Isabella after two grandmothers, was not just the daughter of a car dealer, but the scion of one of Greenwich, Connecticut's, richest families, on her mother's side. That was *who* she was. *What* she was, was in a state of rebellion. She had decided to reject and renounce all that her mother and her patriarch grandfather, Ambrose "Bumper" McCoy, represented. Waddington learned that, while their political sympathies were on the right, Muffy rode an outrigger on the left. Their pursuits were material; hers were philosophic. They cut down trees, she hugged them. They ate animals and wore their skins; she ate veggies and gave money to PETA. They wanted the homeless locked up; she marched in support of giving them voting rights.

Her protests were often for causes, or in opposition to causes and perceived oppressions that her mother had not even heard of. Muffy carried banners against wearing fur and joined the revolt against higher ATM fees. She protested the creation of casinos on reservations, and then marched in favor of Indian rights. She protested against foreign oil imports, offshore drilling, and then rallied for more and cheaper home heating oil and lower gas prices. When Waddington pointed out that some of her protests tended to be in direct opposition to one another, she tossed his observation aside with a simple, "Nothing's perfect."

While Waddington never joined her marches,

on occasion he would drive her to a staging area. Often, she would have to ask someone what they were protesting against. The only difficult moment in their courtship came when Waddington wondered aloud if maybe it wasn't the *cause* that mattered to Muffy, as much as the pure joy of protesting–*anything*.

In retrospect, Waddington realized that he should have performed due diligence on the woman with the head full of herbs. Had he managed to look at her more objectively and less lasciviously, he would never have married her. Unfortunately, as a man caught in the riptide of unrelenting passion, he was simply not capable of such detached analysis. She was the flame and he the moth. There was no avoiding her allure and every night, sometimes in the afternoon as well, he would seek her out to satisfy his growing addiction to the sweet ambrosia he found in her arms.

When not in bed, and when Muffy was not involved in a protest, he would call for her at home. The first time, knowing that he would meet her mother, he had worn a suit and arrived with flowers in hand. Muffy deposited him in the living room, then abandoned him for a moment to run upstairs. No sooner had she disappeared than Mrs. Petula Poor entered the room. She was a large, imposing woman just under six feet tall who carried herself in an imperious way. She had a manner of addressing lesser mortals with her head tilted back, while viewing them down the bridge of her nose. Her eyes took a quick inventory of the figure standing in front of her. She looked as if she had just discovered a stranger in her living room holding a bouquet of poison ivy and tracking mud on her Aubusson. Her first words were not "Hello" or "You must be Preston" or "It's nice to meet you," but rather, "Who are your people?"

"My people?" he repeated, not comprehending her question.

His apparent inability to fathom the nature of her question irritated her. "Your people. Where are you from? What does your father do?"

"Do?" he asked.

Exasperated, she shot back, "What I am asking, young man, is whether you have anyone who you might offer as a personal reference?"

"Well," he said tentatively, "I work for your husband."

"You work for my husband?" She was incredulous. "I wouldn't let that get out if I were you. At least not in Greenwich."

That was the high point of their conversation. Petula's interrogation took only a few minutes, but time enough for Waddington to develop a large degree of sympathy for Jack Poor who, until that moment, he had found to be anything but a sympathetic person. When Muffy finally rescued him, he was holding the flowers upside down behind his back. Muffy must have overheard much of their conversation, because she immediately took Waddington by the arm, looked at her mother, and said simply, "You better get used to him. This is the man I intend to marry."

From that moment on, his fate was sealed.

The phone rang and for a moment

Waddington thought it might be Jack Poor calling him back. It wasn't Jack. It was Muffy's mother. There was no small talk, no pleasantries, only, "I want to talk to my daughter." Her tone was not unlike that of someone demanding to talk to a relative being held hostage. Muffy freed herself from the Butt Buster, poured herself a cup of coffee, and took up residence on a stool next to the phone. "Mummmmy," she began. Her tone was obsequious and subservient. "I was just about to call you. Any sign of the colitis this morning?"

As Waddington studied the face behind the phone, he found remnants of the woman he married, the one with the herb garden in her hair. Of course, her hair was different now. Very different. The lovely brown cascades that had fallen around his face as she rode up and down on him during those months of premarital sex in his one-room apartment had, somehow, been transmuted into long, blonde, frizzy strands that burst from her head in a million different directions. It seemed to Waddington that no comb or brush would dare attempt to bring discipline to that mane.

"Oh, Mummy," her voice dripped with solicitous concern, "You must call Dr. Weiderman this morning and have him give you something. I just can't bear to think of you being uncomfortable the entire weekend.

She hadn't always spoken with her mother in such endearing tones. In fact, for years they did little but yell at each other. Her mother hadn't even shown up for their wedding, saying she could not bear to witness her daughter repeating the same mistake she had made by marrying so far beneath her station. In her place, Petula sent a lawyer with documents, officially revoking Muffy's trusts, canceling her checking accounts, credit cards, and generally casting her out of the family.

"I feel badly that your mother didn't come," he had said after the wedding ceremony, thinking that Muffy needed to be consoled.

"Pres ... I don't care that she wasn't here. Look at me. You're looking at someone who is actually happy she didn't come. I have rejected her. And in rejecting her, I have been liberated from her money and her right-wing regressive politics. She doesn't own me anymore. You have no idea how I've hated being the rich McCoy girl, having to put up with all those prep-school Ivy League types buzzing into our driveway in their Mercedes and Porsches, thinking they could corrupt me with their credit cards and country clubs."

"I kind of envy them," Waddington said. "I mean, I'm driving a six-year-old Dodge Dart, and I don't belong to a country club, and I'm probably never going to be able to afford to live in a town like Greenwich. Not a very exciting prospect for someone like you."

"Pres, Pres ... don't you understand? I married you because I want to live like *real* people in a *real* house, or *real* apartment, or even a *real* trailer park with *real* people. Not these Greenwich snobs. I want to live in a real city like Detroit."

Detroit?

Detroit would not have been Waddington's

first choice or any numbered choice for that matter. And it probably would never have been on Muffy's list either. But fate had a hand in their decision. As they traveled west after their wedding, his Dart broke down on the Edsel Ford Parkway. Muffy immediately proclaimed their breakdown was a divine harbinger. She decided she had been called to serve in the urban desolation that was downtown Detroit. "Real people live in these hovels," she said. "People whose needs and causes I will make my own."

Waddington acceded to her heady sense of purpose and agreed to settle in Detroit. However, after a week in a rented room at the corner of Grand and River Road listening to gunshots in the streets, coping with aggressive drug dealers, and fending off drunks intent on grabbing a quick feel of her breasts, Muffy had an epiphany. She announced to Waddington that the *real* people she was talking about actually lived just west of the city limits in the town of Livonia. And so, they moved–immediately.

In Livonia, Muffy resumed her pursuit of activist causes. Unfortunately, with so many protest opportunities, she found it hard to focus on or stay interested in any one issue or cause for more than a month or so. While she was always asked to march or join a sit-in, it was evident to Waddington that her dedication to any cause, including their marriage, tended to be transitory. What once he regarded as the curiously erotic affectation of a dilettante activist had, for him, run headlong into the reality of getting on with their lives as husband and wife.

He did his best to ignore, and when that was impossible to accept, Muffy's determination to spend her days searching for ways to save Greater Detroit. Her mission, as she put it, was "to rescue the city from the social inequities perpetuated by a corrupt government and the residues of corporate pillaging." What he could neither ignore, nor accept, was Muffy's roller-coaster mood swings. She could ignite at the slightest provocation. It might be something as simple as him forgetting an item on her shopping list or as major as not getting an expected raise. Waddington soon gave up trying to anticipate when, or even why, the next eruption would occur.

Living, as he did, in a state of constant uncertainty drained him of affection. This is not to say there weren't good times in their marriage, times when he'd fallen back in love with her. But there were more times when he was out-of-love. The imbalance slowly dimmed the distant vestiges of his original love for Muffy, leaving only small residues of feeling surrounded by an empty indifference.

Waddington came to understand that time, and nearly twenty years of proximity, had succeeded in transforming him, in her mind, into just one of the several appurtenances necessary to maintaining the appearance of family. But that was not all that had been transformed in Muffy's mind. The travails of the downtrodden had slowly taken a backseat to causes closer to home. When, six years ago, Wayne County, which is where Detroit is located, announced they were going to bus her youngest daughter, among numerous others, to a school in downtown Detroit to help relieve racial imbalance, she said, "Whoa!" meaning: Not with my daughter, you don't! She rallied like-minded mothers in Livonia to stage a protest. It was in vain. The decision to bus was irrevocable. At that point in her life, Muffy finally admitted to Waddington that she needed money. Lots of money. A whole lot more than Waddington was making. While his creation of the *Company Eyes Only* report had provided job security, it had little impact on his salary. Money became her obsession. With money, she was sure she could spare their daughter from the ignominy of becoming one of the pawns in remedying racial imbalance and sent her off to private school. Her political pendulum was in full swing, and she announced to Waddington that it had come time to end fifteen years of filial enmity and seek a rapprochement with her mother.

Waddington drove her to the airport and bid her goodbye as she began her pilgrimage back to Greenwich–a penitent seeking absolution. "I still say we don't need your mother's money. I can find a way to pay for private school." Muffy's response was a short, mildly derisive, "Ha!" She spent a week in her old home, showing proper remorse for the excesses of her youth. When she returned to Detroit, she came bearing Petula's promise of regular and substantial contributions to her checkbook.

In addition, Petula made immediate arrangements for their oldest daughter, Julie, to transfer to Miss Porter's School for Girls in Avon, Connecticut, and to spend her vacations in the cultured environment of Greenwich. Their youngest, Hildy, was enrolled in The Bloomfield Hills Country Day School, just North of Detroit. At Christmas that year, Petula surprised her daughter with a Russian Sable coat. Muffy resolved to wear it only in her basement or when visiting Greenwich out of deference to her two PETA-devoted Livonia neighbors.

Waddington came to regard Petula's beneficence as her way of belittling his less-than-stellar performance as a wage earner. Admittedly, the fount of money that had flowed into Muffy's checkbook over the last five years improved their lifestyle. But at the same time it had, in subtle ways, diminished his status, even his importance, in the eyes of his children. They no longer had to listen to him say, "I'm sorry honey, we just can't afford it." Whenever his children needed money, they went directly to their mother, who denied them nothing. The financial floodgates had opened. There was no way Julie and Hildy could know that their girlish joy and excitement at *being rich* fed and sustained his belief that he had failed his family. Waddington suffered his humiliation in silence.

"Why are you looking at me?" Muffy hung up the phone and began to strap herself into the Butt Buster again. "You know when Mummy calls, I have to talk with her."

"I'm looking at you because there's no one else in the kitchen to look at."

"No, no," she said, shaking at accusing finger at him to indicate she rejected his explanation. "I *know* that critical look of yours. Whatever you're thinking, I want you to stop thinking it right now."

"I was just thinking that I liked your hair when it was normal. Meaning *normal*."

Muffy let out an exasperated sigh. "Paulo-Marcel" (Petula's hairdresser, who was always on stand-by when Muffy returned to Greenwich) "loves my hair the way it is."

"And Paulo-Marcel, of course, is our guru of things having to do with those parts of our anatomy that sprout hair above our neck."

Muffy did not appreciate his sarcasm. "How can you be so out of touch?" she spat. "Don't you ever read W? Don't you ever read the style section in the New York Times? Honest to God, Pres, you are a fucking idiot when it comes to women's fashion."

Egg-walking time, he thought. *I'm in no mood for a fight.* "I am indeed an idiot," he said, *for having subjected myself to this,* he finished silently.

"Oh, I almost forgot," Muffy said, "we're invited to the Fair's next Sunday afternoon for a brunch."

"The Fairs?" he asked, totally taken aback. "The Charlie Fairs? Us?"

"That's right."

"Since when did we qualify for Charlie Fair's Grosse Pointe invitation list?

"Since I've become close friends with Olivia Fair," Muffy answered haughtily.

"You're close friends with his wife?" he asked

71

incredulously.

"Well, friends, anyway. We're working on a petition together." The old Muffy would have called it a protest. "She's having this party to say thank you to all the women who are supporting the petition. And she was nice enough to ask that we include our husbands. So, for your information, Charlie Fair has nothing to do with the invitation list. I'm really looking forward to this. Working with Olivia on her committee has opened the door for me to meet an entirely different class of people and make new friends."

"How many times have you met with Mrs. Fair?"

"I don't know. Two, maybe three, times." Then apparently realizing she needed to justify her claim of friendship she added, "But they have been very, very intense meetings."

"What kind of petition are you working on?"

"A petition to prevent the state from building low-income housing in Grosse Pointe. The birdbrains up in Lansing have decided that every community has to have a certain amount of low-income housing. And they've selected Grosse Pointe as their first location. Can you imagine? They want to take some open land right along the beachfront and build low-income housing? What do they think we were doing five years ago when we spent all that time sitting in at the Mayor's office insisting that he allocate money to rehabilitate those old buildings on the Detroit River? That's low-income housing, and they have a water view. Our question to the state is, why not build more low-income housing on the river so that the people who are already there will have neighbors who are more like them? I mean, you would hardly expect low-income people to do much socializing in Grosse Pointe."

"Maybe the banks of the Detroit River aren't a good place for people to live. It's polluted."

"What does that have to do with anything? The river is there for them to look at. No one is saying they have to swim in it. That's what pools are for. I mean, how many people in Grosse Pointe do you think actually go swimming in Lake St. Claire? Most of them just look at it. And something else, if you live on the Detroit River, you can see Canada."

"Of course, you can; it's just on the other side."

"Well," she laid down her trump card, "you *can't* see Canada from Grosse Pointe. All they have to look at is the lake. If they build those housing units, a lot of people in Grosse Pointe aren't going to be able to see the lake."

"We certainly can't have that, can we?" he responded in mock dismay. "To deny those poor people their view of the lake would be criminal." He stared at her, now in full recognition that the transformation was complete. She was like a butterfly that had somehow morphed back into a caterpillar. It had taken years, but her political pendulum had found a new resting spot. "Muffy, I have to say it's amazing that you, once the queen of the economically trampled, are now backing a petition *against* the downtrodden. On the other hand, I'm sure you could argue that deep inside, there still burns the old activist passions. Even if they are just a little more to the right than the old days."

Muffy didn't respond. She had freed herself from the Butt Buster and was heading for the shower.

As Waddington watched her leave, he wondered whatever happened to the girl with herbs in her hair.

7
Easy

It was late the next afternoon *that* Waddington walked into Axel's office and handed him a manila folder.

"What's this?" Axel asked.

"The brain droppings of a wannabe copywriter," Waddington answered. "You know how marketing has been struggling to come up with a campaign concept for the Le Vent?"

"Yeah. So far, Charlie thinks everything they've come up with is shit."

"Well, this sort just came to me," he said pointing to the folder.

Axel read the headline and the short copy that Waddington had written. It took him only a moment. "Sonofabitch. I love it. Have you shown this to anyone in marketing?"

"Like Popper, you mean?"

Axel nodded. "On second thought, why bother? He wouldn't know good advertising if it bit him in the ass."

"You know as well as I do, if an idea doesn't come from the advertising agency, he's not going to look at it. In his mind, only a fully anointed adverting agency copywriter is capable of writing good ad copy."

Axel thought for a moment and then said, "I've got an idea. Screw Popper. I want to take this direct to Charlie. Do you mind?"

"Be my guest, but he'll probably kick it back

to Popper."

Axel had a wry smile on his face. "I don't know. You never know about Charlie. I think he might go for this." Axel closed the folder and jumped to another subject. "I hope I didn't put you on the spot by asking you to call Jack Poor. I hope you understand why I thought it best if you call him."

"Well, I did and he's not heard anything from the wife or a lawyer…nobody." Waddington walked over to the window and looked out. "What's your take on this?"

"It's bullshit. How can anyone sue us for takin' a twenty-five mile an hour curve at sixty? Not our fault."

"True, but …" he said turning back to Axel.

"But what?"

"Remember Audi's unintended acceleration debacle back in the eighties? The woman is pulling into her garage. She thinks she's stepping on the brake, but she hits the accelerator instead and runs over her daughter. First, she tells police that her foot missed the brake and landed on the accelerator. That was what the police put in their report. But then, a few weeks later, her story suddenly changes. Next thing we know, there she is on *60 Minutes,* claiming her foot was on the brake and that the car took off all by itself."

"Which, of course, is technically impossible."

"Right. And as you know, after years of claims and counterclaims, that's exactly what was . However, when the woman started blaming the car, what did the Audi execs do?"

"Absolutely nothing. Big mistake."

"Exactly. Thanks to the ass-hole media and their own ineptitude, Audi sales went from somewhere around 88,000 cars a year in the U.S. to about 15,000. I appreciate that we don't want to do anything that might scare off the fuckin' French, but I don't think we can pretend to ignore this. What if Charlie is wrong, and this woman and her lawyer *don't* fade away? What if they sue and this becomes our very own version of unintended acceleration?"

Axel said nothing for a moment as he weighed Waddington's comments. "You may be right," he said at last. "I guess the bottom line is we have to be ready with some kind of response if they do come at us. You never want to wake-up one morning, surprised to find yourself knee-deep in shit without a shovel. Charlie may be betting he can ignore this, but not Perk. He's not going to stir the pot needlessly, but he's not going to stick his head in the sand, either. That's why he wants to find out if Jack Poor has heard anything from the woman's fuckin' lawyer."

Waddington never ceased to be fascinated by the way Axel spiked his conversations with obscenities. He made them so much a part of his natural speech pattern that somehow they didn't seem all that offensive. His wife, Mary, had tried to break him of the habit. She assumed she'd succeeded because Axel never used an obscenity in front of her. As a man who spent his life wrestling with dealers and fending off competitors, it took a good deal of effort to park his business language in the driveway and switch on his Sunday-go-to-meetin' vocabulary. But he did it, simply because Mary had asked him to. She had married him against her family's wishes. They had seen him as coarse, hard, and unrefined. She had seen something else and he felt incredibly lucky that she would have him. Tragically, a number of years ago, a bad fall from a ladder put her in a wheelchair. Even with years of therapy, she could stand in braces and use a walker for only a short time each day. Mary did manage to walk down the aisle, with assistance, when their daughter got married, but mostly she lived her life in the chair. Axel did everything possible, including redesigning their house with ramps and elevators, to give her maximum mobility. He worked hard to leave his business problems in the office so that he could devote his evenings and weekends to her. At home, with her, he was a much softer man–gentle, caring, considerate to a fault. Had he brought his home personality to the office, no one would have recognized him.

   To look at Waddington and Axel together, one would never have guessed that the two men were friends. Maybe it was the attraction of opposites, a quirk of human chemistry that explained their friendship. Physically, and in their personalities, they appeared to be yin and yang. If Waddington was medium, Axel was well done. Axel was not a face, or a body for that matter, that anyone would ever forget or mistake. As a teenager, he was the kind of boy a football coach puts at guard. As a teenager, Waddington's mother put him at the piano. Axel's heavy black hair, which he wore in a near crew cut, framed his chiseled square face. His dark eyes peered from beneath heavy brows, giving him a piercing, intimidating countenance that tended to make people uncomfortable. Many of his associates regarded him as the company bully.

Waddington started to leave Axle's office and turned back as he approached the door, " Let me know what you think about my Le Vent ad copy."

***

"You should look at this." Axel handed Waddington's advertising concept to Charlie. "It's dead-on and better than anything that fuckin'
agency of ours has come up with for Le Vent."

"You're telling me our training manager is writing advertising?" Charlie asked incredulously.

"It was something Waddington came up with while he was putting together his sales training programs. I'm tellin' you, Charlie, it's fuckin' terrific. It'll take you five minutes to look at it. Maybe three if you read fast."

Charlie remained skeptical but acquiesced. "Okay. I'll give it three minutes."

***

On Wednesday, Waddington got a call just before nine in the morning.

"Pres? Charlie Fair. I'm sitting at my desk looking at the page of advertising copy you wrote.

79

This is terrific. I absolutely love it. It's exactly what I was looking for."

"I'm glad you like it."

"Of course, you understand that while *I* like it, our ad agency is going to hate it. They're going to hate it because they didn't write it. But fuck em. Now, here's what we're going to do. The agency is coming in from New York tomorrow. In the morning, they're going to show me the ad concepts they've developed for Le Vent. After lunch, I want you to join us and present your idea."

"I don't think Popper Poppenhaus is going to be very happy about that."

"I don't give a shit what makes Popper happy or unhappy. His job is to do whateverthehell I tell him to do. And he will. And that includes falling on his knees and kissing my ass anytime and anywhere." He hung up.

Neither Waddington nor Axel liked Popper Poppenhaus. The man, in their opinion, was an overblown, empty suit. He was VP of Marketing for only one reason: he was Charlie's butt boy. Prior to Popper's arrival, Charlie believed there was no need for a VP of Marketing. In his estimation, no one had better marketing instincts than he. But after several years of sagging sales, Perkins Byrd and the board decided the VP of Marketing position required a full-time effort. Charlie was told to find someone or the position would be filled for him.

Charlie tried to argue his case in front of the board for maintaining both his CEO and marketing responsibilities. He offered a list of reasons why he could, and most definitely should, continue to perform both jobs. When Charlie finished, Perkins wasted no time presenting an ultimatum. "Charlie, when you get back from your ego trip, you've got a decision to make. It's an either/or decision. And it's really simple. You either find a VP of Marketing in the next thirty days or take the job yourself."

"Look no further. I'm the best man for the job." Charlie tumbled into the trap.

"Okay, then I intend to ask the board to make you our Vice President of Marketing." He paused for what seemed like a full minute, "Once that's been done, we will begin the search for a new CEO and President to fill the job you've just agreed to vacate."

Charlie came back from his ego trip in a big hurry. "Wait. I don't want to give up CEO."

"Great! We like you in that job. Now find yourself a VP of Marketing. And do it in the next thirty days or we'll do it for you."

The look on Perkins' face said he would suffer no further discussion. That made the decision easy for Charlie. However, finding the right man was not so easy. At least, not from Charlie's perspective. Had he admitted what kind of person he was really looking for to be his VP of Marketing, it would have been quite different from the typical human resources boilerplate of :

Candidate should have impressive credentials as an automotive marketer, demonstrate proven creative skills, have had years of managerial experience, etc., etc.

Charlie's job description, the *real* job description as far as he was concerned, would have read:

The ideal VP of Marketing will be required to sit at his desk and hold it in place so that it doesn't fly away. He will make no decisions relative to anything beyond where to have lunch. He will answer only to, and follow the instructions of, the CEO and President. He will understand that he is never, ever to be anything more than an errand boy with a big title and excellent pay. Finally, the ideal candidate must be prepared, on a moment's notice, to show his fealty to the President and CEO by bending over and knowing on which cheek to plant the kiss.

In Popper Poppenhaus, he found the perfect floor lamp. Like a floor lamp, he filled a space, he looked like he might be useful, and he responded only when the person with his hand on the switch decided it was necessary. With Popper in the job, Charlie could continue as de facto VP of Marketing.

***

It was as if she had won a Bon Bon-for-life contest. Waddington's secretary, Doreen Walfish, who sat in a cubicle directly across from his, never failed to have a box of the chocolate morsels sitting open on the far corner of her desk. She always placed it there as an open invitation to any and all to help themselves. One of her more regular visitors to the Bon Bon box was Popper

Poppenhaus whose office–he had a real door–was located on the same floor.

Just after lunch, Popper was on his way to the conference room for the afternoon meeting with Charlie and the ad agency. He leaned over Doreen's cubicle wall and asked how she was. She responded with some unintelligible sound which he assumed was intended to be interpreted as an I'm-okay-I-know-why-you're-here. Having dispensed with the social niceties, he proceeded to survey the selection of Bon Bons.

"No more than two, Popper," Doreen said sternly, without looking up for even a moment from her computer.

He grunted his acquiescence and took the allotted two. One went immediately into his mouth, the other he cradled in his hand. As Popper turned to leave, he noticed Waddington sitting in his office. "I understand you're going to join us this afternoon. What the hell for?"

"Charlie wants me to make a presentation," Waddington answered.

"A presentation? On what? Training?" he asked incredulously.

"No, on an idea that I had."

"An idea?" Popper echoed. "What kind of idea?"

"Just an idea," Waddington answered evasively.

"I gather you're not going to tell me what this idea of yours is?"

"I think Charlie would prefer that I wait."

Popper shook his head as if to say, what a

83

waste of time. As he turned to leave, a thought struck him, "Oh, I've been meaning to ask you, what did your father-in-law have to say about the Swenson suit?"

"As I told Charlie, Jack hasn't heard a word from the lawyer. He doesn't think they have a case."

"Maybe not. But will they sue anyway?"

"He has no idea."

"I'll guess we'll just have to wait and see."

As he stepped out of Waddington's office, Popper noticed that Doreen had left her desk, apparently to go on an errand. Quickly he darted inside, popped a third Bon Bon in his mouth, and beat a hasty retreat to his office. Three of the Bon Bon Queen's chocolates in one afternoon. A major coup.

At one-thirty, nine agency people, along with Popper and two members of his marketing staff, were seated in the conference room waiting for Charlie. The buzz around the table indicated they were worried. They'd presented their advertising that morning, but Charlie had said nothing other than he'd meet with them again after lunch.

Waddington had been told to wait in his office for Charlie's call. *The less time with what Axel calls our agency assholes, the better,* he thought. In whatever venue he encountered them, they always presented themselves as the ultimate creative authority. Their smug, disdainful, self-congratulatory attitudes seemed geared to keeping lesser mortals, like Waddington, in their place. God forbid that anyone from the company should have a good idea. What if Charlie actually liked an idea that had not come from the creative minds of the agency? Why, he might begin to wonder if the company really needed the agency. Blasphemy!

***

Charlie waited until Emma Rae told him that everyone was assembled in the conference room. "Let 'em know I'll be a few minutes late. And tell Pres Waddington to come up to my office."

Waddington walked into Charlie's office, hoping that his presentation was going to be canceled. From where he sat, there was absolutely no upside to pissing off Popper and the agency.

"Are you ready with your presentation?"

So much for any hope of cancellation. "Yes, if you think it's worth presenting. I have it all on PowerPoint." He gestured to his laptop.

"Good. Now, once you're done, be prepared to have them rip both it and you apart. Let 'em. Just sit there. Don't say a thing and don't try to defend your concept. Let 'em have at you." Charlie smiled the smile of a man savoring an opportunity to practice a management technique reportedly perfected by Lee Iacocca, namely, to keep underlings anxious and off-balance.

"Once they've all told us how off the mark and rotten your idea is, I'm going to announce that not only do I love it, but that 'Easy' *is* going to be our advertising message. In fact, I'm going to make it clear that your 'Easy' concept is the best advertising we've had in years. Then you watch how they start to tap dance. By the time they're through, they'll have turned 180 degrees from hating it to loving it." He slapped his hands together with glee. "Oh, I really love fuckin' with those guy heads. They are a bunch of conceited, overpaid bastards who need to have their knees whacked every now and then."

Great, Waddington said to himself, *they're going to want me dead.*

As he and Charlie walked into the conference room, Waddington was instantly able to identify the roles each agency person played. The two men in dark business suits were the account executives. They lived their lives in constant fear that Charlie might erupt one day and pull the account. Indigestion and Maalox were intrinsic to their jobs. For men who had mortgages, kids in colleges, debt, and a lifestyle they had gotten used to, the prospect of instant demise manifested itself in a well-honed ability to discern which way the wind was blowing, even before it started blowing. They fully understood that their role was to appear confident and supportive of the company's objectives, but always properly sycophantic and deferential to the whims of the leader. When Charlie liked their work, they went out of their way to credit him for his inspiration and keen discernment. When he hated something, they offered up a sacrificial lamb for him to dispatch. Behind their compliant demeanor lurked a deep-seated abhorrence for the man.

The three women in very tight skirts and silk blouses were basic agency functionaries that

Waddington suspected were there primarily to keep Charlie distracted. The two men in turtlenecks and leather jackets opposite the women were the copywriters who wore the arrogance of men who felt they deserved the Pulitzer Prize for their riveting, impactful ad copy. At the far end of the table, doodling on large pads of paper, were the art directors who looked like they'd dressed themselves out of a Good Will clothing donation box.

"You all know Pres Waddington," Charlie said, as he and Waddington entered the conference room. "As you are no doubt aware, Pres has been developing the sales training program for the Le Vent launch. As it turns out, his training program has given him an idea for our advertising. I know this is a little unorthodox, but I thought it might be interesting to have you take a look at it and let me know what you think."

Waddington looked at the faces around the table. It was as if someone had just broken wind and while no one could avoid it, no one wanted to acknowledge it for fear that it might have come from Charlie.

"Pres, it's all yours."

He decided to adopt an I-am-humbled-to-be-in-the-presence-of-such-creative-greatness approach. "Needless to say, I don't pretend to have the expertise that you folks do when it comes to creating ad concepts. But if there's something here you can use, well, we're all in this together. We all want the Le Vent to be a major success."

He punched up his first slide. It showed a

picture of the Le Vent and the word, "Easy."

"As we know, the market for Le Vent is the person who wants the driving experience that a sports car offers. This person would, if he or she could, go out and buy a Mercedes SLK two-seater. But the people we're targeting can't afford to spend more than about twenty to twenty-five thousand dollars. The copy platform I'm suggesting for both the print ads and TV would be very simple and straightforward. The objective is to focus the ads on the realities of our market's needs and financial limitations. The message would be totally transparent: namely: 'It's easy for you to afford what you really want from a sports coupe.' The copy might read something like:

Le Vent
Easy
Easy to look at.
Easy to handle.
Easy on fuel.
Easy to own.
Easy to mistake for a sports coupe
costing three times as much.
Easy. Le Vent

"Of course, each one of the 'Easy' headings could be expanded to talk about styling, performance, fuel economy, and our financing options. The last one, 'Easy to mistake for a sports coupe costing three times as much,' is to give our prospective customers the feeling that they can be driving around in a car that will get the same kind of admiring stares that people who drive MBs and Beemers get. Finally, the tag reinforces the message, 'Easy. Le Vent.'" He was done. "That's essentially it."

Waddington looked around the table. It was as if all the agency people had turned to stone as the result of suffering some form of lethal attack on their nervous systems. No one budged.

"Comments?" Charlie asked.

Slowly the stones turned toward Charlie, each trying very hard to see if they could read his reaction to Waddington's presentation before they ventured to offer theirs. There was no wind blowing, and it made everyone uneasy. Seconds ticked away like minutes and still no one spoke.

"Walrus. Talk to me. Your reaction," Charlie said. George Wallarus, the agency account executive, who everyone called "Walrus" because of his size, his large, tusk-like mustache, and because his last name invited it, did not answer immediately, but rubbed his chin in contemplation. Waddington decided he looked like a man who had been asked to venture out on a frozen pond to test the thickness of the ice. Wallarus glanced at the stone figures around the table, apparently hoping that one might say something to get him off the hook. There were no volunteers.

"Well, it certainly is an idea that shows some thought on Waddington's part," he began tentatively. "I think maybe Frank might want to comment on the copy." Walrus had tossed the ball down the table to his head copywriter.

Frank glanced up with a look that said, 'You shit, Walrus, why put me on the spot?' He rocked back, then leaned forward and ran his hands through his hair as if he might find something there worth talking about. "Well, as copy goes it's short. Short is good. I like short. The question I would have to ask is whether an ad like that says what we want it to say?" Then Frank tossed the ball back to the other account executive. "Bruce, I'd be interested to hear your reaction."

Bruce had just joined the agency. He had apparently not developed pain avoidance skills and tore right into the ad. "Well, let's be perfectly candid. No need to waste a lot of time on this. 'Easy' just doesn't do it. It doesn't communicate. It doesn't resonate. It's not impactful. It's not fresh. It doesn't sing. And it's not great copy." Once he exhausted all the clichés, he added, "To me, the word 'Easy' degrades the car."

All eyes turned to Charlie. There was just a very slight suggestion of a nod. That was all it took; everyone began to pile on.

The art director felt the environment in which the car had been placed was wrong. The other art director hated the type font. One of the three decorative women offered that she felt the ad did not speak to her. Frank, the copywriter, feeling released from his self-imposed restraint, began to ridicule the simple copy. "Amateur night in Dixie."

When it looked like it was really, *really* safe to pile on, Popper laughed and said, "Pres. I think you better stick to training. Nice try, but copy writing just isn't your bag. Maybe this might work in one of your training sessions. But as an ad campaign, nobody here likes it. That's the bottom line."

Charlie looked around the table. "Anyone else want to offer an opinion?" There were no takers. They'd done all the demolition work they felt needed doing.

"Well, I guess it's my turn." Charlie paused. It was a long, purposeful, almost pain-inducing pause designed to let waves of concern turn to waves of doubt, then to waves of trepidation, and finally wash like a Tsunami over the conference table into the laps of the agency and marketing people. Walrus was the first to realize they'd been set up. "May I add something?"

Charlie held up his hand to Walrus as a signal that the comment period was over. Now it was time for the leader to have his say. "I like it. In fact, I *love* it. To me, it's simple, clean, to the point. It speaks to our potential customers in a way that they'll understand. This, ladies and gentlemen, *will* be our Le Vent platform. I would like you to scrap what you presented this morning, all of it, and build the Le Vent campaign around 'Easy.'" He turned to Walrus who looked like he'd just realized he missed the "Thin Ice" warning sign and was about to fall in. "Are we agreed on that?"

"Ahhhh. You know, sitting here and thinking about 'Easy,'" Walrus said, doing his best to sound like a man given to reasoned discourse, "I'm wondering if maybe we were a bit hasty and owe it a second look. Sometimes when you're thinking one way, you don't always see a new idea for what it is." He turned to Frank, the copywriter. "What do you think, Frank?"

Frank was no fool. He wasn't about to send out his resume and start looking for other work. "Well, this does present Le Vent from a different perspective and it does ..." he searched for a word, "communicate. Yeah, it does communicate a message."

Within five minutes, everyone around the table had made a full one-eighty and was expressing his or her enthusiastic acceptance.

"Well, that does it. We're all agreed on 'Easy.' Great job, Pres. Brilliant concept." Charlie slammed his hand on the table like a judge rapping his gavel at the end of a trial. Then, looking directly at Waddington, but fully loud enough for everyone to hear, "Makes me wonder why we pay our agency so goddamn much." He laughed and looked at Wallarus. "Hey, you know I love you guys. You generally do good work. But you can't get it right every time."

That's one plane going back to New York that I wouldn't want to be on, Waddington thought. The agency assholes and Popper were doing their best to smile and show their support for Charlie's dictum, but it was clear their egos had been sliced and diced. They were walking wounded and bleeding all over the room as they got up to evacuate.

"Popper, I need a word with you," Charlie called as Popper neared the door.

Popper bid the agency people goodbye and walked back to the table where Charlie waited, his expression grim and his arms folded ominously across his chest.

"Popper," Charlie said with a coldness that could have dropped the room temperature by ten degrees, "don't *ever* again ask me to sit through the kind of garbage they presented to me this morning. If you can't steer the agency into producing better advertising for us, I'm going to start looking for somebody who can. Take this as fair warning; if they don't shape up and if you don't shape them up, I'll cut their balls off and yours along with them."

Popper's forehead began to glisten with perspiration. He fidgeted as though he was sitting on tacks but dared not stand up to remove them. Charlie had him on the hook and the only way to get off was to try and distance himself from the agency. "You know, Charlie, the fact of the matter is that I was actually a little disappointed myself. But I thought maybe with some work, you know, maybe with your input and your suggestions … you always have great ideas … you might see some way to save it."

"Please. Popper, don't kiss my ass here in front of Waddington. If you were a little disappointed, why didn't you say so?" Charlie answered his own question. "I'll tell you why you didn't say so, because you *loved* the crap they showed us. And frankly, I don't understand *why* you loved it. The commercials were so goddamn artsy-fartsy, even I had no idea they were trying to sell a car. Those commercials were designed to win the agency Clio awards, not to sell our car. In case you've forgotten, Popper, we're here to sell cars. None of what they showed us did that. What the hell were you thinking?"

"Well, I was thinking ..."

Charlie cut him off, "Do me a favor. Don't think. When it comes to our advertising, from now on, I'll do the thinking just like before I hired you. But I'll tell you what you *can* do. You can start kicking some agency butt. You tell Wallarus that the renewal of his contract with us is riding on how well they execute our 'Easy' campaign. If they screw it up, I'm going to put on my steel-toed shoes and start kicking butt myself. Have I made myself understood?"

Oh, had he ever. Popper looked like a man who'd just been told by a judge that he had to give all his assets to his ex-wife. Popper nodded and instantly assumed the role of a contrite and appropriately penitent supplicant. Yet, Waddington was sure that beneath the rueful façade, the loathing was running rampant. It would not have surprised him to see Popper leap across the table and give Charlie something to remember him by. But at the same time, Waddington knew Popper to be the ultimate pragmatist. Where else was he going to make the kind of money Charlie was paying him? No, Popper would say nothing and do as he was told. At least for now.

Popper stood up, searching for some way to affect his escape without offending Charlie. He found a perfect exit line. "I agree with everything you said, Charlie. And I think it would be a good idea if I started kicking a little agency butt right now, before Wallarus and the others leave for their plane."

"Good. You do that. And while you're at it, tell Walrus that I expect print and television executions of the 'Easy' concept next week."

Popper couldn't get to the door fast enough, but Charlie was not about to let him go without adding insult to injury. "I think we owe Waddington an 'attaboy' for his concept. Don't you?"

Popper forced a transparent smile. "Yeah, attaboy." The words said one thing, the tone said, fuck-you-and-the-horse-you-rode-in-on.

As the door closed behind Popper, Charlie grinned broadly. Clearly, he'd found that exchange to be fun. He loved keeping his people anxious and off-balance. He turned to Waddington and slapped him on the back. "You know, Pres, I'm beginning to think you're absolutely indispensable."

8
Louis XV Redux

The first time Charlie Fair likened himself to Louis XV, his wife presumed he was kidding. Every time after that, she was not so sure. On occasion, Olivia would find Charlie in front of his mirror, admiring himself and saying, "Je sui le roi. Le roi pouvoir non faux. *(Translation: I am the king. The king can do no wrong.)* He had no idea if the French grammar was correct and frankly didn't care. It was the intent that mattered. One of Henry Ford's wives reported that Henry said exactly the same thing–but, in English. Charlie felt that he showed a lot more class by saying it in French. While the house he lived in was not Versailles, it wasn't your typical center hall colonial either. Not with twenty-eight rooms, a guesthouse, a pool house, and an attached five-car garage with servants' quarters.

Charlie surrounded himself with things French, ranging from period *bureau placs* and commodes, *Limoges's* porcelains, classical and neo-impressionist paintings, to his butler, who hailed from Maubeuge, and two tempting French truffles from Marseilles. He also imported two gardeners to maintain the grounds. To save money, he recruited them from Quebec. Though they were not French, they sounded like they were to everyone but the butler and the Marseilles truffles, who claimed that whatever it was they spoke, it certainly wasn't *their* French. While Charlie's backyard was a mere fraction the size of Louis' at Versailles, it did have fountains, garden pools, many flower beds, and crushed white gravel walks.

In fair weather, Charlie, like Louis, would invite his guests to promenade with him through the gardens. And, like Louis, those who strolled with him took note of who Charlie chose to have walk with him. If you were asked to walk alongside Charlie, you were considered to be "in." If you were assigned to follow behind, you were on shaky ground. And if you weren't there at all, it meant you were either temporarily out of favor or in line to be axed.

Charlie looked forward to any and every opportunity to hold court at his home. He found a perverse delight in demonstrating his ability to bring a smile to the face of a manager one minute and then shoot an arrow of fear into his heart the next. He also enjoyed confounding his guests with obtuse, cryptic remarks that defied concise interpretation, but intimated that he was in the process of reevaluating, and adding to, the list of those who would feel the ax. In his mind he may have been Louis XV, but to many of his managers, he was Robespierre.

It was such fun to be the king, surrounded with endless opulence and obsequious supplicants, all in the comfort of his very own Versailles. Yet for all the pleasure Charlie took from the house, it was a house he would never have shown to his stockholders. It was a house that spoke of a man who had made a great deal of money, a man who had earned the title, Captain of Industry, a man who had the genius to make his stockholders rich. What the house did not speak to, did not even hint at, was that it was the home of a man whose company ranked dead last in the American car market A man whose company stock price hovered regularly just above having itself delisted on the New York Stock Exchange. In fact, it was the house of neither man, but of Charlie's wife, Olivia Byrd Fair. She had inherited it from her maternal grandmother, a Chrysler married to a Vanderbilt. Grandfather Vanderbilt had wandered west for a time in 1903 and built what he regarded as a summer retreat on the shores of Lake St. Clair. Along with the house, Olivia was the recipient of a trust that was well-nigh bottomless. She was truly of old money.

The brunch for her petition committee was, of course, Olivia's idea. Her original guest list had numbered no more than thirty. But Charlie felt that no affair at his house–other than a selective dinner– should number less than one hundred. So, he expanded the guest list with invitations of his own. When he informed Olivia to expect about seventy more than she'd planned, she was angry. She became furious when she looked over the additional names and found at least three women who, rumor had it, claimed a recent history with Charlie. Did he think he could hide them from her? Did he think she wouldn't notice? Again, as so many times in the past, she knew she would be the subject of Grosse Pointe gossip: "How can she not know?" "Did you see who Charlie was talking to?" "I can't believe Olivia would allow him to invite *her.*" "The story I heard was …" and so the tittle-tattle would go. It was not limited to just the women. The men took even greater delight in speculating on Charlie's conquests until, on one occasion, two men found themselves confronted with the embarrassing fact that they were talking about their own wives. While the gossip was always titillating at the Fair's parties, no one ever understood how Olivia could rise above the humiliation engendered by Charlie's reputation. She resolved never to emulate Ann McDowell Ford and create a scene by hauling her husband off a dance floor when her husband's dance partner became overly aggressive. Olivia Fair was far too proud, too dignified for that. If she suffered, and the assumption was that she did, she did so in private. She was liked and respected by her friends but pitied as well. If she had been aware of their pity, it might have crushed her.

Yes, Olivia thought as she finished dressing, *I will endure this as always. And if the vodka helps ease the pain, well …?*

9
The Man in the Mud-Brown Suit

Muffy and Waddington were greeted at the front door by the Fair's butler from Maubeuge, who directed then into the enormous living room. "Cozy" was not a word that Waddington would have used to describe the room in which he stood. *You could play basketball in here,* he thought, although it was hard to image someone dribbling through the ornate furnishings and driving for a backboard nailed over the great marble fireplace. It was even larger than Muffy's Grandfather's house in Greenwich, which, by comparison, was a mere handball court.

The walls were covered in red damask, which served as a background for so many paintings that Waddington expected, at any minute, to see a museum guide leading an art class on a tour. The ceiling had been faux painted to give the impression of looking through a large oval opening into a blue sky where puffy, white clouds provided perches for naked cherubs. Waddington decided that the artist had displayed his sense of bourgeois resentment in the facial expressions he painted on the cherubs. Each peered down from the ceiling, appearing dismayed and disgusted by the bejeweled women and grey-suited clones who ravenously accosted waiters carrying trays of hors-d'oeuvres, stuffing their faces between hugs and handshakes as they vied for recognition and favor from the King.

As Waddington surveyed the guests, he immediately began to suspect that every man, other than himself, had been privy to a pre-party notification that the uniform-of-the-day was a dark-gray suit, white shirt, and conservative tie. Waddington had presumed that a Sunday afternoon party the first of June might find the guests in more summer-like attire. So, he opted for an electric blue shirt, bright-yellow tie, and his mud-brown suit. He had ignored, or possibly forgotten, that the suit always wrinkled badly, creating the impression that he'd slept in it. One thing was for certain– there was no way Muffy would lose him in the crowd. For a moment, he thought about going home and changing, but Livonia would have been a two-hour round trip, and the party would have been over by the time he got back.

Waddington took cover behind Muffy, who was wearing a lavender Mary McFadden frock with big puffs and poufs on her shoulders and waist that made her look twice her size. It was a curious choice on Muffy's part, as the outfit tended to obscure her hours on the Butt Buster. He decided that she must be making a fashion statement. From his wifely redoubt, he scanned the room and recognized Popper and three other men from the executive floors, all of whom were titled with VP or higher. The rest of the guests were unknown to him.

Olivia Fair pirouetted her way through the milling bodies and greeted Muffy as a true sister of the cause. The cause, of course, being the effort to block the building of low-income housing in

Grosse Pointe. The women exchanged compliments on each other's dress, hair style, what have you, and then Muffy stepped aside to reveal the man in the mud-brown suit, looking as if he were attempting to emulate Harry Houdini and vanish.

"Olivia, this is my husband." She said it with the same enthusiasm that she might have said, "This is my pet goldfish."

Olivia was working the crowd with her left hand, the right appearing glued to a tumbler of what Waddington presumed was vodka. Water did not seem to be a likely alternative since she seemed to list slightly to the left when she spoke. She looked at Waddington's mud-brown suit, then turned to Muffy and gushed her approval, "Oh, your husband is an iconoclast. I just adore a man who isn't afraid to stand out in a crowd. It says so much about his sense of self."

With that she held up her left hand to Waddington upon which rested something that looked like the Hope Diamond. "I'm Olivia Fair, so delightful to have you here."

Waddington looked at the proffered hand and wasn't sure whether protocol at this level of society called for him to shake it or kiss it. He took the ends of her fingers and wiggled them in a ridiculous fashion, then retreated to a position behind the puff on Muffy's right shoulder. From that vantage point, he had a chance to assess Mrs. Fair. He found himself quite taken with her appearance. She was not at all what he'd expected, but then, he wasn't exactly sure what he had expected. He guessed her to be in her mid-to-late forties. She was small, with a well-defined figure that had certainly held the years at bay. A little liposuction maybe? A face-lift? Maybe. Maybe not. It made no difference. Her black, shoulder-length hair was so perfectly coiffed that, for a moment, he thought it might be a wig. It wasn't. But it was her face that fascinated him. What was it about her face that he found so mesmerizing?

"Waddington!" Charlie's loud greeting cut through the rising din of the vapid cocktail party conversations. "Olivia, have you met Pres Waddington?"

"I just did," she responded.

"Pres has just created the best advertising concept we've ever had."

Olivia looked at Waddington, "Are you in advertising?

He never had a chance to answer.

"No, that's what's so amazing. Pres is our sales training manager and editor of the *Company Eyes Only* report. But he probably should be in advertising. A truly multitalented man. Great asset to the company." Having favored Waddington with his praise, Charlie made it clear that he did not intend to linger long. He had barely said "… to the company," when his eyes began darting about the room in search of something or someone of more immediate interest. Finding it or her or them, he immediately excused himself. "Catch you later."

"Well," Olivia said, "I must say, you seem to have impressed my husband. It's not like him to go on like that about his employees. Are you as talented as he suggests?"

It was a leading question, but before Waddington could suggest that Charlie had been a bit overly generous with his praise, Muffy and Olivia were swept up and carried off by several women whose faces had that I-must-tell-you-about-this-now look of urgency that women at cocktail parties often have.

As he stood alone in the crowd, enduring the occasional stares of guests who seemed to be wondering why the man in the mud-brown suit was out of uniform, he felt very much like a Toyota in the Cadillac parking lot. No one ever dared park a Japanese import in front of a GM facility, just as, apparently, no one ever came to a Fair party in a mud-brown suit.

Waddington could not help but notice that Muffy, on the other hand, literally glowed with delight. She was like someone who, after many years away, had returned to familiar and comfortable surroundings. For her, the Fair's house and Grosse Pointe must have seemed like a small corner of Greenwich transported to the hinterlands. Waddington watched as she infiltrated a group of women who all looked as if they had picked their way through display trays at Tiffany's and were currently in some type of competition to see who could drape, pin, stick, or in some manner affix the largest amount of plunder on their fingers, necks, ears, and clothing.

Marooned as he was in the middle of the room, he tried to appear absorbed in admiring the art on the walls. In fact, he was looking for a refuge. On the other side of the room, across from the entrance to the foyer, he saw what appeared to be a forest of Ficus trees, at least a dozen. A man could wander behind those and disappear, he decided. He had barely taken a step in that direction when a voice said, "I don't know if you're aware of it, Pres, but your pants don't match your suit coat."

Reflexively, Waddington looked at his pants. *My God, he's right.* He had accidentally put on a pair of brown slacks, almost the same color and material as his suit pants, but not quite. Then, in an attempt to mount a face-saving defense, he said. "The light bulb in my closet was burned out." He looked up to see who had nothing better to do than comment on his wardrobe. *Oh my God! Perkins Byrd.*

Perkins looked him up and down and smiled. "Well, Waddington, it looks like you didn't get the memo on the uniform of the day."

Waddington did his best to hide his embarrassment behind a short laugh. "I guess there's always one guy who doesn't get the message."

"Your wife involved with Olivia, is she?"

Waddington nodded, "She's on the petition committee."

"Good for her," Perkins said. He leaned close to Waddington and said, "Charlie tells me your father-in-law hasn't heard anything from the woman's lawyer."

"Nothing. I talked to him again yesterday and he said he doesn't expect to hear from her. He contends it was totally the driver's fault, and the police records will back him up. Or as my father-in-law so eloquently put it, 'It's all bullshit.'"

Perkins was thoughtful for a moment and then said, "Well, let's hope so. But for some reason, I have a bad feeling about this." For a moment he lapsed into some private thought, then snapped back and clapped Waddington on the shoulder as he glanced around the room. "I guess I better go mix. My daughter's orders. Enjoy yourself," he said, lifting an eyebrow and shooting a last glance at the two-tone mud-brown suit. A large grin lit up his rosaceous complexion, "You know, Pres, you might want to consider buying a light bulb on the way home."

Waddington felt naked from the waist down. Maybe from the waist up as well. If he'd been wearing a clown suit, he could not have felt more out of place, more self-conscious and humiliated. This was not a recommended approach to impressing management. Maybe it would be best if he just waited in the car. He was weighing that option when an arm hooked into his and pulled him toward the center of the room. It was Olivia.

"You just must meet some very dear, dear friends of mine," she said. "Actually," she lifted her mouth to his ear and spoke in a confidential tone, "they are not all that dear, but they are big supporters of our petition. I think they work for General Motors." With that she set about wedging Waddington into a group of three men who were involved in what appeared to be a very private discussion.

"Do you three gentlemen know Mr. Waddington? No, you probably don't. But now you do. You all work in the automotive industry, different companies, of course, but I'm sure you have a lot in common. Mr. Waddington is the company training manager, and I presume he writes other things too. Isn't that right?" she asked for confirmation.

"Essentially," he said modestly.

Having her presumption confirmed, she turned back to the three men, "Since you're all involved with cars, I'm sure you'll have a great deal to talk about."

Waddington had no idea what Mrs. Fair's normal relationship was to vodka, but it was clear that it was having its way with her, at least on this afternoon. She exhibited a muddled perkiness, surrounded by a frothy gaiety that she did not wear well. The three men from General Motors did their best to appear not to notice. After she'd fluttered off, the men turned to Waddington, their expressions were all the comment needed to express their instant disdain for the writer of training programs in the two-tone, mud-brown suit. Just before they took evasive action and expressed urgent reasons to be someplace else, the GM dark-grey suits gave him a collective look that said, please disintegrate.

Waddington again found himself in a group of one, with not even a drink in his hand to make it look like the waiters, at least, were prepared to acknowledge his presence. A waiter with a tray of white wine passed near, and he was able to snag a glass. It wasn't much cover, but it was some. At least he looked like he belonged there. *Ah, the ceiling. I will look like I'm intently studying the ceiling. Maybe people will mistake me for an art aficionado ... or a painter ... or in this suit, I could be a building inspector. Take your pick people. Whatever assumption you make,* he thought, *that's why I'm standing alone looking at the ceiling.*

Like a hummingbird revisiting a promising flower, Olivia swooped in on him, once again hovering directly in front of him, staring. "Has anyone ever told you, Mr. Waddington, that you have a very sensitive face? You look like a man who feels ..." she paused sifting words through those brain cells that had not been anesthetized by the vodka until she came up with the right one, "deeply. Yes, I sense a depth."

Like a woman taking charge of a reluctant dance partner, she took his hand and led him to an older, somewhat despondent-looking fellow whose current interest seemed to be that of holding up a wall. When he spoke, his jaw and lips barely moved, giving the impression that he was a ventriloquist without a dummy.

She introduced him as Dr. SomebodyorOther and began to give Waddington a short biography of the man, as if knowing the ventriloquist's accomplishments might help Waddington initiate a conversation. Waddington appeared to be listening intently to Olivia, but, in fact, he barely heard a word. His entire inner being was fixated on her face. He knew he was staring but could not force himself to look away. So intense was his gaze that at one point, Olivia interrupted herself, gave him an embarrassed smile as if to ask, What? Have I got food on my lip? Has my mascara run? What is it you're staring at? Instead she said, "I'm sorry, I am rattling on. Was there something you wanted to say?"

In fact, there was a lot he wanted to say, none of which would have been appropriate at the moment. Instead, he fumbled for an apology, "No, no, I'm sorry if I was staring; I was fascinated by what you were saying." He hoped it didn't sound too lame; especially considering he had no idea what she'd been talking about.

Olivia's smile indicated she accepted his explanation and continued.

Waddington availed himself of the first opportunity to return his attention to her face, this time covering himself by bobbing his head as one fully absorbed. What was it that was so unusual, so compelling about her face? Then it dawned on him. Her face was off-center. All her features, her nose, her mouth, her chin, her eyes were just slightly off-center to the left. It was as if a clay sculptor had created the face and then accidentally bumped it. The slight distortion had left her with a visage that demanded to be looked at, absorbed, appreciated, and studied from different perspectives. He had no idea if anyone else shared his appreciation of that face, but like most art, beauty is in the eye of the beholder, and he suddenly had an urge to behold her, to possess that face, to capture it, to hold it in his hands. He was about to ask her to dance, and would have, but fortunately gathered his wits in time to realize there was no music. He resigned himself to imagining what it would be like to orbit within inches of that face.

Dr. SomebodyorOther turned away to accept another drink from a passing waiter. Olivia glanced first to the left and then to the right, as if checking to confirm that no one could overhear her. She drew up close to Waddington and put her mouth near his ear and whispered, "May I tell you something?"

Waddington nodded.

"I feel like I'm on display. Would you believe it? There are people here I've never seen before who have come just to see what kind of woman Charlie married. I'm sure I must disappoint them." The vodka was now attacking the part of her brain that controlled her ability to enunciate her words.

Before Waddington could argue that she could not possibly be a disappointment to anyone, she said, "You have the face of someone who looks like they'd be easy to talk to."

The butler from Maubeuge appeared and whispered something in her ear. Olivia drained the last of her vodka and excused herself saying, "I must see to our brunch." She nodded toward Dr. SomebodyorOther. "I'm sure you two will have much to talk about."

Waddington noticed that as Olivia walked away, she seemed to alternate first on a leeward tack and then to starboard. *Mrs. Fair is not going to be vertical much longer,* he thought.

10
Où Est le Toilette?

He watched her until the sea of dark-gray suits and Tiffany ornamentation swallowed her up. This was unlike him. What kind of spell had this woman put on him? It wasn't Waddington's nature to find himself so muddled by the mere physical presence of a woman, particularly one who happened to be the president's wife. Strange, he thought. Strange the effect she'd had on him.

It had to be the excess of testosterone, which he claimed was building up since Muffy had decided sex was a stimulant that made her hungry, and by making her hungry, made her eat, which, in turn, made her fat. So much for exercising his conjugal rights. Yes, that had to be it. He was oversexed and under satisfied. Nevertheless, it certainly wasn't good form to begin fantasizing about the president's wife. He turned to Dr. SomebodyorOther, who was now letting the wall hold him up. Like a horse, his knees were locked and he was nearly asleep on his feet.

Once again, he was alone. This time with a standing, sleeping ventriloquist. His thoughts turned to finding Muffy. He last saw her with a group of women in yet another animated discussion near the French doors that opened onto the terrace. She would not look kindly on having to provide him with social cover. That left him with nothing else to do but wander around the room, looking at the paintings and antiques. It was an incredible home, marble floors, marble columns, and marble staircase; an entire marble forest must have been sacrificed to build this house. The period art, the French antiques, the Oriental rugs, it was not just the quality of the items that impressed him, but the abundance.

The living room and what he could see of the terrace leading to the gardens were very crowded now. Obviously, more people had arrived and the frequency with which the waiters came and went with wine and Champagne glasses and special drink orders suggested that they had not had time to attend to the brunch. Maybe there wasn't going to be a brunch. Maybe, at this level of society, the mimosas and Bloody Marys and hors d'oeuvres were considered to be brunch enough. *One thing is for sure,* he thought. *If this group doesn't get some food, and a lot of coffee, they'd better get the kids and old ladies off the streets of Grosse Pointe.* If there were designated drivers among the guests, they had certainly lost their designation.

Waddington became aware that the decibel level was rising. Conversations seemed to have taken on a lighter note, or so he presumed, because the buzz of voices was now frequently being broken with throaty guffaws and shills of high-pitched peals of laughter. Waddington made his way through the open French doors and found a spot on the terrace that offered tacit invitation to view the magnificent flowerbeds and garden walks.

He noticed Muffy with a group of people on the far side of the terrace. He could not help but admit that she looked very comfortable there, so much a part of that gathering. Her patrician roots were flowering. He edged closer, keeping himself mostly out of sight behind a large cement lion standing guard on the terrace. Waddington counted seven people, Muffy, Olivia, who had alighted there momentarily, plus three other women and two dark-gray suits. They were laughing with the kind of alcohol-liberated hilarity that causes tears to roll down cheeks and breath to come in gasps.

As he watched Muffy orchestrating the conversation, clearly having won acceptance as an equal, he realized just how total the transformation had been from social rebel to social climber. There she was, enjoying the company of people who, like her, were lending their names (she was using her Grandfather's last name), their pocketbooks (ditto), and preparing to give a day out of their important lives (which day had not been decided) to picket the governor's office to express their opposition to the Grosse Pointe low-income housing project.

Muffy's voice rose from the group, moving an octave higher as it did when she was in a snit, though there was no sign of that.

"I told him I had no intention of becoming a breed sow." Muffy announced. "My God, he wanted six kids!"

Three, Waddington corrected silently.

"Can you imagine what six kids would do to your uterus? After Hildy, I told him he had to keep a sock on Mr. Winky." All the women and one or two of the men standing in the conversation laughed convulsively. She was certainly on a roll. And at his expense.

Waddington realized that Olivia had spotted him and was watching for a reaction. He determined he would maintain an indifferent expression, just a guest strolling casually about the terrace. He wandered back toward the house, stepped into the living room, and wondered if anyone would notice if he slipped out of sight behind the drapes.

A call from nature. An excuse to escape, at least for a while. *Now where would whoever designed this house have put the bathroom?* He asked one of the waitresses to point him toward "the powder room." While a 'powder room' sounded a bit effeminate, it seemed more genteel than *john* or *toilet*; certainly *privy* was inappropriate. The waitress directed him toward an arch that led to a long hall. Waddington found the bathroom, as had several other guests who waited patiently exchanging waiting-for-the-bathroom small talk. He returned to the living room and cornered a waiter, "Is there another bathroom, I might use? That one," he gestured toward the hall, "has quite a line. It's a bit of an emergency," he confided in a whisper.

"You might try upstairs. Goddamn, man, this place has got more toilets than a bus station." The waiter's graphic description suggested he was new to the Grosse Pointe catering scene. "Just look around up there and take your pick."

He climbed the stairs and found himself with a hallway on the left and one on the right. He felt like the protagonist in the Lady or the Tiger. He chose the left hall and tried the first door. It opened onto an enormous, formal bedroom, which had to be the master. Probably off-limits to guests. The Fairs certainly wouldn't appreciate his peeing in their bathroom. But there was no one around and his bladder was saying, I'm not going to wait much longer. I intend to explode and what a mess that will be. Off to one side of the room he could see a partially open door. That had to be the bathroom. The oasis beckoned. He'd be in and out in just a minute.

Waddington stepped into the bathroom, turned on the light, and found himself in a bathroom that must have required the sacrifice of another marble forest. He unzipped his fly, lifted the seat on the toilet, and sighed with relief. Oh, nothing like the feeling of relieving a full bladder. And then he heard a voice. "Thank you for lifting the seat."

11
Trapped in the Bedroom

Waddington reacted as if he's just stuck his finger in a light socket. Immediately he tried to stop the flow. Not easy and very uncomfortable.

"Charlie never raises the seat, and he drips. I hate that. That's why we have separate bathrooms. You're very considerate, Mr. Waddington."

He quickly stuffed his member back into his pants and glanced over his shoulder. Olivia, drink in hand, was leaning against the doorframe. She was smiling at him, but at the same time having a problem keeping her eyes open. She teetered slightly, but appeared to enjoy watching him standing at her toilet. "Please, don't stop on my account. You'll find soap and a towel there on the sink." She started to leave, then turned back to him, "I'll be waiting in my bedroom. I want to talk."

Talk to me? About what? About joining AA? She was very, very drunk. Waddington turned his attention back to the toilet. *Damn! Why didn't I at least lock the door?* His sphincter released and the flow began again. His stream showed no signs of letting up. He was sure he was about to qualify for the *Guinness Book of World Records* for the longest pee. And it was making so much noise. He reached down to flush the toilet to mask the sound from Olivia. When she tells Charlie she found me pissing in their bathroom, I'm history.

Waddington flushed the toilet a second time, put the seat down, and took longer than was necessary washing his hands. He was hoping that if he delayed long enough she'd either leave or pass out on the bed. Judging from her condition, the latter seemed to be a distinct possibly. He replaced the towel, then stepped to the door and peered into the bedroom, praying he'd be able to escape. No chance. She was sitting on the bed, waiting for him.

"Well, Mr. Waddington, isn't it nice to get away from the crowd? I needed a quiet break. Cook is having problems with the Eggs Florentine. I told Charlie we should have fired him. Very noisy … very noisy down there." Her head bobbed. "I do like it quiet. Please," she said, patting the bed, "sit with me for a while."

The last thing Waddington wanted to do was sit on the bed with Mrs. Charlie Fair. There would be no way he could explain the situation to Charlie. He decided to appeal to her hostess role. "Don't you think maybe we should be getting back to your guests?"

"Why? No one will miss me. They're all here to see Charlie. Even the women of my petition committee. They've all come to see my beautiful Charlie." There was resignation in her voice. She looked directly into his face, her eyes searching, evaluating, assessing. "Has anyone ever told you that you have a very kind face, Mr. Waddington?"

Waddington fumbled for a response, but none seemed appropriate. Again, he found himself fascinated with the slightly off-center face. He had the curious impression that she was sending him a tacit invitation, but to what?

"Do you have a first name, Mr. Waddington?" Her eyes locked on his.

"Preston. But most of my friends call me Pres."

"I would prefer to call you Preston if you don't mind. It sounds so much more serious than Pres. Are you serious, Preston?"

God, where was this going? Wherever it was headed, he didn't have a road map.

"Please, I would like it so much if you'd sit here," she patted the bed again, "next to me."

Waddington sat down, but a full body width further away from the area she'd patted.

"You haven't answered my question, Preston; are you serious?"

"Serious? I'm not sure I understand the question. About my work, you mean?"

"No, about your life ... about ..." She stared off at a large Hudson River School painting that hung over the fireplace. "About the things that really matter ... art ... music ... literature ... the theater. When I was younger, I wanted to be an actress. I was in several plays while I was in college. Are you familiar with *Streetcar Named Desire*?"

"Of course. I loved the movie with Marlon Brando and Vivian Leigh."

"I played the Vivian Leigh part. I was Blanche Dubois. I loved that part. I loved acting."

"Why did you give it up?"

She sighed deeply. "For the same reason I've given up so many things in my life: Charlie Fair."

Waddington decided he wasn't going to press for any further explanation.

"Back to my question, are you a serious person?"

Waddington had no choice but to answer, although he was careful to avoid appearing *too* serious. "I suppose I am. At least, somewhat serious. I like classical music. I guess that qualifies me as serious. I used to be serious about acting. I actually spent time in New York trying to be an actor. But I got serious about trying to make some money to pay the rent and gave it up for a real job."

She looked at him as if he'd just told her he was Russell Crowe. "So, you're an actor?"

Such an adoring look. It thrilled him, but he felt compelled to correct her, "*Was* … an actor and for hardly more than a couple of months. Now I just read plays for the fun of it."

"Maybe you and I should read together." The idea gave her a sudden burst of sober energy. "We could act out some of the great scenes." She slid off the bed and crossed to the French doors that led to the bedroom balcony and opened them. "We could do Romeo and Juliet, right here. You could climb up the trellis. It's almost like this was made for us."

I don't think so, Waddington thought. *Can't imagine Charlie Fair having any interest in sponsoring theatricals on his balcony.*

Olivia walked slowly, and not too steadily, back to the bed and sat very close to him, her leg touching his lightly. Waddington felt a ripple of excitement. She had grown serious and her eyes searched his again. Even his optometrist never looked at his eyes this close.

"Forgive me for staring, Preston, but when I look at you, I see something I don't see in men very often– sensitivity. You strike me as a man who has the ability to express his deepest emotions. You strike me as a man who would understand how a woman might–" She stopped herself in mid-sentence, as though someone had deleted lines from her script. Then she appeared to pick up a totally different script. "Does your wife always talk about you like that in public?" She didn't wait for an answer. "I thought I was going to like Muffy, but now I'm not so sure."

Waddington didn't exactly spring to Muffy's defense, but he offered an excuse. "I think maybe she's had a little too much to drink. She'd been on a diet and, well, you know."

"I suppose you're aware of what they say about my husband?"

Now where are we going? He began to wonder if Mrs. Fair had a problem staying with one subject. Conversational continuity didn't seem to be one of her strengths. He framed his answer as ambiguously as possible. "They say a lot of things about him. What is it that you've heard people say?"

"They say he's not an easy man to work for."

Waddington would agree with that, but not out loud.

"I would add that the only thing more difficult than working for Charlie Fair is to be one of his sons. He's ruined them, you know?"

He didn't know, but he certainly wasn't going to ask why. This conversation was beginning to put him on edge. Again, he danced away. "How many children do you have?"

"Two. Two boys, twenty-four and twenty-one. They don't live with us anymore. They call me but refuse to come home." She became melancholy. "He demanded so much of our boys. He would accept nothing less than perfection in their schoolwork, in their sports, in everything, and they just weren't capable of perfection. Look at them today. They're worthless, no accounts. Neither has a job. They spend all their time rock climbing and bumming around ski slopes. I don't think either has had a haircut in a year. It hurts me to say it, but they'll never recover from their father. I blame myself for that. I should have been more of a mother and less of a referee. Maybe, if I'd just been stronger with Charlie, I might have ..." Her voice trailed off.

Waddington was learning a lot more about the Fair family that he cared to know. Her eyes welled up and a tear found a path down her cheek. He pulled his handkerchief from his breast pocket and offered it to her. Instead of taking the handkerchief, she took his hand and leaned toward him as if she wanted him to wipe the tears away. All he needed now was for someone to walk in and see him sitting on the bed with Olivia, wiping away her tears, and who knew what that someone might think, or worse, say, when he, or she, went back downstairs. He had to find a way to gracefully extract himself.

12
The Love Sponge

For several moments she sat quietly, her eyes closed, lost in her thoughts. *Maybe she'll fall asleep,* he thought. Waddington waited, hoping she would lie back on the bed so that he could leave before anyone saw him. He was about to ease himself off the bed when her eyes popped open and she turned, looking at him with an intensity that he had not seen before.

"I'm thinking about making a change in my life, Preston. A significant change. My life as it is now just isn't working. Would you like to hear what I have in mind?"

"If you'd like to tell me, that's fine, but ..." He decided his best option was to make another attempt at getting her downstairs. "Aren't you concerned that your guests might be wondering where you are? I wouldn't want anyone to get the idea that I've run off with you." He laughed nervously to make sure she understood that he was joking.

Olivia didn't laugh, but looked at him with even greater intensity, "I might like it if you did."

She's coming onto me. Me! Why me, for God's sake? A voice deep inside said, *You have got to get out of here ... now.* He knew it was good advice. Yet, he had to admit, he liked what was happening. This woman, albeit vodka numbed, was attracted to him. *Remember where you are,* the voice warned.

Waddington stood up, actually bolted up, which caught Olivia by surprise. He walked over to the mantle and picked up a large, framed wedding photo. It showed Charlie and Olivia in front of a church altar, smiling at the camera. "You made a very pretty bride."

"And an expectant mother," she added. "I was about two months pregnant when we got married."

Waddington put the picture back, gingerly. Here was something else about Olivia and Charlie he didn't need to know.

"Don't' get me wrong, we didn't *have* to get married, we wanted to get married. We just did things in reverse and got pregnant first. If I hadn't gotten pregnant, we might not have gotten married and we wanted to get married. Do you understand?"

Waddington didn't understand at all.

Olivia read his confusion and felt compelled to explain. "You see, my father didn't like Charlie; he didn't trust him, and he didn't want him within a hundred miles of me. He thought Charlie Fair was a fortune hunter, and maybe he was, but that didn't matter to me. I had never had anybody that handsome in love with me. I wanted to kill my father the first time I invited Charlie to come visit. He'd been there for less than twelve hours. He was sleeping in one of the guest rooms and my father woke him up at about five-thirty that morning and said, 'Young man, I don't like you. I don't want you in my house, and I certainly don't want you dating my daughter. I have, in my hand, a ticket for a bus that will be leaving in exactly thirty-five minutes. I expect you to be on it. Get my drift?'"

"What did Charlie do?" Waddington asked.

"He caught Daddy's drift and caught the bus."

"Obviously, he came back."

"Oh, yes, he was very determined. But so was Daddy. He wouldn't let him in the house. So, I began to meet him in different places. It became a kind of game. Charlie really seemed to love me in those days, and I loved him. I tried to talk Daddy into giving him a chance, but he felt he was just a pretty boy looking for a meal ticket. Of course, later, he learned that Charlie had a lot to offer, and that he really had a feel for the car business. But that was later. So, with Daddy refusing to let us get married, Charlie decided there was only one thing we could do. I had to get pregnant."

"A natural problem-solver, your husband." Waddington's cynicism had just slipped out.

A soulful smile crossed her face. "Yes, I guess he is. Anyway, I got pregnant and when it was confirmed, he went to Daddy and told him he was prepared to do the *right* thing. Daddy gave in. Charlie really didn't give him much choice."

"I'm surprised that your father ever forgave him. I guess he did, though. Otherwise, how could Charlie be where he is today?" That really sounded cynical, and he decided to backtrack. "I don't mean to say that Charlie wouldn't have been made president on his own merit, but ..."

Olivia jumped in and finished the thought for him, "... but it helped to have his father-in-law running the company, was what you were about to say."

"Well, I ..." Waddington had no idea how to respond.

Apparently, she needed no response. "Actually, I'm not sure that deep down in his heart Daddy has ever really forgiven him. Daddy did not appreciate being boxed in and having no option but to let us gets married."

Waddington decided to become supportive, "Well, it seems to have worked out. You two have been married a long time and there's something to be said for that these days."

"Yes, we have been married a long time," she replied flatly. When she began again, there was resentment in her voice. "But it's no secret that my husband has ... well, shall we say he has any number of other interests, which he pursues with far more vigor than our marriage, if you know what I mean?"

Waddington knew very well what she meant, but there was nothing he could say. He wondered how best he might derail the direction of this conversation before it went places he didn't want to go. Again, words failed him.

"I know the question most of my friends would like to ask is whether I am aware of his infidelity." A wan smile crossed her face and she repressed a brief laugh. "If they asked, I'm not sure I would have the courage to answer. I'm not a good liar."

It had to be the vodka talking or whatever else she had been drinking. He could simply not understand why she had selected him, someone she had never laid eyes on, to be her confidant. All the signs said quicksand ahead and he wasn't about to venture any further. He would simply say that he and Muffy had to go home, excuse himself, and leave.

She wasn't about to let him. "I'm afraid, I owe you an apology," she said abruptly.

"What for?"

"For confiding in you the way I have. I know I'm talking gibberish, and I'm embarrassing myself. I'm sure it's the vodka. I really shouldn't have burdened you this way. I have no idea what's brought this on. I guess …" her eyes seem to plead for his understanding. "I guess I just needed to talk to someone. And when I first saw you downstairs, I said, 'There is a man who will listen.' I don't know what it was, but I felt I could confide in you. And I needed someone to confide in. Please, Preston, sit down beside me again. I find talking to you to be such a comfort."

He hesitated.

"Please," she held up her hand, the one without the Hope Diamond, and let her eyes do the rest. He sat down. She moved very close to him. *Very* close. She pressed her leg against this thigh. "You see, Preston, I'm about to make a significant change in my life." Her tone had become somber, even slightly ominous. "I've decided to do something. My mind is made up and no one is going to convince me otherwise. I'm going to … I'm going to …" She paused and looked away, taking a moment to compose herself for the announcement. She picked up where she'd left off. "I'm going to … go …" her eyes close slightly as the vodka reasserted itself. "… shopping …"

Shopping? he asked himself. *She's going shopping? This is the change in her life? What is she talking about?*

And then she told him. "I'm going to go shopping for an affair. I want to take a lover."

He choked back a chuckle. "That should be *some* shopping trip." He really hadn't meant his response to sound as flip as it did. It just came out that way.

"Then you approve?"

"Of your taking a lover?"

"Yes."

How to answer? "I guess you could say … aahh … I don't think I'm really in a position to pass judgment on any decision that someone decides to make. I mean, if that person wasn't me making the decision … then passing judgment isn't my place … if you know what I mean?" Waddington wasn't sure that even he knew what he meant.

Her eyes danced with excitement. She had presumed acceptance. "What you're saying is that you want what I want." She was looking at him intently again; the passion was building like a magnetic force. "And all I want is someone who will truly love me. For me. And not for what my father can do for them or for my money. Just me. You see, Preston, I am just a love sponge."

"A love sponge?" Certainly Webster wasn't going to define that term for him.

"I need love." She was slurring her words badly and fighting to keep her eyelids open. "But it's been so long since there has been any love for me to soak up. I've become very dry … emotionally, that is." She took his arm and laid her head on his shoulder. "For what it's worth, Charlie and I haven't shared a bedroom or even a bed for years."

In that instant she had assumed the shopping position and Waddington began to feel like merchandise on the shelf.

Me? he asked himself. *She wants to have an affair with me?* It was surreal. Here was this rich, attractive woman shopping for a man at a Walmart when she could have been scooping up good-looking studs at Ralph Lauren. All of them would be more than happy to wet her sponge. Clearly, the vodka had prevailed. And yet, he had to admit he was flattered that she had chosen him, short-lived as that choice was destined to be. Other than Muffy, no woman had even found him remotely attractive or come on to him like this.

Sitting there, feeling her leg pressed against his, her face within a breath, he sensed that all he had to do was raise his hands, take her breasts, and she would respond by bringing her mouth to his. The prospect of holding those marvelous breasts and kissing that mouth made him light-headed. No, he was actually dizzy. For a moment, she opened her eyes and looked up at him. He sensed in that moment that she was waiting for him to take charge, to do something. But what? He was a little short on experience when it came to seduction.

Particularly when the seducee is one, totally inebriated, and two, the president's wife. It echoed in his ears, the president's wife. *The president's wife? Are you nuts?* the voice inside him screamed. *Being found with the president's wife, sitting on the president's bed, will put you on a fast-track to losing your job, your wife, and your head.*

Her eyes closed again. She could fight it no longer. Her empty glass rolled onto the floor, her head fell back off his arm, and she began to slip off the end of the bed. Waddington caught her before she reached the floor, picked her up, and carried her around to the head of the bed. For a moment, her eyes opened and looked up at him with a satisfied smile.

"Whoever you are, I have always depended on the kindness of strangers." With that she passed out.

Whoever I am? She's so drunk, she's forgotten my name. Maybe that was a good thing. Waddington slowly positioned her on the bed with a pillow under her head. Her last statement before passing out sounded familiar to him. What was it? Then it came to him. Blanche. In *Streetcar Named Desire.* That was her line as they took her off to the loony bin. What a great exit line for Olivia, he thought. Waddington covered her with a blanket and bent close to her face and whispered, "I'm a little bit in love with you, Olivia Fair." He hadn't felt this kind of excitement for a woman in a long, long time. *I should feel guilty about what I'm thinking, but I don't.*

Waddington took one last long look at her fascinating, slightly off-center face. It would probably be the last time he would see her–this close, certainly. In the morning, she would wake and, hopefully, have little, or no, memory of their conversation. He prayed that would be the case. He noticed her lips parted slightly. Waddington found himself confronting an overwhelming desire to kiss that mouth. Oh, what a mouth that would be to kiss. And then he did, lightly.

Waddington walked quickly to the bedroom door, opened it, and peered into the hallway to be sure it was empty. It was. He slipped out, closed the door, then hurried to the staircase and began to amble down, stopping to admire the paintings, just another guest on tour. As he reached the bottom of the stairs, he noticed it was after four and that the brunch had finally appeared. Most of the guests had already foraged through the opulent display of food, leaving it looking like a garden stripped by locusts. He paused and glanced back upstairs, dwelling on the kiss he had given Olivia. He felt like a schoolboy who had copped his first feel from a date who had fallen asleep in a car at a drive-in. He wasn't exactly proud of it, but he'd do it again … anytime.

13
This is Not a Good Idea

Waddington's phone was ringing as he entered his office the following Monday morning.

"Waddington," he answered.

"Pres, this is Charlie Fair."

Oh my God, Waddington's pulse jumped. *Why is he calling me? What does he know? What did Olivia tell him? I am dead!*

But he wasn't dead. "Listen, I have a favor to ask of you."

"Sure," Waddington answered tentatively.

"You know my wife and yours are involved in this campaign to keep those do-gooder assholes from building that low-income housing project in Grosse Pointe. Well, my wife has decided she needs some kind of brochure. You know, a kind of statement of their position. They want people to understand why they should oppose this thing. Goddamn, who needs a bunch of indigent riffraff living across the street? They'd block my view of the lake. Besides, they'd probably break into every house in town. Anyway, Olivia needs a writer and, since you're a writer, she wondered if I might lend you to the cause, so to speak. I'm sure it wouldn't take all that much of your time."

This is not a good idea, was what Waddington wanted to say. But how to beg off diplomatically? Easy. Next week he would be involved in a week-long presentation at the proving grounds for the writers from the car buff magazines. He offered that up as his reason for having to decline.

Charlie made short work of that excuse. "There's no big hurry on this. You can work on it the week after. This thing is going to drag on for a long time, I suspect."

So much for that attempt. Waddington decided to turn him down by offering a better alternative. "I'm flattered that you and Mrs. Fair would consider me for something like this, but I really think she'd get a much better writing job from someone at the advertising agency. I mean, they are masters at selling things and it seems to me what you're talking about here in this brochure is a sales job. One of their copywriters would be a lot better choice than me." Waddington felt he'd made a strong case.

"Naw, those bastards would charge me an arm and a leg if I asked them to do this. They're expensive. You, I've got for free. Well, not free exactly, but almost free since you're on the payroll."

"But …"

Charlie cut in. "I won't take no for an answer. Neither will Olivia. Consider this an irrevocable request from your CEO. Okay? Call her at your convenience. She can fill you in on what they're looking for. As I said, this shouldn't take a guy like you hardly any time at all. And my wife says she'd really like to work with you. I guess you must have impressed her. Not many people do, you know. So, I'm counting on you to get in bed with her on this."

Now *there* was an interesting choice of words. Waddington choked back a laugh before it could escape into the phone. In truth, since the kiss and the fight he'd had with Muffy on the way home from the party over her discussion of their sex life with a bunch of strangers, the thought of "getting in bed with Olivia" had become a late-night fantasy.

"Yes, you can count on me," Waddington answered. The thought of her breasts, her lips, that off-center face, rose like an ocean wave breaking over him, pulling him under. *Talk about courting potential disaster. Whoa!*

14
The Verite Truth or
They Shoot Messengers

Every year during the first week of June, Axel McPherson, Waddington, and his training staff coordinated a week of the long-lead press previews for those automotive magazines that had deadlines well in advance of their September publications. The writers and photographers were invited to spend a day at the company's Michigan proving grounds for a full day of marketing and sales briefings and hands-on driving on the test track. The purpose was to give the automotive writers an opportunity to hear the company's marketing pitch and then experience the cars, safely, at top highway speeds and under conditions that only a controlled track environment can provide.

The highlight of the event came at the end of the day. The writers put on racing helmets, belted themselves into the seats, and then took the cars out on a special road course that featured high-speed straight-a-ways and an infield road course that looked like so much spaghetti on a plate, curving, dipping, and twisting with its different surfaces, wide arcs, and hair-pin turns. The course was well-marked with speed limits and safety cones to assure that the writers would drive within the dynamic limits of the car.

The objective was to let the writers dazzle themselves so that they would come back into the staging area convinced, or reasonably convinced, that the company's Verite 300 or new Le Vent was, at the very least, a discount version of BMW's driving machine. It was an illusion, of course, but then that's what most automotive writers write about,–illusions.

"I told them specifically to hold it down in the curves. I even put up forty-five miles-per-hour signs on the hairpins." Hap Burlington ran the proving grounds, and he was clearly angry. "There's always one guy whose gotta prove he's got a bigger dick than anyone else." As he, Waddington, and Axel walked around the badly damaged blue Verite 300 that had just been towed off the track, he added, "The last thing I told those writers after lunch was, 'easy in the hairpins.' The car won't hold really tight curves much past fifty. I figured putting a forty-five mile-per-hour limit would give them a bit of a cushion."

Waddington was well aware that most automotive writers believe, deep down, they have the makings of stock car drivers. Hey, they write about cars, so they must be able to drive them. Fast. The trouble was more than a few of them really didn't know how to drive fast in the same way that professionals do.

"What it looks like to me is that the guy came into the curve too fast–I'm guessing maybe fifty-five–and realized too late he wasn't going to make the curve. He's got his wheels turned, he's plowing toward the cement barriers, he panics and stands on the brakes. The rear end breaks loose and we have one less Verite to drive tomorrow."

"Nobody was hurt, right?" Axel asked.

"No, he was belted and wearing a helmet. Shook him up a bit, maybe. But I'll bet you the house he'll be telling everyone back in his office about it for a month. Nothing like driving into a wall to make a guy feel like a race car driver."

Hap Burlington kicked at a rear tire that was now leaning at a forty-five-degree angle. "I'll tell you what's really scary. We put those cement barriers on the curve just last month. If they hadn't been there, the wheels would have dropped in the drainage ditch, and this car would still be rolling."

"I guess we better change the layout so that they won't get into the corners as fast," Waddington said.

Axel nodded his agreement. "Yeah, bring 'em to a dead stop a couple of times, especially before they get into the hairpins. That'll slow 'em."

"I can loan you a couple guys if you need help changing the course," Hap said.

"All I need is some more yellow cones. My trainers and I can take care of it tomorrow morning."

Axel had wandered to the other side of the car and was now on his way back. "You know why I think the guy lost it in the curve?" He didn't wait for an answer. "Perception. The perception we've created in our advertising is that the Verite 300 is a true performance car. What we have, in reality, is a terrific automotive design that *looks* like a sports coupe, *sounds* like a sports coupe and has a *name* like a sports coupe. The reality is that if someone is looking for a true sports car, a car they really can throw around, power through the curves and blow everyone else off the road, it's going to cost them another thirty to fifty grand. And need I say, they won't find that in any of our showrooms."

"Then, why in hell are we making commercials showing the Verite looking like it just won the French Grand Prix?" Hap asked.

"Marketing," Waddington answered.

"Fuck marketing. We're pitching performance when we should be promoting precaution," Hap said. "How about if we put a warning tag on the car, like they do on cigarette packs. 'This car could be dangerous to your health in sharp curves.' Maybe we should suggest that when people come up on a tight turn, they stop the car, get out, and push it around the curve." It was a funny image, but nobody was laughing.

Axel stared at the car. "I don't understand it," he said after a few moments. "Other than just driving the Verite back and forth to the office, I really haven't had a chance to ring it out. But I clearly remember several years ago, it must have been maybe five or six months before the introduction, I was out here giving it a workout. While nobody was going to mistake it for a Benz or Porsche, I would have sworn there wasn't a corner or a curve on this track that I took under sixty. Maybe it was all in my head, but as I recall, I was able to ram it through that same hairpin, and the car gave me just the right amount of oversteer to hold my track. It really felt good to me, I almost believed I was in an Audi TT."

"Maybe the accident was just driver error. Automotive writers spend a lot more time driving desks than they do driving cars," Waddington said.

"Maybe. But if he wasn't doing more than fifty-five, then the rear end shouldn't have broken loose like that." Axel turned to Hap. "Where are the rest of the Verites?"

"They're setting them up for tomorrow's session."

"Do you guys want to take a ride with me?"

"Sure, as long as you don't run us into a wall." Waddington's jest was tinged with a hint of apprehension. Axel's heavy foot had put the fear of God in more than a few of his passengers at the proving grounds.

"I'd do my best not to," Axel grinned.

The three men walked over to the staging area where the Verites and Le Vents had been parked in a long, neat line. Waddington called track control on his two-way radio and let them know they were going out on the track and to hold all other cars. Hap sat in the back and Waddington took the passenger seat. Axel eased onto the track and then floored it. He made one complete circuit and was well into the second before he was ready to pass judgment.

"This is not the car I remember," Axel said as he navigated the twisting infield road course. "Much too much over-steer. It feels like I'm going to lose it in the corners every time I get over fifty.

What the hell happened? Is it the tires? Are they low on air?"

"Nope!" Hap replied. "Got 'em at forty pounds for high-speed performance. The reason it feels loose is because the rear suspension in this car is totally different from the one you drove two years ago. The original Verite design had a very different suspension system."

"Are you saying this *isn't* the suspension in the original specs?"

"That's what I'm saying. A couple of my friends in engineering told me that about six months before we began production, word came down that we had to take some content out of the car. There was no way we were going to be competitive pricewise and make a profit if we didn't cut costs. Every memo that came down from management said the same thing, 'Cut costs.'" One of the places they found to save a few bucks was in the suspension. By the time they were done, the suspension was nowhere near as hefty as it was in the original prototype you drove."

"I'd like to take a closer look at the suspension," Axel said. "Hap, can you get someone to put that wrecked Verite on a lift?"

"No problem." Hap pulled out his two-way radio and called for a forklift to take the car to the proving ground's service garage.

The three men arrived at the garage just as a big forklift put the Verite onto a car lift. They saw it immediately; one of the links between the suspension and the wheels was twisted and broken.

"No way that should happen at sixty-miles-an-hour. No way," Hap said.

"Look at the stabilizer bar," Axel said. "It can't be more than a half inch thick. It should be at least an inch. You can't have a sports car with a curtain rod for a stabilizer bar."

"Here's something else you should see," Hap pointed toward the springs. "The original specs call for variable rate springs. Those are constant rate springs."

"What's the difference?" Waddington asked.

"First, there's cost. Constant rates are a lot cheaper. Then there's performance. When you get into a corner and the constant rate springs start to depress, they do so at a constant rate of resistance. Doesn't take much for them to hit bottom. When they do, your rear end will be driving itself. With variable rate, the springs are designed to provide an increasing amount of resistance as the springs flex. That way, they are not likely to bottom out. The result is the car is going to be much more stable in a curve."

"How long before they released the Verite for production was the change made?" Axel asked.

"Not long. Which is why I don't think they put a lot of thought into what they were doing to the performance of the car. We got the new version out here well after it was in full production and were told to rerun our standard performance tests, which we did. That's when we found there are certain driving situations in which the rear end will come around and kiss the front before you can say

'Oh shit!' When we sent the results of the tests to corporate …"

"Who at corporate?" Axel interrupted.

"Who else? The Verite is Charlie's baby, as he has made very clear to us all. From design through production, everything and anything having to do with Verite went through him. Every time somebody complained that this or that change was cheapening the car, his response was, 'I don't give a shit; I want you to cut costs.' The man had spoken, and that was that."

"But what did he say about the results from your rerun of the performance tests?"

"Two words, 'Results unacceptable.'"

"So, what did you do?"

"We made them acceptable."

"How?"

"We did what Charlie told us to do. We ran all the tests at slower speeds. It was pure bullshit."

"What an approach to problem solving: Forget about fixing the car; just fix the test results," Waddington said.

Axel shook his head. "How come I never heard anything about this?"

"Are you fuckin' kiddin' me? Nobody was to hear nothin' about nothin, if you get my drift. Mine is not to reason why; mine is to hang in here two more years until I can retire. But." he held up his hand in a gesture that said there was more, "in my report, I went on record saying that the Verite 300 released for production did not meet the original performance specs. I made it damn clear that the changes in the suspension system had compromised performance integrity and that there was a strong, I emphasized *strong,* probability that it had increased the safety risks."

Waddington found it all incredible. "Now all we need is for Ralph Nader to find out about our bogus test and write a sequel to *Unsafe at Any Speed.*"

"Well, the Verite isn't anywhere near as bad as the old Chevy Corvair. Let's just say the car is unsafe at *certain* speeds."

"Terrific!" Axel said in disgust.

"Now we come to the bottom line. If you ask me, and nobody has, I'd say the fact that we all but totaled a car here today proves that the Verite is an accident waiting to happen."

Waddington looked at Axel. "Considering what happened in Westchester, maybe our accident hasn't waited."

"What are you talking about?" Hap asked.

Waddington told him what they knew about the Swenson accident and the threat of a lawsuit.

"It sounds like Mr. Swenson discovered just how *unsafe at certain speeds* this car can be," Hap said.

"How difficult, which is to say, how expensive would it be to retrofit the Verite with the original suspension system?" Waddington queried.

"Interesting you should ask," Hap said. "The other thing I included in my report, and this was something I'm sure sent Charlie through the roof, was my recommendation that we consider a recall."

"Ohhhh, now you're talkin' big bucks," Axel said.

"Yeah, but what would a class action lawsuit cost?" Hap asked.

"Bigger bucks," Waddington volunteered.

"Right," Hap said. "And money isn't the only thing at stake here. Consider this: What if the Swenson woman decides to sue. What do you think would happen if her lawyer were to discover that someone very high in management had ordered the downgrade of the suspension system, okayed advertising that claimed the Verite was something akin to another 'Driving Machine' and then authorized bogus tests designed to conceal the fact that it had serious performance limitations?"

"That someone in high management would probably end up spending time gettin' to know the guys from Enron."

"The French would go home, and we'd all be looking for work," Waddington added.

"Frankly, I could give a shit about what happens to Charlie," Axel said. "But you're right; if Charlie were to go down the tubes because of this, so would the company."

Waddington suddenly felt like the Dutch boy who's found the hole in the dike. The question was, did anyone have a big enough thumb to fill it?

Waddington left the two men to get ready for the next day's press presentation. Axel and Hap watched him drive off and then made their way to Hap's office. As they crossed over the track and entered the administrative offices, Axel said, "You know, considering what you've told me about

Charlie's decision to downgrade the suspension, I'm a little surprised that he's not more concerned about the potential of a lawsuit. For his own neck, if nothing else."

"Maybe he is. A week ago, Harry Spar showed up giving me some B.S. excuse for going though all our test track files. What he was really after, I discovered, was all the documentation of the Verite tests, before *and* after the suspension redesign."

"How do you know that's what he was after? Did he say he was?"

"No. He didn't tell me anything. After he left, I went through the files myself and everything related to the Verite was missing. He took 'em. Smell a rat? I do."

"I smell Charlie."

"One and the same."

"So, all the Verite test results are gone?"

Hap smiled the smile of a man who had been playing in this ball field for a long, long time. "Well, the ones in my office file are gone. But not the ones I keep in my insurance files."

"Insurance files? What insurance files?

"'Remember back in 1970, Ford had their Pinto problem?"

"Of course, the exploding gas tank."

"That was the symptom; the problem was that they *knew* about it, and according to people close to the car, everyone was afraid to tell Iacocca about it for fear of being fired. In our case, Charlie has been told. I've got letters and reports that have Charlie Fair's heavy hand all over em. Plus, a couple of his initials. I could cook him. But I have no interest in l. ting the stove. The reason I'm keeping my copies of the file is just in case he starts shopping for a fall guy. If he decides to save his ass and begins to look for someone to fall on his sword, it sure ain't going to be me," he said emphatically.

"Charlie doesn't know it, but you're one dangerous guy," Axel said, half serious.

"He doesn't know it now, and he won't know it ever, unless one day, he tries to put the finger on me or one of my people. We find the problems out here. We don't create 'em. We leave that to the assholes like Charlie back in Detroit." He laughed.

"So, you have copies of the last Verite performance tests?"

"Like I said, in my insurance file."

"You mind making me copies for my insurance files?"

"Nope. As long as you're able to forget where you got them."

"I've got a very short memory."

Axel and Hap left the proving grounds and drove to Hap's home. He poured them both a beer and then went down into his basement office to retrieve the thick test file and make a copy. When Hap returned, he handed the pile of documents to Axel and said, "For what's it worth, I suggest you be very careful with these. It's like giving a guy a load of dynamite to blow up a tree stump. You hope he knows how to use it and doesn't end up knocking down the whole forest. This little pile of paper could cause this company a lot of trouble."

"It's time to talk recall with our leader."

"Do you think Charlie will listen to you?"

"Maybe not, but somebody has to tell the emperor he has no clothes."

"You're aware, of course, that the man is known for shooting messengers."

"So, let him start shooting." He picked up the copy of the Verite file, "With this, I'm wearing a bulletproof vest."

"Then, l hope he doesn't aim for your head."

15
Green Sally Rands

The driver of the car hauler couldn't believe it; nine, count 'em, nine green Sally Rands on his truck. *(Translation: Car industry lingo for a "stripper"– i.e., base cars equipped with no options or accessories. The least expensive and least desirable cars a dealer might have on his lot.)*

Da sheet iz gonna hit da fan, he thought, as he pulled off the Connecticut Turnpike at a rest area. It was 8:30 p.m. *Don't wanna get der too early*, he thought. The driver turned off the motor, crawled back into the sleeping area at the rear of the cab, and set his alarm for 1 a.m. At 2 a.m., he pulled up in front of Jack Poor Motors and parked under a sign that read: "They call me 'Poor' because I practically give cars away." As he swung down out of the cab, he looked up at the load of Kelly Green Defiants. Everyone a "Sally Rand."

Dis guy is gonna luv seeing deez cars, he thought and then laughed. "Hee, ha, ha, haw, haw, hack, hack, hack!" The driver put on his gloves and began to pull out the long metal car ramps and set them in place so he could begin to back the cars off the carrier.

16
Poor Jack Poor

At 2:45 a.m. Jack Poor was having a fitful night. In fact, he had hardly had any sleep at all. His thoughts kept pondering Waddington's phone call earlier that morning, the second one in ten days. Waddington never called him. They didn't like each other much, so there was really nothing for them to talk about. *But then two calls in the same week to ask how my month is going. Suddenly he's concerned if I'm selling cars. I don't think so. No, he called to pump me about the Verite accident. For two weeks, I don't hear anything from Detroit about the accident, and then I get a call from Waddington. Wants to know if I've heard from Mrs. Swenson's lawyer. Why should that concern him? It shouldn't. But it should concern the company. So why hasn't it. Or maybe it has?*

Jack rolled over and continued to fret. *If anybody should have called me, it ought to have been Charlie. What are they up to? I gotta believe they'd like to keep Mrs. Swenson quiet, at least until the French deal is signed. If she starts to squawk, it could cause a real public relations problem. But hell, she hasn't got a case. Her husband's mind was on his dick and missed the turn. They should know that. But then, maybe they don't. Of course, they don't. Who would have told them?*

Then another thought occurred to him. *Those bastards couldn't be setting me up, could they?*

149

Maybe there's something going on here that I don't know about and they plan to hang me out to dry. That would be just like those sonsabitches.

The phone rang on Jack's nightstand.

"Hello." He fumbled to turn the clock to see the time, 3:15.

"Mr. Poor, this is Gartner from Greenwich 24/7 Security. You told me to call anytime a car hauler arrived after midnight. Well, there's one here now, and he's unloading a whole bunch of green cars."

"Sonofabitch!!!" Jack exploded, propelling himself straight up in bed. "Those fucking bastards!" Jack Poor was sitting on the side of the bed now. He stood up. "Did you say *green*?"

"Yes, sir. You planning a St. Paddy's Day sale or something? In case you haven't noticed, it's June 10th, so you're either too late, or too early."

Jack never heard anything past "Yes, sir."

"What's wrong?" Petula Poor asked, raising her head slightly off the pillow. From the tone of her voice, she was making no effort to hide the fact that she was far more irritated at having been awakened than concerned over what fucking bastards he might be referring to. There were so many fucking bastards in her husband's life, the salespeople who worked for him at the dealership, the mechanics, the zone managers, the factory representatives, his customers. There seemed to be little distinction; they were all, at one time or another, fucking bastards.

"The bastards are dumping cars on the lot," he said, letting his accent regress to his Brooklyn roots. "I gotta get down there and break some fuckin' knees."

Petula was now fully awake and propped up on an elbow, prepared to vent her pique. "I cannot believe that after all these years, you are unable to manage that dealership better." Her irritation with her husband bore a weary edge, like that of a woman so long suffering that she could barely muster a decent level of indignation. She let out a long, deep sigh, "Once again, Daddy and I will probably have to bail you out. If it weren't that it keeps you out of the house, I'd sell the whole thing in about two minutes flat." Having made her point, she seemed to lose interest in whatever the 'fucking bastards' had done and rolled over. "Be a dear, Weasel, and turn off the light."

Weasel? She hadn't called him that in a while. It was her pet name for him, based on a corruption of his middle name, Wessel. The fact that she had called him that indicated one of two things: Either she retained some small residue of affection or, more likely, he thought, she had forgotten the endearment and was expressing her opinion of him. Life at the Poor house, and it was anything but poor, had not been a bed of roses since she had discovered that Jack was something less than fully devoted to her.

Jack switched off the light, mouthed a silent "bitch" to her back, and left the bedroom.

Jack Poor, like many car dealers of low-priced, high-volume cars, was often subjected to what the trade referred to as midnight deliveries or factory dumping. When factory inventories got too high, the factory would initially try to convince the dealers to order more cars, along with the promise of financial support in the form of a "program" or a consumer deal, like "$1000 Cash Back," or "Zero Financing." In each case, they designed the program to enable the dealer to sell the cars to the consumers for less and still make a reasonable profit. So intent are the manufacturers to keep their inventories at reasonable levels, they are usually willing to try anything short of a buy-one-get-one-free deal to get the cars off their books and onto dealers' lots. If, as in the case of the Defiant, the dealers elected not to participate in a "program" or to beg off saying they already had too many cars, the trucks would roll at night, and the dealers would arrive at their lots the next morning to discover a sudden increase in their inventory.

Jack Poor did not bother dressing. He put on a raincoat over his pajamas, jumped in his car, and tore out of the driveway. He arrived at his dealership just in time to see the truck driver unloading the last of the green Defiants.

"Chu Jak Poor?"

"Yes, goddamn it! What the hell do you think you're doing?"

"Deliverin' boats. What's it look like I'm doin'?"

"Don't get smart-ass with me. Put these cars back on the truck and get them the hell out of here."

"Not my yob. I jess unload 'em and park 'em. You wanna sign for these?"

"No fuckin' way."

The driver shrugged, "Sign or no sign, no farkin' matter ta me. Der yer cars now."

What the hell kind of accent is that? Jack wondered. "Where are you from?"

"New Jercee."

"Before that."

"Sumplace else."

"Why am I not surprised?" Under his breath, he mumbled, "Goddamn foreigners are ruining the country. We oughta deport 'em all." Jack decided he'd given enough time and thought to U.S. immigration policies and turned his attention to the line of Green Defiants. *Green Farkin' Defiants.* Jack opened the door to the Defiant closest to him and looked inside. Doesn't even have a cassette player. "Shit! Every one a Sally Rand." *(Or 'stripper.' Car dealer parlance for a car stripped of all amenities.)* Jack hated the Defiant. There were times he made so little markup on the car that he felt it would be cheaper to pay people to buy them.

"Chu sell alotta green cars? Green for Green Witch, right?" Hee, haw, haw, ha, ho, ha!

"Get your foreign ass and your goddamn truck off my property," Jack commanded, having elected to screw the PC shit. He wasn't about to be ridiculed by some immigrant. Hell no! The trucker backed up slowly toward his truck shouting something, actually a whole lot of somethings, in a language that Jack had never heard before. Nevertheless, he understood the message and responded with an obscene gesture.

He understood another message as well. It had come from the company's Northeast Zone Manager. "That asshole," he shouted at the load of Defiants. It was bad enough that he dumped the cars on him, but *green* Sally Rands? This was more than just reducing factory inventory. It was a message. And the message was that Jack hadn't properly taken care of the zone manager in the last several months. A year ago, when this had happened with sunset orange Cadences, Jack had gone out and bought a gold Rolex and sent it to the zone manager as a birthday present, with no idea, or caring, whether it was his birthday or not. The orange cars disappeared and the more salable White, Blue, and Maroon ones, fully loaded, suddenly appeared in their place. This shitload of green cars was the zone manager's way of saying that the Rolex was fine for last year, but what have you done for me lately?

The trucker climbed into his cab, revved his diesel for a full two minutes, doing his best to wake everyone within eight blocks, and pulled away.

As Jack cursed the Sally Rands, his zone manager, Charlie Fair, and the company in general, he found himself wondering again about the real purpose of Waddington's call. Was all this part of some plan by the company to fuck him over? Standing on his car lot in the middle of the night, his raincoat over his pajamas, he felt very heavy, weighed down, as though even gravity had it in for him.

17
Reversing Gravity

As Jack opened the door to the dealership and made his way up to his office, he asked himself the question that he'd been asking for the last three years: *Why in hell did I agree to take on the franchise?* Even Waddington, whose opinions he generally had little use for, had tried to discourage him.

"These are not the kind of cars that are going to sell in an upscale market like Greenwich," Waddington had counseled him. "Why take the risk when you've got Toyota and Jeep lines that are doing great?" Jack had dismissed his advice out of hand.

"The Verite 300 is going to make a lot of dealers very rich men," Charlie Fair had assured him, as they sat in the Las Vegas suite. Jack was on his fifth martini and was being tortured by a woman with enormous breasts. "The only way you can get a piece of the action is to buy a franchise." Charlie had leaned close to Jack and put a reassuring hand on his shoulder. "I shouldn't be admitting this to you, but I need a location in Greenwich. To have the Verite 300 sold in what's probably the richest city in America," he paused. "well, I don't have to tell you what that could mean for our image."

As if on cue, the woman with the large breasts pressed close and put her hand on Jack's thigh. Charlie recognized that Jack had tacitly accepted the proposition–his–and was about to make one of his own to the woman crawling into his lap. Charlie eased himself out of his chair and started for the door. "I can promise you this, Jack; if you buy our franchise, you're going to have a direct line to me any time of day or night." Charlie's sincerity virtually oozed across the room like an oil spill. "I'm going to work very hard to make sure you are one of our most successful dealers. You have my word on that, and you can take my word to the bank."

"I went to the bank and his fuckin' word bounced like a bad check," was the way Jack put it to Waddington a year later. "The son-of-a-bitch conned me, big time." In truth, what really embarrassed Jack was that Charlie had succeeded in conning a con man.

While the Verite 300 was a good-looking sports car, it could do nothing to improve the appearance of the Cadence and Defiant. It was like putting Nicole Kidman next to Janet Reno and Madeline Albright. Jack would have sold the franchise in a New-York-minute, but he knew that no dealer in his right mind would even consider buying him out. He couldn't just close it down; he had too much money tied up in it. Petula's money, to be specific. And if she lost so much as a nickel after the sell job he'd done on her, she'd probably lynch him in front of the dealership.

As Jack pulled out of the lot, his headlights swept across the crushed Swenson Verite 300 that had been moved behind the wash rack to hide it from public view. *I'd like to take that piece of shit and shove it and this whole fucking franchise up Charlie Fair's ass.*

It came to him slowly as an amorphous possibility, full of promise, but badly in need of shaping and refinement. *Maybe I could do exactly that.* It occurred to him that the combination of the Swenson accident, the company's financial problems, and the negotiations with the French consortium might just give him the leverage to get out of the franchise financially whole. He had no idea how that combination might work to his advantage, but at least he'd think about it. Certainly, the last thing Charlie Fair wanted was for someone to toss a monkey wrench into the French deal. Maybe Alfie Swenson's Verite could provide Jack with that wrench.

Jack turned south and headed for Belle Haven, driving through one of the tony sections of Greenwich. He glanced at the still dark mansions whose occupants would never deign to lower themselves to visit his dealership. *Bastards*, he thought, not because they were actually bastards, but more because he was not one of them. In their eyes Jack Poor was ... *a car dealer.* How bitter the residue of the words *car dealer* left on the tongues of those who shunned him at parties. Maybe if he'd sold the prestige marques like Ferrari, Mercedes, or Rolls, they would have regarded him differently. But no, he sold ordinary cars. His early attempts at earning the respect of his neighbors were not helped much by Petula, who seemed to find it amusing to tell people that when she met Jack, he was selling *used* cars. "In Brooklyn, no less. Can you imagine?" she would add, as if totally bewildered by the circumstances that had lured her to Jack's bed. While there was speculation as to why she had married someone of such low standing - no, their daughter was born three years after the wedding - Jack might have argued that he hadn't actually married her, he'd sold himself into indentured servitude.

Petula's father, Armwell "Bumper" McCoy, was one of the more privileged of Greenwich society. As Bumper's only child, Petula was worth tens of millions, and it was said that Brink's trucks were standing on reserve, waiting to deliver a lot more once the old boy died. Not surprisingly, McCoy had been vociferous in his opposition to Petula's announcement that she was buying him a car dealership. Petula's rationale was that she was not about to be accused of harboring a kept husband. A compliant, deferential husband was sufficient. So, she built him a dealership that was the envy of all the high-end dealers up and down the Post Road. However, as her father's daughter, Petula's largess came with a price. Jack could have his name on the door, but she would retain eighty percent of the ownership, a fact Petula was quick to remind him of whenever he tried to exert some control over the dealership. "Your twenty percent doesn't give you the right to do anything but what I tell you to do."

Jack followed Field Point Road to the guard shack that protected the homes of Bumper, Petula, and a few other fortunate few who had the hundreds of millions necessary to maintain this address. Ahead he could see the ornate iron gates that had been purchased from an estate in England, which now served to keep the uninvited at bay just outside the McCoy estate. The place looked like an English castle, and Bumper certainly enjoyed playing Lord of the Manor ... Lord of the Realm ... Lord of the Flies ... Lord of whatever. Most men in Jack's position, married as he was to a woman like Petula McCoy, would have just bided their time, waited for Bumper to kick-off and then moved into this Greenwich castle and become Lord Next. But Bumper made it clear that if he couldn't take his money with him, he was sure as hell not going to leave it behind for Jack Poor.

For all but the first year of their married life, Jack Poor had lived in the wake of Petula's money. When they entertained, he barely attracted any more attention than the wallpaper. Many of the guests had no idea who he was. Those that did limited their conversations to, "Hello, Jack, how's the car business?" Or "Too bad you can't get a good franchise like Mercedes or Lexus." Or "What kind of deal can you get me?" Never anything like, "Where do you and Petula plan to vacation this year?" Or "What do you think of the new French restaurant on Putnam Avenue?" Or "Would you like to join me for a round of golf?"

Once in the early years of their marriage, Jack shared his feelings with Petula about being ignored and neglected. "What am I, chopped liver?"

All she could bring herself to say was, "Please Jack, don't use that chopped liver expression. It's so ... so lowbrow."

Jack had long ago come to accept that he would never be more than consort to Queen Petula. He was to be on call, ready to do her bidding. Emasculated though he was, his role was to be the male figure in the home. But even that became less important as the years passed. Petula and her money had achieved independent status. She was the person *to know* in Greenwich. It mattered not to those who sought her company if she arrived at a party with a husband, an escort, a lover, or alone.

It was predicable that Jack's diminished status in Petula's life would eventually lead to an affair. He fell in love with an automotive insurance claims adjuster from Port Chester. It would be hard to imagine that the woman was truly enamored of Jack; she could easily have done better for herself. However, she became addicted to the extravagant gifts he bought her, and that proved to be enough to sustain her interest in showing up for their trysts at the Roll Inn Motel.

Regular copulation with an attractive, compliant woman made Jack a different man. He had something other than the dealership to look forward to each day. He was more cheerful around the house. There was a lightness to his step, and he began to work out in the basement with weights. It was the weights that made Petula suspect something was going on. She hired a private detective, who quickly discovered there was an insurance claims adjuster in Jack's life. Petula cried, pouted, lamented, grieved, and spent three days locked in her bedroom, available only to her maid, her cook, and her masseuse. But, when the detective reported the insurance claims adjuster was the recipient of gifts paid for with company money, the tears stopped, the lamenting ended, the bedroom door opened, and she erupted with a visceral anger that could have knocked down walls.

"Bring me that bastard! I want his head on a plate! I want him arrested, beaten, drawn, and quartered!" Clearly an affair was one thing but supporting it with her money was an entirely different matter.

Petula declared that no punishment would be severe enough. But then she thought of one. She commandeered the books, barred him from any and all financial transactions, and installed her own accountant. No more would Jack be able to dip into the cash drawer in the Service Department or help himself to a few hundred dollars from the petty cash drawer in the accounting department or pocket a cash down payment for one of his cars.

Ivan Krumpe, who Jack referred to derisively as "my Commie Kraut," was a short, extremely thin little man with wide eyes, who had worked for the IRS. "If you ever," Petula had thundered, "catch that son-of-bitch with his hand in the till, you are to chop it off. "

As Ivan was about one-third Jack's size, the potential for violence, on any level, was out of the question. In fact, Ivan was terrified of Jack and resorted to carrying out his assignments, figuratively at least, from behind Petula's skirts. Almost every conversation began something like, "Mrs. Poor wants this," or "Your wife told me to do that," or "Mrs. Poor will have to be told so-and-so." Even though Jack took personal pleasure in thinking of ways to physically intimidate Ivan the Terrified, he understood, full well, that Ivan was Petula's eyes at the dealership. Jack even suspected he might have planted a hidden listening device in his office. Although when he searched, he found nothing. Still, when he had private calls to make, he used his cell phone. Life at the dealership wasn't much better than a minimum-security prison.

Things weren't all that much better for him at home, either. Petula refused to speak to him other than on those occasions when necessity demanded it, like, "Pass the butter." For almost two months, she wore an expression that made her appear as if, any minute, she expected him to break into the silver chest or run off with the China. But then, as other things, more important social things, vied for her time, she seemed to want to return to life with Jack as it was before. She began to speak to him more often and in longer sentences. "You better call the plumber, because I think my toilet is leaking." Slowly, he returned to his role as a home furnishing. At the dealership, Ivan the Terrified never left his post, but some of the restrictions were lifted when it came to expense advances. Jack felt like a parolee on a work release program.

During that time, Jack made up his mind to escape his incarceration. To hell with Petula and the dealership. He would break free of his servitude. Over the years, he'd managed to squirrel away nearly three hundred thousand dollars in salary and other monies that he'd liberated from various dealership cash boxes. But that sum, he knew, wasn't going to be anywhere near enough. To live comfortably off the interest, he estimated that he was going to need something like two and a half million dollars. That could easily earn him almost two hundred thousand a year, which would sustain life in the Florida Keys. The question, of course, was how to make up for the current shortfall.

No sooner had he asked the question than the good fairy dropped Popper Poppenhaus into his dealership. Before Popper was made VP of Marketing, he had been the account manager with the agency that handled the company's advertising. Popper liked the looks of Jack's main showroom and saw it was an ideal location to shoot the company's car commercials. It did not take long for the two men to find a common interest–they were both looking for money. Chunks of money. *Biggggg* chunks.

The deal they made was simple. Popper would see to it that the ad agency paid Jack an exorbitantly generous fee for the use of the showroom, in cash, of course. Jack, in turn, would return a portion of his payment to Popper. In the three years Popper was with the agency, the arrangement had netted Jack over one hundred thousand dollars.

When Popper accepted Charlie's offer to be VP of Marketing, he had to cut in his replacement at the agency on the deal. Jack was not happy to see Popper have a second kick-back to pay, but there was no other way to keep the money flowing.

The sun was coming up. *Looks like a nice day,* Jack thought. *And if things don't get fucked up at the dealership, I should be able to slip out around noon for a quick visit to the Roll Inn.* He felt his member begin to swell against his pajamas.

He really hadn't intended to renew his liaison with the insurance claims adjuster. She'd come to the dealership to appraise a fender-bender. He had seen her in the lot and, within hours, it was back to Roll Inn Motel. Of course, having her back in his life, as pleasant as it was, meant he had to dip into his savings. Every time they had sex, she had an insatiable desire to go shopping. Jack wondered if it might be some kind of psychological affliction. *We have sex, and she goes shopping. Sex and shopping. Shopping and sex.* They seemed to be irrevocably linked in her mind, to the point where this cause-and-effect relationship summed up their affair.

Occasionally, Jack would be lucky enough to have sex after the stores were closed, so there was little else for them to do but talk. During one of their after-sex conversations, they agreed to escape together to Key West. Sun, sand, and sex. Shopping might be a cut well below New York, but … well, a woman can't have everything. Jack did some research. He talked to several travel agents and even made two calls to a real estate person in Key West. After doing some careful figuring, Jack determined that two million wouldn't do it. He'd need at least two-point-seven million to assure that he and the insurance claims adjuster could spend their days on the beach and their nights in bed with nary a financial care.

His thoughts drifted back to his emerging plan. Wouldn't it be great if he could screw Charlie Fair and get free of Petula all at the same time? Free from Petula! There had to be a way. He was sure there was. He just hadn't found it yet. As he turned into his driveway and turned off the engine, he felt as if gravity had eased up a bit

.

18
Dressed Up for the French

"Well, what is it, a wedding or a funeral?" Muffy asked as Waddington entered the kitchen in his blue suit. Then she remembered. "Oh, this is the day you're to meet with Olivia Fair." She looked at him slightly askance. "Putting on our Sunday best for Mrs. Fair, are we?"

The tone of Waddington's reply was more defensive than called for by Muffy's playful innuendo. "I have a very important meeting this afternoon, with the French, and I won't have time to come home and change." Waddington had fully expected Muffy to say something about the suit. It was, after all, a suit he almost never wore to the office. He decided that a meeting with the French sounded like a plausible excuse. He was sure that Muffy had no idea how perceptive she had been. He *was* putting on his Sunday best for Mrs. Fair, because his ego demanded that he give her the opportunity to see him as something other than the sartorial embarrassment in the mud-brown suit with mismatched pants.

"I think it's a waste of time."

"What is?" Waddington asked.

"You're writing a brochure for the low-income housing petition. We've already got press releases, letters, handouts, signs. Whoever heard of creating a brochure to protest something? I'm afraid Olivia Fair just isn't cut out for this kind of thing. To her, it's like some Junior League project."

"Believe me," he lied, "there are a whole lot of things I'd rather be doing this morning than spending a couple hours at the Fair's." But in truth, there was nothing else he would rather be doing. For one thing, he wanted to look at that wonderful, engaging, slightly off-center face again. For another, he wanted to see if the sober Olivia, assuming she wasn't some kind of morning alcoholic, was different from the one he'd gotten to know before she passed out.

He fully expected to find a more formal, reserved woman bent on presenting a more conservative image. Certainly, if Olivia had any memory of that afternoon, she would, no doubt, want to make it clear that she did not look upon herself as a love-impoverished female. In fact, he would not be surprised if she found some way to characterize their intimate conversation as nothing more than an unfortunate by-product, resulting from the chance nexus of happenstance, proximity, and vodka.

Waddington had no illusions about Olivia reciprocating his affection, even on a platonic basis. The image he confronted in the mirror each morning was not one that would inspire a woman to leave home. Especially not one who lived in a knock-off Versailles. No, he expected nothing more from his visit to Olivia Fair than to have the opportunity to play the part of a tourist, returning to a fascinating place for the sole purpose of enjoying the view once more. Of course, he reasoned, I might find that when she's sober, she's a shrew, and I'll end up feeling sorry for Charlie. He hoped not. Olivia had become his fantasy affair.

"What did you think of her?" Muffy asked.

"Who?" He tried to appear preoccupied with matters other than Olivia Fair.

There was some exasperation in his voice. "Olivia. What do you think of her?"

"What do *you* think of her?" He bounced the question back to Muffy.

"Well, at first, I sort of liked her, but now I'm not all that impressed."

"Really? What made you change your mind?"

"I think she's detached."

"Detached?"

"Like her husband said …"

"Her husband said she was detached?"

Muffy began to laugh. "What he said was …and I love this, 'Olivia has about as much grasp on reality as Marie Antoinette, who thought she was being really helpful when she suggested cake.'"

"Charlie told you that? When?" Waddington was taken aback that anyone, especially Olivia's husband, would have described her in that way.

"At the party. I had a long talk with him."

"About his wife?"

"About his wife," she sounded evasive, "and us."

"You and me *us* or you and Charlie *us*?"

"Well, Charlie and me *us*, I guess. He wanted to know who I was, and I told him about Greenwich and…" she broke off in mid-sentence.

She'd explained about all she intended to explain. "Let's say it was just a nice, friendly, at times, *very* friendly and interesting conversation." The word 'interesting' was accompanied with an enigmatic smile that hinted at volumes left unsaid.

"Did he come on to you?"

"In what way?"

"In any way."

"Well, a little, I suppose. He said I had a nice figure." She smiled sheepishly.

Waddington wondered how he could tell what kind of figure she had with so many puffs, poufs, and bows hung all over her dress.

"You know how a woman senses those things. Actually, I was a little flattered. I mean it's been a long time since any man has given me - *the look.*"

This had to be some kind of perverse justice, Waddington thought. While he was sitting on Olivia's bed doing everything he could to remember where he was and who he was with, Muffy was downstairs letting Charlie hit on her. Had Charlie actually come on to her? With his stable of compliant cupcakes, why would he bother with Muffy? Or was he just confirming, for whatever transitory amusement it gave him, that no woman could resist him whenever he decided to prove his irresistibleness. Charlie did things like that. He considered come-ons and sexual innuendoes as a form of social work for the plus-forty set. Nothing like boosting an older woman's ego, he would say.

"Is it true that Charlie Fair plays around?" Muffy asked.

Waddington was not about to get into that. "There are rumors. But since I'm not among his more intimate acquaintances ..."

"Well, I thought maybe you might have heard something at the office. Eppy Frappernell, she's on the petition committee, pointed out two women at the party that she is almost positive have had affairs with Charlie." Muffy had a flirtatious smile that Waddington had seen her flash at parties when she'd had a little too much to drink. "But can you blame them? I mean, the man is *gorgeous*," she said drawing the word out for emphasis. " Half the women at that party would have lined up to hop in his bed."

That might have been interesting, he thought. *Olivia and me in her bed and Muffy and Charlie in his.* "Which half were you in?"

She became instantly indignant. "Well, I hope you know which half I was in."

The eggs were starting to roll out and Waddington put on his egg-walking shoes. "Of course, I know."

"And?"

"And what?"

"Which half do you suppose I was in?" Her tone was indignant.

"My half, of course," he said solicitously. His answer seemed to mollify Muffy, as she ducked into the closet and reappeared with her Butt Buster.

"What's your big meeting about?" she asked as she unfolded the contraption.

"What meeting?"

"The one you're wearing your suit for?"

Amazing how muddled one becomes when hiding the portent of an affair, however fanciful or unlikely its possible consummation. "It's just sort of an ... of a meeting ... with the French."

"I know it's a meeting with the French. But what's it about?"

"They want me to review our training strategies."

"Are you going to speak French with them? You know, 'Bone Jure Mon Sewer.'" She laughed at the way she had mimicked the language.

"Hopefully, if they want to speak French, I'll be able to do a little better than that."

"I know," she said peevishly, "you're so cultured. You speak French and German. La de da."

"What? Does that make me a bad person?"

"No, but sometimes I think it makes you a real snob."

He had no idea what was bugging her about his ability to speak more than one language, but he had neither the interest nor inclination to find out why.

At that point, Muffy lost interest in his meeting and in disparaging his language skills. "Oh, you'll have to take Hildy to school this morning. I've got to get my workout in now because I promised Mummy I'd give her an hour today on the phone. We've got to go over our checklist for Bumper's surprise birthday party." Bumper was not only her grandfather's nickname, it was what she'd always called him.

"When is the party?"

"Damnit, Pres," she exploded, "I told you specifically to put Friday, June 21st on your calendar. I have plane reservations at 11 a.m. Now don't tell me you've got a goddamn company meeting or something. You are going to be there." The look she gave Waddington made it clear that Muffy was giving no quarter.

Suddenly, the frown left her forehead as she remembered something she'd been meaning to tell Waddington. "Oh, some good news. Mummy has bought Julie a horse, and she's going to give her riding lessons this summer."

"Here, in Livonia? I didn't know we had stables in Livonia."

"Don't be ridiculous. The lessons will be in Greenwich. Julie's going to spend the summer with Mummy. You know how much she adores Greenwich. Livonia and Detroit just aren't Julie. For that matter, they aren't me either."

"But Greenwich is you?"

She avoided his question. "You know, Pres, I'm seriously thinking that Hildy and I will join Julie and spend the summer in Greenwich with Mummy. It would be such a relief to spend some time, quality time, in a more refined environment."

A more refined environment. Every day she sounds more like her mother. God help me. "I guess Grosse Pointe isn't refined enough."

"Of course, it is, but let me be brutally honest. We will *never* be accepted in Gross Pointe society. How could we? You haven't got any financial clout or even a corporate title. Manager doesn't cut it there. You're lost in middle management, which means that in Gross Pointe you're …" she paused to weigh her words and when the scale tipped toward cold candor said, "… you're a *nobody*. By association, so am I. But in Greenwich, well, there, I'm Bumper McCoy's granddaughter. And, as you know, Mummy virtually controls the social scene for everybody who's anybody in Greenwich. There I've got an identity. I'm somebody."

"And by association, what am I in Greenwich?"

She rolled her eyes and said nothing. But he knew the answer. Even by association, in Greenwich, he would still be a nobody in her eyes and Petula's.

"So, is this definite? You and Hildy are going to spend the summer in Greenwich?"

"Yes," She answered definitively.

"And when were you planning to tell me this?" he said making no effort to hide his irritation.

"I'm telling you now," she shot back. Then, quickly, appearing to make an effort to justify her decision, "Pres, you won't even miss us. Summer is your busy time, what with running your sales training programs and producing the dealer meeting. You know very well that you'll probably be up to your behind in alligators for the next three months." She sighed a sigh of mild exasperation as she strapped herself into the Butt Buster. "Why is it every year your summer is such chaos? You'd think after all these years, you'd have things under control. I don't know what it is, but you always seem to have problems. Maybe you just don't manage your time well."

Waddington could feel his blood pressure jump about fifty points. What the hell was she talking about? He ran his department extremely well. Axel never tired of pointing to him as a model of how a department should be run. Everybody gave him high marks for the way he ran the sales training programs and the dealer announcement shows. For a brief moment, he thought about defending himself, but then decided it wasn't worth the effort. Muffy had long ago made up her mind that he was a failure, and there was not much that would change her mind. And anyway, arguing with Muffy about anything was an exercise in futility. What's more, he simply didn't give a good goddamn what she thought anymore.

"Of course," Muffy added, "you will be welcome to come visit us on weekends, if you like."

How nice, he thought, *she's thrown me a bone.* He felt like throwing it back but resisted the temptation. Waddington finished his coffee and said, "I better get Hildy to school." Then to himself he added, *and I don't want to be late for Olivia.*

19
Not Doin' It Anymore

Though he would never have admitted it to Muffy or to anybody else, for that matter, Hildy was his favorite daughter. While Julie seemed to take an instant dislike to him the moment she emerged from the womb, Hildy, as a child, had been his little furry caterpillar that would climb into his lap before bedtime and ask him to read a story. At ten, she had spun herself a cocoon and refused to talk to either of her parents.

Now at twelve, the butterfly was emerging from the cocoon. She had begun to show signs of approaching womanhood, and he suspected that it would only be a matter of time, a short time, that she would fly off to test her wings. He normally treasured his times alone with her, times like now, as they drove alone to school. It gave him a chance to plumb the depths of Hildy's emerging personality.

"So, what are you learning in school, these days?" Dumb question. Guaranteed to immediately irritate a twelve-year-old. It drew an obvious answer.

"Nothing."

"Nothing? Well, then I guess we won't need to pay next semester tuition. Maybe I should get you a job at Hudson's."

She was not in a mood to be trifled with. "Oh, Dad, like, get real."

Like get real? What did that mean? What did he have to do to get real? The conversation had fallen into a pothole, and it was only after several minutes of silence that Hildy decided to pull it out.

"Can I ask you a question, Dad?"

"Of course."

"Are you and Mom still … like … *doin' it?*"

What kind of question was that from a twelve-year-old daughter? "What do you mean?" He hoped he had either misinterpreted her question or, at the very least, his return question would give him time to muster a proper parental response.

"You know, are you still … *doin' it?"*

Waddington did his best to compose himself. "If I understand what you mean by *'doin' it,'* and I think I do, I have to wonder why you're asking?"

"Cause I want to know if you and Mom plan to have any more kids? We're studying reproduction in biology and learning about, you know, *doin' it."*

Good grief. Where had the years gone? His little caterpillar was old enough to learn about *doin' it.* He'd read how today's teenagers were becoming sexually active at a younger age and, for a moment, he was tempted to ask if she was *doin' it.* Fortunately, he had the good sense not to. Hildy hadn't even been on a date, and as far as he could tell, she had not developed an active interest in boys.

"No," he said at last, "your Mom and I are happy with the two we have."

"So, you're not, like *doin' it* anymore?"

The truth was they weren't *doin' it* anymore, but not because they were trying to avoid procreation and not because he enjoyed the celibate life. In short, it wasn't his decision as to when or where or even if they would be *doin' it* anytime soon or, God forbid, ever. He decided to change the subject.

"Are you learning about reproduction in biology?"

"No, in biology we're learning about global warming, and how we're ruining the environment by using up all the resources and leaving the rest of the world with just about nothing."

"That's what you're learning in biology?"

"Yep."

I knew that school was too extreme, he thought. *But Muffy wouldn't listen. She and I are going to have to talk about this.* He decided to probe another subject. "I saw you reading your history book the other day. Have you studied the Civil War."

"Sorta …"

"Sorta?"

"Our teacher said that the only thing we had to know was that the war freed the slaves, but not really because they are still oppressed, and that we should give them reparations." She looked up at him quizzically, "What are reparations?"

He wanted to answer, "a sham" and leave it at that. But he decided he had to come up with some type of definition. "Well, it's sort of a penalty paid to a group of people who haven't been injured by another group of people who had nothing to do with the injury the first group never had."

Hildy looked up at him blankly and said, "Oh."

He decided to continue with his probe. "What have they taught you about the Revolution?"

"The sixty's revolution?"

"The *American* Revolution." And then with a tinge of frustration he added, "The one we celebrate on the Fourth of July."

"A little, but our teacher said it was mostly about some dead white guys who aren't all that important to our lives in the 21st century."

"George Washington isn't important anymore?" He asked incredulously.

"Yeah, because … I guess, like … well, Dad, he's, like, dead."

"True." It was hard to argue with absolute fact. For a moment he began to consider how best to begin the process of deprogramming his daughter, who was obviously being brainwashed by a cult of radical Bolsheviks passing themselves off as teachers at the Bountiful Country Day School. "Just out of curiosity, what does your teacher look like?"

"Mr. Sporze?"

"Is that his name, 'Sporze?'"

She nodded. "He's really cool looking."

"Cool looking?"

"Yeah, he has real long, black hair and a long braid down the middle of his back which he sometimes, like, wears wrapped around his head. He's got a beard, which is kinda scudzie."

"Scudzie?"

"It's really blotchy lookin' … like … remember when Puddy Tat had that skin disease?"

"You mean when her fur came out in handfuls?"

"Yeah. It sorta looks like that."

"A Bolshevik with a black, blotchy beard," he said mostly to himself. "What an appealing looking fellow he must be."

"Mr. Sporze dresses like an Indian. I mean, like, he doesn't wear a feather or anything, but he sorta looks like an Indian. But what's really cool is that he lives in the back of a great big truck."

And I'm paying for this? he asked himself. He wasn't, of course; Petula was. Then it occurred to him how much of an absentee father he'd been, at least since Hildy had left the Livonia public elementary school for the private day school. Once Petula's money had arrived, he had, for all practical purposes, abrogated most of his parental responsibilities. Did she condone this nihilist education or was she as ignorant as he was about what was going on in Hildy's classes?

He decided to try another tact. "What's your favorite class?"

"English."

"Oh, are you reading stories?"

"No, we're writing."

"Writing? Like what?"

"Poetry. Wanna hear one of my poems?"

"Absolutely. I'd love to."

Hildy opened up her schoolbag and sorted through some papers. "Here it is. You ready?"

"Read on, Wordsworth."

Hildy laid the poem in her lap and took a moment to compose herself for the poem's premier presentation.

"I see a world of death and pain.
There is no sun, there is no rain.
The earth has turned to dust and sand,
It's all the fault of wasteful man.
Down with all of nature's foes,
Smash 'em, burn 'em, anything goes."

Waddington was speechless and did his best to appear to be giving her work serious consideration. "Well, that's quite a statement," he said leaving out the adjective "subversive." *Who is this person next to me, he wondered? I'm taking a stranger to school.* Or had Hildy suddenly become a latter-day version of the Muffy he had married, a budding activist?

"What did you think of the poem?"

"Well … ahhh … everything certainly rhymes."

"Stop!" She shouted suddenly.

Waddington jumped on the brakes. "What? Did I hit something?"

"No, I just want to get out here."

"But we're still two blocks from school."

"I know," she said, opening the door.

"Why don't I drive you up to the front?"

She hesitated, and then, clearly hiding the truth said, "I'd just rather walk, Dad, like, if it's okay with you."

Did she have a rendezvous with a boy? Someone she planned to walk the last two blocks with? Was she going to meet some friends? Or maybe the Bolshevik with the beard? Like he needed to know. "Sure, it's okay with me, but I don't understand why you don't want me to drop you off at the front door?"

"Well, Dad, like, this is our clean air week and … ahhh, my teachers know you work for a car company … and since cars pollute … well, it would be, like, embarrassing if they were to see me with you." Before she closed the door, she leaned her head in, blew him a kiss off her fingers and said, "Love ya, Dad."

With that, his butterfly flew off to a bunch of radicals waiting to fill her mushy brain with garbage. At that moment, he made up his mind not only to become an involved parent, but an antiactivist one as well.

He watched as she joined several other girls and then turned his pollution producer, this scourge of the environment, toward Grosse Pointe. For the first time, he felt totally disenfranchised from his family. Not only didn't they need him anymore to provide the basic necessities, they didn't need him for much of anything. They were all flying on Air Petula.

20
This Is Madness

Less than two weeks ago, Olivia Fair had spent nearly half an hour sitting on her bed, within inches of a man with whom she felt instant rapport, and yet, she could not remember what Waddington looked like. She remembered thinking that he had a kind face, a face that invited her confidence and trust. She recalled his mud-brown suit and remembered thinking that he appeared utterly lost and out of place each time she came to his rescue at the cocktail party. But his eyes, his nose, his mouth, his face? It was all a blank. Try as she might to retrieve it from the hard disc of her memory, the screen came up with an error message. "We can find no link to this page."

What distressed her even more, however, and to a much greater degree, was that she remembered *everything* about what had happened in her bedroom. To have embarrassed herself, no, humiliated herself, with a perfect stranger was not only totally out of character, but unforgivable. Why had she opened so much of her personal life and revealed so many frustrations to a man she had just met? Then, to have announced she was shopping for an affair; how could she have been so crass? It was, she decided, behavior beyond the pall. None of it should ever have happened. It must have been the vodka.

Normally, she drank very little. In fact, she often made one drink last an entire party. But, when she realized she was in the same room with three women–three she knew about, anyway–who had, at one time or another, *entertained* her husband, she decided to drown the indignity in her glass.

What she drowned were her inhibitions. She had given in to her desire to *get even,* to show Charlie that two could play at philandering. How could she have given in to so base a desire?

The question she could not answer–the one she was afraid to answer–was whether she would actually have made love to him had Waddington decided to avail himself of her not-too-subtle invitation. She could, of course, have written off the incident as a weak moment in which nothing, literally nothing, happened. She could easily have chosen never to ever see him again. But she *had* chosen to see him again and she would, in a matter of minutes. That reality both added to her disquietude and heightened her anticipation.

She had invented the ruse that her anti-low-income housing committee needed a brochure and didn't Charlie know of someone who could help her write it? "What about Preston Waddington? You said he's a writer, developed the Le Vent advertising, and his wife is on our committee. Couldn't you spare him for a couple of hours … *dear*?" Of course, Charlie could.

As she stood in her bedroom, looking out the French doors into her gardens, the memory of "the kiss" flowed back. Even in her semi-consciousness haze, she had been aware of his gently picking her up and placing her head on the pillow. Then, just before she fell asleep, he kissed her. It was not the kind of kiss one gives a person out of pity. That kind of kiss lands on the forehead or cheek. He had kissed her on the lips. Nor was it the kind of kiss one would expect from a man bent on seduction. Waddington's kiss transcended that. It was, she decided, a cosmic message.

The thought had no sooner made its way through all her synapses than she began to admonish herself for getting carried away. *Exactly what I need,* she chided herself, *a cosmic message from a man without a face in the mud-brown suit that looked as if he'd slept in it. And yet,* she thought, *maybe that's exactly what I need in my life right now.*

Olivia turned back to her bed where she'd laid out different outfits. What to wear? How did she want to present herself to him? As the "Oh-I'd-almost-forgotten-you-were-coming-by-today"
socialite?" Or the "Thank-you-for-coming-Mr. Waddington-shall-we-get to-work?" activist? Or the "I've-been-looking-forward-to-spending-time-with-you … again … alone" woman shopping for an affair.

The distinct difference in her choices perplexed her, particularly because she hadn't made up her mind if she was going to just work on the bogus brochure, apologize for her behavior, or God help her, take him to her bed. No, the last option was defiantly out. Why was she even entertaining that thought? She was beginning to sound, to herself, like a character from a trashy novel. What had gotten into her? She wasn't some tramp like the women her husband pursued, Emma Rae, for example. No, nothing like them.

Olivia Byrd Fair had never violated her wedding vows, despite the fact she had more than sufficient justification to emulate her husband's adulterous behavior. Even though she knew that arranging this meeting with Waddington was venturing out on the high wire of temptation, she was determined to remain prudent, proper, and providential.

Olivia looked at her watch. He was due at 11:00. The slacks and blouse would create the impression she was spending a casual morning at home ready to dig into brochure writing. There was the tight blue cocktail dress that Charlie said was a showstopper. Absolutely not appropriate, though she loved wearing it because it showed her figure to such advantage. She could imagine meeting him wearing that, "Oh, you'll have to excuse how I'm dressed, but Charlie and I were out all night and we just got home." At 11 in the morning? Some image that would present.

Back in the closet went the showstopper. Then there was the tennis outfit with the cute little skirt that showed her legs off nicely. She could tell him she'd been playing tennis all morning. But that would mean working up a sweat to create believability, and the last thing she wanted to do was meet him in a lather.

Then she remembered the lemon-colored summer frock she'd bought earlier in the spring.

Perfect, she decided. It was demure, yet its scooped neckline was inviting. If she sensed that he thought her a bit overdressed, she could tell him that after their meeting, she was off to the Grosse Pointe Garden Club luncheon. Yes, the lemon frock. In it, she demanded to be looked at.

She dressed quickly and then found herself back in front of the mirror primping, adjusting, finalizing. It had been a long time, she realized, since she had been this concerned and spent this much time worrying about how she looked. Maybe, deep down, she actually *was* shopping for an affair. Or was she just in search of some happiness?

There had been happiness in her life, of course, but in retrospect, it seemed to have been unsustainable. She was the last of four girls born to Perkins Byrd and Floressa (Flossy) Vanderbilt Byrd. Flossy was willing to try one more time in hopes of having a son, but the doctors advised against a fifth child. Poor Flossy. Her only contribution to the family, other than four girls and her wealth, was her colitis, which she complained of in such exquisite detail that it seemed only fitting that her malfunctioning bowels should have sent her to an early grave.

Perkins Byrd, a widower at 38, remained faithful to his dead wife and took his business as his full-time mistress. He was an attentive father when he was around and constantly professed love for his daughters, never once suggesting that he wished one had been a boy. Yet, they all knew how he really felt. Even when Flossy was alive, the girls were like China dolls to be dressed, lined up, and shown off to friends. "Aren't they just adorable?" was the expected response. Had there been a son among them, the girls might have grown up invisible except for appearances at confirmations and weddings.

For years, Olivia felt it incumbent upon her to find ways to compensate for the lack of a male heir. As a little girl, she tried to play the role of the tomboy, climbing trees, getting dirty, and even occasionally picking fights with boys from her school. She was badly miscast. For her efforts, little Olivia received only reprimands from her mother and a broken arm in a fall from a Beech tree.

After her mother died, she worked harder to become Perkins' surrogate son by proving her athleticism. The only thing she proved was that she could not catch a baseball with her nose. The doctor who set it was near-sighted, which, Perkins claimed, had left his daughter's face slightly off-center. In high school, she did her best to share her father's interest in hunting and fishing. She did not have the heart for shooting animals and got seasick easily. In prep school, she wanted to join the band and play the trombone, just as her father had when he was a teenager. She thought he might be impressed. He wasn't.

When she went off to college, she declared engineering as her major. She had no aptitude for it. Upon graduation, she announced to her father that she'd like to work in the car industry. Perkins squashed that idea, telling her that it was no place for a woman, at least not in any job that mattered. Anyway, he was a traditionalist. His daughters would marry and be what their mother had been until she died, a supportive companion and a proper corporate wife.

It was his hope, frequently voiced, that one of the son-in-laws would fill his void. The three other daughters married beneath their station. Pooh wed a bank teller from Goshen, Indiana. Tappy married a geologist who spent most of his time on a North Sea oil rig, and CeeGee married a Frenchman with no discernable means of support. Of the four sons-in-law, only Charlie came close to being the missing son, and the jury (i.e., Perkins) had yet to deliver a final verdict on him.

Olivia went back into the bedroom and called the butler from Maubeuge on the house intercom to let him know that Mr. Waddington would be arriving at any minute and to show him into the South salon.

She sat in front of the open French doors and looked down in the garden where the two Québec gardeners were, for some unfathomable reason, wading in one of the fountain pools carrying a chainsaw and a broom. Whatever they were up to she could not have cared less. At that moment, she was consumed with the realization that she had to be out of her mind. Her decision to meet with this faceless man was madness.

21
"Rosa, Rosa, My Mexicali Rose"

As Waddington pulled up to Charlie's Versailles, he noticed two ornate, gleaming, brass signs imbedded impressively in large rocks. One directed guests to the front main entrance, the other pointed off to a drive on the right and read "Service." Were it any other house, Waddington might have felt it an esthetic sacrilege to park his two-year-old Defiant in front and opted to join the Dusters, Darts, and Valiants back where the help parked. But as this was the home of the man who guided the company that made the Defiants, he drove through the front gates into the courtyard, swung to the right on the oval drive, and parked just short of the front entrance.

As he got out, he looked up at the magnificent mansion and realized that the house was not a scaled-down Versailles, but a smaller version of the hundred-room Grand Trianon that was built for Louis the XIV. The architect had apparently eliminated all but the two flanking wings, giving the house an H-shape. The exterior was brick, finished with near-white terra-cotta tiles, made to resemble stone. In a word, Waddington thought, it was truly imposing. The unimposing medium man from Livonia would not have been surprised if some member of the staff appeared and instructed him to use the servant's entrance.

He rang the bell and, after a moment, the large oak door opened. The butler from Maubeuge was dressed in full morning attire, tails, vest, and all. Waddington noticed that he wore a breast pocket badge that read "Flaubert," which had to be either his name or his favorite author. "Vous été Monsieur Waddington?"

Waddington had heard that Charlie liked his servants to speak French, not that he understood it, but it did help maintain a certain aura. For an instant, Waddington was tempted to echo Muffy and respond, "Bone Jure Mon Sewer," but held himself in check. Instead, he answered in the perfect French that his mother had taught him as a boy. "Oui. Je suis Preston Waddington." And then, maybe for his ego's sake or just to prove to Flaubert that he was more worldly and educated than he appeared, he commented on the house, the weather, and his purpose, all in French.

Waddington assumed that Flaubert would be delighted to speak with someone fluent in his native tongue. But the butler from Maubeuge was unmoved and seemingly unimpressed, as though this American person had violated some unspoken French law that forbid anyone but French to speak their language well.

"Follow me," Flaubert said in monotone English, accompanied by a look that suggested he intended to accord Waddington only slightly more respect than the Terminix man. Waddington decided that the prudent course was not to favor the butler with any more French. He followed Flaubert into the great hall that had been the site of the cocktail party. Without the crush of people, the full magnificence of the room became fully apparent. They crossed the room and started down a wide gallery-like hall, resplendent with art works that had been painstakingly lit with tiny pin spots located in the ceiling. He'd not seen this hallway on his first visit. Not surprisingly, he thought, since he'd spent most of his time trying to dissolve into the woodwork in his mud-brown suit or trying to escape from Olivia's bedroom.

The marble floor clicked under the butler's shoes. *Was he wearing taps? Odd*, he thought. The gallery ended at massive double doors, which extended the full height of the gallery, at least ten feet. The butler swung the one on the left open and stepped inside, indicating for Waddington to follow. "Madame Fair has asked that you wait for her here."

Waddington stepped into what looked like a small concert hall. The room was a half oval. Ornate French doors lined the curved outer wall, letting in the sun and revealing the riot of colors from the garden that could be seen just past the balustrade that rimed the narrow terrace. An intricate, heavily carved, deep-gold colored molding spanned the entire arc above the doors. From there, a deep-blue domed ceiling with gold ribbing rose over twenty feet, drawing the eye to a mirrored medallion from which hung an enormous crystal chandelier. Directly below the chandelier, in the apex of the half oval, was not just a grand piano, but a full concert grand piano. Chairs, no doubt period pieces, Waddington assumed, were placed theater style, as if the Fairs were expecting to host a recital at any moment.

Waddington heard the heavy door close behind him with a deep and expensive *ka-clunk*. The butler had left him alone. He turned his attention back to the piano. *What a magnificent looking instrument*, he thought. As he approached, he realized that this was not just your ordinary hundred-thousand-dollar Steinway, but a Bosendorfer. And this one, from the look of it, had to cost at least two hundred thousand dollars.

Once, when he was about eleven or twelve, his mother, a piano teacher, had taken him to New York and, on a whim, had stopped in at the Bosendorfer showroom on Lexington Avenue. She pointed out that this extraordinary instrument had not eighty-eight keys, but ninety-seven, nine additional keys being placed at the base end. Here it was again in this extraordinary room, inviting him to sit down. As he slid onto the piano bench, he tentatively pressed middle C and then followed it with a C-major chord. And another and another. Oh, the sound. What a sound. The piano, the acoustics of the half dome, what a combination! He ran an F-major scale up and then down the keys. Now, this was what a piano should sound like.

He glanced briefly at the door to be sure it was closed. For no rational reason, he tore into a bouncy, raucous version of "Rosa, Rosa, My Mexicali Rose." Many years ago, it had been a favorite in his fraternity house among the brothers who loved to sing a bawdy adaptation of the lyrics. Abruptly he stopped. How dare he desecrate this incredible instrument with "Rosa, Rosa"? Immediately, he made amends with the piano by playing a Brahms sonata.

The music seemed to swirl up from the sounding board into the dome, enhancing it, giving each note extended life. Never had he had such an experience with a piano. After the Brahms, he segued into Mozart's "Eine Kleine Nacht Musik." When his memory failed to produce the remainder of the notes, he rolled into Cole Porter's "I Get a Kick Out of You." And then, with an arpeggio transition, his fingers chose "If This Isn't Love," from *Finian's Rainbow*. Everything he played sounded better than it deserved to sound. Oh, to have access to a piano like this in a room like this instead of the used upright Wurlitzer in his basement in Livonia.

When he completed the last flourish, the applause began, and he turned to find Olivia leaning against the doorframe. For a moment, the memory of seeing her leaning against the bathroom door flashed through his mind.

"Mrs. Fair!" Waddington said quickly rising. "Sorry, I didn't hear you come in. I hope you don't mind ..." He said gesturing toward the piano. "I just couldn't resist. What an extraordinary sound. It's ... it's ... well, it's unbelievable."

The only thing I mind is that you called me Mrs. Fair. Please, Preston, call me Olivia."

Olivia walked toward him and held out her hand, the hand without the Hope Diamond. He presumed, correctly, that protocol called for him to shake it. "Thank you for coming. I hope this won't be too much of an imposition." She was very formal, but the essential demureness he had sensed was still there. And the face–the slightly off-center face was, if possible, more compelling, more magnetic than the first time he saw her, especially here in this room, bathed in the deflected sunlight.

"I had no idea you were so accomplished. Play something else."

"What would you like to hear? Show tunes? Classical?"

"Classical. Do you know any Chopin?"

"A little. I'm not sure how far I'll get. It's been awhile, and I may be a little rusty. But I'll give it a try."

"I'm sure you're being modest." She put her hand on his arm.

"No, just cautious." He played the "Etude in B Flat Minor" with no problem.

She applauded when he'd finished. "That was wonderful. I think you may have missed your calling, Preston. How long have you been playing?"

"Oh, since I was about four. My mother was a piano teacher, and it wasn't until I was seventeen that she finally admitted to herself that I'd never make it to Carnegie Hall unless I bought a ticket." He laughed.

"Do you have a piano at home?"

"Yes, but it's a distant cousin to this one. In fact, they probably aren't even related. It's got white keys and black keys, but there the similarity ends. Do you play?" he asked.

"No one would ever call it that. I've been taking lessons for the last three years, and just last week, my music teacher told me she was moving to Chicago. I think there was a message there. I'm afraid you'd have to add the piano to my long list of nonaccomplishments."

"Do you play any other instrument?'

"Yes. Well, let's say I did ... a long time ago," she answered tentatively.

Waddington waited for her to tell him what it was. He noticed that she actually appeared embarrassed.

"If I tell you, you won't laugh, will you?"

"Of course not."

"The trombone."

He assumed she was joking, and it was all he could do to choke back a laugh. Olivia Fair, the queen of this Grosse Pointe version of Versailles playing the trombone? That would be something to see. "Are you serious?" he tried to make his question sound complementary just in case she was.

She smiled. There was an apologetic tone in her response. "I know, I don't seem the type. But there was a time when I actually played the trombone. I still have it."

"Really?"

She began to laugh in a way that, to Waddington, rivalled the sound of the Bosendorfer in the pleasure it gave him.

"I sense that you don't believe me, Preston."

"Well ... I ..." he fumbled, "of course, I believe you."

"No, you don't." She was smiling, so he knew he hadn't offended her. "I'll have to prove it to you." She walked over to the wall near the double doors and pressed something. Immediately, an entire wooden panel swung open revealing a large storeroom. She disappeared inside for a moment and then reappeared carrying a trombone. "Now, do you believe me?"

"And you actually played it?"

With that she lifted the trombone and played about three bars of "When the Saints Go Marching In." Waddington was stunned. The image of this very attractive, sophisticated woman in a lemon frock, standing in this magnificent room holding a slide trombone in front of her face and producing the most dreadful sounds was a study in incongruity.

He sat frozen on the piano bench, having no idea of how he should, or even could, respond. She stopped abruptly, turned, and disappeared back into the storage room. Several moments passed and Waddington began to wonder if she had gotten lost in the closet or had decided not to come out. Finally, she appeared, her head bent slightly forward as she closed the panel behind her. She was doing her best to make light of what, for her, had clearly been an impetuous act.

"I don't know what possessed me to do that. I seem to have a penchant for making a fool of myself."

Waddington sprang to her defense. "No, no, that was terrific. I admire a woman who isn't afraid to … to … to have a little fun at her own expense."

He would like to have added, you could have brought out a tuba and marched around the room playing John Phillips Sousa marches and I would still adore you. How could he tell her that for three bars of "When the Saints Go Marching In" he was jealous of the trombone's mouthpiece? He couldn't, of course. Instead, he stood up and as soon as she was close enough, he put his hand on her arm. "I like your spirit. I really do. You're … fantastic."

She looked up into his face, "Thank you, for that. But you have to admit, it was pretty awful." She smiled a smile that melted Waddington completely.

"Come with me." She held out her hand, offering him to take it.

He did not hesitate. He took her hand and followed.

22
Her Private Corner

She described the room as, "my private little corner." Her little corner, Waddington observed, was as big as the entire first floor of his house in Livonia. It was a combination library, office, and sitting room. As Olivia began to gather some papers and documents on her desk, Waddington made a quick tour of the room. As he walked along the wall lined with books, he was impressed with her selection of biographies, nonfiction, and classic novels. On one shelf, he found about two dozen of what he would have described as the kind of women's novel where the heroine gets raped ten times before she meets Mr. Right.

"Those are my escapist books," she said. "I have to confess that every once in a while, I like to just lose myself in a good trashy read."

"That's the way I am with spy novels. Nothing wrong with pure entertainment." Waddington then turned toward the fireplace wall and stepped back to look at the half dozen paintings displayed there. They appeared to be by the same artist. He stared at them for a moment before Olivia broke in.

"This is the only place in the house that Charlie will let me hang those."

"Why?"

"Well, they aren't exactly museum pieces."

"Maybe not, but they're very nice. I'd say the artist is fond of Monet."

"He's a favorite of mine."

He had guessed right; they were hers. He decided to take full advantage of his discovery. "Well, all I can say is that I'd hang these on my wall anytime. I think they're very good. Nice depth to them." Waddington stepped up close to one of the paintings and looked for a signature. Then he looked at a second and a third. "They're not signed. If I were the artist, I sure would have signed them."

"Thank you," she said quietly.

"These are yours?" His feigned surprise was convincing.

She nodded. "I'm afraid they really aren't all that good."

"Hey, I'm no art critic, but I think you're selling yourself short. These are really well done."

"You're making my day, Preston."

No, he thought, *you're making mine.*

She moved out from behind her desk. "Here's all the information on the petition. Why don't you sit here," she motioned toward the desk, "and look it over?" She handed him a typed sheet. "This is some of what I've written. I'm afraid it's not all that good. I mean, I don't pretend to be much of a writer. Hopefully, you'll be able to do something with it."

Waddington sat down at the large eighteenth-century *bureau plac* that served as her desk. It was probably worth ten times what he made in a year. Olivia sat on an ottoman in front of the desk, hands folded in her lap, looking like a student waiting for the professor to grade her term paper.

Waddington read the copy and, before he could say anything, she began apologizing for it again. "As I said, it's not very good, but I hope you get the idea of what I think we want to say."

Waddington, from his slightly higher vantage point behind her desk, looked down at the woman with the slightly off-center face in the delicious lemon frock and realized just how vulnerable, how insecure, Olivia Fair was. She seemed to have so little self-confidence. It surprised him. He had always assumed that money would buy confidence. It certainly worked for Petula Poor. Here was a woman worth tens of millions of dollars, maybe hundreds of millions, who could buy and sell anyone in Detroit, who could have wielded her fortune like a truncheon and demanded homage from the entire city. Instead, she was more like the shy teenager with a slight case of acne, hoping that someone might ask her to the prom.

"You won't hurt my feelings if you tell me it's pretty amateurish."

"To the contrary, it's pretty damn good. Olivia, forgive me for saying this, but I think you underestimate yourself both in terms of your artwork and your ability to write. When it comes to playing the trombone ... well ...." He rocked his hand back and forth to indicate a so-so talent. They both laughed.

"I shouldn't waste my time taking lessons, right?" she continued to laugh.

"Unless you think you can find a job with a Dixieland band."

"Not many of those in Grosse Pointe."

"But seriously, so far as this copy goes, there is no way anyone is going to improve on what you've written here. In my opinion, you've spelled out your position and done a very convincing job of it."

Her reaction to his praise was tentative, "You're not just saying that?"

My God, he thought, *she really has her doubts.* "No. I'm serious, you write very well."

She looked at him for a long admiring moment. "You're really such a breath of fresh air. Would you mind just sort of hanging around all the time? You're very good for my ego. Or at the very least, would you mind giving Charlie some lessons in ego boosting. You really are a tonic."

"That's me," he joked, "I just go through life boosting egos and making people happy."

"Well, you can make me happy if you'll stay for lunch."

"I don't want to put you out."

She was adamant, "I absolutely insist that you do stay for lunch."

She wasn't going to have to ask him twice.

"I'll arrange to have it served in the garden gazebo."

"You're sure it won't be too much trouble?"

"No trouble at all." She gathered up the petition copy and put it back in her file. "May I ask you something, Preston? And may I depend on you to give me a totally honest answer?"

"Absolutely." *Where was this going*, he wondered? "If you can count on me to boost egos, you can certainly count on me to give honest answers. Same price."

"Do you think this petition is frivolous? Are we wrong in opposing low-income housing? I mean, does it look like all we're saying with this is that we don't want poor people in our neighborhood?"

Waddington hadn't expected a question like that. He took a moment to gather his thoughts and answered as best he could, "I guess it would depend on your perspective. You made a point in your petition about esthetics; I agree with what you said about it being wrong to plop down an ugly piece of architecture right in the middle of Grosse Pointe, just for the sake of creating some housing. I get the impression that no one from the State has given much thought to the design. Also, as you said in your copy, just because it's low income doesn't mean it has to look like a slumlord's tenement. So, I guess I'm against it on an esthetic basis.

"From an economic perspective, again, you made a good point. Does it make sense to provide low-income housing in a town where everything costs twice as much as it does anywhere else? Where will these people shop? Is the State going to bus them to a Walmart? On the other hand, if low-income housing gives people a chance to live better lives and provides their kids with a better shot at life, who can be against that? I guess my bottom line is that, like most of what the government does, it hasn't really been thought out all that well."

Olivia nodded in agreement. "I like the way you think, Preston. You're right. The entire concept hasn't really been thought out." She held out her hand to him, "Come. Enough of this. It's much too nice a day to be inside. Let me show you my garden. Do you like gardens?"

I'd tiptoe through your tulips any time was the answer that passed through his mind, but he reduced it to a simple, "Yes."

23
Lunch with Olivia

They sat down to lunch at a white wicker table located in the center of the ornate French gazebo in the Fairs' garden. Just after twelve, Waddington poured them their first glasses of Montrachet. The conversation was prudent, exploratory at first, designed to help two people mark off their common ground. There was more in common than either would have expected. The conversation flowed from one topic to another and bore the kind of unguarded intimacy that two strangers on an airline might share, knowing full well that they will never see each other again. They were explorers, delighting in how many of the same things they enjoyed and appreciated. It may have been partially the wine and partially the need to find someone who was willing to listen and understand that gave them the confidence to share feelings that had been pent up for a long time.

Over the endive salad, Charlie's name disappeared, and by the second glass of wine, Muffy was put aside. They were alone in the garden, except for Monique, one of the Truffles from Marseilles, who appeared with the main course and shortly thereafter, with the second bottle of Montrachet. After that, she was seen no more. At one point in the afternoon, the careful observer would have noticed that there were two conversations, one spoken, the other implicit. An emotional connection had been made, two people irresistibly drawn like magnets, unable to resist the attraction to one another. Any attempt to give what was happening between them language would have been superfluous and invasive. Instead, they found reasons, under the cover of supportive conversational gestures and the passing of table implements, to touch now and again, to lay a hand on an arm, to brush a shoulder. They drifted into the stupendous timelessness of suspended reality.

After Waddington had poured the last of the second Montrachet, Olivia said, "About last Sunday, I'm afraid I may have said too much about my marriage and Charlie. I hope you won't hold that against me. I was, as I'm sure you noticed, intoxicated. I want you to know that's not me. I guess it was the vodka that let it all out. If I'd talked the way I did to one of my friends, everything I said would be all over Grosse Pointe by now. So, I guess I'm lucky it was you with me when I had my … eruption." The residue of her embarrassment showed on her face.

"I'm glad it was me too. Otherwise, I might not be here with you today. You know, in thinking about what you told me about your marriage and what I've experienced with mine, I've come to realize that living with someone is like drifting down a river. If you both don't paddle like hell from time to time, you can get caught up in a current and drift into places that are hard to get out of. Sadly, sometimes only one of the two realizes what's happened. Sadder still is when one of the two isn't all that interested in doing his or her share of the paddling. So, there you sit, going nowhere and not very happy about it."

She nodded her agreement and then added, "And you make yourself promises that you'll find some way to change things. Or if that's not possible, to get out and move on by yourself. But then one day, you realize that years have passed and that all you've done is find excuses for doing nothing."

"It occurred to me today, while I was driving my daughter to school, that nothing in my life is as it should be. The children that I thought I knew are strangers to me now. My wife ... well, I have no idea where she's coming from these days. On second thought, maybe I do and that's the problem. Sometimes I feel like my life is on cruise control. It's all so mechanical ... predictable. But then, a day like today comes along, and I find myself in this beautiful place, having lunch with an extraordinary woman and talking about things I have not talked about with anyone, maybe ever. And suddenly, I feel good about myself. I believe I can paddle right back into the river. Earlier, you said *I* was a tonic. I think *you* are."

"I think it's wonderful when two people can talk so openly. The only problem is that you have to be very selective. Even when you find someone who appears to want to listen, it's hard to let your guard down. Because you know if you do, there's a good chance that person will either end up thinking less of you or using what you've told them to contribute to their quota of gossip. So, we go through life wearing no trespassing signs around our necks."

"I don't see that sign around your neck today."

"No, today has been different. I haven't needed it."

He began to simile as though enjoying a private joke.

"What?" she inquired.

"I was just thinking, that being here with you, talking the way we have, could become addictive. And my only regret about today …"

"Regret?"

"My only regret would be if today is the only time we'll be together like this."

"I don't think we should let that happen," she said taking his hand. "I would like there to be many days like this. It may be selfish on my part, but I need someone to talk to, someone I can trust. Someone who I know feels the way I do. Look around. What do you see? All the things money can buy. I could have luncheons and dinner parties here every day and surround myself with dozens and dozens of people. But the truth is, I'd always be alone. Today, for the first time in a long time, I was not alone."

"I am not very good at saying the things I feel, Olivia. Words tend to escape me at the most inopportune time. But I can say that today meant a great deal to me. Like you, I want there to be other days like this. And yet, I know that eventually it's going to hurt to be with you."

"Hurt?" She looked perplexed.

"Yes, it will hurt to be so close to something so perfect and know that you will eventually have to let it go."

She smiled, but there were tears in her eyes. She squeezed his hand with both of hers, as though she had no intention of ever letting go. "You are a romantic, Preston. I like that very much. Believe me when I tell you that I won't let go if you won't."

In that instant, they had become like travelers who, intentionally passing the last exit, have committed themselves to an uncertain destination.

After a while, she excused herself, promising to be right back, and went into the house. Waddington closed his eyes, the sun and the wine inviting sleep. He dared not give in. He stood up, walked around the table, and sat down. His back was to her when she approached, his head had already slumped to his chest. In the half consciousness that precedes sleep, he became aware of her hand on his shoulder. He felt her breath on his ear; her hair brushed the back of his neck. "A penny?" she asked.

Full consciousness returned in the nick of time, "A penny?"

"For your thoughts."

What an opening. What a cue line. What an opportunity to deliver a truly great response. *Think. Think. What would Cary Grant have said or Robert Redford or even Ben Stiller? Think.* Suddenly, his mind was flooded with inane responses. He wanted to say something romantic that would provide a perfect curtain line for a perfect day. Then it came to him. He decided to rehearse it once in his mind: I was wishing that I could paint, so that I could capture forever this afternoon on canvas. Too late, she was looking at her watch.

"Do you know what time it is? It's almost four-thirty!" she said.

He'd blown it. He missed his cue. All he could muster was a lame attempt at humor. "I guess that means I'm going to be a little late for work today."

"Just a little," she agreed.

As they started down the gazebo steps, she took his right arm in both her hands and leaned lightly against his shoulder. Their pace was slow, like lovers in a Seurat painting on a Sunday stroll in the park. They walked along the white gravel pathways, past the perfectly manicured flower gardens, around the fountains that seemed to be playing for their benefit, onto the terrace, and through the French doors. They lingered for a moment in the great hall, Waddington using questions about this or that piece of art to delay his departure. Finally, they made their way through the grand archway that led to the foyer and front door.

Neither Olivia nor Waddington happened to notice that the second French Truffle, Jeanette, was deep in the Ficus forest at the end of the room, watering the trees. She noticed them, however, and murmured an "ooh, la la" at the way Olivia was holding onto Waddington. She edged her way to a vantage point where she could remain hidden in the Ficus forest and yet maintain a clear view of the foyer.

Waddington was about to open the front door when Olivia reached up and took his face gently in her hands. "Thank you for today, Preston," it was almost a whisper. "I wish I could put today on canvas so that I could make our time together stand still."

Talk about two people on the same page, she's even reading my line, he thought. But, oh, how much better it sounded coming from her.

She wasn't finished, "I don't know where we go from here, Preston. I think we should just ride the tide and see where it takes us. And by the way, I intend to bring a paddle." She grinned.

"Me, too."

Her hands fell to his shoulders and he assumed she'd give him the perfunctory social buss on the cheek, maybe both cheeks. That was not what she had in mind. There was no feint to the left or right; she took direct aim at his mouth. He felt her lips meet his. It seemed that all the wine he had consumed was rushing back to his head. Her mouth began to open, beckoning him to do the same. There was nothing social about this kiss. Olivia wanted him.

Her body pressed into his and for a moment they moved slightly, purposely against one other. His pulse jumped, his lungs put in an emergency requisition for more air. For a moment, he thought he might have to pull away to catch his breath. Waddington could feel himself start to respond to the movement of her body against his. Within moments, he knew she should feel him too. She made no effort to pull away. Unbelievable.

Incredible. She wanted him. He wanted her. It had to happen. It was going to happen.

No, it *would not* happen! At that critical moment, Waddington broke the *Guinness Book of World Records* for premature ejaculation. Goddamn! He'd shot himself in the foot, or more accurately, in his drawers. How do I explain this to Olivia? From somewhere a phone began to ring. She pulled back and released him, her eyes never leaving his face.

"I know, I know," she said misreading the look of consternation, "we've got to get control of ourselves. But I really don't want you to go."

Waddington was now confronted with a serious dilemma. He didn't want to give Olivia the impression that he was in a hurry to leave, but at the same time he was in a hurry to leave. He had to take care of his *problem* before it began to show up on his suit pants. Talk about the ultimate humiliation. If she found out, his ego would deflate faster than a punctured tire.

"Mrs. Fair!" The butler from Maubeuge was calling her. "It's Miss Pooh on the phone."

"That's my sister," she said. "Her daughter went into labor this morning. She promised to call when the baby arrived."

The butler's footsteps could be heard clicking on the marble floor as he approached the foyer. Immediately, she backed away and, for the benefit of Flaubert, took Waddington's hand and shook rather like she might shake the hand of someone from whom she'd just bought a set of Encyclopedias.

"Well," she said in a full voice, "we did manage to accomplish a lot today." She whispered. "Did we ever." Then at full volume again, "On behalf of the petition committee, I want to thank you for your help. I look forward to our next meeting." She turned toward the butler, "Here I am, Flaubert," she called, "just seeing Mr. Waddington out." She shook his hand again, then gave him a brief social peck on the cheek that gave her an opportunity to whisper in his ear. "You know those trashy novels you saw in my library?"

He nodded.

"I feel just like one of those women. Except this is going to be even better than anything I've ever read in one of those books." With that she turned and left him to give her attention to the phone call. Waddington let himself out and hurried toward his car. *Some Don Juan, I am.*

The only other time he could remember this happening was just after he'd gotten his driver's license, and he took Rita Maccarelli to the drive-in. He lost it just after she'd slipped out of her bra and presented him with her 36Ds. That time his misfire gave him away and for months Rita had the temerity to refer to him in front of his friends as The Fastest Gun in Teaneck, New Jersey.

He drove south to where the Grosse Pointe dramatically ends and the Detroit City limits begin. Dramatically, in that crossing the city line is like falling off a ledge. The elegant homes, the expensive shrubbery, and the stately lawns instantly disappeared as he passed Jefferson Avenue. In their place, a wasteland of rubble from buildings demolished years before and never rebuilt.

He pulled into the first gas station he saw and went directly to the restroom. What a mess it was. The toilet had overflowed; there was water on the floor, no toilet paper, and only one dim bulb. It would have to do. He carefully took off his trousers and laid them over the empty towel dispenser. Then he stepped out of his underpants and tossed them in the wastebasket. As he did, he caught a glimpse of himself in the mirror. He looked ridiculous in his blue suit coat, white shirt, tie, and no pants. He noticed that someone had pasted a small sign in the corner of the mirror. It had one of those round smiling faces over the words. "Smile, things could get worse."

Suddenly, it occurred to him that they most certainly could. What if Muffy had called the office and his secretary had told her that he had not been in all day and that she knew nothing about a meeting? What if Charlie were to find out that he'd spent the entire day with Olivia, drinking two bottles of his very expensive Montrachet, no less? What if his suit pants slipped off the paper towel holder onto the wet floor? As indeed they just had. That raised a fourth question: How would he explain the wet trousers to Muffy?

Already, Waddington felt that the fates were conspiring to punish him, not just for what he was thinking about doing with Olivia, but for what he was bound and determined to do.

24
Jack Poor Needs More Jack

Popper Poppenhaus had reinvented himself so many times even he wasn't sure who he was. His life was a total fabrication. Several years ago, at his divorce hearing, his wife told the judge that she had gotten tired of waking up to a different man every morning and decided to move in with an accountant and live a more predicable life.

Popper coveted money. It was his passion. And it was this passion that had motivated him to recruit Jack Poor in his kickback scheme. In the three years that he was overpaying Jack for the use of his dealership, he'd managed to squirrel away twenty-five thousand dollars. But he needed more, much more, to live the life to which he wished to become accustomed. That goal, as always, was number one on his to-think-about list.

Popper did his most creative thinking about getting money and anything else that was on his list immediately after the physical act of sex. It had, he felt, the therapeutic ability to clear his mind of extraneous thoughts so that he could focus on a given issue with greater clarity.

He had arrived at the Greenwich Hyatt the night prior to the shoot in Jack Poor's dealership. Jack had procured a friend of his Insurance Claims Adjuster to share Popper's bed for the night. Popper awoke and looked over at the woman lying next to him. Whatshername? Helen, Betty, Jane?

Whatever. It made little difference what her name was. He'd made it a practice to protect himself from addressing a sex partner by the wrong name by calling every woman he bedded "sweetheart" or "babe" or "honey." In the case of the young lovely next to him, it wasn't a matter of confusing her with another woman; rather, it was a case of his having forgotten her name all together. How, he wondered after spending the night with her, do I tactfully ask her name? Sex for Popper was becoming almost an impersonal pastime. Like picking up a tennis game and never knowing anything more about the guy on the other side of the net than he's got a weak backhand.

Sitting on the edge of the bed, he reached over and patted her behind with mechanical disinterest and said, "Last night was terrific, Babe. If you could put that in a box and market it, you'd make a million bucks." He laughed at the thought. "I love you, Sweetheart, but now I gotta think."

"About what?" Helen or Betty or Jane asked.

"About business," came the reply. " Why don't you take a shower?" And then in his mind added, *or take a powder, take a hike, take a bus, just don't take my wallet.*

Having cleared his mind of any thoughts relating to the young woman, Popper started to think about getting his hands on more money. Lots more money! He would be the first to admit that he lived beyond his means, a house in Detroit, a condo in Vero Beach, a forty-eight-foot fishing boat and lots of women to impress. His need to finance his lifestyle led him into doing special favors for specific dealers, much like he'd done for Jack, and, in turn, reaping their appreciation in such a manner as to enable him to substantially augment his monthly income.

But with the French deal pending, the bean counters had been taking a close look at all expenses. As a result, Popper had been forced to cancel his quid pro quo arrangements with more than a dozen dealers. All that was left was his deal with Jack Poor and that was hardly netting him enough to buy gas for his boat. He needed a major infusion of cash, and soon.

At 8:30 a.m., Jack Poor pulled up in front of the Hyatt, and Popper got in for the short ride to the dealership. After a few minutes of discussing last night's accommodations and the performance of Helen or Betty or Jane, Popper got down to business.

"Jack, I've got a problem."

"Yeah?"

"The French Consortium has been doing their due diligence on the company. I've got bean counters on me like flies on sugar. Which means, I've got to be very careful that they don't discover our little arrangement."

"What are you saying?"

"I'm saying that your fee for the use of your dealership is going to be a little less this time."

"How much less?"

"About two-thirds less."

Jack sighed. "Damn!"

"It would be too risky to give you the usual. The last thing I need is for those Frogs to start questioning how I allocate the money in my budget. Actually, you're lucky."

"Yeah? In what way?"

"I've had to shut down all my other …" he hesitated, "arrangements. Maybe after the French are on board, we can go back to the full amount."

"That's assuming you still have a job," Jack said. "You know, Popper, a lot of times when new investors take control of a company, they clean house. Hell, you may end up working for me, selling cars." His laugh had a touch of mockery in it.

"Jack, I'd fuck your wife before I'd work for you."

"Obviously, you've never met my wife. That woman would scare off a rapist." They both laughed. Then Jack said somewhat enviously, "Well, you've got nothing to worry about, not with Charlie Fair looking out for you."

"Yeah, right," Popper said sarcastically. "I hate that bastard. He'd sign me up for the guillotine in a New-York-minute if it meant protecting his ass with the French."

"But he's the guy that hired you."

"Yeah, to be his butt-boy. I'm his front. I'll tell you this, Jack– if ever I get a chance to screw that sonofabitch, I will. Big time."

Jack laughed. "Join the club, Popper. The bastard talked me into taking on this franchise. Worst decision I ever made. He's broken every promise he ever made to me and to all the other dealers I've talked to. They are really pissed off. All I've gotta say is he better be wearing Kevlar when he gives his speech at the dealer meeting in August."

Having both vented their anger at Charlie Fair, they said nothing and it was several miles before Jack broke the silence. "Popper, you and I have at least two things in common: We both hate Charlie, and we both want to get our hands on some money, *lots* of money. I want out of this dealership, this town, and my life with that bitch I'm married to. I want enough money to go down to Key West, buy a little house and a small fishing boat, and live happily ever after screwing divorcees. There's got to be some way that the two of us can make some real money. And hell, if we can screw Charlie Fair in the process, all the better. But the money comes first."

"You're preaching to the choir, Jack. I don't care what I have to do to get it, short of shooting your wife or my ex. I'm open to suggestions. If you've got any ideas, let's hear 'em."

"Goddamn, I'm doing my best to try and think of something. And that would *include* shooting my wife." He began to laugh. "Only trouble, shooting her wouldn't net me a nickel. All her money goes to my daughter and granddaughters." He looked over at Popper who was staring ahead intently. "For the record Popper, I'm kidding about shooting her." He waited a moment. "I'd prefer to run her over with her Goddamn Bentley." He laughed again. "Of course, she's such a moose she'd probably do more damage to the car than it would do to her." He let out a long-resigned sigh. "I don't know, Popper, this may be a lost cause."

As they pulled into the dealership, Popper caught sight of the crushed Verite 300. He knew exactly what it was but decided to play dumb. "What the hell happened to that? A present from Charlie Fair?" He laughed.

Jack glanced over at the Verite. "That's physical proof that you can't take a twenty-five-mile-per-hour curve at sixty-miles-an-hour."

Jack told him the whole story, with embellishments. When he was through, Popper asked, "Has the lawyer filed a suit yet?"

"No. But if he does, so what? I guarantee he'd be laughed out of court."

"Why? Because Swenson was breaking the speed limit?"

"No, because Swenson was getting a BJ from the bimbo when he hit the tree."

The blow job comment took Popper by surprise. "You want to run that by me again?"

"Yeah, according to the cops, they found his fly unzipped and her head in his lap. Of course, the lawyer probably doesn't know that."

"Yeah? How come?

"Well, when the tow truck operator brought the Verite in, he told me that the police decided to leave the BJ part out of their report."

"Really? Why?"

"I guess you might say they did it out of consideration for the guy's wife. I mean, having to tell Mrs. Swenson they found her husband with another woman was bad enough. But to tell her what he was doing when he died would just be rubbing salt in the wound. His having a BJ might answer why the car went off the road, but it sure as hell wouldn't make his wife feel any better."

"However, if Mrs. Swenson's lawyer decides to sue, that would have to come out in court."

"Which is why it will never get to court. Once he learns that Swenson was getting a Monica Lewinski, he's going bail out."

Inside, on the showroom floor, the film crew was lighting the featured cars for the commercial. The director came up to Popper and started asking questions which he needed answered before they finished the set-up. Ivan the Terrified spotted Jack and announced that he had to go over some figures.

"Catch you at lunch," Jack called as he started upstairs to his office.

"Right," Popper answered.

Just before noon, Popper walked into Jack's office and closed the door. He pulled up a chair in front of Jack's desk and sat down.

"You buying today?" Jack asked.

"Yeah, but first, let's talk. I've been thinking. In fact, I've been doing a lot of thinking for the last couple hours. I've come up with a way for us create a major payday for ourselves and, in the process, screw Charlie Fair. Unfortunately, we can't let him know that he's been screwed, which will take some of the pleasure out of it. But that's the price we'd have to pay to be able to keep the money."

"What kind of money are we talking about?"

"I can't put an exact figure on it right now, but I'd say in the neighborhood of five or six million."

"You're shittin' me, right?"

"Dead serious."

"So, what's the plan?"

"First, let me ask you a couple of questions. "The news story said the lawyer's name is Slipwalker. Do you know anything about this guy?"

"Actually, I do know something about him. I had my lawyer check him out. The guy is a typical bottom-feeding ambulance chaser. He will sue everybody and anybody, especially a corporation, if he thinks there's a buck in it. Most of the time, he's looking for the defendants to settle out of court to avoid getting their asses hauled through the mud."

"Legal extortion."

"Exactly. Take the money and run. You know the type."

"Yeah, I know the type."

"However, in this case, I get the feeling that Slipwalker may not even file. It's been almost a month since the accident. I think we would have heard from him by now."

"Not necessarily. Filing a suit like this takes time. Especially if he's having to dig up some experts to help support his contention that it was the car's fault."

"But why are we talking about Slipwalker? If he tried to sue me, I'll bury him. Of course, I'd rather he didn't sue me. Suits like his are a pain in the ass. But what's he got to do with five-million dollars?"

"He's got a whole lot to do with five-million dollars. And you're wrong about one thing, Jack; I would rather he *did* sue. Popper read Jack's disconcerted expression. "You heard me right, Jack. You and I *want* Slipwalker to file suit."

"Why? So I can make the guy look like a fool? Can you imagine a trial in which the main testimony has to do with the effect a blowjob can have on a guy doing sixty in a twenty-five mile an hour curve? He wouldn't get a nickel going to court with this."

"You're absolutely correct. And congratulations, you've just nailed the essence of my plan."

"I did? I guess you better explain it to me."

"Let me be sure I have all the facts. Per your tow truck operator, the police made no mention in their report of how they found Swenson and the woman, right?"

"If they had, the reporters would have been all over it. They love that kind of stuff. There's a guy here in Connecticut not long ago that racked up his car while this babe was doin' him. Only in that case, the broad survived. So, what did the cops do? Believe it or not, they charged her with reckless endangerment."

So, I can assume that Slipwalker doesn't know?"

Jack nodded, "I think that's a safe assumption."

"Good. Now, it's extremely important that neither Charlie nor our legal department find out what really happened. So don't say anything about the BJ to anyone."

"Popper, you're losin' me. I hate to seem dense, but how does Slipwalker suing me and the company make us any money?"

"It's not the *lawsuit* that we cash in on, it's the *negotiation* and what I'm betting will be the company's willingness to settle out of court. The settlement is what will put money in our pockets."

"I don't see how."

"Trust me. It will. But, before I explain how this is going to work, there are a couple of details I need to figure out. In the meantime, your number one job is to let me know the minute you get word that they've filed suit."

"Whatever you say."

Popper stood up. "Let's go lunch." A thought occurred to him. "Oh, one more thing I want you to do," he said with a big grin on his face. "I want you to start thinking about how you're going to outfit that fishing boat down in Key West."

25
What the French Maid Saw

The next morning, Waddington arrived at the office early. The voice mail on his office phone was from Olivia. He'd left his briefcase at her house. She would be home all day, if he wanted to stop by and pick it up. It was an invitation that he fully intended to accept, once he was sure that Charlie was out of the house and in his office.

As he pulled into the Fair's driveway just after ten, he found it crowded with various service trucks. One identified itself as belonging to a window washer, another had a sign advertising a drapery firm, and there were two others that gave no indication as to why they were there.

The utler from Maubeuge answered the door.

"Mrs. Fair called and said that I'd left my briefcase here the other day."

"I'll let her know you're here."

Waddington stepped into the living room. There were men taking down the drapes, and he could see window washers clinging to the windows leading to the terrace. From somewhere in the house, he heard what sounded like the hum of electric buffers polishing floors.

Olivia appeared and immediately began to apologize. "Pres, I'm so sorry. I forgot when I called that today was going to be chaos here. They're taking the draperies off for cleaning and the window washers have been scheduled for a month. And upstairs they're polishing the floors."

"Please don't apologize." As her eyes met his, he realized that behind the apology was a question. Did he have any regrets about the other day? "I'm the one who should apologize for not calling and telling you how much I enjoyed yesterday. It was very special."

Olivia's face made no secret of her immediate relief and joy. "Come," she said, holding out her hand.

Without hesitation, he took it and followed her up to her *private little corner.*

"Your briefcase is still by my desk where you left it."

As they climbed the stairs, they passed several workmen who never looked up. It was as though Olivia and Waddington were invisible to them.

She opened the door to her little corner, and Waddington followed her in. She closed it behind him and all the sounds of the work activity, particularly the whine of the floor-buffing machine, faded to a muffled hum. She turned back to him, lifting her face toward his and said, "I like having you here, Preston."

"And I like being here."

Immediately, she was in his arms, and he was kissing that inviting mouth. He hadn't felt like this in years. He wanted her more than he had wanted any woman since his days with Muffy in his one-room apartment back in Greenwich. Suddenly the room was filled with noise. Voices, hammering, the whine of the buffing-machine. They pulled apart and glanced toward the door.

Jeanette, one of the French truffles was standing in the door and staring at them.

"Excusez moi, I did not realize. I was coming to dust and ..." She lowered her head to avert her eyes and did not finish the sentence.

"I think that can wait until later, Jeanette," Olivia said casually, as though to suggest that what Jeanette had seen was not at all what it appeared to be. "We're rehearsing a scene from a play that I might try out for."

Waddington's back was to Jeanette, and it was all he could do to keep from laughing.

"Romeo and Juliet," she added as further explanation.

"Mais, oui! But of course," Jeanette said. Her eyes remained averted as she backed out of the room and closed the door.

"Rehearsing a play? Romeo and Juliet?" Waddington laughed. "Where did that come from?"

"Weren't we talking about doing a scene from Romeo and Juliet in my bedroom?"

"As a matter of fact, we were."

"So, today we're rehearsing it. What else could I say? Considering how she found us, my options were somewhat limited. Of course, I could have said you were my new Yoga instructor and were teaching me a new relaxation technique. But somehow, I don't think she would have believed me." Olivia was clearly enjoying what Waddington was seeing as a serious dilemma.

He was both amazed and amused at how lightly she was treating the matter. "I must say, you are very quick and very cool under fire, Olivia. Do you think she really believes we were rehearsing?" he asked, making no attempt to hide his own doubts.

"You know, I am at a point in my life where I really don't care what anybody thinks."

"Will she say anything?"

"To Charlie? No. Charlie never talks to the maids. He thinks they're beneath him. He only talks to Flaubert. He regards him as his personal valet."

"Well," he said grinning broadly, "in that case, I think we should get back to our rehearsal."

"May I take that to mean you can stay for a while?"

"An hour, anyway."

They sat down together on the *Pierre Deux* sofa. Had Waddington been placed on a witness stand and asked to tell the court what they talked about; he would have had to plead temporary amnesia. At times, he felt like a teenager experiencing his first girlfriend. At other times, in his lucid moments, he found himself wondering what had possessed him to leap into an affair with the president's wife. *I've lost my mind*, he thought. When, after a while, she leaned over and kissed him, he found himself tempted to begin to unbutton her blouse, but that temptation was quickly reined in with the appearance of a window washer, wielding his sponge and squeegee outside her windows. They both began to laugh.

"I'm beginning to feel that our rehearsal has turned into a performance."

The window washer, a gentleman of some foreign extraction, peered in at them, smiled a mostly toothless smile, and waved.

"I think our performance has turned into a peep show. Maybe we should just invite everyone in."

"And charge admission." They laughed again.

"This is crazy, you know? Us. Here, like this," he said.

"Absolutely crazy and that's what makes it so wonderful."

"I feel like I've just boarded a train with no idea of where I'm going."

"We could be headed for a colossal train wreck."

"I don't suppose there's any way we can avoid it?"

"None, whatsoever," she slid her hand over to his, well out of sight of the window washer who appeared to be talking to them, although they could not make out anything that he was saying.

"Well, if we can't avoid it, then I think we should just enjoy the ride."

The squeegee was making squeaky sounds as the window washer wiped down the panes. Within a few moments he was done and his head began to sink below the windowsill. She brought her lips to his again. It was a light, tender kiss, as if she were programming it to make him want more, a whole lot more.

There was a knock at the door. They separated.

"Do you believe this?" she asked.

"Let me see," "Waddington said, "I'm betting it's the carpet layers."

"I'll take the drapery man."

Waddington moved to the far end of the sofa and Olivia picked up a stack of papers and put on her reading glasses so as to make it appear they had been working on her petition.

"Yes?" she called. "Come in."

It was Flaubert.

"Madam, if you have a moment, the man from the drapery firm needs to confer with you."

"Well, I was close," she said to Waddington. And then to Flaubert, "I'll be right there." Flaubert stepped just outside the room in the hall and waited dutifully by the door. She turned to Waddington, making sure Flaubert could hear. "Well, I think that about wraps it up for today, Mr. Waddington. I do appreciate your taking time out of your busy schedule."

"My pleasure," he said. "Anytime." *Anytime very soon,* he added silently.

Waddington retrieved his briefcase and headed for the door. Olivia followed. As he passed Flaubert, he could have sworn that the butler from Maubeuge gave him a knowing look. Had the French maid told him what she'd seen? She might have. All those "backstairs" English movies always had the servants gossiping about their employers.

Olivia walked him to the front door. As he opened it, he said, "I suppose we should be more careful. I don't think Charlie would appreciate hearing that I've fallen in love with his wife."

"I don't care what Charlie would or would not appreciate. I care only about what I care about." She gave him a quick kiss on the cheek. "My drapery man awaits. Call me."

Waddington had barely left Grosse Pointe when he began to consider, seriously, the possibility that the French maid might have told Flaubert what she saw. If she had been an American maid, she might have believed Olivia's rehearsal ruse. But Jeanette was French, and she probably knew an affair, even a budding affair, when she saw one. What if she told Flaubert? And what if Flaubert felt obliged to pass on what he'd been told to Charlie? If he did, then there was one thing Waddington could count on for certain: Charlie would make him instantly *dispensable.*

26
Happy Birthday Bumper

Petula Poor, apparently, had not expected Waddington to accompany Muffy and the girls to Greenwich for Bumper's birthday. She greeted his arrival with about the same level of enthusiasm that she would have welcomed a meter reader from the electric company. Like the meter reader, Waddington had come unannounced, had little to do, wasn't expected to stay long, and Petula would barely notice when he left.

Jack Poor arrived home at about six, just an hour before Bumper McCoy's surprise party was scheduled to begin. His attire immediately brought a disapproving grimace to Petula's face. His powder blue sport coat and light yellow slacks might be acceptable in the dealership, but not at Bumper's party. "We are going to change our clothes, aren't we?" It wasn't a question; it was a demand. "Your grey suit has been laid out on the bed." Jack nodded, said nothing, and obeyed.

While Waddington had done his best to avoid more than twice-a-year visits to Petula and Jack, he was always amazed to find that the master of Jack Poor Motors was, in his own home, more like a boarder who had come to live under Petula's roof and was expected to appear only at meals. Generally, Jack found refuge in his den, watching television and reading the car ads from his competitors.

By six-thirty the guests started to arrive so that they could be in place by seven to surprise Bumper. Waddington wondered just how much of a surprise it would be considering the driveway was full of cars. Jack and Waddington were assigned by Petula to stand by the front door like doorstops. They greeted the guests who had little inclination to offer more than a "hello" or "where's the bathroom" and then moved on to the foyer to mix with more socially appropriate company. At the appointed hour, Bumper's chauffeur found that he could not get past all the guest's cars, which meant the old man had to walk halfway up the long drive, past all the cars in order to be surprised. Well, if not surprised, he was certainly pleased to be serenaded with a chorus of Happy Birthday, Bumper.

He made the rounds of the guests, greeting them by name and thanking them for helping celebrate his seventy-fifth birthday. He proudly proclaimed, to one and all, that, for reasons unknown, it was only fitting that his birthday was on June 21st, the summer solstice. Jack and Waddington were the last to receive his attention.

Bumper looked at the two men as if he had just happened upon two party crashers. He jumped right over the more conventional greetings like "Hello. How are you?" and leveled a verbal karate chop. "You two still haven't figured it out, have you?" Without losing a beat he continued, "The car business is for losers. Wall Street. That's where smart people and smart money live. It's obvious where you two live. Or I should say, 'don't live.'

Hell, if you tried to move where the smart money lives, they'd probably burn your house down." He broke into paroxysms of laugher. "Haw, haw, hen, haw, hee, ho, hack, hack awhoop, awhoop, hack, arggggb, swapshssss!" He bent over, phlegm shooting from his mouth. He sounded as if he might choke and die. Petula heard the hacking, ran to his side, and started slapping him hard on the back.

"A little harder," Jack said in an aside to Waddington, "and she might kill the old bastard. Wouldn't that break your heart?" He bit down hard on a short laugh.

After a few moments Bumper recovered. The butler appeared and announced to all that dinner was to be served.

As soon as dinner was over, Waddington and Jack slipped outside. The front courtyard was filled with Benzes and Bentleys and Rolls and a Ferrari or two.

"Looks like a used car lot for the financially handicapped." Jack lit a cigar. "Can you believe it; not a Verite, Cadence, or Defiant among them?" His tone was ripe with sarcasm. "Want a cigar?"

"No thanks, I'll pass."

"Have you ever seen so many phony fuckers in one place in your life? Most of them hate Bumper. It's like they're afraid if they don't kiss his behind, they'll be excommunicated from the country club."

"They did seem to grovel a bit."

"Unctuous bastards." He took a long draw on his cigar and then turned to Waddington and said,

"Did you know we're having a Sell-A-Thon tomorrow?"

Waddington shook his head.

Slowly, the master of Jack Poor Motors was reemerging. "It's our biggest tent sale of the year. This will be a hell of an opportunity for you to see how we move the iron. You guys in Detroit could learn a thing or two about what it takes to sell cars, if they spent a couple days with me. This business that you guys preach in your training programs of suckin' up to customers is bullshit. Maybe those assholes at Mercedes and BMW can kiss the customer's ass and get 'em to buy cars, but not us. At our end of the market, we have to nail the weasels to the floor and squeeze 'em. That's what works for us." Jack took another long drag on his cigar. "You want to stay here tomorrow or come down to the dealership with me and learn how to sell cars?"

Now there's a Hobson's choice, if there ever was one, Waddington thought. *I can spend the day being insulted by a mother-in-law who hates me or I can sit in a dealership and listen to my obnoxious father-in-law pontificate about the art of selling low-end cars to weasels.*

27
Sell-A-Thon

Jack and Waddington arrived at the dealership early to get ready for the Saturday morning sales meeting. Waddington was well aware of how much Jack loved sales meetings. Other than selling a car for full sticker, there was little he enjoyed more than to get up in front of his fifteen salesmen and set the tone for the day by motivating them to achieve even higher levels of sales.

Ivan 'the Terrified' Krumpe arrived at 7:45 and Jack, as was always the case before a Sell-A-Thon, signed what he had come to call a "Petula receipt" for $1500 to provide incentive money for the salesmen–sales*men*–no sales*women*, no sales*persons* in Jack Poor's shop.

While Jack bent over Ivan's desk recounting the money, Waddington noticed that Ivan, his eyes fixed on Jack, slowly lowered his hand to the bottom right-hand drawer and pushed it closed. It looked to Waddington that Ivan was trying to hide something from Jack. That something appeared to be a small radio. He found it a strange place for a radio. *Odd*, he thought, and left it at that.

The recount done, Jack picked up the stack of bills and said, "Well, you little dickhead, you counted it right." He turned to Waddington. "Last time, he shorted me a hundred."

Ivan the Terrified said nothing as the two men left his office.

Jack slapped Waddington on the back as they walked toward the training room. "I'm really pumped this morning. We're taking no prisoners today."

Waddington realized that the man who walked with him down the hall was no longer Jack Poor, car dealer. He had transformed himself into an automotive General Patton, ready to lead his boys into battle. Jack looked like a man who could smell the action. Taste the blood.

"By the time we close our doors today, the sales floor is going to be running green ... green with money," he said confidently.

The man was obsessed, Waddington concluded.

"Everyone here?" Jack asked his sales manager, Spud Korman, as they stepped inside the room.

"Looks like it." Spud said looking around the room. "Oh, Owens won't be here. Called in sick."

"Bullshit. He's hung over. Fire the bastard."

"Done," Spud Korman said.

The training room was about twenty by forty with chairs lined up schoolroom style facing a large American flag and a white marking board. Waddington found it interesting that Jack purposely avoided eye contact as he walked toward the front. Clearly part of the show.

Jack slowly turned to his salesmen, all of whom were dressed in coats and ties. Waddington took a seat in the back of the room. A quick glance told him that, despite Jack's arrival, the salesmen were, variously, half asleep, bored, scared, detached, interested in whatever they were reading in the newspaper, or finishing the last of the coffee and Dunkin' Donuts that Spud always brought in for these meetings.

"Okay," Jack said, "let's get started. For any of you that are too hung over to have noticed, this is Saturday, June 22nd.It's a *Jack Poor Sell-A-Thon* day. *You* are going to make money today. *I* am going to make money today. We are *all* going to make money today!"

With that, he opened his briefcase and held up the fifteen-hundred-dollar wad of bills. "Listen up. Here's the skinny: I'm paying $100 to each of the first three guys who close deals this morning. I got $200 for the best gross. I am giving $400 to the guy who sells the most cars today. And there's $200 for the guy who can get rid of that '97 Blue Dodge that's been sitting on the lot for the last four months."

Jack unfolded a newspaper and held up the full-page ad that had appeared in several local papers. "In our Sell-A-Thon ad, you will notice that we feature the Red Verite that's sitting out under the tent for '$1.00 Over Invoice.' Be aware that we are not, I repeat, we are not selling any other Verite for $1 over invoice, just that one. Got that? Just *that* one. Now, listen carefully: There's a reward for any guy who sells that car. And the reward is ..." Jack paused for effect and looked at every man in the room, "... the reward is *you lose your fuckin' job.* Your ass is outta here! Let me repeat that for the benefit of you rookies: That Red Verite under the tent does *not* leave this lot. Your job is to convince people that they *do not want* that Red Verite. You'll say or do whatever it takes *not* to sell that car. I don't care if you have to pry their fingers off the door and drag 'em away. That car stays right where it is. You will sell them *off* that car and *onto* one with a full markup or I will personally come out on the lot, rip off your head, and shit down your neck!"

Jack was loving himself, Waddington thought. He was in overdrive and cruising until one of the rookies raised his hand.

"But that doesn't sound very ethical, Mr. Poor," the rookie said with concern. "How can you offer something in the paper and then not deliver?"

Now there's a question worthy of philosophical debate, Waddington thought.

"What the fuck does ethics have to do with it? You're not here to feel sorry for these weasels. You're here to put their asses in a car and to clean out their wallets."

Jack took a breath and looked around the room. "How many of you live in Greenwich?"

No one raised his hand.

"Exactly. Not one of you. You can't afford to. But the people who walk in here today *can* afford to live in Greenwich, which means they have money and that makes them the enemy. If they can screw us out of making a profit on one of our cars, you can bet your sweet bippy that they will. Well, they can't screw Jack Poor because I screw 'em first. Read my lips: These people are not your friends. They are people with money. But when they walk in here, it's no longer their money. It's

238

my money and I want it. Your job is to get my money, *your* money, out of their pockets and onto Spud's desk. I don't care if you have to squeeze 'em, bump 'em, bush 'em, or whack 'em; your job is to get every last nickel out of their pockets."

Jack paused to catch his breath. Waddington suppressed a laugh. Jack had worked up a significant sweat. Then, without thinking, he began to mop his forehead with the eraser from the white marking board.

"One more thing, and this is for the benefit of you rookies: Nobody, and I mean *nobody,* walks. *(Translation: A customer leaves the showroom without buying a car.)* If you can't close 'em, you pull the alarm and turn 'em over … T.O. 'em, to Spud here. You rookies can learn something from Spud. When he puts a customer in the hot box, they don't come out until they've lost ten pounds and signed on the dotted line. Then, when they come to pick up the car, he bangs 'em for a few more bucks just for having been such an asshole and given us a hard time. I love it when he does that. If I could only clone him." Jack looked admiringly at his sales manager who was basking in the adulation. "Any questions?"

Waddington had a bunch of questions, but this didn't seem to be the time or place for a discussion of ethics. He looked around the room. The rookies looked shell-shocked. The veterans shrugged with same old, same old expressions.

Jack clearly did not expect any questions. He clapped his hands and shouted, "Okay, troops, let's get out there on the floor and … MAKE … ME … SOME … MONEY!"

For a moment, Waddington expected to hear a rousing "let's go get 'em" response, like a gung-ho football team leaving the locker room or the dough boys going over the top. Instead, he saw three incredulous, dismayed rookies and a dozen veterans wearing vague, ambivalent expressions shuffle out of the room like a bunch of people with no particular place to go and in no hurry to get there.

28
Mrs. Swenson Pays a Visit

Just after twelve, Waddington heard screaming. Mrs. Delia Swenson, a seriously overweight, middle-aged women with flaming red hair, dressed in what looked like sweat clothes, had commandeered a place in the middle of the showroom and started screaming, "Jack Poor killed my husband! He sells cars that kill people! Jack Poor should be arrested and sent to the electric chair for what he did. He's a killer! A mother-fucking killer!"

If her objective was to attract attention, she certainly achieved that in short order. She looked like the kind of wild-eyed, bent-on-revenge woman that would, at any minute, produce a machine gun out of her sweatpants and start shooting up the place. Customers who had just walked into the dealership did an immediate one-eighty and fled. Others cowered behind their salesmen, most of whom were also looking for cover.

Waddington, who had parked himself at an empty desk to check his emails, stood up, and looked around to see if anyone was going to deal with the woman. It appeared that everyone had suddenly found someplace else to be.

"Are you Jack Poor?" She screamed as Waddington approached. "Are you the miserable bastard that sold my husband that deathtrap on wheels?"

"No, I'm not Mr. Poor. I'm sure he'd be more than happy to talk with you. But first, you've got to calm down and control yourself."

"Control myself? You mean like my husband couldn't control your fucking car?"

Waddington reached out to lay a reassuring hand on her shoulder, "Please believe me, Mr. Poor was truly saddened to hear of your loss."

"Lay a hand on her, and I'll sue your ass for sexual molestation and assault and battery." The voice belonged to a squat, little clone of Danny DeVito.

"Who are you?" Waddington asked.

The clone reached into his pocket and handed Waddington a card that identified him as Abner Slipwalker, Personal Injury Lawyer. "I'm Mrs. Swenson's lawyer. Any attempt to remove my client from these premises will be documented." With that said, he pulled out a small digital camera and held it up, preparing to shoot any attempt to remove the hysterical Mrs. Swenson.

"Wait here," Waddington said, "and please try to calm your client. I'll find Jack Poor." Waddington left Mrs. Swenson and Slipwalker and ran up the stairs that led to Jack's office.

Jack met him at the door. "What the hell is going on down there? What's all that screaming?"

" Swenson's wife is here and she wants to see you. She's hysterical. She's screaming that you killed her husband."

"What?" Jack was incredulous. "Get her the fuck off the floor before she scares away all my customers."

"Should I bring her up here?

"Does she look like she might have a gun?"

"A gun?" Waddington asked.

"You can't be too careful these days. If you're sure she hasn't got a gun, bring her up."

Waddington returned to the floor and asked Slipwalker and Mrs. Swenson to follow him back upstairs. Mrs. Swenson remained reasonably restrained until she entered Jack's office. Once inside, she let fly again.

"You killed my husband! You knew that car was a deathtrap! You're going to pay for this! I'll have you in court. I'll take you all the way to the Supreme Court if I have to. I'll see you in the electric chair!" She had gone over the edge, a fact not lost on her lawyer, who decided that he'd better step in before Mrs. Swenson started breaking things.

"Delia, Delia," he said stepping in front of her. "I think you should sit down and let me handle things from here." He looked at Jack, "As you can see, she's very distraught over this."

"I can see that," Jack said with matter-of-fact frankness.

"Mr. Poor, my name is Abner Slipwalker, and I represent Mrs. Swenson. We plan to bring suit against your dealership, you and, of course, the manufacturer, for the death of Adolph Swenson." Slipwalker pointed toward the couch adjacent to Jack's desk, "May we sit down?"

"Be my guest," Jack said in his most accommodating tone.

Slipwalker and Mrs. Swenson settled onto Jack's couch.

"Excuse me for asking, but isn't this a little unusual for you and your client to announce in person that you're going to sue me? I don't want to tell you how to do your job, Mr. Slipwalker, but I don't believe this is the way these things are supposed to work."

Mrs. Swenson interrupted, "I have to go to the bathroom. Bad."

Jack pointed to a door on the other side of the room. "That's my private washroom. Please feel free."

Waddington couldn't get over Jack's measured and calm demeanor. It was not like him. By now, he'd fully expected him to toss both Slipwalker and Mrs. Swenson out of his office.

As soon as Mrs. Swenson closed the door, Slipwalker stood up and took a seat next to Jack's desk. "Understand, this was not my idea. In fact, I advised strongly against it. But this is the one-month anniversary of Mr. Swenson's death, and she insisted on visiting the scene of the crime."

"Excuse me?" Jack retorted incredulously. "Scene of the crime? If my memory serves me correctly, the *accident* happened over in Westchester."

"True, but the car came from here and, well ..." he shrugged, "she's been under a lot of strain since the funeral." He turned and checked to be sure that the bathroom door was still closed. "I had no idea she would react the way she did. But you have to understand, her husband's death has been a terrible blow."

Jack got up from behind his desk and stared at the little man for a moment, then picked up a chair and set it down very close to Slipwalker. Godfather close, which is to say, uncomfortably close. "Abner, may I call you Abner?" he began.

Abner nodded.

Waddington could not begin to guess what Jack was up to.

"Abner, based on your performance so far today, I'd say as a personal injury lawyer, you'd make a great lamp shade. Let me give you a bit of free advice; if you're going to sue someone, you don't pay them a social visit first."

"I told you, my client insisted on coming."

"And you let her?"

"I had no choice. If I had refused, she would have come without me."

"I'm not a lawyer, Abner, but if I were, I certainly would not have let her put on that performance in my showroom."

"She ran inside before I could stop her. She is very determined."

"She is also nuts."

"I would prefer distraught to nuts. I don't think you'll be able to defend yourself, based on her emotional state of mind. Her case is truly tragic. And you and your company are going to have to answer some very serious questions."

Again, Waddington thought Jack might show some anger. But he remained exceedingly calm and controlled.

" You're new at this, aren't you Abner?"

"New? New at what?"

"PI. Personal injury law. I mean, you don't strike me as having had much experience in matters like this."

"If you think you're going to put me off with insults ..."

Jack cut him off. "My apologies. I am sorry." He said it with such sincerity that Waddington though he might even mean it.

"Far be it from me to insult you or your client. Here at Jack Poor Motors, everyone who walks in the front door is entitled to our utmost respect. I insist on it. Even personal injury lawyers. In fact, especially, PI lawyers."

Waddington was sure that Jack was playing with him now.

Jack leaned even closer to Slipwalker, laying a paternal hand on the little man's shoulder. "Let me make sure I understand your intentions. Mrs. Swenson feels we were responsible for her husband's death, and she's considering a lawsuit."

Slipwalker nodded slightly, growing increasingly uncomfortable at his close proximity to Jack.

"That's your right. Far be it from me to suggest you do not exercise your rights. I invite you to sue. In fact, I would like you to file it very soon so that this matter can be settled in court and not on our showroom floor. When can I expect you to file?"

Slipwalker was taken aback. He probably had never had a potential defendant invite a lawsuit. "What are you up to, Poor?" Slipwalker rose from his chair and moved to the center of the room.

The sound of the toilet flushing arrived as Mrs. Swenson opened the door to the toilet. "I think you better get a plunger. It's stopped up."

"Thank you for letting me know," Jack said most graciously.

Slipwalker put on his best PI face and tried to regain the initiative. "I don't know what kind of game you're playing, Poor, but this Mr. Nice-Nice act of yours is not going to put us off. We are going to sue."

"You're damn right," Mrs. Swenson volunteered.

"If you feel you have a case, I invite you to do just that." Jack stood up, walked to his desk and fished for a business card from the middle drawer. "This is my lawyer," he said handing Slipwalker the card. "Now, I ask you again, when may we expect you to file?"

Slipwalker was clearly nonplussed. "We'll be filing in the next couple weeks, you can count on it," he said, clearly determined to show this car dealer that he could not be put off with whateverthehell he was trying to do.

"Fine," Jack answered pleasantly. "I look forward to it." Jack smiled like a chess player who has just called checkmate after three moves.

Waddington was at a total loss to understand Jack's tactic. He knew his father-in-law well enough to know that all was not as it seemed. Jack had a plan. What that plan was, he could not even venture to guess.

Slipwalker looked like an actor who had forgotten his lines. He did not know what to say. He turned to Mrs. Swenson and took her arm. "We need to go, now."

She pulled away from his grasp. "What? Wait a minute! Let go of me! When do I get my money from this sonofabitch? You said he'd want to offer a settlement to get us off his back."

Jack smiled the smile of a man very much in control.

"We'll talk about it in the car," Slipwalker said, guiding her out the door before she could protest further.

"You know," Waddington said, "I always ranked personal injury lawyers well down on the food chain. And I assumed that most are connivers, opportunists, sneaks, and a whole lot of other terms. But I never assumed they were dumb. This guy I would call dumb. It's like he got his degree from a home study course. But he *will* sue."

"Of course, he will. Or at least, he'll file. Mrs. Swenson let the cat out of the bag. He's looking for some type of settlement."

"Extortion, pure and simple."

"As far as I'm concerned, he can take his lawsuit and cram it up Mrs. Swenson's substantial behind." And then as an afterthought Jack said, "Did you see that woman's rear end? It looked bigger than the one we've got on the Cadence." Jack found his choice of imagery very funny.

"For argument's sake, let say you and the company refuse to settle, and it goes to trial. That's when you lose control. You never know about juries these days. They like to stick it to corporations every chance they get."

Jack shook his head confidently. "Not in this case. Believe me, Slipwalker can't win. Trust me."

Jack's confident attitude, his self-assured aura seemed so much out of character that Waddington began to wonder if he'd missed something. Waddington thought about what Perkins had said. A lawsuit, if it got out of control and caught the attention of a cable news network, could derail the French deal, to say nothing of the impact it could have on Verite 300 sales. Maybe that was it, Waddington decided. Basic dealer myopia. Jack was looking at this just in terms of his dealership. He had no idea of the bigger picture.

"Pres, do me a favor, wouldja? Go and check to see what kind of damage that crazy bitch did to my Sell-a-Thon. I'll be down in a couple minutes. I just remembered I have an important phone call that I need to make."

"I need to make a pit stop." Waddington nodded toward Jack private bathroom.

"For your sake, I hope that daffy broad was wrong about the toilet being stopped up."

Waddington laughed, "I'll let you know."

"If you need it, the plunger is under the sink." Jack picked up the phone. He waited until

Waddington had closed the bathroom door and then dialed.

As Waddington settled himself on the toilet seat, he thought he heard Jack say, "Popper?"

29
The Vote

Waddington and Jack left the dealership about five. No sooner had they walked into the house than Petula announced that the four of them were going to the Country Club with a dozen or more of her friends. Petula billed it as a welcome home, Muffy, dinner. By the time the main course arrived, Waddington viewed it more as a celebration for the return of the Prodigal daughter. Petula, it seemed, had the chef at the club kill the fatted calf. Waddington had never seen such enormous slabs of roast beef.

Just after the salad and before the cheese course, it became clear that neither Jack nor Waddington was doing much to lift the level of conversation. Jack wanted to talk about the car business and Waddington was doing little to dissuade him. As soon as it seemed appropriate, Petula dispatched them to the men's locker room where they sat with the locker room attendant and watched the Mets lose to San Diego by what Waddington, never an avid baseball fan, guessed to be about a hundred runs.

The next morning, Waddington quietly slipped out of bed, making sure not to wake Muffy. He dressed quickly and went into the kitchen where one of Petula's maids was laying out breakfast. It was a beautiful morning, the temperature in the mid-seventies. He downed a small glass of orange juice, poured a cup of coffee, and helped himself to a Danish. He left the kitchen and made his way across the expansive, rolling yard His destination was a Gazebo hidden from the house, overlooking the Long Island Sound and well away from Petula's critical gaze or Muffy's laments about her exile in Detroit.

The air was sea fresh, sweetened by the smell of the Jasmine that hung in baskets from the roof of the Gazebo. His thoughts drifted back to his lunch with Olivia. What a pleasure it had been to spend an afternoon in a garden with an attractive, intelligent woman who had not one critical thing to say about his appearance, his opinions, or his mediocre career. If only life had reruns, he mused. He would replay that afternoon in the garden over and over.

The potential for a relationship of any real depth or longevity was, he knew, pure fantasy. Even those times when he had kissed her, he felt it might rightly be considered opportunistic on his part. While he sensed Olivia was very fond of him, he wondered if maybe he was guilty of taking advantage of a woman trying to gain a measure of revenge for her husband's infidelities. She had to be looking for the means to retaliate. Was Waddington just her subconscious instrument?

The last time they were together, besieged as they were by the French maid, the window washer, and the butler from Maubeuge, had actually been fun in a perverse sort of way. Olivia had a wonderful sense of humor, and he loved that about her. What they had laughingly called their rehearsal had turned out to be the performance of a farce. Yet, even in the midst of all that chaos, he sensed that she actually loved him. But why? Same answer. Timing. He decided she had come to a point in her life when she desperately needed someone to whom she could relate. Someone who would love and respect her. By the luck of the draw, she had selected him to fill the void. But fill it with what? He had nothing of substance to offer her. Preston Waddington from Teaneck, New Jersey, was hardly up to Gross Pointe standards.

It was only a matter of time until Olivia would come to her senses. He could write the script. At first, she would struggle to find a way to let him down, easy. She would fret over the how and when. At last, she would call him and in her sweet, considerate, almost self-effacing way, apologize for having been so selfish as to have entangled him in her life. She would finally get around to suggesting that it might be best if they did not see each other again. Of course, he would agree. And that would be that. All that would remain would be his memory of their brief affair, unconsummated as it was. What a miserable ending to his script, he thought.

He began to serenade Long Island sound. "Thanks, for the memories …"

"Singing? You're out here singing?" Muffy seemed to appear from nowhere. "I think you may have really lost it."

"Possibly. That's why I came out here, to find it."

"Why do I get the feeling that you're hiding from us?"

"I have no idea. I'm not hiding. I'm here in plain view, having my breakfast and enjoying the fabulous view."

She looked out at the Sound and offered confirmation. "There is no other view quite like this."

"It's not all bad," he agreed.

"Wouldn't it be nice if you could enjoy a view like this every day? "

Waddington looked at her curiously. *What kind of question was that* he wondered?

She did not wait for him to ask. "Pres, I've made a decision. I've had it with Detroit. Completely and totally had it. In fact, I hate Detroit. I hate the weather. I hate the flatness. I hate the way people drive. I hate the downtown, which doesn't exist. I hate everything about the city and the state of Michigan, and the whole Midwest. They should bomb it. How can any thinking human being live there? Especially, if they had the opportunity to live in a place like Greenwich."

The new Muffy, the one Waddington had seen go through a metamorphosis over the last several years, had developed a tendency to take a thing and beat it to death. The city of Detroit this morning was near moribund.

"I'm sure the Detroit Chamber of Commerce will be interested in your assessment."

"You're not funny. But I'm serious. I want out of Detroit."

"Unless what I'm looking at is the Detroit River," he said, "you are not presently in Detroit.

And based on what you told me, you will not be returning to Detroit until the end of summer. So why this attack on Detroit?"

"Because I hate it."

"So, you said."

"And I have decided that I intend to be here *all* the time."

"Here? At your mother's?" Waddington needed clarification.

"Not necessarily at my mother's. But in Connecticut. It makes sense. With Julie going to Wesleyan and now that Petula has gotten Hildy accepted at Miss Porter's in the fall, this is where we ought to live."

"Your mother got Hildy into Miss Porters?"

"Yes, she has a great deal of influence up there."

"Does Hildy want to go to Miss Porters?"

"She will."

"She hasn't been asked?"

"I know what's best for her. And I know she'll love it."

"Excuse me, Muffy, but I think a decision like this should be made by you and me. Not your mother."

"That's a subject for another discussion."

"Then I'm confused. What are we discussing?"

"We are discussing the decision to leave Detroit and come back to Greenwich."

"What in hell are you talking about?"

"I'm talking about what I consider to be a very generous offer from my mother. Once we sell our house in Livonia, she has offered to make up the difference in what we make on the sale with whatever more we need to buy a house here in Greenwich."

"Did I miss something? Are you suggesting that we sell the house in Livonia and move here?"

"You're not paying attention, Preston. You're tuning me out. You always tune me out."

"No, I hear you loud and clear. Every word. I just don't believe what I'm hearing. Maybe you've forgotten or maybe you've just chosen to overlook the fact that I work for a car company. And, through no fault of mine, they are located in Detroit. So far as I know, they do not have any plans to move to Connecticut. Now, in regard to your dislike of Detroit, may I remind you there are suburbs like Bloomfield Hills and Grosse Pointe that are as nice as Greenwich."

"Except for two things," she said, locking the lower part of her jaw as she was wont to do anytime she was determined to win a point. "We don't happen to live in Grosse Pointe and never will. And even if we did, Grosse Pointe does not have a view of Long Island Sound."

"Well, I'll give you that," Waddington said, realizing that as far as Muffy was concerned, this was not an issue that lent itself to impassive discourse. Poor old Detroit. That wilderness outpost in flyover America had lost its appeal to Muffy.

"Leaving here and going to Detroit twenty years ago was the biggest mistake I ever made."

"As I recall, that was your choice."

"I'm not denying that. However, I do not intend to pay for that mistake by doing penance in Livonia for the rest of my life. My girls deserve what Greenwich and the East have to offer."

"My girls?" he bristled. "What happened to *our* girls?"

"Let's not get technical," she retorted. "Now, Mummy and I discussed this last night after you went to bed. I told her that you certainly would want to find work here in Greenwich and that it should probably be something to do with cars. What Mummy suggested, and I think this was very considerate of her, is that you work for my father for a couple years until he retires. Then you can take over the management of the dealership."

Waddington just stared at Muffy incredulously. Then he said, "I would rather drown myself in the Detroit River than work for your father."

Muffy made no secret of her exasperation. "Now there's a perfect example of why I hate Detroit. You'd die in that river of some disease before you had a chance to drown."

He dropped his head in his hands. *What did I do to deserve this, this morning?* he wondered.

"I am serious about this, Pres. I want out of Detroit. However, this is a decision that will affect both of us. So, I think it only fair that we vote."

"Vote? On what?"

"What I've been talking about. There are two choices. One, we can stay in Livonia, where I will do my best to endure a living hell," she paused for emphasis. "You can believe that I will not endure that hell in silence. Or, two, we can move to Greenwich so that we can give *our*," she put added emphasis on 'our' this time, " daughters the kind of life they deserve."

"And that your mother is willing to pay for," he added sourly.

"Well, *you* certainly aren't in a position to pay for it."

Waddington looked out at the sound and counted five sailboats leaving the harbor that had to be eighty feet in length or more. One might even have been Bumper McCoy's. Muffy was right, of course. He couldn't afford to give them the kind of life Petula was tempting them with. But then, there was certainly no guarantee that Petula's largess would make better women of his girls. Waddington was fully aware that he was fighting a losing battle.

"So those are my choices. Hell with you in Livonia, or heaven with your mother in Greenwich?"

"I do not appreciate your cynical attitude. Now, I've given you the choices."

"Is this to be just a family vote, or are we going to give a ballot to Petula and Jack?"

"This is just between us."

"Well, at least that will make the votes easy to count. I presume you've already casts yours for Greenwich?"

"This is a secret vote. When you cast yours, we'll count."

Good God, he thought, *she's serious. We're going to count votes? Only two people are going to vote, and she's going to do the counting. The woman's gone over the edge.* "What if I don't like either choice? What if I don't want to vote for either of your cockamamie choices?"

"Well, nobody's forcing you to vote. You can always abstain."

"And if I do?"

Her jaw tightened and there was a look of no compromise, no prisoners on her face. "Then you might want to think about making other living arrangements. As you know, the house in is my name. That gives me the right to sell it. And that's exactly what I intend to do. Immediately."

As she turned her back on him and walked back to mummy's house, he realized that this was the beginning of the end. The girl who used to wear herbs in her hair was going home, without him. And he didn't mind it at all.

30
Well, C'est la Vie!

Petula was more than happy to have her chauffeur drive Waddington to the airport. Only Hildy, who had not yet been told that she would be permanently relocating to Greenwich, bid him goodbye.

On Monday, he got to the office late. Doreen was not at her desk, and his phone was ringing. It was Olivia. The conversation quickly turned to the weekend and "The Vote."

"Muffy has decided to stay in Greenwich," and then with emphasis, "permanently," Waddington said.

"Permanently?" Olivia appeared not to understand.

"Permanently, as in she's not coming back to Detroit … ever. As you might have suspected from our conversation that day in your garden, it was bound to come to this."

"I've missed you," she said softly. "I guess I'm not sorry that your wife won't be coming back to Detroit."

He was glad that she missed him. But at the same time, he began to wonder, as he had for the last several days, *why him?* He was simply not in her league. *She's first class, I'm steerage.* As much as he wanted to be with her, he felt that it was up to him to do what was right. And what was right was to back away before he compromised her. She was too special to have their affair become fodder for the rapacious gossips of Gross Pointe. It was time they both faced up to reality.

She had no intention of discussing *reality*. "Preston, do you like Mahler?"

"I have all nine symphonies."

"The London Philharmonic is performing at the Max Fisher Music Hall this Thursday night. If I were to leave a ticket for you at the box office, would you join me?"

Perfect, he thought. *She has just given me an opportunity to start backing away. I can certainly find some reason that I'm busy with training or the dealer meeting. I can make myself unavailable for weeks. The longer we go without seeing each other, the easier it will be to finally go our separate ways.* All he had to do was tell her that he was sorry, that he had another commitment. That would do it. That's all he had to say. But that's not what he said.

" I'd love to go." Then for no rational reason, he found himself adding, "And I promise not to wear my brown suit."

"I'll hold you to that," she said, laughing. "It starts at eight." And softly she added, "I love you."

Well, so much for his new resolve.

Waddington's seat at "The Max" was in the sixth row, on the aisle. At five of eight the seat next to him was still empty. Just as the lights started to dim, she arrived. Quickly, he stood up and moved into the aisle so that she could take her seat.

"Would you believe it? We had a flat. On the Edsel Freeway, of all places. Thank goodness a taxi stopped, otherwise, I'd have never made it."

She was wearing a formal black dress with a modest neckline. Waddington couldn't take his eyes off her. "You do not look like a woman who just stepped out of a taxi. Out of the pages of Vogue maybe, but not a taxi."

She smiled up at him and squeezed his hand. "You're so good for my ego, Preston."

The lights dimmed and the conductor took the podium.

The program featured two works. Mahler was scheduled for after intermission. The first work was by Saint-Saens.

The lights came up for the intermission. Waddington was about to stand up when a matronly woman, whose voice cascaded over him, said, "It *is* you. I thought I saw you come down the aisle. The woman was leaning over him, placing a rather substantial pair of chintz and lace-covered mammilla in his ear.

"Olivia, I just wanted to tell you how much I enjoyed the Petition Committee brunch at your house. It was simply fabulous, and I apologize for not having called or sent a note to thank you. But my schedule has just been out of control. There just never seems to be enough time."

For all intents and purposes, he had become invisible to the woman who, even as she pressed her ample upper body into his face, never once acknowledged him. Realizing that Olivia was a captive audience, the woman appeared to be planning to stay awhile. Olivia had no choice but to smile, nod, and hear her out. Waddington could not help but notice that the interloper had a near terminal case of halitosis. She could have killed cockroaches at twenty feet with that breath. To avoid the olfactory discomfort, Waddington turned his head away so that he was looking directly at Olivia, whose eyes seemed about ready to glaze over. She was suffering too.

Finally, the woman appeared to realize that there was a live body under hers, and she pulled back and looked at Waddington with a curious expression. "I know you," she said. You were at the bunch. The brown suit."

I've achieved immortality in Grosse Pointe, Waddington thought.

"Well, we must have lunch one day very soon, Olivia. I promise to call you just as soon as I have a moment." And with that she left.

"Let's hope she never has a moment," Olivia, said. "I think, had she not left, I would have asked the usher to have her removed bodily and tossed into the orchestra pit."

"That I would have liked to have seen." He laughed as he stood up and stepped into the aisle to join the crowd as it made its way to the lobby for intermission refreshments.

Olivia stepped into the aisle and took his arm. "I hate to admit it, but I have forgotten her last name. Sandy something. She doesn't look like a Sandy, does she? And she rambles. Half the time, I have no idea what she's talking about, and I don't think she does either. I am absolutely convinced that her late husband died just to escape her."

As they walked slowly up the aisle, Waddington became concerned that someone might see them. He could hear the tongues in Grosse Pointe. *Who was that medium-looking man you were with at the concert?* And if someone from the company saw him, how would he explain having the President's wife on his arm? He thought about suggesting it might look better if she let go of his arm. At least that way, they might appear as two people who just happened to have accidentally met at the concert and were exchanging pleasantries. From the firmness of her grip, Waddington realized she had no intention of letting go, for any reason.

He looked down at her slightly off-center face. She simply glowed. *God, I love your face,* he thought. His eyes dropped to her dress, and he found himself looking at her well-formed breasts. He gave into a moment of speculation. "I think I'd like to make love to you, Olivia," he whispered in her ear.

She looked up at him, beaming, "I think I'd like you too," she said.

Well, there it was. He jumped off the cliff. *Well, c'est la vie,* he thought. *What happens, happens.* With that, he put his hand on her arm. He was not about to let her go.

31
Sleep-Away-Camp

"I don't know about the rest of you, but the idea of three years in a Federal sleep-away camp is not my idea of a great vacation." Axel was doing his best to keep his temper under control.

Charlie looked like a man in a tax audit who has just been confronted with proof that he has not reported all his income. He was naked, vulnerable, and caught totally off guard. Of all the things Charlie worked hard to prevent, number one was being confronted with the unexpected. He glanced at the pile of documents Axel had dropped on his desk and then glanced over at Harry Spar. Had the glance been bullets, Harry would have been on the floor bleeding.

Spar, realizing what Axel had put on Charlie's desk, looked like a Taliban terrorist who had just been lashed to a bomb and was having second thoughts about an early visit with Allah to collect his seventy-two virgins. Popper picked up Charlie's state of shock and gave the impression of a man who had happened upon a budding street fight and was retreating to a safe place from which to observe the altercation.

"This is a fuckin' disaster waiting to happen," Axel said emphatically.

Charlie decided to buy some time. He opened the report slowly, purposely turning each page. The impression he wanted to create was that he was reading the document for the first time. He realized that might not play when he saw that many of the memos and reports had his name on them and several bore his handwritten initials. Charlie grabbed for a straw, hoping it would keep him afloat long enough to defuse whatever Axel had in mind. It was not, he knew, his strongest defense, but it was the best he could conjure up without making a full retreat. Purposely and with a forced air of unconcern, he leaned back in his chair and flipped several pages of the report toward the edge of his desk, deliberately intending that they slid off the desk onto the floor. They did exactly that. Axel instinctively stooped to pick them up. Standing, Axel had been in a dominant position. Stooping, he had momentarily compromised himself and, while Axel was still squatting, Charlie began his offensive.

"It might be well if you'd stick to sales and let me handle engineering. That report is not what I presume you think it is. It means nothing."

"How so?" Axel was ready for combat.

Charlie's practiced cool exterior was in marked contrast to Axel's tight jaw and aggressive body language. "Those were some tests we ran on a special set of cars. The purpose was to see how much content we could pull out of the Verite without impacting performance."

"By 'content,' I presume you mean quality. Since when have we taken to reducing quality on purpose?"

"You don't get it do you? People in sales never do. What you'd really like is to build a

Mercedes CLK and sell it for under twenty grand. That would make your life really easy, wouldn't it? If we do could that, we wouldn't need a VP of Sales. The cars would roll off the line right into the customers' garages." Now it was time to begin to demean Axel in front of Spar and Popper. "I'm surprised, Axel. You came up through the factory. Which means that you, better than most, should understand that building cars for our end of the market is first, a matter of styling, and second, a matter of controlling production costs. Every time I can eliminate a nickel of cost here or a dime there, I end up saving the company hundreds of thousands of dollars. And do you know what that does?" He intentionally let himself sound gratuitously pedantic, hoping that Axel might lose his temper and give him all of the high ground. "It lets me keep the company profitable and pay the salaries of the people who work here. This may come as a surprise to you, but there's a lot of pressure on me to bring in our cars at a very competitive price."

Axel did not try to mask his disdain for Charlie's lecture in Business Economics 101, and he gave it back to him in kind. "I suppose that justifies our building cars that can derail in a curve and smash into a wall, or roll off a cliff, or maybe hit another car. Golly gee," he said with broad sarcasm, "I guess this means the more Verite's that get smashed up, the more we'll sell. What a marketing strategy."

Charlie had borrowed a Ford process from years back which they had called "thrifting."

Charlie renamed it "content evaluation," but the purpose was the same, to pull costs out of the car. The key to the process was to eliminate as many components from under the skin as possible, without substantially affecting the performance of the car. Charlie could feel his blood pressure rising and would have liked to have tossed Axel out of his office, but he knew he needed to maintain his cool and get on the offensive. "Axel, I don't think this cynical attitude of yours is conducive to an intelligent discussion. What you have to appreciate is that we're walking a tightrope. I realize there is always a fine line between controlling costs and reliability risks. That's why, when we did those tests, we were trying to identify just where that line was. There is no way I would knowingly permit this company to build a car that has not met industry safety standards."

"Charlie, maybe you better reread those reports. It's pretty clear to me that you authorized the redesign of that suspension system, knowing full well it could potentially cause excessive oversteer. It's all there. Complete with your initials and even two signatures."

"That may be true, but you're wrong about these reports. The tests shown here were run on special cars that we modified for the tests. Isn't that right, Harry?"

Harry nodded robotically.

"Bullshit. I read the fucking report, very carefully. Those were production cars, right off the line. I checked. There were no modifications to those cars. They have the same suspension system that every fucking Verite 300 on the road today has."

"So?" Charlie wasn't sure how to respond.

"So, each one is a potential death trap."

"Says who?"

"Says me." Axel opened his briefcase and pulled out a black-and-white eight-by-ten picture of the Verite that had crashed during Waddington's press preview. "Look at this."

"What is it?"

"It's a Verite that was totaled during the first day of Waddington's press preview at the providing grounds. The driver lost it a tight curve."

Charlie began to rub his forehead. He needed time to formulate a rebuttal. "Let me ask you a question: Can I presume the guy driving this car was taking the curve at a pretty high speed?"

"Just over fifty."

"And this was a sharp curve?"

"Right."

"Well, it sounds to me like he was creating a situation which is far from what the typical driver is going to encounter. So far, I haven't heard any complaints from Verite owners about loss of control."

"What about that guy Swenson in Westchester? Sounds to me like what happened out at the proving grounds happened to him. He lost it in the curve."

"We looked into that. Harry, tell Axel what you found."

"Driver error. One hundred percent. I called the Westchester County Police, and they told me that this guy Swenson took a twenty-five mile-per-hour curve, marked big as life, at well over fifty. Close to sixty, maybe. It was the law of physics combined with a guy who probably wasn't a very good driver in the first place."

Charlie chimed in, "I think you'll agree, Axel, we can't be responsible for every asshole who decides not to obey the speed limit."

"Well, from the article I read, it looks like his wife and her lawyer think otherwise."

"They haven't got a case," Harry Spar snapped.

"Maybe they don't. But let's say, for the sake of discussion, that Mrs. Swenson's lawyer ... what the hell's his name? Slipwalker. Let's say this dirtbag decides to go to the press and label this a case of 'Unintended Spinout.' How long do you suppose it would be before a whole bunch of people looking for a quick payday would come out of the woodwork, claiming their cars have the same problem? They'd be like flies on sugar. Then maybe Slipwalker tips off *60 Minutes* to the 'unintended spinout' problem, and they decide it would make a good story for their program. Now, let's really add some gasoline to the old fire: What if the lawyer or CBS were to come across these test reports and find your name all over them? Can't you just hear one of those *60 Minute*s hosts saying, 'And it appears that the CEO, Charles Fair, *knew* that in certain situations, the Verite was a death trap. Company records indicate that he tried to cover up the performance limitations by ordering new tests at lower speeds.' Jesus, our sales would sink lower than virtue in a whorehouse. And forget the fuckin' French. They'd be out of here on the next flight home."

Charlie said nothing. He suddenly realized just how exposed and vulnerable he was. It would be his head the press and Feds would come after first. And right here, on his desk, were the incriminating test reports that he thought Harry Spar had collected and shredded. He glared over at Spar who grimaced like a man who'd just been told that he'd been moved to the head of the guillotine line.

Charlie stood up. "Excuse me a minute. I need to take a pee." He also needed a couple of minutes to decide how he was going to handle Axel.

32
Pandora's Box

Charlie reappeared from his private bathroom. His demeanor and tone suggested he was not so much making an observation as issuing an order. "There is one thing we won't have to worry about. No one is going to see this report." He walked back to his desk and sat on the edge. He made every effort to look relaxed, comfortable, and not at all concerned. "Have you got more copies of this in your office?"

"No," Axel answered.

"Harry," he asked pointedly, fully intending not to reveal the mission he'd sent Harry Spar on to destroy all the reports, " are you aware of any additional copies of this that might be floating around?"

"I'd like to know where Axel got that one?"

"Maybe Axel will tell us," Charlie said turning back to his VP of Sales.

"What the hell does it matter where I got it? That's not the issue here. It's what's in the fuckin' report."

"Is this the only copy you have?"

"That's the only one," he said, "and I'd like to have it back, if you don't mind."

Charlie assumed that Axel was telling him the truth. At least he sounded like he was telling the truth. Chances were, he decided, this *is* the only copy. It was hard to imagine Axel standing at the

Xerox machine, copying two hundred pages of documents. No, this was probably the only one.

"I think, under the circumstances, that it will be better for all concerned if I keep it here under lock and key. The last thing we need is for this report to get into the hands of one of those assholes from the <u>Free Press</u> or *60 Minutes* or one of those cable networks. Rest assured, Axel, this report is not going to leave this building." Charlie picked it up and dropped it into his bottom desk drawer and locked it.

"You can burn it, bury it, or have it for lunch, for all I care. Whatever you do with that stack of paper, it doesn't deal with the problem. I want to know what you're you going to do about the Verite's rear suspension? Swenson may have been the first to spin-out, at least that we've heard of. But what if there are others? Morally, ethically, and from a pure business perspective, we have to do something about the rear suspension. For what it's worth, I've talked to engineering, and they say it would not be all that difficult to fix."

"You're not suggesting a recall?" Charlie asked incredulously.

"I think that's the way most car companies step up to eliminate defects."

"A recall would break the company," Charlie said pointedly. "You're talking millions and millions of dollars in retrofits, and that's money we don't have. Plus, if we were to announce a recall, the French would scream like frogs in a vivisection class."

"If you think *that* would be expensive, what do you think a class action lawsuit will cost if the Verite owners decided that their cars have suddenly taken to steering themselves off the road? What you've got here, Charlie, is a Hobson's choice. If we do nothing, we risk a lawsuit, which we can't afford and which could potentially bankrupt the company. If we issue a recall, we strap ourselves financially and probably piss off the French."

"And the recall won't do much for our image," Popper added. "Plus, the dealers will have apoplexy. The last thing those bastards need is to take any more heat from their customers."

Charlie slid off his desk and began to pace in front of his windows. "Well, Axel, since this seems to be your show, what choice would you have us make?"

"There's only one to make."

"Which is ...?" he asked, turning back to Axel.

""Go to the board. Give 'em the facts and do the ethical thing–issue a recall. We've got to do what's right by our customers or we have no goddamn business selling cars."

"And if I should decide *not* to issue the recall? Are you going to be a team player and go along? I mean, we are a team here, aren't we?"

Axel stared at Charlie for several seconds. "True. We are a team. Like most teams, there are rules in our game. And if you don't follow those rules, somebody steps in and takes the ball away from you."

"So, what are you saying? Are we to expect you to make a surprise appearance on *60 Minutes* this Sunday?"

"No. One guy doesn't make the decision for the team, unless he's the captain, and I think that's you, Charlie. I'm not going to blow the whistle. I'm not going to tell the world that you thought you'd save a few bucks and fuck-up the suspension. No one needs to know that. But" he paused for emphasis, "we either do something about this, and by do something, I mean issue a recall and beef up the suspension, or I'm going to the board with my resignation. I'm going to tell them about those test reports with your initials all over 'em. I have a feeling if you leave me no other option than to go to the board, Perkins Byrd will cut your balls off, issue the recall, and tell you and that punch board secretary of yours to take a hike." Axel made no effort to suppress his anger. "You are fucking with people's lives, Charlie. You are fucking with the future of this company. And I am not going to sit by while you roll the dice in hopes that no customer of ours is ever going to find themselves in a situation where that suspension gets pushed beyond its limits."

It was all Charlie could do to restrain himself. He knew he had to maintain control and get Axel out of the room so he could decide how best to deal with the situation.

After a long moment, he said coolly, "Ok, Axel, you have me by the short hairs. I'm going to bring in Walt Nut from engineering and our suspension guy, whatshisname? Overstreet.

Hopefully, they can figure a way to handle the fix without breaking our backs."

"Let's hope so," Axel said.

"Does that make you feel better?"

"I'll feel better when you issue the recall."

"Oh, one more thing. You never told us where you found that report?" Charlie did his best to sound only mildly curious.

"In a box."

"A box?"

"Yeah, Pandora's box." Axel stood up. "I look forward to the recall announcement, which I will expect this week. We've got a dealer meeting in six weeks. We better get word to them well in advance of the meeting. Otherwise, you better bring out the riot police." With that he turned and left.

As the door closed behind Axel, Charlie exploded, "Shit! I'll kill that fucker. That's all we need, a bunch of pissed off dealers at the announcement show. He's got to be stopped."

"Well, at least you've got the report," Popper said.

"I've got the copy he brought in. How the hell do I know I'm not going to find more copies on Amazon.com next week on the best seller shelf?" He turned to Spar, "Harry, you might want to find a reason to visit Axel's office tonight."

Harry understood the assignment.

Charlie shook off the assignment, "No, forget it. That fucker is probably too smart to leave a copy there. Shit! Double shit!" He picked up his phone, "Emma Rae, get me Walt Nut and Bill Overstreet." Then a thought occurred to him.

"Wait. Cancel that." He hung up and pulled out the company directory and looked for the extension number of Harvey Nickels, the company's Chief Legal Counsel. Before he dialed, he looked up at Harry and Popper. "You guys are leaving, now. And don't forget to close the door."

When the door clicked shut, Charlie dialed the extension. "Harvey? Charlie here. I have a question for you. When officers sign our employee confidentiality and nondisclosure agreements, does that cover *any and all* information we consider to be confidential?"

"Absolutely," Harvey said.

"Good. So, if a VP or above, even an ex-VP, should violate that agreement, we could take legal action against him, right? We could make his fucking life pretty goddamn miserable, right? And we could probably wipe him out financially, right?"

"We could take legal action. We could make him very miserable. We could leave him very broke," Harvey echoed.

"Ok, now consider this. Let's say we have an ex-employee who violates that agreement, are we in a position to deny him his pension and his deferred compensation?"

"Probably, but I'd have to know the specifics."

"We need to talk. Like right now."

33
Okay

Waddington had returned from a sales training session in Chicago and gone straight to bed. For a while, he lay looking up at the ceiling, thinking about the state of his life. His immediate conclusion? It was a mess. A train wreck. *I'm a mediocre man in a mediocre job. My marriage is in the toilet.* But then, he reasoned, it had been on a very shaky ground for a long time. *My mother-in-law has bought the affections of my children ... well, maybe not Hildy. Not yet. And what form of insanity makes me think that Olivia and I have a future? A few stolen hours together here and there. Maybe we'll even make it to bed. That I'd like. I'd like that very much. But then what? When Charlie finds out, and eventually he will, things are bound to get messy and, God forbid, ugly.* Waddington read the signs, and they all said the same thing: *Disaster Ahead. Initiate Avoidance Procedures.* Impossible. There was nothing he could do to head off the inevitable, whatever the "inevitable" turned out to be. He was riding the riptide unable, maybe even unwilling, to swim against it.

He dozed off and began to dream. He was in a small airplane, and people with parachutes on their backs were laughing as they jumped out the open door. Suddenly, a man was beckoning him toward the door. Next thing he knew, he was outside the plane; his arms were wings, and he was flying. The sensation of the free fall was exhilarating. Like being with Olivia, it was a totally heady experience. As the ground rushed up at him, he became aware that he was not wearing a parachute. He wondered if there was any chance that he might bounce.

He never found out. The phone woke him. It was 10:45. He'd been asleep for only a few minutes.

"Hello."

"Pres," Muffy said, "were you asleep? A little early for you to be in bed, isn't it? I guess I woke you."

She sounded irritated to find him asleep. "You did," he said turning on the light.

"I'm calling because we have decided …"

"Who is 'we'?" He interrupted.

She corrected herself, "That *I've* decided to start divorce proceedings. Unless," she drew out the word, "unless you agree to come to Greenwich, I can see no way for our marriage to survive."

"Okay," he answered simply.

There was a long pause on Muffy's end of the line. "What do you mean by 'Okay'?"

"Just, Okay."

"Are you saying, 'Okay,' you'll come to Greenwich or 'Okay,' I should call a lawyer?"

"Okay, you should call a lawyer."

"Okay? Okaaaay?" She was shouting, "Is that all you've got to say?"

"What more do you want me to say?"

"After all these years, I should think you'd have more to say than 'Okay, call a lawyer.'"

"Muffy, I think 'Okay' sums up about all I have to say. I'm not going to Greenwich, so do what you have to do."

Muffy began to sputter. "I certainly will. And for starters, you sonofabitch, I am hereby informing you that my house, *my* house, goes on the market immediately. And I will thank you to get your ass and your stuff out of there by next Monday morning."

"By my stuff you mean …?"

"Just your clothes and personal things and that Wurlitzer in the basement. But don't you *dare* try to take any of the furniture, the lamps, the beds, or the TVs. All that was paid for with my mother's money, which makes it mine."

"I'm sure the Motel 6 will have all the furniture I need, including a TV. However, I'm not sure if they'll have room for the piano."

"Motel 6?" she said haughtily. "That fits. You are soooo Motel 6." The derision in her voice was like a gasoline spill. Any spark would ignite it.

Waddington took a deep breath, determined to say nothing that would provide that spark, "For the girls' sakes, I hope we can do this amicably."

"Don't count on it!" she shot back.

"Okay," he said and hung up.

34
The French Maid Does Housework
and Charlie Fair

He had spent a miserable night. The thought of Axel's threat and the potential damage it could do to him had made for a fitful sleep. He had to neutralize Axel, permanently, and Harvey Nickels had given him the way.

Charlie rolled out of bed in a brown mood that turned dark brown when he looked out the window. It was, Charlie thought, almost as bad as the Perfect Storm. The wind was whipping Detroit like an angry schoolmaster, and the rain appeared to be falling sideways. He always regarded it as a personal affront from God when, during the summer, his weekends were ruined by rain. Today was one of those days that God was on his "no cookie" list.

As he stood in the kitchen with a glass of juice, looking like a model out of a golf magazine, he shook his head as the clock chimed nine and his tee time at the club got scratched. Damn rain. Now what the hell was he supposed to do with the rest of his Saturday? Olivia had gone to Chicago to visit her sister, Pooh, and to see Pooh's daughter's new baby. She had told him she planned to stay through July 4th and wouldn't be back until July 6th.

Flaubert, in full morning dress, was in the pantry polishing the tea service. For a moment, he thought about having Flaubert help him with his

French. With the Frogs taking over half the company, it would be in his best interest to bone up on his French. His pronunciation was terrible, his grammar atrocious, and his vocabulary limited to such sophomoric phrases as *Voulez vous couché avec moi?* No, he didn't feel like putting up with Flaubert today. Anyway, he thought, the way to learn French is not in the pantry with the butler, but by lying in bed with a compliant French woman. Umm. Monique was off this weekend. Good, that left Jeanette, and she would probably be in her room. Yes, why not a little French lesson and French everything else from his little Marseille cupcake. Jeannette was his favorite, not just because she was more attractive than Monique and not just because her bed was always available to him, but because she also gave incredible massages.

He found her in the large, oversized tub he had installed in the maids' quarters, beneath a mountain of bubbles. A tub for two he called it. Charlie sat down on the toilet seat. Her eyes were closed, but by the way her nose and mouth were twitching, it was obvious to Charlie that first, she knew he'd come in, and second, she was, for some potentially perverse reason, making a concerted effort to ignore him. "Good grief, Jeanette, did you pour in the whole bottle of bubble bath?"

"Oui," she said without opening her eyes to him.

Ummm, Charlie thought, *we are in a pouty mood today. Maybe it's the weather.* No, more likely the fact that he'd not been alone with her for well over two weeks. She got testy when he neglected her. Maybe it was a good thing the game had been rained out. This was definitely an account that needed servicing.

"So," she said, making no effort to hide her pique, "today it rains, so today we come to visit Jeannette, no? If the sun comes out, Monsieur Fair plays not with Jeanette, but with the golf ball."

"Are you upset with me, Jeannette?" Charlie asked casually. Ah, neglect. What an oppressive affect it had on women, he mused.

"No, of course not. Why should I be?" Jeannette still had most of her residual French accent. It had been somewhat corrupted when, as a teenager, she was brought to Toledo. To most of her high school classmates, French was a type of potato.

Charlie lifted a foot and crossed his leg over the opposite knee as he unlaced his shoe and took off his sock. "Well, you don't seem to be your cheery French self today."

"It's the weather. I don't like it when it rains like this. But then, only when it rains or it's too cold, that's the only time my master has time to come visit. Or, those times, like today, when his wife is out of town."

Charlie considered it discreet and personally prudent that he never visited Jeanette when Olivia was in the house. How would Olivia, who served him well as a corporate wife and astute hostess, ever come to understand that his relationship with Jeanette was not emotional. She was more like one of his classic cars. She was to be well taken care of, enjoyed on occasion, and never loaned out to friends.

Charlie put his bare foot down on the floor and lifted the other onto the opposite knee. "I apologize, Jeanette. I know it's been a while since we've had any time alone, but as you know, we are in the process of making a deal with the French. The new model line is about to be announced, and I have to prepare for the dealer meeting in six weeks. With all that on my mind, along with so many other problems, it's hard to find time to enjoy the company of the one woman in the world who truly knows how to orchestrate the subtle sensual harmonies of physical love." Whoa! What a gem that line was. If he had a pen, he'd have written it down. It must have gotten to her because she was smiling. She rose up slightly from the tub, her breasts peeking through the bubbles like the eyes of a submerged crocodile. Then, almost as quickly, she sank back into the tub, puckered her mouth and adopted her "I'm pouting' look."

"Well, I'm sorry," she said peevishly. "I have no time for you today. I must polish the silver."

"Flaubert is taking care of that. And I've just given you the day off. With full pay, of course." He decided to test her. "But if you'd like me to leave ..."

"What and go visit the little tramp, Monique?"

"She's gone for the day," he answered.

"And does that make Monsieur, unhappy?"

Charlie began to unbutton his shirt. "Not at all. I am very happy to be where I am right now. In fact, I should like to stay and play all day."

"Or until the sun comes out, and you can go play golf," she said in mildly accusatory tones.

He knew she was testing him. The fact that she was dead-on correct was another matter. "Let the sun shine when and if it will. I'm not going anywhere until you tell me to leave." That really worked. Her face had morphed into that coquettish, come-hither look that she always had just before they made love.

Charlie stood up and released the buckle on his pants and slipped out of his shorts.

"May I share you bubbles?" he asked with mock formality as he stepped into the tub.

"I think I would like that."

He eased himself next to her, submerging all but his head beneath the mounds of white froth.

"*Bienvenu, mon amour.*" She kissed him.

"Ah, nothing like a warm bath with a beautiful woman on a rainy day."

For a moment, neither said a word, then Jeanette sat up and turned to Charlie, who had almost drifted off. "Charlie?"

"Ummm?" he responded.

"Do you love me?"

He wasn't going to let himself fall into that trap, so he jumped over it. "I adore you." For a moment, she said nothing. Good, she wasn't going to press him for a more detailed commitment.

"You say you adore me, but sometimes weeks go by and you do not come to visit me. Maybe I should take a lover for the times you're not here, no?"

"What?" Charlie looked at her quizzically. "No."

She sat up and looked down at him. There was a knowing, superior look on her face. "Well, if Madame Fair can take a lover for when you're not here, why can't I?"

Charlie frowned, "What are you talking about?" *What kind of game was this?* he wondered.

"I'm talking about Mrs. Fair's lover."

Charlie was growing slightly annoyed. She was obviously playing some kind of game to punish him for his lack of attention and to pry out some profession of greater love. "Mrs. Fair does not have a lover. Of that, I am very sure. Now, why don't you pop out of here and get the massage table set up."

"Just like an American. Why is it American husbands are always the last to know?"

"Jeanette, please, no games. You know I don't like to play these kind of silly games."

"I'm not playing games. But your wife may be. I mean, she is a woman. A very attractive woman. Her husband is always very, very busy. Maybe she needs love, and since she's not finding it in her bed, she's looking elsewhere."

Now he was perturbed. He was not in the mood to try figure out the innuendoes and imputations of his French truffle. But Jeanette was clearly suggesting something. What? He decided he needed to know. "Ok, what are you trying to tell me?"

She was coquettish, "Well, it could be nothing. But one day last week, there was a man here. I'm not sure which day. He played the piano for her. They had a long lunch, and then, when he left, well, I have not seen Mrs. Fair kiss *you* like that."

Incredulous, he asked, "You saw my wife kissing someone? Where were you?"

"I was hiding in the Ficus trees. That was the first time. The second time, I opened the door, and there they were, kissing."

"You saw my wife kissing some guy ... twice?"

"Oui."

"Well, that doesn't mean anything. She kisses people hello and goodbye all the time."

"But, not like this." She leaned toward Charlie, opened her mouth and parted his teeth with her tongue. For the moment, Charlie's mind was on Jeannette, who was pressing her bubble-bath-slippery body into his. When they finally parted, Charlie was ready to skip the massage and hop into bed.

"I don't think my wife was kissing anyone quite like that. She wouldn't know how." While he felt sure that Jeanette was simply involved in a feeble attempt to get a rise from him, Charlie decided to probe further. "Who was this man that you saw?"

"I dun know. I was not introduced. Maybe he was the postman. Or maybe he was someone to fix ze toilet."

"How was he dressed?"

"He was wearing a blue suit."

"If there were no U.S. Post Office patches on his suit, that eliminates the postman. We know the UPS man wears brown, which means it must have been the man who came to fix the toilet." Charlie laughed at how he had deduced the lover's identity.

"You do not think it possible Mrs. Fair has taken a lover?"

"Possible, yes. But very, very unlikely. She's much too loyal to me to take a lover. Maybe it was Father Whatshisface from her church. You're sure he wasn't wearing a black suit and white collar?" He laughed. The idea was so ludicrous, and Jeanette's fabrication so transparent, that it had become a joke to Charlie.

"Next time I see your wife with this man, I will ask him who he is?"

Charlie was having fun now. "Good idea. Just walk up to him and say something like, 'Excuse me, what is your name, and are you fucking Mrs. Fair?'" He laughed so hard his head began to rattle on the edge of the tub, and he sat up.

Jeanette stepped out of the tub and wrapped herself in a towel. "Okay," she said with an assurance that unsettled Charlie slightly, "You make the jokes, while this man he makes it with your wife. As for me? I am waiting for you on my bed."

Charlie shook his head and smiled. He had no idea what had brought on these wild accusations, other than some manifest expression of her jealousy. It was all so preposterous. Clearly, if Jeanette was out to punish him for his lack of attention, she could have done better than make up a story about Olivia and a lover. But then, it was so far-fetched, he found himself wondering if, possibly, there could be something to it. Was it possible that Jeannette had actually seen Olivia with another man? But who? Was it somebody from the petition committee or maybe a new piano teacher? And the kiss–Olivia wasn't into passionate kissing, at least not in the last dozen or so years. Jeanette must have been mistaken about the kissing part. Maybe the man she saw was Preston Waddington. Charlie knew that he had talked to her on the phone. But had he ever come over to the house? If he had, she never mentioned it. But no. There was no way Preston Waddington could be this mysterious man. He was most defiantly not Olivia's type. Charlie felt sure that, if his wife was going to have an affair, unimaginable to him as that was, it would be with someone like himself. He tried to set the issue aside, but it kept imposing itself on his thoughts. What if Jeanette was right? What if Olivia did have a lover? It was hard to believe she could hide that from him. He was not an idiot. He would have noticed a change in her attitude, her demeanor. No, he concluded, Jeannette was either exaggerating or making it all up.

Charlie got out of the tub, released the drain handle, and toweled off. He could smell Jeanette's perfume all the way from the bedroom. If there was anything that could clear his mind of extraneous thoughts, even those having to do with the possibility of his wife having an affair, it was the smell of that French perfume. He walked into the bedroom and found her propped up on the pillow, wearing the French maid costume he liked so much. Last time she'd worn something that looked to be straight out of Marquis de Sade, he'd told her to get rid of it. Even the mere hint of anything to do with S&M horrified him. This was more like it. It left just enough to the imagination to provide ample titillation. He found Jeanette fantastic and incredibly versatile. She provided him with all the benefits of an experienced, dissolute, morally profligate libertine who, when not entertaining him in her bed, did housework. What a package.

As he crawled in next to her and began their game of French Maid and Her Master, his thoughts drifted to the golf course. Too bad about the weather. He was hitting the ball so well this summer. Any day now he felt sure he would shoot his first par round. Maybe tomorrow. All things considered, however, with the gale force winds and torrential downpour, he had to concede that lolling away a few hours or more in Jeanette's bed was, after all, a pleasant way to spend a rainy day.

35
In Love or In Need?

She had been with her sister in Chicago for almost a full day before she blurted it out, "I'm having an affair, and I plan to divorce Charlie. Well, actually, I'm *about* to have an affair. I mean, I'm *having* an affair, but it's really not a physical affair yet."

Pooh was Olivia's oldest sister by twelve years. She had assumed the role of surrogate mother after Flossy Byrd died when Olivia was but six. It was she that all the younger sisters came to, even now, when they needed motherly advice and counsel. She was, frankly, shocked by Olivia's confession. To her, the affair and the decision to divorce her husband seemed out of character for Olivia. Not that Pooh had anything against affairs or divorces. Her marriage to the banker from Goshen had produced a daughter but lasted only two years. She jettisoned the banker and moved to Chicago, where she married a man of more substantial means. He was considerate enough to die and leave her his entire fortune before he discovered she was having a scandalous affair with an ex-football player. Her current husband had been snatched from the arms of a woman who ran a local public relations firm. To the victor go the spoils.

"I take it this affair, or this *about to be* affair, is a recent development?"

"Yes. Very recent."

"He's single?"

"No, he's married."

"A minor impediment."

"But he's leaving his wife."

"Because of you?"

"No, at least I don't think so. There hasn't been much love in their marriage for years."

"Did he tell you that or do you know it for a fact?"

"Both. I know his wife."

"What's his name?"

"Preston Olivier Waddington."

"Well now, with a name like that, he sounds like he might be English. Is he titled?"

"No, he's not English. He's not titled. He's American."

"But the name does sound like *old* money."

"Names can be deceiving."

"Where's he from?"

"He's originally from Teaneck, New Jersey."

She was incredulous. "People in Teaneck, New Jersey, name their children Preston Olivier?"

"His mother was French."

"Where did you meet him?"

"He was in my bathroom," she said. The words were no sooner out of her mouth than she realized her sister was going to jump all over them.

"He was in your bathroom?" she asked to be sure she'd heard Olivia correctly.

"Yes," she said reluctantly.

"He's a plumber?"

"No. He was a guest at a cocktail party I was

giving."

"Let me guess, he was not there to take a shower."

"No, he was not taking a shower."

"I presume then, he was doing what people usually do in a bathroom. But what were you doing in there with him?"

"I wasn't exactly *in* the bathroom. I just opened the door and sort of surprised him." She had no intention of admitting she was inebriated and that she and Waddington sat on her bed and talked. "Let's just say that after he came out of the bathroom, we had this long talk. It was wonderful."

"Wonderful." Pooh repeated.

"I needed somebody at that moment, somebody to talk to. Someone who would listen, and he did exactly that. He was … well, wonderful. That's the only way to put it."

"Okay, I'll accept 'wonderful.' Next question: This affair you're having, or about to have, is it just a fling or do you have something more permanent in mind?"

"I would like it to last."

"Does he have a job? Gainful employment?"

"Of course,"

"What does he do?"

Olivia hesitated. She was already anticipating Pooh's response. "He works for Charlie."

"He works for Charlie?" she was incredulous. Then she started to laugh. "Well, I guess there's some advantage in that. At least you won't have to introduce them to each other." Pooh shook her head in disbelief. "Good heavens, Olivia, do you know how bizarre all this sounds? You meet a man in your bathroom, who works for your husband, and have an affair that isn't physical. I don't think you want to let that story get around, if you know what I mean."

"The only thing that matters is that he is the most wonderful, considerate, decent man I have ever known. More important, he loves me."

"Or does he love your money?"

"That's unkind."

"No, that's realistic."

"Well, he loves me."

"What does this Don Juan of the bathroom look like?"

"Well, he's medium height, medium build, medium brown hair."

"He definitely sounds … medium."

"Let me describe him this way: he's not like Charlie. Women are not going to fall all over him when he walks into a room. But it's not his looks that matter; it's what I feel when I am with him. There is something … I'm not sure I can describe it … a kind of magnetism that just makes me want to be with him."

"But handsome, he's not. Is that what you're saying?"

"What I'm saying is that he is truly beautiful on the inside."

"My God, Olivia, you sound like you're reading lines from some trashy true-romance novel. Take it from an expert, the only thing inside most men are libidos. Huge, bloated libidos, and they are seldom beautiful."

"Preston's not like that. He's different. Sure, he wants me, and I fully expect that we will make love and soon. But there's more to a relationship than bed. I like being with this man. He listens to me. He makes me feel good about myself. And most importantly, he respects me. And respect is something I've had very little of over the last twenty years."

Pooh pondered all of what her sister had told her, then offered her support, followed by some questions. "Let me say first, that I fully approve of you divorcing Charlie. He's a philandering shit. He's used you, he's used Daddy, and you both deserve a lot better. But I'm concerned about this man, Preston. Maybe he's everything you say he is. But you must be aware, Olivia, that sometimes when a woman hasn't had love in her life for a long time, she tends to blindly grab for the first guy who pays attention to her. Which raises a question, a question only you can answer."

"Which is?"

"Are you in love or are you just in need?"

Olivia thought about it for a moment and then said quietly, "Maybe both."

36
Axel Gets the Ax

It was Sunday night and Waddington was starting to pack for his departure from the house that had been home for almost fifteen years. No longer would he have to try and anticipate Muffy's mood swings. Just after nine, the phone rang. Muffy, he assumed, making sure he'd be out of the house by morning.

It was Axel with news. And it wasn't good.

"So, he calls me into the office tonight. A Sunday night, no less. I'm sure he didn't want any witnesses. Our CEO and moral leader invites me to sit down and make myself comfortable, then asks if I would be so kind to lay my head on the chopping block while he sharpens his ax. Whack. Off it rolls. I'm gonezo."

"Why? What the hell did he do that for? Did you have any idea this was coming?"

"Well, no, but I guess I should have. I'm on my way home from church, and I get a call on my cell from Emma Rae Dickbreath, who tells me that Mr. Fair would like me to stop by the office at about five for a *"word."* I guess if 'whack' is a word, that was it."

"I don't get it. Did he tell you why?"

"He didn't have to tell me. I knew."

"So why?"

Waddington heard Axel sigh, "I confronted Charlie with some information that, if it got out, could kill the deal with the French, and more importantly to him, hang his ass out to dry."

"It's got something to do with the Verite 300, right?"

"It's got everything to do with the Verite and what you and I both saw happen out at the track. Do you remember the Ford Pinto problem years ago?"

"Of course, the exploding gas tank."

"That was the symptom; the problem was that they *knew* about it, but kept it covered up until the cars started exploding. Well, it turns out that we have a problem with our suspension. Worse, we *know* about it. Or more specifically, Charlie knows about it. I found a file full of reports that spells out exactly what happened. Charlie opted for a cheaper suspension system to save costs. The safety engineering tests showed the car couldn't handle high-speed corners without the rear end breaking loose. The new suspension created a major oversteer problem. He knew it, but insisted we go with the cheaper system. I confronted him and demanded he issue a recall. I threatened to resign and go the board and expose him if he didn't. He agreed to the recall. But surprise, surprise! He reneged and gave me the ax instead."

"Do you have proof that he knew about the results of the tests?"

"Yeah! Absolutely. The test reports have his name and initials all over 'em. I even have a memo from him to engineering which says in so many words, 'The hell with the tests. Read the design and cost objectives and do what I tell you to do.'"

"If it's on paper, then you've got him between a rock and a hard place. All you have to do is go to the board and expose the bastard."

Axel sounded almost apologetic, "I could and I would, but … he sort of has my balls in a vice."

"How?"

Axel didn't answer. Instead he said, "We need to talk. You and me. But not on the phone. Can you meet me for breakfast tomorrow?"

"Sure, where?"

"Do you know Gabe's Kitchen on Telegraph at Seven Mile?"

"Sure, I pass it every day on my way to the office," or at least I used to, he said to himself. "I've never eaten there."

"It's a humbling experience. It will be good for you."

"I'll take your word for it."

"See you at 7:30. Novena mass at eight. Bring your rosary."

Gabe's Kitchen was a diner frequented only by the kind of people who bought the company's cars, "X" generation, blue-collar people, men who wore baseball caps backwards (when they ate), and women in desperate need of Richard Simmons, none of whom would have had a clue to, or even cared about, the identity of the two individuals sitting in the booth next to the front window.

In fact, with Waddington in a suit and Axel in a sweatshirt and jeans, they gave the impression that the master of the estate was interviewing the owner of a lawn service. Axel looked like those men in the business of hauling young men, with limited English vocabularies, in open trucks laden with lawn mowers and rakes from house to house in Bloomfield Hills or Grosse Pointe to free their owners from this menial task. His scruffy beard showed that he had not bothered shaving. The heavy folds under his eyes suggested he'd had little sleep.

The waitress approached, holding up the coffee pot as a tacit question. Axel nodded toward his cup, and she filled it, then did the same for Waddington. Axel poured in some sugar and began to stir.

"What can I get for you boys?" she asked.

"Just coffee for me," Axel said.

"I'll have eggs over easy, bacon, and whole wheat toast." Waddington handed the menu to the waitress.

"Comin' up."

"You know, Pres, for all the problems we've had and for all the crap I've personally had to take, I love this company. It's been my life. Never really had any other job that I liked as much. I hope you understand that, despite whatever bitterness I feel toward Charlie, I want the company to survive. I want you guys to pull this out, and then I want to see you make it grow like I know it can."

A company man to the last, Waddington thought. While another man might have wished the company every ill, Axel seemed to have focused all his anger on Charlie.

"I don't want history to nail our scalp up next to the likes of Packard, American Motors, Yugo, Sterling, and all the other car companies that ended up taking the pipe." He pounded the table with his fist, "Goddamn it, we're better than any of them. I really believe that." His eyes wandered out the window and stared vacantly into a steady stream of cars on Telegraph Road.

"Axel, I think you should put up a fight. Go after Charlie. Take it up with the board. Hell, they ignore something like this at the risk of getting sued."

"Going to the board could be dangerous."

"To who? To Charlie? To you? I don't understand."

"Think about that for a moment. If I hang Charlie out to dry over his cover-up and we get into a public fight, you might just as well put a padlock on the front door. The French would fly home, and you'd have the banks and our suppliers breaking down the walls to try and get their money. Everyone from the Wall Street Journal to the Detroit Free Press has got our obituary set-in type and ready to run. All they'd need is an all-out brawl between Charlie and me; it would be 'Call the embalmer, they're dead.' As much as I'd like to get even with that bastard, and goddamn it, one day I will, I've got to think about the thousands of people in this company that are looking for paychecks every week."

"I understand that, but ..." he stopped. There was something wrong here. This was not like Axel. The man loved a fight. Waddington restated his case, "Axel, there's no reason this has to go outside the company. It never has to leave the boardroom and you can win easily. Particularly when you're

300

holding all the trump cards. If you've got proof that Charlie tried to hide the test results, Perkins will listen with all ears. I am sure of it."

Axel averted his eyes from Waddington and stared at his coffee cup for a moment. "Unfortunately, as I told you, Charlie's got me where it hurts, and he's not likely to let go."

"On the phone, you said he had your nuts in a vise." Waddington could see a pained expression grip Axel's face. He knew that he did not need to pry. Whatever it was that Charlie had on him was about to come out.

"I have always appreciated Charlie, the president, because he's led the fight to build cars that somebody might actually like to buy. But I never liked Charlie, the man, very much. We are just too different. Nevertheless, when it came to our relationship at work, we were on the same team. Or so I thought. About four years ago, as you know, Mary was in a very bad way. Living in a wheelchair for six years after her fall had gotten to her psychologically. Basically, she'd gotten tired of being an invalid. Moving around the house had become an incredible chore. She would lapse into long bouts of depression. Sometimes, when I'd come home from work, I'd find her in exactly the same spot as I'd left her in the morning. I had to do something.

"I hired an architect who specializes in designing handicapped facilities, and he created a plan for totally redesigning our house. You've seen it; ramps, an elevator, and transfer devices to help her get in and out of the tub. All kinds of state-of-the-art stuff when it comes to making life for a wheelchair person a whole lot easier. It was fantastic. The only problem was that the cost was nearly a quarter of a million, and I was already mortgaged to the hilt. So, and I'm not proud of this, I found a way to … well, let's say I siphoned about $250,000 from my operating budget to pay the architect and contractor. Took almost a year and I thought it would never be missed out of a multimillion-dollar budget. But I didn't count on Harry Spar.

"Charlie called me into his office and confronted me with the proof of what I'd been doing. He asked me why. And I told him the truth. He asked me if that was to be the end of it. I told him it was. Then he said, 'Okay, you're too good a man to lose. If you will assure me this is the end of it, then it never happened. I'll take care of it.' And with that, he tore up what I presumed were whatever documents he had that proved I'd taken the money. Except he didn't. I don't know what he tore up, but it wasn't what he said it was. Well, Sunday, he produced the invoice and requisitions that had my signature okaying payments to the architect and contractor. Charlie's message was simple, 'You rat me out, and I'll return the favor.' About that time, Harvey Nichols appeared out of the woodwork. That bastard is really in Charlie's pocket. Anyway, Nichols said that if they decided to prosecute, the company could garnish my pension, my profit sharing, and seek criminal charges. They could bust my balls financially.

"If it were just me, I'd say screw it. I'd love to

take that bastard down, even if it meant my going with him. But there's Mary. If they took away my pension and benefits and I were to die, where would that leave her? My daughter and son-in-law are in no position to take care of her. Bottom line, I just can't take a chance that I'd come out whole if I took the fight to Charlie. They've got me boxed in, tied up, and ready to screw me up the ass if I so much as fart in Charlie's direction."

It was a different Axel sitting across from him now. Different from the man who had been waiting for him a half-hour before. The macho, compelling bravado that had both impressed and amazed Waddington over the years was gone. Waddington understood what had motivated Axel to do what he did. He remembered listening to the pain in Axel's voice as he talked about the woman he loved slipping away into deep depression. Maybe he would have done the same thing in Axel's position. Hard to say he wouldn't have, particularly if he'd been as devoted to Muffy as Axel was to Mary. It was not for him to judge. Instead, he felt sorry for the man and a little sorry for himself as well. The company would be very different without him, and the sales department would be a lot less effective. Of that he was very sure. Axel stared into his coffee cup, as though waiting for Waddington to pass judgment.

Waddington offered an observation, instead. "Nothing like a little extortion to guarantee Charlie a free pass."

The waitress appeared at their table with Waddington's order and set it down, then beat a retreat. Waddington looked at the plate. "Scrambled. Didn't I ask for eggs over easy?"

Axel nodded. "You ask for one thing. You get another. That's what life is all about, isn't it? You want to send it back?"

"No, this will be fine."

Axel became reflective, "What gnaws at me, I mean, what *really* chews at my gut is that the sonofabitch will never issue the recall. No one will ever find out what's he done. We'll have customers out on the road running around in so-called sport cars, our bogus *Driving Machines,* like a bunch of accidents waiting to happen. Eventually, the suspension problem is going to come back and bite us in the ass. The sad part is that it doesn't have to. It can be fixed. Now. Expensive? Sure. But not compared to what a class action lawsuit could cost us." Axel reached under the table, picked up a briefcase, and placed it in front of him on the table. "Are you familiar with Pandora's box?"

"Sure, it contained all the ills of the world."

"Well, this isn't Pandora's box; it's pandora's briefcase."

"Recognized it right away," Waddington said, attempting to inject a little lightness into the conversation.

"In here are the Verite 300 test results that Charlie tried to bury. I told our moral leader that I had given him the only copies. Shame on me; I lied to the sonofabitch. Anyway, it's all here. There are dozens of documents that have Charlie's initials and signatures, proving that he'd read the tests results and that he was the guy who directed engineering to ignore them."

"So, what do you plan to do?"

Alex leaned forward, pressing his chest against the table, and slowly pushed the briefcase over to Waddington. "Pres, you're a smart man and an ethical man. You're one of the few guys I completely trust in the company. I know this is going to seem like a cop-out on my part, but I'm hoping, *really* hoping, that you'll take this information and find some way to force a recall. It would give me a great deal of satisfaction to have you walk out of here with this briefcase, knowing that you'll try. However, if you decide to slide it back across the table and dump it in my lap, I wouldn't think any less of you, and I'll never mention it again. This conversation will never have taken place."

Waddington was clearly taken aback and temporarily at a loss for words. Axel's request didn't seem to have any upside for him. The company? Yes. But for him? No. Waddington had never envisioned playing the role of a corporate savior and sacrificing himself for the cause. But that, essentially, was what Axel was asking him to do. Certainly, somebody had to do something. Letting Charlie stick their corporate heads in the sand made no sense. Axel was right; eventually the suspension problem would lead to accidents and maybe deaths and then lawsuits. If that happened, he wouldn't have to worry about hanging onto his ledge. It wouldn't be there to hang on to. What options did he have? None.

He turned his thoughts to potential strategies.

He decided to use Axel as a sounding board. "The question, of course, is how do I use this as leverage without letting it get outside the company. No way I could play Daniel Ellsberg and leak it to the press. That would bring the roof in on us. If I were to use it as a way to nail Charlie in front of the board, then there's a good chance the French would find out, and that might be all she wrote. Not a lot of options, are there?"

Axel shook his head and took another sip of coffee, "To be honest, I don't have any suggestions. But there has got to be some way to make Charlie feel like he's in real danger of being exposed, criminally exposed even, without going public. Somehow, he's got to be made to see that issuing a recall is his only option. He's got to believe that it's the only way for him to save his ass from the board, from the press, and maybe even from the Feds. I admit this isn't going to be easy. But I honestly believe that the future of this company depends on getting this recall out before the lawsuits start pilin' up. The time to deal with it is now. Hell, if we're smart, we could probably position the recall in such a way to make us look like responsible corporate citizens. GM and Ford and Chrysler issue recalls all the time and hardly anyone seems to notice. It's on the news one day and history the next. I don't think it will hurt our deal with the French. In France, they don't buy cars, they buy visiting rights because their cars are in the repair shop so often. It's having Charlie's cover-up discovered that could kill us."

Waddington turned his head and stared out

the window. His mind was racing over several possible scenarios. Suddenly he had an idea. "There's always extortion."

"Extortion!" Axel repeated taken aback.

"You could even call it blackmail. Although, I think maybe *leverage* is a more businesslike word. And the *leverage* I'm talking about is in this briefcase. What if I were to publish these reports in the monthly *Company Eyes Only* report."

Axel was about to object to the idea, but Waddington cut him off, "And, what if I were to limit the initial distribution of that report to just one person?"

"Charlie."

"Right. The rest of the copies, all 200 of them, I'll keep locked up. Then I'll give Charlie two options: He can issue the recall and all the reports disappear. Or he can refuse and within twenty-four hours, two-hundred executives in the company, along with the entire board of directors, will have copies in their hands."

"I like it," Axel said grinning. "I really like it. Considering the damage that report could do to Charlie's reputation, he's got to issue the recall."

"One thing for sure, it doesn't give him a lot of options."

"I only have one question for you: Are you sure you want to do this?"

"Honestly?"

"Honestly."

"I can think of a long list of other things I'd rather do. But I can't find a good reason to tell you that I won't do it." Waddington looked at the briefcase for a moment. He thought about Olivia and how an office confrontation with Charlie might look to her. The potential usurper calling the king out to do battle. That last thing he wanted was for Charlie to learn that he was having an affair with his wife. Charlie would use it to claim that Waddington's real motivation was to dethrone him and take his place in the castle. This could become very messy, even a disaster, on several different levels. He needed to talk with Olivia. He certainly didn't want her to end up in the middle of all this. And she wouldn't, so long as Charlie never found out about the two of them.

I am out of my mind, Waddington thought, as he closed his fingers around the thick leather handle of the Pandora briefcase. Slowly he pulled it off the table and set it on the seat beside him. He glanced over at Axel. "If I had any sense, I'd probably walk out of here and drop this thing in River Rouge."

"Haven't you heard, it's against the law to throw toxic materials in the river? And believe me, what's in that briefcase qualifies as toxic. I know. It's already made me sick. "

"Remind me to think twice next time you ask to meet me for breakfast."

"What are you bitchin' about? I'm buying."

Waddington looked at the check, "$7.28. Can you afford it?"

"I've still got an expense account. We'll let Charlie pay for it."

37
Some Low Profile

"Preston?"

The sound of her voice quickened his pulse. "Hello," he said, careful not to say her name in the event the cubicle walls had ears.

"Will I see you tomorrow?"

"Yes. We need to talk. Or maybe, more correctly, I need to talk."

There was a long pause on her end of the phone. Then, "If, this is what I think it is, I'd rather us just a say good-bye now."

God! What was she thinking it was?

"I mean," she said, "if you and Muffy … I mean if you feel … Well, I'll understand if this is where it ends."

"Olivia, the only thing you need to understand is that, if I had my way, I'd wake up every morning for the rest of my life with your face next to mine. There is no way that I want this to end."

"Thank you. I so much needed to hear you say that."

"I'd be happy to say it a lot. Just so you know, in so far as Muffy is concerned, she called me Friday night and asked me to vacate the house."

"Why?"

"She's going to sell it. Muffy has decided she prefers Greenwich and the company of her mother to me. She's filing for divorce."

"This is not because of me, is it?" Her voice was laced with concern.

"No. She has no idea about us. As I've told you, this has been coming for a long, long time. Years actually. To paraphrase Allen Greenspan, our getting married was the result of a youthful irrational exuberance. We should have attended the Brittany Spears school of marriage, "One night and good-bye.""

"I'm sorry."

"I know it sounds crass, but I'm not sorry, or even a little bit sad. It's hard spending your whole life walking around on eggs, knowing that if you broke even one, there would be hell to pay. It will be nice to feel the floor under my shoes for a change. But enough of that. The reason I need to talk to you is that … well, the company is faced with a potential problem."

She interrupted, "With the French?"

"No. This has no relation to the negotiation. Although it could. Axel McPherson has been fired. Charlie gave him the word last night. This morning, Axel asked me to do something that puts me in a very difficult position. If I don't handle it right, I could create a great deal of trouble for your husband. I could also damage your father and because you are who you are, it might even spill over on you. Obviously, I don't want that to happen. That's why we need to talk. I want to tell you what I plan to do. Your opinion means a lot to me."

"I think," she said slowly, "this sounds like something that might be better discussed away from my house. Too many ears, if you know what I mean? There's a large mall in Mt. Clements. I'll meet you in the farthest northeast corner of the parking lot at 9:30. We'll drive to my summerhouse up north. It's hardly ever used. We won't be disturbed there."

"Sounds good."

"Oh, and Preston, I'd like to wake up with your face next to mind as well." She hung up.

He was fifty-one, and he felt like a schoolboy in love for the first time. His head was spinning, but not just because of what he felt for Olivia. It was as if his life had been dropped into a blender. Here he was, involved in an affair with the president's wife, planning to virtually blackmail Charlie into making the recall decision, faced with the tribulations of his divorce, all the while trying to produce the dealer meeting and the Le Vent new car introduction. *Is all this happening to me? At one time?* He answered his own question. *All this is happening to me.* From somewhere he thought he heard is father's voice. "Remember, son, the key to survival is to keep a low profile."

Some low profile.

38
A Serf from Livonia

If the Grosse Pointe house was Charlie's version of Versailles, then the cottage on the shores of Lake Huron was Olivia's Petit Trianon. His observation was supported when Olivia explained that her great-grandmother had visited Versailles in the early1900s and had taken pictures of the Petite Trianon to use as inspiration for the cottage. The drive up Route 25 had taken just over an hour, and Waddington had done his best to tell Olivia everything about the Verite 300 problem. He explained how Charlie's decision to reduce the costs in the suspension had compromised its performance and created a car that could, in certain situations, spin out of control. He told her what he and Axel had discovered at the test track, about Mrs. Swenson, and Axel's confrontation with Charlie. He had even made copies of the key pages from the test reports for her to read. Then he told her about his breakfast with Axel and the Pandora briefcase. By the time he had finished, they had arrived at the summerhouse and were sitting on the back terrace, looking out at the backyard and the lake beyond.

"You know," Olivia said, "most men I know would have given the briefcase back to Axel."

"Are you saying I should have?"

"Not at all. In fact, I'm discovering that Mr. Waddington is a very gutsy guy. I admire courage in a man."

"Well, I'm not sure how much courage is involved here. It's more a case of survival. I mean, if the boat looks like it might sink, and I'm the only guy with a bucket, then I'm bailing for me along with everyone else."

Just before noon, Olivia decided they'd talked enough about Charlie and the recall. "Come with me," she said. "Let's walk down by the lake. Bring that blanket." She pointed to a beach blanket on the chair next to him. "I know a great place to sit and enjoy this extraordinary day."

As they left the terrace, he said, "Funny how being here on a day like this, with you, changes my perspective on things."

They walked across the lawn, past a miniature barnyard, again inspired by Marie Antoinette's Petite Trianon, but now devoid of animals. Olivia pointed out different places that she and her sisters had played as children. There was a barn and stables, large enough only for children and their pet animals. White rail fences defined small pastures. On the far side of the little farm was the playhouse, modeled after a French cottage. Everything had been kept up as though any minute children would arrive to populate the farm with their pets.

"This was such a happy place when I was a girl. My sisters and I used to spend the entire summer here. But then, after my mother died, we hardly ever came back. At least, not until I married Charlie. When the boys were little, we spent summers here. Or, at least, the boys and I did. Charlie would come up on weekends when he could. Or to be more accurate, when something more interesting had not presented herself. Now, no one comes. My sisters haven't been here in years, and I get up only occasionally, mainly to assure myself that it hasn't burnt down and no one has thought to tell me."

"It's a shame. It's so beautiful here. Whoever you've got maintaining the place does a great job of keeping it up. But it cries for someone to enjoy it. It needs life."

They walked through a well-manicured stand of trees. Waddington noticed that there wasn't so much as an errant branch or excess of leaves anywhere on the property. It looked like a stately park. They stopped where the trees gave way to the sandy beach and spread the blanket in the shade and sat down. For several moments, the view left them mute, the only sound of a single speedboat, passing well offshore, and the gentle lapping of small waves.

Olivia had found some distant place on the horizon that had caught her imagination and fixed her gaze. Waddington, sitting slightly behind her, found himself mesmerized by the way the gentle breeze rippled through her hair. Sitting there, so close her perfume seemed to seek him out, all thoughts of the recall vanished like idle chatter. *Maybe here, maybe now*, he thought. He put his hand on her shoulder. She turned to him, a smile on her lips as she began to press herself close.

"I am going to leave him, Preston. I've already begun conversations with my lawyer. I'm tired of playing 'Poor Olivia doesn't know.' Because I do know and I want a life with someone

I can trust, someone I can love and be loved by."
She looked at him. Her eyes asked for a response,
for confirmation.

"And I'd like that someone to be me." But
from somewhere, in the far recesses of his mind,
the doubts began to bubble up. He had so little to
offer her. No money, no looks, no position, not
even a house anymore. And chances were, even if
he was successful with Charlie, he would probably
be out of a job within a matter of days. Charlie
would certainly want to retaliate, to have his pound
of flesh. Waddington felt compelled to confess his
sense of how inadequate he felt to have her think of
him as that someone in her life.

"Olivia, if I were to conjure up the perfect
woman in my mind, she'd be you. At night, I
fantasize what it would be like to live with you, to
spend every day with you. But in the morning, I
begin to think of what your friends will say behind
your back and maybe even to your face. 'Do you
believe it; she's taken up with a manager of sales
training? Is she out of her mind? How can she
expect him to join the country club when we never
accept anyone less than an Executive Vice
President? Certainly, she can't expect …'"

Olivia started to object, "Preston …"

"No, please, let me finish. This needs to be
said. You can't dismiss who and what you are.
Like it or not, you're Grosse Pointe royalty and by
comparison, I'm really not much more that a serf
from Livonia. I don't bring much to your party,
Olivia. What concerns me is that one day you
might look at me and say, 'My God, what am I

doing with this man; I must have been out of my mind.'"

It was a righteous anger that erupted from Olivia. He had never seen her get angry before. But she was angry now. "Okay, enough. "Stop right there! I will not accept your assessment of yourself based on what you think my opinion might be at some time in the future. What you see in the mirror is one thing. What I see in you, Preston, no one is going to find in a mirror. What I see is somebody very special, who, if he gave himself a chance, could be anybody and do anything he wanted. I'm not sure you've ever met that guy yet. Or, if you have, you've forgotten. Mr. Waddington, I would like to introduce you to one hell of a man who is kind, caring, smart, full of integrity, and capable of enormous love. And let me tell you something else; if you don't love me, that's one thing. But if you do, well then, mister, I'm not leaving. I plan on hanging around. Because I'd like to introduce you to the man beyond the mirror. I happen to like that man a lot. And I want to be with him."

Her initial anger had slowly softened until it had been reduced to an intimate whisper. "More than like, I love him, and I want him for myself. As far as what people might say, frankly, my dear, I don't give a damn."

They both started to laugh, recognizing she had just borrowed Rhett Butler's line. She had simply blown him away. "Well, then, I don't give a damn either … about other people. But I do give a damn about you, which is to say that … I love you."

"Come here," she said leaning back and pulling him down to her. Her arms held him tight as her mouth drew close to his. "Preston, make love to me," she whispered.

Slowly his hands found her breasts and began working their way down over her abdomen.

"Fetch boy! That's a good doggie."

The voice came from the beach. Two women in shorts were walking along the water's edge, throwing a ball for their Golden to retrieve. If they had seen Olivia and Waddington, they gave no notice of it.

Olivia began to laugh. "Do you get the feeling we're not alone?"

"Now that you mention it …"

"Here boy. Here boy," one of the women called.

"I think my bedroom would be more comfortable."

He got up, grabbed the blanket, and they hurried back toward the house. As they approached the back terrace, they were met with the sound of a small engine, like that on a lawn tractor. The sound grew louder until the tractor, which turned out to be a four-gang mower, appeared from around the far side of the house, followed by two men in work clothes carrying hedge clippers and rakes.

One of the men saw Olivia and shouted to her over the sound the mower, "Hullo, Misses Fair! I no see you for so many long time! You come to stay for a while, I hope?" He did not wait for an answer, "You see how good we take care of everything?" He made a broad gesture to include the entire property.

"That's our gardener, Spinelli. Been with us for forty years," she whispered to Waddington who had stopped just under the portico that covered the terrace. His face was in the shadows, which must have obscured his features from the gardener, who shaded his eyes from the sun.

"I cannot see. Is that you, Mr. Byrd, or is it Mr. Fair?"

"Ahhh, no, neither," Olivia said, quickly improvising, "This is a gentleman from …"she hummed and fumbled and then blurted, "Home and Garden Magazine. He's thinking about doing an article on the house."

"Oh, good choice, Mister. I show you all the flowers and the ornamental trees. I am very proud of what I do for this house. This is my pride and joy. I take special care of this place. I give you a tour. This house make good article for your magazine. Maybe you mention my name? I spell it for you." Which he did. "This house, this whole estate, this is Spinelli's pride."

"Well, he's just looking for now," Olivia interrupted. "If he decides to do the article, I'm sure he'll want to spend time with you."

"Why not now? Now is the best time. It's a beautiful day. No better time than right now. My name is Spinelli. Oh, I told you that already. I will give you my card, so you spell it right. I give you tour now." There was no refusing Spinelli. He grabbed Waddington's arm and the tour began. Spinelli knew every flower, every shrub, every tree by name and made sure that Waddington saw them all.

Olivia had taken a seat on the terrace to wait for him. Waddington glanced back at her several times. Each time he could see she was smiling. No, laughing. *My God, the fates are conspiring against us,* he thought.

When finally, and mercifully, the tour ended, Spinelli announced that he and his merry gardeners would be there for the rest of the afternoon. The bedroom would have to wait for another time.

As they drove south toward Grosse Pointe, Waddington opened the console cover and pulled out a CD. "La Boehme."

"One of my favorites."

"It's the recording of Pavarotti and Mirella Freni's first performance together in the U.S. It's magnificent."

They listened for a while, and then Olivia reached over and put her hand on Waddington's arm. "I wish, right now, you and I could get on a plane and go to Paris and find some wonderful little hotel on the Left Bank and be our own version of Mimi and Rodolfo."

"You wouldn't have to ask me twice."

"Funny, I just remembered. I will be in Paris next week."

"What?"

"The wrong Paris, however. I'll be in the Paris Hotel in Las Vegas. Charlie has requested that I accompany him for the Dealer Council meeting out there."

"We're also holding Le Vent preview at the same time at the Las Vegas Speedway."

"Then you'll be there too?" she said excitedly.

"Three days. I'll be coming back on Sunday."

"I really don't like going with Charlie on his business trips. In most cases, he doesn't want me to come along. I tend to qualify as excess baggage. But there are times, like now, when he finds me useful. Oh, how I love to be thought of as *useful*."

"What does he mean, 'useful?'"

"Since all of the dealer council members are bringing their wives, you can imagine what they'd say if the President and CEO showed up in Sin City without his adoring and devoted wife."

"Does he keep you busy?"

"Charlie only parades me out for the cocktail receptions and the dinners. The rest of the time I'm told to entertain myself. I don't gamble, so there's not much for me to do. Las Vegas is not exactly a culture center."

"Subculture maybe," he offered.

She looked over at him, "Is there any reason why you and I shouldn't be able to find some time to pick up where we left off today?"

Waddington glanced over at that slightly off-center face. No more self-doubts. No more new resolves. *I love her and she loves me for what I am. That's all that matters.*

She prodded him, "There isn't, is there?"

"No reason, whatsoever."

39
The Purloined Report

Popper was in need of a chocolate fix. As he returned from lunch, he made a slight detour past Waddington's office. Doreen Walfish was at her desk, scanning a stack of documents into her computer. She looked up as Popper approached, then looked back at her computer screen and said, "Read the sign."

On the box of chocolates she had a yellow Post-it reading. "Take one! And ONLY one!"

Popper lifted the lid and assessed the assortment in the box like a man given permission to break off his diet. "Oh, a box with nothing but chocolate cherries today," he said popping one into his mouth. "Love to pop a cherry from a box," he said, fully intending to get a rise from Doreen.

Doreen's face scrunched up, and she fired off an acerbic response, "You are a disgusting sleaze-ball, Popper. You know that?" This was a woman who did not mince words. If you had it coming, she was not averse to delivering.

"Of course. That's part of my charm. That's why you secretly adore me."

"Yeah, right," she said caustically. "And don't finger the candy, okay? You probably haven't washed your hands since your last crap."

Popper decided to stay and "play" for a while. "You do have a way with words, Doreen. Clearly, your Dale Carnegie course was of real benefit." She ignored him. He waited until she turned her back and quickly popped a second piece in his mouth.

"Okay," she said, seeming to have eyes in the back of her head. "You've had your second, you're over the limit, now get lost. I've got work to do."

"Where's Waddington?"

"Out."

"I haven't seen him all day."

"Maybe that's because he's been out all day."

One of Popper's more well-honed talents was his ability to read upside down. This skill had served him well in meetings with clients and in learning useful information from documents left carelessly on top of other people's desks. As he looked for something on which to wipe his fingers, he noticed that the documents Doreen was scanning had to do with test results on the Verite's suspension system. He picked up phrases like,

The vehicle has cornering
limitations and does not react well to higher than normal 'g' forces
in turns.

"What are you working on?" he said, availing himself of her Kleenex box to wipe the chocolate from his fingers.

"It's this month's CEO report."

"Did Waddington put in anything about me or my new ads?"

"No," she replied flatly.

She finished scanning another page and placed it on the pile. Again, his inverted reading skill picked up several key lines.

The safety engineering department suggests that the decision by top management to use constant rate springs as opposed to the more expensive variable rate springs and to reduce the thickness of the stabilizer bar by half is a mistake and antithetical to its goals of offering sports car performance.

Well, sonofabitch, he thought, *what the hell is that all about?*

"Can I read some of this?"

"No. A copy will be on your desk next Wednesday. You can read it then. And if you take another chocolate, I'll cut off your fuckin' fingers." Doreen was not one to be intimated by a title or job position.

"And you have a nice afternoon as well," he said backing way. "Oh, you might want to move your box away from the computer. I think some of your candy is melting. But then, some people like soft, warm cherries. Chocolate covered ones, of course."

"You're sick, Popper," she said, moving her box of chocolates from the computer. "Always thinkin' with your dick."

"It not only thinks, it does tricks."

"Out! Or I'll call HR and scream sexual harassment."

And he knew she just might. A purposeful retreat was in order. As Popper strolled back to his office, he had but one mission to accomplish that day. He had to get his hands on the report. If the rest of the report was as damaging as the parts he'd managed to read upside down, it could represent a major problem for the company.

Popper waited until everyone had gone home for the day, then he returned to Doreen's desk, bypassed the chocolates, and began to look for the copy of the Verite test report that he'd seen her scanning into the computer. *Damn*, he thought, *she must have locked it up.* Then he noticed her computer was still on. He wondered if maybe, just maybe, she might not have logged off. He hit the space bar. Voila! Up came the screen with the first page of the scanned report on it. He began to scroll down on the screen. It was all there. *Careless Miss Walfish*, he thought as he clicked on the print icon and helped himself to a chocolate. For the next twenty minutes pages piled up in the document tray of the Hewlett Packard printer.

Later, as he sat in his office skimming through the pages, he realized that these test results and the reports from Hap Burlington's were lethal material. No way should any of this be appearing in the CEO report. This must be what Axel had dropped on Charlie's desk. Axel had been right; it was Charlie's ticket to sleep-a-way camp. And that raised a question: What was Waddington up to? He had to know that once Charlie saw this, all hell would break loose.

He locked his copy of the CEO report in the bottom drawer of his desk and left the building. Driving home, his thoughts turned to the crumpled Verite 300 behind Jack Poor's body shop and the prospect of Mrs. Swenson's lawyer filing a suit. *Could it be*, he wondered, *that Waddington's CEO report has just given me an incredible opportunity?* An idea began to take shape in his mind. A much better idea than the one he had hinted at to Jack Poor. It was an idea that deserved some serious thought.

40
The Fine Print

It was like being backed into a corner by a Doberman who had been too long without red meat. Petula went right for his jugular.

"Your life is over, OVER!" she snarled. "You thought I made your life miserable that last time I caught you with that tramp, you bastard. Well, you don't know what miserable really is. You are going to wish you were dead!"

Jack Poor had not intended to see his Insurance Claims Adjuster again. The sex had gotten ordinary and she had, quite frankly, become too expensive. This business of sex in exchange for shopping had simply gotten out of hand. He hadn't seen her in over two weeks when she showed up at the dealership, on legitimate business, to look at a car that had been rear-ended. He watched her walk around the damaged car from his office window. A gust of wind caught her skirt and lifted it up around her thighs. That was all it took. The thought of those smooth, slightly tanned, soft thighs inviting him to slip between them was temptation beyond resistance. *What the hell?* he thought. *One more time and we move on.* He called to her and within less than thirty minutes, they were once again ensconced in the Roll Inn. In retrospect, Jack suspected that he'd been spotted talking to her by Ivan the Terrified. Obviously, the little shit had followed them and reported back to Petula.

"Ivan. He's the one, right? He's your spy. Well, you might ask him how he's going to like life as a eunuch?"

"Don't you dare touch Ivan. He was doing what I told him to do."

"This crap has got to end, Petula."

"Well," she said through a wide, nasty smile, "it is. I forgot to tell you. I'm selling the dealership. By this time next month, you'll be out of a job, and you know what that means?"

Jack did not venture a guess. He knew he would be told what it meant.

"You will be here, with me. *Every* day. You will not leave the property unless I give you permission. You will go nowhere without me or Muffy to keep an eye on you. You, you conniving, philandering bastard, are going to be on a short leash until your Mr. Happy can't get itself up for more than its morning pee."

Jack fired back. "Go ahead. Sell the dealership. I could give a shit. I'm tired of this fuckin' business anyway. But remember, I own twenty percent, and you and I both know it's worth millions. Once I get my hands on my twenty percent, that money and me are history. I'm outta here."

Petula began an icy, derisive laugh. It sounded like the laugh of an executioner holding the release on the guillotine being told by the man with his head on the block that he wanted permission to blow his nose.

"What twenty percent? You *don't have* twenty percent," she roared with victorious glee.

"The hell I don't! When Bumper bought that dealership, he and you gave me twenty percent of the business. It's spelled out in my contract, my dear Petula. Big as life and in bold print. Twenty percent!"

Her laughed stopped in mid "ha" and she spat her words at him. "You never read the fine print, did you? No, of course you didn't. I even told my father you wouldn't read it."

Jack looked like a man who just realized he'd stepped into an open elevator shaft. "Fine print?"

***

Jack's first order of business when he arrived at the dealership was to find Ivan and dismember him. But Ivan's mother had borne no fools. That or Petula must have called him because by the time Jack arrived at the dealership, the little man had cleared out his personnel effects and disappeared. Jack went up to his office, brushing past his salesmen like grey ships passing in the night. There was hardly a nod or greeting among them. Once inside his office, Jack closed and locked the door. He was not going to chance an interruption. His private phone indicated he had a message. He knew it wasn't Petula because he'd purposely avoided giving her that number. Jack punched up the play button.

"Got it last night." He recognized the voice of his lawyer. "Slipwalker has filed. I've got a copy of the complaint, and I'll bring it over on Monday. Nothing you need to do now. It'll be weeks before we even hear from the court to schedule depositions. I'm presuming Detroit got their copy as you're both cited. Have a nice weekend. And don't worry. The schmuck is just blowing smoke up your ass." And that was it.

He started to call Popper's home phone and then remembered he planned to be in Las Vegas for the dealer council meeting. Jack glanced at his watch, 8:30, and counted back three hours to determine the time in Las Vegas. Immediately he searched for Popper's cell phone number, found it, and dialed.

"Jesus, what time is it?" he heard Popper say as he opened the cell phone.

"It's time we fuckin' did something and soon. You told me to call when Slipwalker filed. Well, he has. If you've got a way for us to make some money off this, now's the time to make our move. I don't want to go into details now, but I've really got a major problem here."

"Petula?" Popper asked.

"Fuckin' bitch. I'd leave today. But with what I've got in the bank right now, I wouldn't have a pot to piss in within two years. I need to know what you've got in mind."

"We're on track. This is going to work better than I'd imagined. But there's still a couple pieces I need to put in place. Hang tight for forty-eight hours. I'll call you first thing Sunday morning."

41
Viva Las Vegas

"Bone chewer," the door man with a heavy Texas accent said as Waddington got out of the taxi in front of the Paris Hotel. He'd been there before and knew that one of the affectations of the hotel was that it required all its employees, at least those with at least a moderate command of the English language, to greet customers with a few words of French. "Bone chewer," he heard the doorman say as he greeted another arrival. Whoever was in charge of helping employees master their French pronunciation had more work to do.

As Waddington paid the driver, he looked up at the scaled-down replica of the Arch de Triomphe, which was positioned in front of the hotel. Above him soared a scaled-down Eiffel Tower. Together they were enough to confirm a Frenchman's worst opinion of the U.S.

"Gol damn," said a man wearing a cowboy hat and a shirt that bore a bright luminescent collage of all the major landmarks in Las Vegas. The shirt fell tent-like down to his thighs, doing little to hide his substantial girth. "Them French must really be hurtin' to have to sell that Eeefell Tower to us."

Waddington assumed the man was attempting to make a joke, but the awe on his face told him he had intended it as a statement of fact.

"You know, I had a feelin' them Uro-pee-ans was in deep do-do when the Brits sold the London Bridge to America."

Waddington assumed that the man had interpreted his lack of response as an indication of doubt.

"Hey, it's true. Been to see it. Right down there in ol' Lake Have-a-sue, A-Z. Then you come here to Las Vegas and find that they bought one of them Eyetallian bridges for the Veeneetian Hotel. Over there," he said pointing toward the Belaggio. They have emm-ported the Trevi Fountain. Damn! Who needs to go to U-rope when they're bringin' it all here?"

The profundity of the man's observation left Waddington wondering, for the brief moment, if the strong influence of imitative architecture was a homage to our European heritage, a lack of imagination, or just a monument to high tact.

Waddington was not staying at the Paris. Only VP's and above got that privilege. He was booked into a nasty little motel near the airport, which seemed bent on rationing the hot water in the morning. You either got a hot shower early, well before six, or you're out of luck.

The first day of the Le Vent preview for the twenty members of the dealer council had been a success. The normal hyperbole that Charlie laced into to his speeches was held to a minimum. The select group of dealers loved the car. The hope was that during the next thirty days, they would spread their enthusiasm to the other six hundred dealers before the August dealer meeting in Detroit. It never hurt to prime the dealer body with anticipatory enthusiasm before an announcement show.

Waddington called Olivia three times. Once Charlie answered, and he hung up. A second time, there was no answer. The third time he was successful.

"I'll be free tomorrow night," she said. "Charlie has a dinner and God knows what else with the dealer council. If I know Charlie, and unfortunately, I do, he'll be out most of the night. Call me about seven," she said and hung up.

It had taken him the better part of a half hour to drive from his motel to the Paris. It struck him as he heard "Bone Chewer" repeated with the arrival of each taxi and limousine, that either the doorman had a truly limited French vocabulary or hadn't notice that it was after seven.

He pushed through the doors into the hotel, made his way through the forest of slot machines, and found himself amused at the extent of the hotel's pervasive effort to sustain a faux French atmosphere. Signs pointed the way to La Recéption, Les Telephones, Les Show Tickers, Le Salon de Table and Ascensors *(which, out of deference to their clients they translated in a parenthesis as "elevators."),* and Les Toilette, where one could, presumably, take Le Crap.

"Hello?"

"I'm in the lobby."

"He's just about to leave," she said in a whisper.

"Who's that?" he heard Charlie's voice in the background.

"It's room service," Olivia called back.

"Room service? What do they want?"

"Ahh … they wanted to know if we're hungry."

"Room service wants to know if we're hungry?" Charlie repeated. "Since when does room service call the guests?"

Olivia shrugged indicating she had no idea why they called. She turned to the phone. "Mr. Fair is just about to leave for a cocktail party he's throwing for some press people over at The Mirage, and then he's going to the Bellagio for a dinner with his dealer council, so I guess we don't need anything right now."

"Olivia, you don't have to give room service my itinerary. Just say, 'no thank you.'"

"I wonder," she said still talking into the phone, "if you might recommend a quiet restaurant here in the hotel?"

"I suggest you try the bar just across from the reception lobby," he said enjoying the telephone ruse. "The drinks are too expensive, but I can be had for the asking."

"Well, that sounds like a wonderful idea. I'll be down in say twenty or thirty minutes."

"I love you," he said.

"*Je t'aime.*"

"What was that?" he heard Charlie ask.

"It was French for have a nice night." She hung up the phone.

She is quick, Waddington thought. *The woman is very quick.*

Waddington looked at his watch and wandered over to the cocktail bar that was supposed to look like one of the outdoor restaurant pavilions in the Jardin des Tuileries. He sat down in one of the lounge chairs and ordered a Pinot Noir.

Barely fifteen minutes later, he felt her hand on his shoulder.

"Mr. Waddington," she said in too loud a voice. "What a surprise to find you here." Clearly both the nature of her comments and the volume were meant for the benefit of any dealer or dealer's wife that might be in the area. "You know, Mr. Waddington, you promised to give me your ideas on our brochure. I'm sure you've been very busy, what with the Le Vent launch and getting ready for the dealer meeting." She appeared to interrupt herself. "Oh, I'm sorry, are you meeting someone here?"

It was all Waddington could do to keep a straight face. He understood the charade and glanced around to see if there was anyone he recognized. "Actually, I just wandered in off the street in hopes of finding a friendly face and instead, I find a truly beautiful face who looks like she might be interested in dinner."

"Was that an invitation, Mr. Waddington?"

"Absolutely."

Waddington paid his bill. Once they left the hotel lobby, she pointed to a limo. "That's one of the limo's assigned to us. I know a restaurant we can go to that is well off the strip. No one we know will be there from the company because it hasn't got any slot machines."

"Are you concerned the limo driver might say something to Charlie?"

"Haven't you heard the Las Vegas commercial? 'What happens here, stays here.'"

***

At dinner, they talked mostly about the CEO report and the potential ramifications and fallout. "It will be on Charlie's desk next Wednesday morning, which means we'll have a recall issued by late in the afternoon or I'll be looking for work."

"If he fires you, he'll probably be doing you a favor. Every time a whistle blower comes forward, they end up writing a book and getting a big advance." She laughed and he joined her.

"Of course, if Charlie has Harry Spar break all my fingers, I'll have to dictate the book."

She reached across the table and took both his hands in hers and drew herself as close to him as the table would permit. "You *are*, doing the right thing. And I want you to know that I truly admire you for that. It's also one of the reasons I love you."

They were back at the Paris just before 10:30.

"I don't think we need to tempt fate by taking the same elevator. Let me go up first," she said, as they pushed through the revolving doors. "We're in the Charles DeGaulle suite. Top floor. We're so high you can see all the way to the Eiffel Tower." She laughed.

335

Waddington waited five minutes and followed. She met him at the door, checked to be sure that there were no maids in the hallway, and then pulled him inside and threw her arms around him. "Oh, Preston, I've missed you," she said, kissing him.

The Charles DeGaulle suite featured a large, ornate, nicely paneled living room with rather impressive reproductions of Louis XV furniture. At either end were doors that led to the bedrooms.

"I make Charlie sleep down there." She pointed to the far end of the room. "I told him I don't like to be disturbed when he comes in late smelling like a distillery. This is mine," she said, leading him into her bedroom and closing the door.

"And what if Charlie comes back?"

"In case you haven't noticed, we're in Las Vegas, home to almost all of Charlie's vices. If he gets in before sunrise, I'll be very much surprised. No. Preston, we have this suite all to ourselves." Their lips met again, and he began to unbutton her dress. There was no frantic rush, no ripping of clothes; it was if they had a tacit agreement to savor every moment.

"My God, you're beautiful," he said as he lifted her naked body onto the bed.

"I love you, Preston," she said, pulling him down on top of her.

"In here guys! Bar's over there. I'll have Olivia order up some snacks. Turn on the TV, if you like. I think they're broadcasting the Turner/Branfield fight."

Had Waddington been struck with a cattle prod he could not have moved faster.

"Olivia?" Charlie called from the living room, "Are you decent?"

"I'm in bed, dear," she called through the door. "Just a minute while I find my robe." She ran to the door and locked it, then turned and searched for her robe.

Waddington frantically picked up his clothes and shoes, looking for an escape route. "There's no way out of here," he said, "except through the living room, and right now, I don't think that's an option." He looked down at the bed which cleared the floor by only about six inches. "I can't even fit under the bed."

"In there," Olivia motioned toward her bathroom door. "Charlie never uses my bathroom."

Waddington stepped into the large, marble-lined bathroom. It was almost as big as his room at the motel.

"Olivia, it's locked," Charlie called, as he tried to open her bedroom door.

"Sorry," she said as she opened it a crack. "I had dinner in my room and I left the hall door open for them to pick up the dishes. I thought it best to lock my bedroom door. You hear all these stories about hotel help."

Charlie started to push the door open, but she resisted. "I'm not dressed. I'd just gone to bed." Through the narrow opening she could see that the living room was beginning to look a lot like the drunk tank at a police station. Men with cigars and drinks looking as if they'd left more than their money on the tables crowded into the room. They randomly plopped themselves into chairs and onto anything that looked like it might not collapse when they sat on it.

"Ran into a bunch of the dealers over at the Bellagio and decided to bring them back here for a nightcap. Do me a favor; call room service and order up a bunch of sandwiches and hors d'oeuvres. Then you can go back to bed."

"Okay," she said and closed the door, locking it again.

In the bathroom, Waddington quickly put on his clothes. As he dressed, he noticed that the bathroom had two doors. One led back to Olivia's room; the other, he presumed must open into the foyer so that it could be used as a guest bathroom.

"Is this the guest can?" he heard a voice ask on the other side of the door.

"Gotta be," came a response.

"Oh, no!" Waddington said, ready to retreat back into Olivia's room. Then he noticed that the shower stall near her door provided immediate cover. It had tile walls and the opening faced away from the rest of the bathroom. The only way anyone would see him was if they suddenly had an urge to take a shower. *That,* he thought, *might make for a rather interesting confrontation.* He heard someone enter the bathroom and close the door. The seat lid clicked against the water tank and was followed by the familiar sound of a kidney draining into the toilet. It was accompanied by a prolonged series of rectal noises. *Good God,*

Waddington wondered, *what in hell did he have for dinner?*

The toilet flushed, the seat clacked down, and water began to run in the basin. There was a loud knock on the foyer door.

"Hey, Cherfondi, you fat shit what ya doin' in there? Playin' with it?" The slurred words and the tone gave every indication that the man on the other side of the door was in desperate need of the toilet. Chances were he either needed to pee or throw up. "Come on, Cherf, there's a goddamn line out here waitin' to take a piss."

For the next half hour, Waddington stood in the shower, listening to a variety of animal-like sounds and grunts as the men attended to their bodily functions.

Damn, he thought, *why won't one of these guys at least turn on the exhaust fan?*

An hour passed and from his redoubt in the shower it sounded as if the crowd in the living room was growing. Waddington decided that his only chance was simply to walk out of the bathroom as though he had been among the group in the room.

He stepped out of the shower, took a look at himself to be sure everything was on right and zipped up. He opened the door cautiously. There was no one waiting to get in, so he walked out hoping that he looked like just another one of Charlie's guests who had needed to relieve himself.

"Waddington," the voice boomed. It was Charlie. "Didn't see you come in." Charlie appeared to be about one drink away from toppling over. "Glad you could make it. Hey, come here." He draped his arm around Waddington's shoulder and pulled him close so that he could whisper in his ear. "Not for publication in the *CEO*, but I got word today that Motor Trend just might pick Le Vent as the car of the year." He teetered slightly and then slapped Waddington on the back. "An award like that would punch up sales like you wouldn't believe. And with our *Easy* advertising campaign, we've got a winner! The French are going to love us. Fuckin' love us!" He began to laugh. "Hell, we might even be able to give you a rise. What are we paying you?"

Waddington glanced around to see who might be listening. Nobody was. Most everyone's attention was focused on the TV fight. Those that weren't looked as if they had crashed for the night. The room was not going to be pretty in the morning.

"Seventy-five hundred," Waddington answered.

"A week?"

"Ahh. No, a month."

Charlie pulled back to arm's length and looked at Waddington with concern. "How the hell do you live on that? You know, I gotta start taking better care of my guys. Here you are, publisher of the *CEO*, the best goddamn training manger in the industry, and the guy who came up with the best goddamn ad campaign I've ever put my name on. Pres, you are fucking indispensable to this company." He was listing badly, but Waddington sensed there was at least a degree of sincerity in his voice. "Fuckin' in-dee-spen-cy-bull!"

Waddington wondered how in-dee-spen-cy-bull he'd be after Wednesday.

"Gotta piss. Bad," Charlie said under his breath, as if sharing a personal secret. With that he headed off toward his bedroom on the opposite end of the living room, looking ever so much like a tightrope walker using a Scotch glass in place of his balance bar.

Waddington waited until Charlie had disappeared into his room. "I think I'll call it a night," he said to the roomful of men, none of which paid him any attention. He walked across the foyer, opened the door, and made his escape. He hoped he would do as well on Wednesday.

42
Liar, Liar Pants on Fire

Popper had made it a point to stay until the last man had stumbled out of the Charles DeGaulle suite. Charlie had caught a second wind and was itching for entertainment. "Popper, my man, let's go have a drink and catch a titty show. The best ones all start after midnight."

It was the opportunity Popper had been waiting for.

They told the limo driver what they were looking for and he needed no further instruction. The club was a study in red velvet, low lights, and women performing interesting feats on silver poles on a stage. They watched with an intent, prurient interest, occasionally voicing an opinion on this or that girl's anatomy and suggesting what they might like to do with her had they the opportunity. But all look and no touch soon cost the girls the two men's interest. It was like being at a petting zoo where they don't let you touch the animals.

"So," Popper began, "it looks like the French deal is almost signed and sealed." It was more a question than a statement.

Charlie nodded, "Looks like a done deal. Still a couple of loose ends to tie up and a couple wrinkles that Perkins is trying to iron out. But it's a done deal. And you know something? With the French cash in the bank, I got a feeling that this coming model year is going to have our name written all over it. The Le Vent is on track to get

Car of The Year, and the Verite 300 sales were the highest last month since we introduced the car."

How considerate of Charlie, Popper thought. *He's even giving me my cue line.* "Speaking of the Verite, we may have a slight problem there."

"Problem? What problem?"

"Well, I was talking to Jack Poor earlier today about doing some inserts in his showroom for the *Easy* campaign. He told me that the Swenson lawyer has filed. Jack's lawyer got his copy of the complaint this morning. Which means, if Harvey Nichols hasn't got ours by now, he'll probably see it on Monday."

"Let the fucker sue!" Charlie spat. "They haven't got a case. Driver error, pure and simple."

Popper bobbed his head and rubbed his face, working hard to create a convincingly pained expression. "Except that, according to Jack, the lawyer has come up with some information that could bite us in the ass."

"What information are you talking about?" Charlie, never one to receive bad news from messengers calmly, was making no effort to hide his growing concern.

"Well, I'm giving you this sort of thirdhand. I mean, I'm just passing on what Jack told me that his lawyer told him. Seems this Slipwalker, the Swenson lawyer…"

"I know, I know. Get to the point!"

"Well, seems that Slipwalker claims …" Popper stopped. Charlie was like a golf ball on the tee, waiting for Popper to pull out his driver. He decided to take a couple of practice swings.

"You want another drink," Charlie?

"Later. It seems that Slipwalker claims what?"

"You mind if I have one?"

"Have five for all I care. Tell me what the hell the lawyer said."

"Oh. Okay. Sorry, I should get to the point."

"I'd like that very much," Charlie said, barely able to contain his impatience.

"What he said was that Slipwalker claims he has the … I think the words he used were, *The Smoking Gun*." All his years of perfecting the art of sounding convincing when he lied were on full display.

"The Smoking Gun! What the hell did he mean by that?"

"Jack's lawyer said that Slipwalker claims to have some damaging reports relating to the suspension performance of the Verite 300. Frankly, it sounds to me like those reports might be ours. Although, I'm not too sure about that. Anyway, all Slipwalker would say is that …" The waitress walked up and bent over the table, providing Popper with a wonderful view that seemed to extend all the way down the front of her dress to her knees.

"Black Label and Water. No ice." Popper said. "Charlie? Sure, you don't want something?"

"No, no, get on with it, goddamn it. What did he say?"

"Jack's lawyer said Slipwalker claims that, and these are his words, 'he has us by the balls and he intends to squeeze until they pop.'"

"He's bluffing!" Charlie retorted sharply, more in an attempt to convince himself than stating a fact. "What the hell could he have?"

Popper was pleased. This was going well. Charlie had taken the bait. Now the trick was to carefully reel him in. Not too quickly. Just a little at a time. "I don't know. I remember Axel dropping that report on your desk. Did any of that ever get out?"

"It goddamn better not have!"

"May I make a suggestion?"

"As long as it's not stupid," Charlie snapped, making no effort to hide his heightened level of irritation.

Popper's drink arrived, and he took a long purposeful sip. *Charlie,* he thought, *you are an asshole and I'm going to enjoy fuckin' you over more than you will ever know.* The obsequious look on his face gave not even the slightest hint of the fiction that was to follow. "Here's what I suggest," he said at last. "I'm going to be in Greenwich Monday and Tuesday for the Le Vent insert shoot. Jack tells me he and his lawyer plan to have a meeting with Slipwalker. I'm not sure what the hell he thinks a meeting will accomplish. In fact, I told him it was a bad idea and tried to talk him out of it, but you don't tell Jack what to do. My thought is that, since we can't stop him, it would be a good idea for me to be there when he meets Slipwalker."

Charlie balked, "I don't know. Could your being there tip our hand to this guy?"

"What's to tip? That we don't deal with bogus lawsuits? I'm sure you'll agree that it's in our best interest to know what Slipwalker's got, if he's got anything, before he goes public with it. And Jack is giving us an opportunity to do just that."

"Maybe I should have somebody from legal go with you. I can send Harvey Nichols."

God, that's the last thing I want, Popper thought as he felt blood rush to his head. *Easy,* he said to himself. *Don't appear too anxious to deep-six Charlie's suggestion.* "Let me think about that," Popper said leaning back in his chair. His head nodded as an indication to Charlie that he was weighing options. At last he shook his head, "Too early for him. Save Nichols for round two. He'll be a lot more effective if we have some idea what reports Slipwalker's claims he has."

Charlie was clearly vexed and seemed to be teetering on the edge of a decision. Popper decided he needed a push. "Another reason to hold off on Nichols–Jack doesn't like him." In truth, Popper had no idea if Jack had ever met the man. "If you were to suggest to Jack that he take Harvey Nichols with him, Jack would tell you to go to hell. One thing you have to understand about Jack Poor, he doesn't trust us. He feels we've screwed him over on model allocations, hold-back payments, co-op advertising, you name it. Knowing him, he might even get it into his head that we're planning to leave him holding the bag, if there *is* a lawsuit."

"What?" Charlie responded incredulously.

"The guy's paranoid. He's a loose cannon. Given half a chance, he could really muck things up for us with this lawyer, especially if the guy does have something that can hurt us. Now Jack likes me. He trusts me, totally. More importantly, I can control him. He won't do or say anything stupid if I'm with him." Then almost parenthetically he added, "Hey, if Slipwalker is as much of a legal whore as Jack's lawyer says he is, he may even offer to settle right then and there."

"The hell with settle. We need to find out what he's got." Charlie thought for a moment, then made his decision. "Okay. You go with Poor. But make goddamn sure you tie down that loose cannon. You understand?" Charlie rubbed his eyes and began to yawn. "I gotta get some sleep." He stood up, looked around the room for a moment, then turned back to Popper and said emphatically, "Don't fuck this up." With that he turned and left.

Popper watched him weave through the tables of gawkers toward the front door. Assured that Charlie was out of earshot he said, "The only thing I'm going to fuck up is you, Charlie."

43
Buy Your Tickets for Key West

Jack was in his office by eight, staring at the phone waiting for Popper's call. The sonofabitch better call, goddamn it. At ten after nine the phone rang.

"Jack Poor."

"Call the airline and book your tickets to Key West. Your money problems are soon going to be history."

"God, I hope you're right. Tell me how you plan to make me rich."

"It involves risk. Are you up for taking a risk?"

"If the payoff is worth it, I'm up for it."

"Okay. I'm getting on a plane first thing Monday morning, and I'll be at the Hyatt in Greenwich Monday night. While I'm traveling, you have a mission. A mission critical to our success. Here's what I want you to do. Call Slipwalker and tell him that you'd like to meet him sometime Tuesday. Afternoon would be best. Don't mention that I'm coming, just tell him you want to meet. Tell him there's something he needs to know that has a major bearing on his case. Bait him good. Tell him you've got information that could give him a whole new perspective on the suit. Be vague. If he balks, you might even tell him you'd consider helping him against the company, if he'll drop the suit against you. I don't care what you have to say, lie your head off if you have to. But get him to agree to a meeting on Tuesday. Then you and I are going to go in there and make him an offer he can't refuse. When we leave, we're going to have set ourselves up for a ton of money."

"I don't get it. How the hell is talking to Slipwalker going to make us any money?"

Popper laid out his scam in detail. When he'd finished Jack gushed, "Jesus! That's fuckin' brilliant. But if we get caught, we could be in deep shit."

"There's always that risk, of course. But I think we can keep it low."

Jack asked for reassurance, "Do you think you can really pull it off?"

"Let's put it this way; if I were you, I'd put my trust in ol' Popper to make me a very rich man. Right now, your number one priority, the most important thing you have to do in life, is get that lawyer to agree to a meeting. If we don't get that meeting, cancel those tickets to Key West."

"I'll get the meeting. Count on it."

"I am."

44
Dunkin' Donuts

"He told me his office was above the Dunkin' Donuts shop," Jack said as he and Popper pulled into the parking lot in front of the Elmsford, New York, strip mall. It was a tired edifice with an assortment of stores that looked as if any minute they might post "Lost Our Lease, 75% Off" signs.

They found a door between the Dunkin' Donuts and a Laundromat that bore, among others, Abner Slipwalker's name. As they climbed the stairs covered with badly stained carpet, Popper said, "This guy looks like an ambulance chaser who hasn't caught many ambulances. The place is a dump."

They opened the door to Slipwalker's office. The reception area was barely big enough for a secretarial desk and one chair. The desk showed no signs of recent habitation.

The door to the inner office opened and Slipwalker appeared, glancing at his watch. "Two o'clock. Right on time. Who's this?" He looked at Jack but pointed suspiciously at Popper.

Popper did not wait for Jack to respond. "Poppenhaus. I'm a senior VP representing the company."

"Lawyer?"

"No, just an interested party."

Slipwalker became noticeably agitated. "Poor, you said you were coming alone."

Again, Popper injected himself. "I asked Jack if I might join him because, since we're both named in your suit, I thought it might be best if we were both here when we presented our proposal."

"Proposal?" Slipwalker asked, curiously.

"I wonder, Mr. Slipwalker, if we might go into your office. I think we'd all be more comfortable if we could sit down and discuss our ..." he paused purposely and smiled a smile that said, 'I've got a deal for you if you're smart enough to listen.'

Still very much on guard, Slipwalker showed them in.

"I'll say one thing for you, Mr. Slipwalker," Popper said, as he sat down and glanced around a room that looked like the dorm room of a C-minus college student, "You certainly don't waste money on office space. I suppose if you were successful in your suit against us, you might be inclined to upgrade your location. Although, there *is* some benefit to being over a Dunkin' Donuts, especially in the morning, if you haven't had breakfast."

Slipwalker looked like a man who had just discovered he was about to be mugged. "I have a busy schedule this afternoon, so I'd appreciate your getting to the point."

"Of course, my apologies," Popper said solicitously. "Let me begin by thanking you for finding time to meet with us. I realize that a meeting like this is somewhat unconventional in the normal conduct of a lawsuit. However, under circumstances which I'm about to reveal to you, I thought we might be able to save everyone involved, specifically Mrs. Swenson and you in

351

particular, with a good deal of needless expense and aggravation." Popper decided it was time for one of his irritating sidetrack comments. "I don't suppose there's any way we could order up some coffee and a couple of crullers from that Dunkin' Donuts is there?"

Slipwalker was making no effort to mask his irritation. "They don't deliver."

"Of course. I should have known. Too bad, I do like a cruller now and then." Popper looked genuinely disappointed. "Well, maybe we'll get one on our way out. Now, back to what I was saying. As it turns out, there are some circumstances in this case of which you may be unaware. I'm referring to what one can easily surmise to have been a key factor in the accident."

"Like what?" Slipwalker was still suspecting a mugging.

Popper glanced over at Jack, who looked like a man waiting for the magician to pull the rabbit out of his hat.

"Well, according to your complaint, you contend that the suspension system in Verite 300 was faulty and that's what caused the unfortunate spinout and crash. Part of our defense, as I'm sure you've already anticipated, will be that, according to police records, Mr. Swenson was traveling nearly sixty miles-per-hour in a well-marked twenty-five mile-an-hour speed zone."

"Your advertising promotes sports car handling, and that car did not handle like a sports car."

"I'm not prepared to concede that point. However, that advertising does not suggest that one should defy the posted speed limit *and* the laws of physics. However, there is another possible contributing factor that may have to be examined when assessing blame and responsibly. Again, as I said, this is something of which you may not be aware."

From the expression on Slipwalker's face, Popper knew that he had no idea what he was talking about. He also recognized that he had managed to push Slipwalker's patience to the edge. Good, that's what he intended to do.

"You see, Mr. Slipwalker," Popper glanced down at a triangular block with a brass plate on the face reading Abner Slipwalker, Esq. "Might I call you Abner? I'm not keen on standing on formalities in friendly conversations."

"Call me whatever you like but get to the point."

"Of course. Terrible habit of mine, getting distracted as I do. Well, to the point; it appears that the Westchester police, in addition to being diligent, watchful, and efficient, are also discreet. In order to save the victim's survivors from having to endure profound embarrassment, they did not include one rather important fact in their report."

"What are you talking about?" Slipwalker's left eye was twitching.

What a wonderful twitch, Popper thought, purposely staring at it. *It says so much about what's going on in your head, Slipwalker, that you might want to consider sunglasses.* He wanted

Slipwalker to be fully aware that he was aware of the affliction, so he continued to stare at that eye. "It appears ... no, 'appears' is the wrong word. 'Fact' is more accurate. It is fact that when the police found Mr. Swenson and his female companion, his fly was unzipped. All the way. His male member was out of his pants and implanted in the young lady's mouth. The young lady, in turn, must have bitten down hard at the moment of impact with an unfortunate resulting occurrence."

Slipwalker made a sputtering and undisciplined attempt to refute Popper. "That's bullshit!" His twitch became even more pronounced.

"Not in the least, Abner. That, in fact, is the way they were found, and I have three ... no, I'm wrong, four ... very credible Westchester police officers who will, if called to testify, absolutely confirm what I've told you." Popper, of course, had no idea who or how many officers had been on the scene. But consummate liar that he was, he felt confident of his mastery over the lawyer. So much so that he decided to make sure to dispel any doubts Slipwalker might be harboring about the veracity of his claim. "I can, if you like, provide you with the names and contact information of the four officers so that you can include them in your depositions."

Slipwalker looked like a blowup doll that had just acquired a slow leak. He sank back in his chair. Popper imagined that his visions of an office upgrade were vanishing.

"I think you can appreciate that, if you were to pursue the suit against Mr. Poor and my company, there would potentially be two negative outcomes. One for you, and one for us. In your case, we'd find it necessary to embarrass poor Mrs. Swenson, who clearly was burdened enough with a philandering husband. No one wants to bring up blow jobs in court. And of course, you'd look foolish, and God only knows what that would do to your reputation. For our part, we would regard this as a nuisance suit, one that, based on what I've just told you, we would be certain to win. However, suits, whatever their lack of merit, have a way of generating negative publicity. We do not want the Verite 300 to be a punch line in a late-night comic monologue. With all that on the table, I would like, on behalf of my company and Mr. Poor, to propose a cash settlement."

The words "cash settlement" clearly acted like a tonic on Slipwalker. He immediately pulled himself up in his chair.

"In return for a *cash,*" Popper put added emphasis on cash, "settlement, you would have to agree to the following: Your client would have to drop the suit and both you and your client would have to agree, in writing, not to reinstate the suit at any time in the future. Second, and last, the amount of the settlement could not be disclosed to anyone at any time. *Ever.*"

"What kind of money are we talking about?"

Popper could envision Slipwalker already thinking about calling his real estate agent and telling him to start looking.

"I should think that $300,000 is an adequate amount."

Slipwalker smiled like a man who had just found himself in the driver's seat. He shook his head," That wouldn't even pay for the time I've put in. I've got to have at least seven-fifty."

"Four."

"Six."

"Done at half a million. In cash. In ten business days."

Slipwalker hesitated. "Ok, I'll take the five, but you gotta toss in one more thing."

"What's that?" Popper asked.

Slipwalker grinned. "My deal with Mrs. Swenson is forty percent. That's only two hundred grand for me. I'll need a little more incentive to agree to this deal."

"And what kind of incentive are we talking about?" Popper asked, having no idea what to expect.

"I want one of those Verite 300's."

"The car you called a death trap?" Jack injected.

"Hey, I'm not going to be taking corners at sixty with some broad sucking on my dick."

"Well, that's certainly good news for Mrs. Slipwalker," Popper said.

"So is the car in the deal?"

Popper turned to jack, "Jack, can you accommodate Abner?"

"Absolutely. I got a green one on the lot that's got your name on it. Come by tomorrow and we'll do the paperwork."

They all shook hands and Slipwalker opened the door for Jack and Popper and watched them go down the stairs. "Hey, Mr. Poor. What time tomorrow?"

"Any time after nine. Whatever works for you."

"Nine it is," said the happy about-to-be-owner of a green Sally Rand.

As they stepped out on the sidewalk in front of the Dunkin Donut shop, Jack turned to Popper and said. "That was beautiful. Now, the question is, how much are you going to be able to squeeze out of Charlie?"

Popper smiled the smile of a man who has just learned that his ex-wife no longer wanted her alimony. "A lot more than five-hundred thousand. A whole lot more!" He nodded toward the Dunkin' Donut shop. "Want a coffee and cruller? I'll buy."

45
The Scam

Back at the dealership, Popper immediately commandeered Jack's chair, desk, and phone. "You're not here, okay?" he said to Jack, who had opted for the large leather couch. "You can listen in but cover the mouthpiece. Tight." Popper dialed a number, listened for a moment until he heard Emma Rae's voice. "It's Popper; let me talk to Charlie."

"He's been waiting for your call."

Good, Popper thought. He's primed.

"So, did you meet with that lawyer?"

"Just got back."

"And?"

"Well, it's a good news/bad news situation."

"What's the bad news?"

"The bad news is that somehow, he got his hands on our *CEO* report."

"You mean Waddington's *CEO* report?"

"Yes."

"Well, so what? There's nothing in those reports that would cause us any problem. Hell, he usually makes us all look like goddamn geniuses."

"Maybe. But this one seems to be different. The date on it is July 20th."

"That's tomorrow," Charlie said.

"Right. Have you seen it yet?"

"No."

"Well, I had a chance to take a quick look at it while Slipwalker went into one of his partner's offices to call his client."

"And?"

"Charlie, you could strap that *CEO* to a Palestinian terrorist and it would blow him up."

"What the hell are you talking about?"

"I'm saying that I didn't like what I read."

"Which was what?"

"Well, it looked like the same type of information that Axel said was in those engineering safety test results he dropped on your desk. For example, one line I read said something about top management insisting on certain changes in the suspension system to save money, even though those changes had been shown to affect the Verite's driving performance."

"That was in the report?" Charlie asked, sounding both shocked and skeptical at the same time.

Hold on Charlie, Popper said to himself, *I'm just warming up."* "Again, I only had time to read a couple of pages, but what I saw was a whole lot more than should ever be seen by anybody outside the company. Maybe even inside. Slipwalker kept calling it the 'smoking gun' and said it would prove, without doubt, a clear case of purposeful negligence on our part."

"Sonofabitch!" Charlie barked.

"Now let me give you the good news. Jack Poor's lawyer knows this guy and his firm. They're ambulance chasers, pure and simple. Their game is to file a suit, rattle the defendant's cage, make a lot of noise, and then settle before they ever get near a court."

"Maybe we should call his bluff. Let him try and take us to court. Nichols will chew him up."

Ummm, Popper thought, *I better make the jeopardy a little more personal. Charlie needs to feel exposed.* "Ask yourself this: What if Slipwalker should decide that his case against us will be stronger if he gets the Feds to take a look at the *CEO.* If there is even the slightest suggestion that we've covered up a known problem, it's going to be like blood in the water for the sharks at the Justice Department. Those guys can play rough." *And now,* Popper thought, *let's send a rocket up Charlie's ass.* "My question to you is this: If the *CEO* has the same information that Axel had, then your name is all over it. If that's the case, who do you think they will come looking for?" Popper didn't expect an answer, but he paused long enough to give the question time to sink in. "I'm afraid if we don't cut Slipwalker off at the pass, this could get really nasty for the company and, Charlie, for you."

Popper would have sworn that he heard the rocket explode and sweat break out on Charlie's forehead.

"Goddamn it to hell! Where did that asshole get that report? And what the hell is Waddington doing putting that stuff in the *CEO?* This doesn't make sense."

"I asked Slipwalker where he got it, but he just gave me a shit-eating grin and said he had *sources.*"

"Let me be clear on something: Did he actually say anything about turning it over to the Feds?"

"A lot was said, and I remember him mentioning the DOT and maybe some other governmental agency, maybe it was Justice, but I don't remember exactly. Slipwalker is a nut. He rambles all over the place and sometimes you have no idea what he's talking about." *Ummm, let's add a little more instability into the pot.* "I think the guy is psychotic. He's hard to predict. There's no telling what he might do or say."

There was a long pause at Charlie's end. *Good, he's thinking.* Popper smiled to himself.

"You're sure that what you saw was our *CEO* report?"

"No question."

"And it had tomorrow's date on it?"

"Positive."

Popper heard Charlie shout, "Emma Rae, get me Waddington, right now!" he snapped.

Then he said back to Popper, "I want to see this report. I don't believe Waddington could have fucked up like this."

"It's hard for me to believe too. The sooner you get to see a copy, the sooner you'll have an idea of your personal exposure." He put slightly more emphasis on *personal.*

"Shit. That report goes to more than two hundred people in the company and zone offices, plus every member of the board. If what Axel gave me is actually in the *CEO*, Perkins Byrd will cut my balls off."

What a nice bonus that would be, Popper thought. *Of course, it would certainly be disappointing news to a lot of women.*

"Charlie," Popper could hear Emma Rae's voice in the background, "he's gone for the day."

"Well, call him at home."

"He doesn't live there anymore. His secretary tells me that his wife tossed him out. She doesn't know where he's staying."

Again, a long pause on Charlie's end. "Popper, you said you thought this guy Slipwalker was willing to settle."

Jack, his meaty left hand still covering the phone, rolled his eyes in delight. Charlie was playing right into Popper's hands.

"That's his game. In my judgment, a case like this is way over this guy's head." And now, he thought, I'll add a touch more reinforcement. "But, if he decided to get some help from a more experienced team of lawyers, he could probably take the company to the cleaners and send you on a long Federal holiday."

"I don't want to hear that." Charlie snapped reflexively.

A direct hit, Popper realized. *Now it's time to ask for the order.* "Look, the point of my call is to let you know that Slipwalker can be handled. The guy can be bought off and now's the time to do it before he starts showing the 'smoking gun' around. I am absolutely positive that if we offer him the right number, he'll take the money, drop the suit, turn over the *CEO* report, and say, 'thank you very much, goodbye forever.'" He footnoted his comment with a mildly ominous caveat, "*If* the number is right."

"What's the right number?"

Best I not give Charlie a number too fast, Popper decided. "I'm not sure, but I get the feeling he can be bought for a reasonable amount of money."

"Like what's reasonable?"

"Hard to say. I'd have to guess at this point."

"Well, goddamn it, guess!" Popper sensed that Charlie was now fully under his control now.

"Ten million." Popper looked over at Jack and made a face that said, *how about that as a starting place?*

"Ten million! Are you out of your goddamn mind? Ten million?"

Popper quickly supported his number, "Charlie, that's chump change compared to what a jury award could amount to. You know as well as I do that juries like to stick it to corporations, and they love executive blood. Especially when there's a widow involved with kids."

"Swenson had kids?"

"Yeah, Four kids under ten."

Jack waved frantically and mouthed, "He had no kids, none, nada!"

Popper waved him off with a not-to-worry gesture.

"Shit!" Charlie spat.

"Bottom line, Charlie, is that you've got to decide how much it's worth to the company. More importantly, how much is it worth to you to make this guy and his client disappear? I don't see any other option but to settle while we have the chance." Popper decided that he'd said enough. It was time to shut up and let Charlie do the talking.

There was a long pause on Charlie's end of the line before Charlie did any talking. "Do you think this guy will take less? I mean, will he negotiate?"

Yes! He's on the hook! "I think if we offered less and told him he could have it in *cash,* which is what he asked for, we could make a pretty good deal."

"Cash? He wants it in cash?"

"Apparently, he likes cash."

"What's he going to do with cash? Buy drugs? Hide it from the IRS. Leave the country?"

"Maybe all of the above. Hey, he's a lawyer; what can I say?"

"I've got to think about this. And I've got to get a copy of the CEO to see whatthehell Waddington put in it."

"Fortunately, I was able to buy us some time. I got Slipwalker to agree not say or do anything until he heard from us."

"When does he expect you to get back to him?"

"By tomorrow noon."

"That's not a lot of time."

"True, so we've got to move fast. You think about it overnight. Get a copy of the *CEO* and read it. I'm afraid it will scare the shit out of you. Then get back to me with a number you can live with. But remember, it's got to be big enough that we don't insult the guy. The key is to make him happy, so he'll go away. Quietly."

"Goddamn thieving son of a bitch lowlife lawyer! I'd like to shoot the fucker."

Popper couldn't help but add a little wry humor in response. "That's an option, of course, but the penalty is a bit stiff, if you get caught."

There was silence on Charlie's end. Apparently, he didn't appreciate the humor. "Call me tomorrow. I'll let you know what I want to do."

"About ten?"

"Whenever," Charlie said, clearly in a deep funk.

Jack could barely contain himself. He hung up his phone and looked at Popper in utter disbelief.

"Ten million? You're asking Charlie to cough up ten million dollars? Do you think he'll come up with that much?"

"Realistically, ten million in cash would be nearly impossible for him to pull off. He's going to have to find some way to hide it from the French auditors and more importantly, from Perkins Byrd. Perk would never go for this. He'd never authorize a settlement to a guy like Slipwalker. Between you and me, I think if Byrd ever found out that Charlie had rigged those Verite tests, he'd toss him to the wolves. But to your question of how much: I think Charlie can find a way to siphon off about five to six million from the company coffers in one way or another. How he's going to do it without anyone knowing is for him to figure out. But as long as he believes his only choice is between finding the money and going to jail, he'll find the money."

"For my part, I'd be more than happy with five million," Jack said. "That would leave us four-point-five to split after we paid off Slipwalker."

"Not a bad payday."

"With what I've managed to put away from our rental deals and along with the money I've skimmed from the dealership, I'll have just short of four million. You know what that does for me?"

"What?"

"It buys me a first-class ticket out of here. No more Petula or Greenwich assholes or Charlie Fairs or green Sally Rands. Fuckin' bee-you-tee-full!"

46
Waiting for the Call

On Tuesday night, after the building had emptied out, Waddington wrote a cover note for the copy of the CEO that he was about to leave on Charlie's desk.

I would like you to review this. Then we should talk before I release all two hundred six copies for distribution. As you'll see, I've included all the recommendations from Safety Engineering that the Verite 300 be recalled and certain modifications be made to the rear suspension. I believe that each of us company employees have an obligation to consider the welfare and safety of our customers above all else. I'm sure you'll agree and will see the benefits to the customers, the company, and to yourself in issuing a recall.

Preston Waddington

Next morning, he got to the office just after 8:00 and began to mentally prepare himself for dealing with the tirade he was sure would rain down on him within the next couple hours. Doreen arrived at 8:30. He told her that he would accept only one call and that was from Charlie.

Waddington was fully convinced that his was a righteous cause. It was the moral and ethical thing to do. It would demonstrate to customers and would-be customers that the company had a sense of corporate responsibly.

10 a.m. Still no call from upstairs. He picked up the phone to be sure it was working. Waddington decided to call Axel and tell him Pandora's box was open and on Charlie's desk.

After they'd speculated on how Charlie would react, Axel said, "If you're successful, and he does issue the recall, I'm betting he'll find a way to come out of this looking like Mr. Charles Ethical Fair, a CEO more interested in the safety and satisfaction of his customers than he is in making a profit. God, by the time he and his PR department get through, he'll be made to look like the Jesus Christ of the car industry. The bastard should be breaking rocks."

"Maybe, but the important thing is the recall. If that happens, then at least we'll have a moral victory, even if it means I'm looking for work tomorrow."

"Charlie won't fire you."

"You don't think so?"

"No way. You know that axiom in the Godfather movie? 'Keep your friends close, but your enemies closer.' He's going to want to keep you very close."

"Well, if you're wrong and he fires me, it might be just what I need to motivate me to do something worthwhile with my life. Up to this point, it's added up to a big fat zero."

"I disagree with you on that score. You've done a hell of a job for the company against some pretty miserable odds and with some lousy products."

"Maybe, but it still only totals zero. I've come to look at this as a turning point in my life. I'm actually looking forward to seeing how it plays out."

"You're a good man, Charlie Brown. Let me know what happens or if there's anything I can do from here behind Mary's skirts."

"Hey, enough of that."

"I'm proud of you, Pres. I really am. But. I'm embarrassed for myself. I folded when I should have taken Charlie on."

"You had no choice. Mary had to come first."

There was a long reflective pause, "Ummm, I wonder. I guess I'll always wonder. Good luck," he said as he hung up.

At noon Doreen stuck her head in the cubical opening. "You want me to bring you something from the cafeteria?"

Waddington shook his head, "No, thanks. I'm not all that hungry. You're sure there's nothing wrong with the phones?"

She shook her head, "I checked. Again."

The afternoon dragged on like winter in Detroit. It seemed to refuse to come to an end. No call. Not a word. After Doreen returned from lunch, he asked her to do a little reconnoitering for him and check to see if Charlie had even come to work. She reported that he'd been seen entering his office just before eight, but no one had seen him leave.

"One of the girls that works upstairs told me that Emma Rae has been running in and out of his office all morning and looks frantic."

Waddington stayed at his desk until seven and then called Olivia.

"What happened?" she asked.

"Nothing. Absolutely nothing. I didn't even get a call."

"Do you think he saw the report?"

"If he sat down at his desk, there is no way he could have missed it."

"Emma Rae called me about noon to say that Charlie had scheduled some late meetings and planned to stay in the company suite at the Hyatt tonight, so something is going on."

"But what? Maybe he's waiting for the man with the ax to show up. I'm going back to my wonderful room at the Motel 6 overlooking the used car lot and revise my resignation speech. How about if I begin with 'Tis a far, far better thing I do than I have ever done?'"

She laughed briefly. "I don't know if I see you in the Sydney Carton part."

"Besides, Charlie prefers an ax to either the gallows or the guillotine." He laughed. "Why am I laughing?" He answered his own question. "I guess I'm laughing because of something my father told me a long time ago."

"What was that?"

"If you want to survive in business, you've got to keep a low profile. Somehow, I don't think this qualifies as keeping a low profile."

"I want to be with you tonight," she said in a way that left no doubt how much she wanted him.

"And I'd like to have you with me. But not in the Bide-a-Wee Motel. Anyway, I wouldn't be much company tonight."

"I understand. But call me later, okay?"

"Count on it."

47
Holding the Bag

Charlie Fair found the *Company Eyes Only* on his desk, glanced at Waddington's note, and read several pages. He wasn't mad. He was scared. Visions of sleep-away-camp pummeled him. His stomach and chest suddenly became one large knot of panic. If this information got out, if it was discovered that he had okayed the Verite suspension downgrade after his own people had proclaimed it unsafe in curves at higher speeds, he would be dead. The very least that could happen was that he'd lose his job, his pension, and his golden parachute. The worst was something he didn't want to even contemplate. He fought back images of being led out of the office in handcuffs, of the perp walk, of the trial, and of facing a jury of ex-employees who would enjoy nothing more than seeing him put him away. A goddamned nightmare!

Suddenly, every cell in his brain was focused on a single, overriding objective. He had to find some way to save himself. The *Titanic* might be sinking, but he sure as hell was going to get himself into a lifeboat.

But first the questions: *What the hell was Waddington up to? I wonder if that bastard knows that what he's doing is blackmail, extortion even? He has to know. But what's his take out of this? If I issue the recall, what's he get? Nothing. Nada.*

Zippo! Am I missing something here? He half expected the walls of the empty room to answer him.

Charlie reread Waddington's note and focused on the line "before I release it for distribution." If that meant what he presumed it meant, then there was a chance he could escape without any damage. Still, he'd need a plan to deal with Waddington. Charlie turned around to his credenza and pulled out the last black book in his line-up of black books in which he kept the sins, failures, and transgressions of all his employees. "Let's see what I've got on that sonofabitch. He paged down to the W's and then slammed it shut. Nothing! Not a goddamn thing. His name isn't even in here. I wonder if Spar knows if he's screwing his secretary. Then he remembered what Doreen Walfish looked like. "Oh, God, she's a pig. He'd have to be in a pretty bad way to be dickin' that. There's got to be something."

The intercom buzzed.

"Yeah."

"It's Popper on two," Emma Rae said.

"Tell him I'll call him back in fifteen minutes."

Let me focus on the lawsuit for a moment, he thought. *What are my options with Slipwalker? Damn! If that lawyer has a copy of the CEO, then I haven't got any options. I've got to settle with him. If Popper is right and he'll take less, a lot less than the ten million, say five or six, I can make him go away. The only problem will be to get the money out of the company."*

373

Emma Rae came in for her morning grope and was met with a sharp reprimand for not knocking, not that she ever had. "Get your tail out to your desk and glue it down. Don't so much as leave to take a pee. I'm going to need you so stay put."

"Do you want to tell me what's wrong, Charlie?"

"No, I don't want to tell you what's wrong," he snapped. "Do what I tell you and close the door."

The conversation with himself, asking questions, weighing various strategies and alternatives took almost half an hour. Slowly an idea began to crystallize, take shape, and evolve into a plan. He'd need Harvey Nichols and Norton Brewster from purchasing to help him pull it off. They could be trusted because he had enough on both of them in his black books to keep them loyal and quiet. Charlie picked up the phone.

"Emma Rae, tell Nichols and Brewster that I need to see them in my office, like ten minutes ago. Then call Popper back."

Charlie looked down at the *CEO*. Edited by Preston Waddington, it read. He began to smile. *This will work*, he thought. *Not only will it save my ass, but I will also come out of this smelling like a rose. If something should go wrong, I'll still be okay, because I won't be the one left holding the bag. Waddington will.*

48
3, 7, 4, 6, 5

Emma Rae returned the call to Popper. "He's really in a terrible mood," she spoke in a low voice into the phone so as not to be overheard. "Something happened this morning, but I don't know what. He's really having a bad day."

Popper smiled and mouthed the words, "Thank you Preston Waddington; you did your job extremely well."

Emma Rae continued to rattle on, offering no information of further value to Popper. When she stopped to take a breath, he broke in and said, "Well, put him on and let's see what I can do to *make* his day." *Make his day miserable*, he added silently.

Charlie picked up the phone, dispensing with even a basic greeting. "We're going to settle with this guy. There's no other option, considering ..." He left the thought hanging.

"Okay."

"But ten million is out of the fucking question. I don't care what it takes; break his goddamn knees for all I care, but you've got to get him to settle for three million. And the bastard can have it in cash." Popper heard what sounded like an abortive laugh followed by, "then I'll tip off the IRS, because sure as hell he doesn't plan to report it."

"Three is going to be tough. Really tough. I think we want a decision from this guy today. The longer he has to dig into that *CEO*, the more likely he is to discover that he's got a load of dynamite that could be worth tens of millions. If he figures that out, you can guess what he's going to tell us we can do with our three million. My recommendation is we offer seven."

"Screw seven. Break his balls and tell him we'll give him four."

"And if he won't go lower than six?"

"Tell him five is it. In cash. That's as high as I'll go. If he won't accept that, tell him to sue."

"Okay. Five it is. I think I know how to get him to agree to that. He's got some dirty laundry in his closet. I'm sure when Slipwalker finds out what I know about a certain incident with two underage young ladies, he'll take the money and run." *God, I sound convincing*, he thought.

"He damn well better."

"Trust me, Charlie. The settlement is a done deal. You can go to the bank on that." *Or more accurately*, he thought, *I can go to the bank*. Popper was like the painter who was about to give the last stroke to his masterpiece. "Have Harvey draw up whatever agreement we need for Slipwalker and Mrs. Swenson to sign. Get me the money and I'll have this wrapped up by the end of the week."

"I'll need more time. I can't make it happen that fast. I'll need at least two weeks."

"That long?"

"Popper, I don't have five million in cash lying around the office. I can't just go down to the bank and cash a check. I've got to get this out of the company without the French audit committee knowing where it went. But that's not your concern."

The hell it's not, Popper thought.

"All you need to know is that the money will be available in about two weeks. Now, I expect you to make sure that Slipwalker understands that the settlement means he drops the suit and delivers every file, every document, and the *CEO* reports to you before you hand over the cash. One other thing, no one is to ever know the amount we paid."

Popper almost laughed into the mouthpiece. "Slipwalker fully understands that. Don't worry; he may be a shyster lawyer, but he understands how the game is played."

"Okay. I'll let you know when we have the money."

"In cash."

"Yes, in U.S. cash!" Charlie barked back, making no effort to hide his pique as he hung up.

Popper sprang out of the chair and rushed over to Jack and gave him a high five. "In two weeks, Mr. Poor, your name will be Mr. Rich. We'll be spitting four point five million. It's not going to put us in a class with the Rockefellers, but it's sure a lot better than a sharp stick in the eye."

Jack roared. "It sounds fuckin' good to me."

49
Sandbagged

Thursday lasted a week and Friday was closing in on a month, or so it seemed to Waddington. He sat in his office and tried to do some work on the preparation for the Le Vent introduction at the dealer meeting. He accomplished little. Finally, just after two on Friday afternoon, the phone rang. He expected to hear Emma Rae's voice. But it was Charlie. Waddington braced himself for a torrent of rants and a string of expletives. But there were none. Nor was there a telltale angry edge to Charlie's voice, no latent vitriol boiling beneath the surface, waiting for the right moment to erupt.

"It's Charlie, Pres. I've reviewed your *CEO* for this month. Your note suggested we talk before you release it for distribution. Could you maybe come up now?"

Waddington couldn't believe it. For a moment, he wondered if it was actually Charlie on the phone asking calmly, politely, "Could you maybe come up now?" Charlie never asked anybody to do anything. He demanded. Where was his more typical, "Your ass had better be up here ten minutes ago"? What kind of game was he playing? Was this some type of ploy? Or maybe, just maybe, Waddington surmised, Charlie realizes that I haven't given him any options. I've got him sandbagged and he knows it.

As Waddington stepped off on the executive floor, he would not have been surprised to have been met by Harry Spar and a couple of kneecap crushers. But there was no one to greet him other than Emma Rae, who never looked up and only tossed her head in the direction of Charlie's door. Waddington interpreted this as an indication that he was to go right in. And he did.

Charlie was sitting on his couch. His suit coat hung over a chair next to a small conference table. He was puffing on a cigar and holding a coffee cup in his hand. He looked more like a college professor ready to discuss the inner meaning of Walden Pond. Waddington quickly glanced around the room, almost as if he expected hooded ninjas to begin an attack at any moment.

"Have a seat." Charlie gestured to a chair at the end of the coffee table that was supporting his feet. Waddington noticed that the copy of the *CEO* was by Charlie's side. Once Waddington had seated himself, Charlie picked up the report, casually, as though he had no intention of giving it any more of his attention.

"You really sandbagged me with this." He nodded toward the *CEO*.

At least Charlie had the sandbagging part right.

"I gather you took up Axel's flag after he left us and decided to run with it yourself. I must say that your use of the *CEO* to support your argument was a little more persuasive than his." Charlie tossed the report on the coffee table with the kind of casual flip one discards an old magazine in a dentist's waiting room. "There are some who might suggest that what you've done here would come under the heading of extortion."

Waddington was about to argue the word *extortion*, but then, that's exactly what he had called it. It just sounded different coming from Charlie's mouth. "I would hope that you'd regard it as encouragement to do the right thing."

"I have told legal and PR to draft a recall letter and to start mailing to Verite owners next week."

The announcement caught Waddington totally by surprise. This was very un-Charlie. Waddington wondered if his apparent cave-in on the recall was not part of some more nefarious strategy. Charlie was not the kind of man to concede a victory without intending some form of retaliation.

Waddington felt compelled to say something, anything, to at least acknowledge Charlie's decision. "I think your decision is a good one for both our customers and the company."

"Tell me, Pres, do you see yourself as a sort of Ralph Nader?"

"Hardly," Waddington answered. "I like to think of myself as a company man. But a company man who believes that we have certain responsibilities that should never be compromised. I don't want to see us make the same kind of mistake other companies have made trying to cover up product defects. To me, it comes down to corporate ethics."

"Expensive word, *ethics*," Charlie said coldly.

For a brief moment, Waddington thought about rebutting, but immediately concluded there was nothing to be gained by debating morality and ethics with Charlie. Instead, he decided to toss Charlie a bone. "I think a recall shows a lot of leadership and willingness on your part to make the tough decisions. If PR spins it right, you might earn a lot of respect from the press."

"I can promise you that PR is busy spinning as we speak. I'm not going to take a hit on this. Which brings me to some questions I'd like to have answered. First, how many copies of this *CEO* are floating around the company?"

"That's the only copy."

"Where are the rest?"

"Locked away. Once the recall notifications are in the mail, they'll be in the incinerator."

Do I take that to mean you don't believe I've actually authorized the recall?"

Charlie seemed to have removed one of the sandbags and placed it in front of Waddington. He couldn't very well tell Charlie that he didn't trust him. Especially since Charlie had, at least until now, shown no overt animosity or inclination to put up a fight. Waddington had no choice but to give on the point. "If you say you have, then I believe you."

"You realize, of course, you were taking a major gamble by publishing this information."

Waddington started to say something in his defense but decided to against it.

"This report, if it got in the wrong hands, like say the <u>Free Press</u> or some cable TV show, could have done a lot of damage. And not just to me. It doesn't take much for some asshole looking for a

Pulitzer to blow something like this all out of proportion. One little rock allowed to roll down a mountain could start an avalanche. Tip over one domino and they all fall. Start a small campfire in a windstorm and the whole woods could burn down."

The man is a fount of platitudes, Waddington thought.

"If the <u>Free Press</u> or a national cable show had gotten hold of the *CEO,* they'd have shit all over us. Considering our financial position, it wouldn't take much to topple us into the toilet. If that were to happen, it could easily cost thousands of people their Friday paychecks. You might have found them wondering if your need to demonstrate a sense of *ethics* was worth their having to spend weeks standing in line at the unemployment office. No telling what the nice folks from the UAW would have said, or *done,*" he said, ominously.

Waddington had the feeling that Charlie had moved another sandbag to his side of the coffee table. He decided to mount a defense. "As I see it, we ... and you ... were taking a much bigger risk by doing nothing."

Charlie gave no indication of wanting to refute Waddington's argument. He took his feet off the coffee table and set the coffee cup on top of the *CEO.* After a moment, he looked up at Waddington and said, "If, as you say, this is the only copy of the *CEO* that's not locked up, explain, if you will, how the lawyer representing Mrs. Swenson appears to have his very own copy of this very same report."

"What? Are you sure?" Waddington felt as if he'd just been mugged in a dark alley.

"Popper saw it."

"That's not possible."

"Apparently it is," Charlie said with the demeanor of a prosecuting attorney who had just destroyed the defendant's alibi. "Popper had a meeting with Slipwalker in Slipwalker's office and saw a copy of this *CEO*. Popper was able to read some of it. No, there's no doubt in my mind or his that somehow Slipwalker managed to get his hands on this. And that, I don't think I need point out, represents a major problem for us."

"There's something wrong here," Waddington said suspiciously.

"Yes, you bet there is, and that something is probably named Axel McPherson."

"No. No way." Waddington shook his head with conviction.

"It has to be him. He's pissed. At me. At the company. He was mad that I wouldn't recall the Verite. Who else would have any reason to give Slipwalker a copy? Of course, that begs another question. Where did he get a copy of your *CEO*? Has he been in the office in the last week or so? Maybe he dropped in to say hello? Maybe he saw a copy on your desk and decided to help himself. Maybe you were out of your office for a few minutes or maybe you thought he might like to see how you were going to stick it to Charlie Fair. What do you think?"

Waddington saw it now, the seemingly docile, amenable, 'you've got me sandbagged' Charlie

Fair was slowly moving the sandbags one by one to Waddington's side of the table.

"I haven't seen Axel in a couple weeks. And I'm sure he's not been back to the building. If I recall company policy correctly, *your* policy, once someone leaves the company, they don't get back in without a pass. Check security. They keep logs of visitors. See if he's been here."

"I already have."

"And?"

"No record of him having been here. But then nobody checks what you carry out in your briefcase at night, do they?"

Waddington realized that Charlie's relaxed, calm, 'you've won' attitude was just a ploy. He thought he could hear someone putting the ax to the grindstone in the next room.

"I did not give Axel a copy of the *CEO*," Waddington said firmly, showing just a tinge of anger.

"If you say you didn't, then I have to take your word for it until or unless events prove differently. But know that sooner or later, I will find out how Slipwalker got a copy. Right now, my only interest is getting it back. And that's going to cost me five million dollars."

"Five million dollars? What are you talking about?"

"That's what an out-of-court settlement with Slipwalker and Mrs. Swenson is going to cost the company. For five million, he drops the suit, turns over any and all documents, including your *CEO,* and disappears back down the hole he crawled out of."

"You may not believe me, Charlie, but I contend there is no way Slipwalker could have gotten his hands on a *CEO*. I didn't even have a final draft until sometime last week."

"Again, how he got the report isn't important right now. Getting it back *is*."

Because, Waddington thought, *it's your ticket for a long stay in a small space.*

"If we're going to do the 'ethical thing,' and at the same time, protect the jobs of our employees, we have to handle this very, very carefully."

"If you get the *CEO* back and he drops the suit, you're out of the woods."

"True, but there's a slight problem."

"Me. You want me to disappear." Waddington realized that he'd jumped too fast. That was a mistake. Another sandbag landed on his side of the table.

"Oh, no. You're not going to get off that easy. You and your sense of company ethics got this ball rolling. Now you're going to have to help me bring it to a stop."

"What are you talking about?"

"Let me be completely honest with you."

Waddington translated that as, "Let me be somewhat honest with you, but not completely."

"Let's start with objectives. You want the recall because you're concerned about the safety of our customers."

"And the integrity of the company."

"Agreed. In addition, I am sure you don't want to do anything that would knock over the dominos and lead to our going out of business and costing 30,000 innocent, hard-working people with families to feed their jobs."

God, he sounded like a politician talking about working families when he had no idea what the term even meant. "You're right. I don't want to hurt the company or the employees."

"Okay. All of those objectives depend on getting the recall out before Slipwalker decides to hand over his copy of the *CEO* to the media. Whatever wrongs we might have committed in the past have to be buried now in order for us to move on and become, in your words, more ethical. Agreed?"

Waddington nodded.

"Let's add a reality check. The agreement with the French is a done deal. All they have to do is sign and put their money in our bank. The plan is for the head Bull Frog to come to Detroit for the dealer meeting and the Le Vent announcement. The formal signing will take place just before the meeting so that we can announce it to the dealers. In the meantime, the audit frogs are watching every penny we spend. Hell, they even cut out all first-class travel for the entire executive staff."

"But didn't you rent a Gulfstream to fly to Vegas?"

"I did. But they said, "No First Class." No one said I couldn't rent a jet. But that's neither here nor there. What I'm trying to tell you is that if I were to authorize a check to Slipwalker for five million, the French would be all over me like rain. I know those bastards; I've been watching them work for the last nine months. They'd start digging and, sure as hell, they'd get their hands on the *CEO,* and my ass would be hanging out to dry in no time. Good-bye any chance of putting past mistakes to rest."

One of the sandbags back went back to Charlie's side.

"But guess what? I'm not going to let that happen. Which means, I've got to find some way to get five million dollars out of the company, in small increments. I've got to make the five million look like a legitimate operating expense."

Waddington suddenly felt like a man in a dark alley who expected to be mugged at any moment.

"Because your *CEO* is, at least partially, responsible for our being held hostage by this shylock, I need your help with that ambulance chaser being paid off."

"Sorry, Charlie, but I don't think my checkbook will handle five million. At least not this month."

"But your *new* department's budget will."

"Excuse me?"

"As of today, you have been promoted to a Vice President."

The mugger just hit him in the head.

"Your new title is Vice President of Dealer and Customer Relations. Your job is to make us *The Ethical Car Company*. Hey, I like the sound of that."

"You're promoting me to Vice President?"

"That's what I said. Your new job has an initial budget of five million dollars. It just so happens that you've already contracted for the services of ... I think it's seven different consultants and suppliers who exist only as names on bank accounts. You'll find their invoices on your desk Monday morning. Oh, by the way, we won't be able to move your office right away. In fact, it may never be moved because I don't expect you to give up your current responsibilities. That dealer show has got to be great. But first things first. Monday morning you're going to sign those invoices. The payments will be made to the bogus suppliers, then immediately converted to cash and given to Popper so that he can deliver the five million to Slipwalker."

Waddington couldn't believe what he'd just heard. "I'm the ethical VP and my first order of business is to scam the company out of five million dollars? Is that what you're asking me to do?"

"I don't see this as a scam. It's just another cost of doing business. There are out-of-court settlements every week in virtually every industry. Hell, if we weren't wrapping up our deal with the French, I'd just authorize the money and be done with it. What you need to keep in mind is that this little subterfuge of ours will make it possible for you and me to protect all those poor, up-to-their-eyeballs-in-debt employees busting their butts to feed their families."

"And if I should refuse?"

"Then you explain it to your fellow employees, especially the ones with the hungry kids, why they're standing in the unemployment line. You explain to them that they lost their jobs because of your sense of ethics. You make them understand why they can't afford to buy a six-pack of beer." Charlie's frustration was growing. "What's your problem, here? I'm not asking you to do anything illegal."

"Paying money on fake invoices to companies that don't exist is not illegal?"

"Not from where I sit. Anyway, that's not for you to worry about. Nichols and Brewster in purchasing will handle all the sticky parts. All you have to do is sign the invoices and ...

"... and keep my mouth shut."

"That and be the guy who can one day look back and say he helped save this company and the jobs of all those miserable working families. The only alternative is for us to hire someone to break into Slipwalker's office, steal the *CEO,* and then kill the bastard. But somehow that option doesn't seem to measure up to what I presume are your high standards of corporate ethics. Look, I'm issuing the recall. I'm giving you what you want and at the same time doing my goddamn best not to let this Verite thing put the company in the tank. I don't think it's too much to ask for you to help out. Are you a player, Pres? Can I count on you? Or should I just get the pink slips ready to send out?"

Waddington suddenly realized that Charlie had managed to move all the sandbags onto his side of the table and stacked them up to his eyeballs.

50
Object Lesson

An hour later, Charlie walked into Harvey Nichols's office and closed the door.

"Did he go for it?" Harvey asked.

"He's on board. Mr. Waddington is now our Vice President of Dealer and Customer Satisfaction."

"You're sure it was a good idea giving him a promotion instead of canning his ass?"

"Oh, quite sure. I want him close. I want to have him really close. At least until the suit is dropped and I get my hands on Slipwalker's copy of the *CEO*. Once that's behind us, I may have to re-evaluate our headcount and reduce it by a grand total of one. But then, maybe it would be best just to keep him boxed up here, looking very ethical."

"Ethical?" Nichols asked quizzically.

"Private joke," Charlie answered. "I presume you've taken care of things on your end?"

"Absolutely. Mission all but accomplished. I set up seven Limited Liability Corporations who are billing us for their services as we speak. I must say, I was very creative in writing the invoices and contracts. I almost convinced myself that they were real. Anyway, the invoices will be ready for Waddington's signature Monday morning. Brewster is ready to cut the checks. He'll spread them out over a week so as not to raise any red flags. We should have all the cash ready to go in no less than ten days, just as you asked."

"Good work. One last question: If any of this should go south on us and a frog discovers that five million dollars has gone to bogus corporations, are we covered?"

"They won't find our fingerprints on any of it. On the other hand, if there is a problem, our friend Waddington will find himself trying to explain why he has authorized a total of five million in payments to seven different companies, all of which bear his name as the sole proprietor. I think they call that embezzlement. Naturally, if that were to happen, you and I would be shocked, horrified, and gravely troubled that such a fine employee should have attempted to bilk the corporation."

Charlie's smile was smug and reeked of satisfaction. "You know, Harvey, it's a shame we can't tell anyone about this. It would be a good object lesson for all of our managers."

"Object lesson? Meaning?"

"Nobody, but nobody, tries to screw Charlie Fair and gets away with it."

"Unless her name is Emma Rae Gooh," Harvey broke into a throaty laugh that lasted but an instant when the shocked look on Charlie's face brought it to an abrupt halt. He had forgotten, like Emma Rae, Charlie had no idea that *everyone knew.*

51
A Bad Feeling

At three o'clock on a Saturday afternoon, Gabe's diner was not the kind of place lovers would normally choose for a rendezvous, unless they wanted to be absolutely sure that no one would recognize them. In that regard, Gabe's served its purpose well for Olivia and Waddington.

"I'm sorry Olivia. This was a dumb suggestion for a meeting place. I don't know what I was thinking."

"You were thinking," she said playfully, while glancing around at the tired surroundings, "that Olivia Fair has lived a far too sheltered life and needs to experience a restaurant with a more humbling quality about it."

"Humbling is good word," he said, picking up on her light banter. "I just hope we're both not humbled with an attack of who-knows-what when we discover that it hasn't passed the board of health inspection." To support his concern, he held up a water glass that appeared to have bypassed the dishwasher.

"You're assuming that the board of health has the courage to inspect this place."

It had been a week and a day since Charlie had successfully committed Waddington to help relieve the company coffers of five million dollars. He had explained every detail of Charlie's plan, at least that of which he was aware, to Olivia during several phone conversations. She had expressed her concern more than once and suggested they meet and talk about it before he carried out his part of the scheme. But the press of preparations for the dealer meeting and the Le Vent announcement show had kept him at his desk or in meetings with the show producer, Tom Thomas. Waddington finally was able to get away for several hours on Saturday.

"You know," he said, "I'm not all that accomplished when it comes to affairs, but if we're having one, I think we're doing something wrong."

She reached over and took his hand. "Once I'm free, and that should be very soon, we won't need to meet in," she paused as she looked around and began to laugh, "places like Gabe's."

"Speaking of 'free,' what did your lawyers say?"

"They've checked the prenuptial agreement my father had Charlie sign and assured me he has no right to anything more than what he has personally earned." Olivia sighed. There was a look of finality about her. "Now, all I have to do is tell him it's over."

"I don't imagine that will be easy. I guess you'll want to wait for the right moment."

Olivia looked at her watch. "The right moment will be about three o'clock this afternoon. I'm going to tell him as soon as I get home."

"Would you like me to be with you?"

"I'd love to have you with me, but I have to do this on my own. It will be hard enough for him

393

to believe that I'm serious about divorcing him. I think he'd become apoplectic if I introduced you as the new man in my life. " She smiled and took his hand, "We'll save that surprise for later."

Waddington could not contain a short laugh of disbelief. "A year ago, I was a virtual nobody to Charlie Fair. Now, I'm the guy who's blackmailed him into issuing a recall on our bestselling car, and I'm also the guy who is about to run off with his wife. That news just might motivate him to start thinking seriously about bodily dismemberment. Mine."

She made no effort to hide her concern. "I just hope one day you don't come to regret all this."

"Not a chance. Forcing him into making the recall was the right thing, even if it took a little extortion on my part. And I could never have any regrets about loving you. My only concern is how Charlie is going to react when you tell him. He's not going to want to lose you."

She shook her head, "A divorce will be a major blow to his ego, but he'll get over losing me in no time at all. What he won't get over any time soon is the loss of the house, the end of his lavish parties in our gardens, and most of all, the business leverage our marriage gave him with my father."

"I'd say this has not been a good week for Charlie Fair. And things don't look to get much better any time soon. Even assuming his five-million-dollar scam nets him the settlement and he gets his hands on Slipwalker's copy of the *CEO*, Charlie's still going to have to face a bunch of dealers out for his blood. Recalls don't make them happy. And one more thing: Can you imagine what Grosse Pointe society will do to him once they learn he's been tossed out of the house?"

"I hadn't thought about that." A bemused smile crossed her face. "The gossips will have a feeding frenzy. It will be *interesting*." She glanced at the menu for a moment then looked up at Waddington. "There's just one thing that concerns me. Well, actually, there are a number of things that concern me, but one in particular."

"Which is?"

"Charlie is nothing, if not vindictive. He does not like being one-upped or backed into a corner and you managed to do both by using your CEO report to force a recall. I am sure that he will try to retaliate. For all you know, this business of the lawyer having a copy of your CEO could be a setup of some kind."

"The thought has crossed my mind. As I told you, I can think of no possible way Slipwalker could have gotten a copy of the report."

"Popper is sure he saw it on the lawyer's desk?"

"That's what he told Charlie."

"Could he have been lying?"

"Maybe, but why? How would that benefit him?"

She shook her head. "I don't know, but I don't like it."

"I'll tell you something else I don't like. My signature is on five million dollars of bogus invoices."

"You should have refused to sign them."

"But how? Charlie had me between a rock and a hard place. If the Verite cover-up got out, it could potentially bring down the company. Like it or not, I'm the one that ended up with his thumb in the dike. If I'd pulled it out, a lot of people could very well have found themselves out of work."

"You're right. He gave you no choice."

"That's how I rationalized agreeing to go along with his plan."

A cloud of foreboding passed over Olivia's face. "I have a bad feeling about this. A very bad feeling."

52
A Tub for Two

Charlie's smile had begun at the eighteenth green and was still frozen on his face as he drove into his garage. A 72! A par, goddamn it. His drives split the fairways; he reached all but two greens in regulation, and his putts had eyes. Fuckin' eyes. Never in thirty years had he had such a day on the golf course.

To make things even better, he had cleaned the clocks of his foursome for $500. Life was good. *Very* good. Not only on the golf course, but at the office as well. Waddington had destroyed all the copies of the *CEO*, and checks had been written for the bogus invoices. Nichols had assured him that all five million would be converted to cash and packed into two suitcases, ready for delivery sometime in the coming week.

Early reports from the long lead press preview indicated that the Le Vent was going to be a hit. The only downside was the Verite 300 recall. But events were turning out to work in his favor. Harry Spar had come up with a way to blame the decision to cheapen the suspension on Axel McPherson. The press release read:

> It became necessary to terminate Axel McPherson when it was revealed by associates that McPherson was responsible for preventing the safety engineering reports from reaching President Fair. Mr. Fair notes that he

would have acted upon it immediately had he been informed. "The company cannot tolerate such behavior," the President said.

`The fact that Axel was VP of Sales and was in not in any way responsible for reports coming out of safety engineering did not seem to be questioned by the press. And why would they care? All they were likely to remember was that some guy with a name like a shock absorber had been responsible for not passing on the information to the President and CEO. Yes, Charlie decided, he was home free. And talk about lucky timing: On the day the story was released to the press, GM announced a recall of its own on 1.7 million vehicles. Daimler Chrysler reported record losses and some rock star claimed most of the space above the fold of the business section detailing how he was suing Viacom for one hundred million.

The Verite recall rated only a brief mention on the third page of the business section and barely created a blip in the stock price. By the next day, it was old news. By the third, history. Now, Charlie only had the dealers to pacify. The dealer council had contacted him and raised holy hell over the recall. He would have to throw them a bone during his speech at the dealers meeting. God, they were a pathetic bunch. But he was confident he'd figure out a way to placate them. Yes, everything was under control. And he'd finally shot a 72. *Damn! I've got to frame this scorecard,* he thought.

As he entered his house from the garage, he found Flaubert in the kitchen having a cup of coffee. "Is Mrs. Fair here?" He asked.

"No, sir, she went out about eleven. I imagine she'll be home around five."

"Five?" He looked at his watch. Three hours. His eyes drifted up in the direction of the maid's quarters. A French massage would be a proper reward for his triumph on the golf course.

"Hello, Jeanette," Charlie said as he opened her bathroom door and found her up to her neck in fluffy bubbles. *Good grief*, he thought, *the woman seems to spend most of her time in the bathtub. She might not be more than an average housekeeper, but she certainly kept herself clean.*

"Monsieur Fair. Have you come up to visit Jeanette?"

"You could say that."

"It has been some weeks since you visit me. I thought you might be visiting Monique."

"No, I came to see you."

"She is a tart, you know?"

"Who? Monique?"

"She sleeps with the new gardener."

"She does?" Charlie found the idea of Monique rolling in one of the flowerbeds with the gardener very funny.

"No class, that one."

"And who do you sleep with?"

"I sleep alone," she said tossing her head defiantly.

"Have you got room in there for me?" He knew, of course, that she would not refuse him.

"You are the master. You can do what you want."

"I want what you want."

"Well, I suppose I would like you to join me." She sat up so that her breasts were above the bubble line.

Charlie needed no further invitation. He quickly undressed, carefully hanging his slacks and polo shirt on a towel rack and slipped into the tub.

"Ah, the water is perfect. The same as your body temperature, I presume."

"You had a nice golf game?"

"I had a spectacular golf game, thank you. And I can think of no better reward for having played so well than spending an hour or two with you."

"Two hours in the tub?"

"No, five minutes here, two hours in your bed."

Suddenly Jeanette's face turned ashen and she sank quickly below the bubbles.

"Well, don't we look comfortable."

"Olivia!" Charlie briefly considered joining Jeannette under the cover of the bubbles. His only practical option was to immediately begin to mount his defense with a denial, "This is not what it looks like."

"No? Well, let's see, what does it look like? Maybe it looks like you're here because your tub is not working, and I know how you love bubble baths. Or maybe it looks like this tub for two is part of your effort to conserve water. Or could it look like something else?"

"You've got this all wrong. I was coming up for a massage and … well, I hadn't taken a shower after golf." *God that sounded lame*, he thought.

"And you wanted to be extra clean for Jeanette. How considerate." She stared at the end of the tub where Jeanette had remained submerged.

"Do you think she plans to surface again? Or should we just let her drown?"

Suddenly a gasping French truffle broke the surface and, in what seemed to be one unbroken motion, jumped out of the tub, grabbed a towel, and ran from the bathroom.

"I don't think this was in her job description. Or is this something new you've added to her duties?"

Charlie started to pull himself out of the tub. "Please, Charlie, don't get out on my account. But do plan to get out of the house on my account in the next two hours. And you can take Jeannette with you. Tomorrow you may call with the address of where you'll be staying. Flaubert will see to it that all your clothes and personal items are delivered there."

"What are you talking about?"

"I'm talking about divorce. You'll be getting the papers at your new address from my lawyer on Monday."

"Olivia. You're upset. Let's talk about this after you've calmed down."

"Talk? Well, that would be a new dimension in our relationship. If one could call it that. No, Charlie, I've been planning this for some time. Any reservations I might have had about throwing you out will follow those bubbles down the drain."

"I'm your husband. You can't just throw me out."

"I don't intend to throw you anywhere. You will walk out under your own power or I'll have the sheriff help you leave."

"Now hold on, Olivia."

"Hold on? To what? My house? Oh, yes, I'll hold on to my house and most of what's in it. I'll also hold on to my trust. All of it. Good-bye, Charlie. It has been less than a pleasure living with you." With that she turned quickly and left.

Charlie sat stunned in the bubble bath that had all but reduced itself to a soapy film on top of the water.

The door opened again. It was Jeanette.

"Is Mrs. Fair going to fire me?"

"Consider yourself fired."

"No notice?"

"No notice."

"Where will we go?" she was nearing tears.

Charlie looked up at her with an incredulous expression. "What do you mean 'we?'"

He pulled himself out of the tub, grabbed a towel, roughly brushed by Jeanette, and headed downstairs calling Olivia's name. He caught up with her as she was starting up the stairs to her bedroom.

"Olivia. One question: Is there another man?"

"Would that surprise you, my dear?" she said taunting him.

"Well, I'd sure as hell like to know who the bastard is."

"I'm sure you would. Let me just say there might be another man." She paused to be sure the possibility had registered and then added, "On the other hand, there might not be. I guess you'll just have to wait and see."

Charlie immediately assumed there was. "Is he someone I know?"

"Maybe, assuming there is someone," she said.

"There is. I knew it. And I'll bet the sonofabitch is with GM. Those fuckers are home wreckers."

"Of course, he could be someone from Chrysler or maybe even someone from your own company." She had his ego dangling on her hook and was enjoying it.

"You might as well tell me now, because eventually I'll find the bastard."

"But then again, maybe there isn't anybody. I know it may seem inconceivable to you, but maybe I'm just tired of having to play the unsuspecting wife when I meet some of your conquests."

"You know I will fight you on this."

"Suit yourself. But know one thing: As far as I'm concerned, you've already lost. And I am not about to give you a rematch." With that, she turned her back and went upstairs.

53
What, No Brinks Truck?

"Get up here. We have a problem!" Charlie was on the phone the minute Waddington sat down behind his desk. Charlie left no doubt that he was unhappy about something.

Olivia! He's found out about Olivia and me. But how? They'd talked last night, and she told him that Charlie felt sure there was another man but had no idea who it might be. Maybe one of the maids told him. Certainly enough people had seen them together. As Waddington got off the elevator, he decided that if Charlie wanted to have it out with him about Olivia, so be it. He would not deny anything. *What the hell? He's going to have to find out about me sometime. Now is as good a time as any.*

But that wasn't why Charlie had called him to his office. He had other problems.

"Poppenhaus was supposed to pick up the money for Slipwalker today," he nodded toward the two metal suitcases resting on the floor in front of his desk, "and drive it to Greenwich. He and Poor are supposed to complete the settlement tonight."

"Where's Popper?"

"He's in New York. The agency has been screwing up our *Easy* ads, and I told him to grab those assholes by the balls and not let go until they got it right. The ads and commercials have got to be ready for the dealer meeting. I'm not going to have those bastards throwing up some half-finished commercials in front of the dealers. But that problem we can solve. The bigger problem right now is that this money has absofuckinglutely got to be in Greenwich tonight. And since Popper can't drive it there, I've elected you."

"Me? You want me to drive five million dollars to Greenwich? In a car?" Waddington was confused. "Why me? Why not hire a Brinks truck? They're in business to do that kind of thing, you know."

"What a terrific idea. Why didn't I think of that?" the derision dripped with every word. "We can hire a Brinks Truck and let everyone in the building wonder why a Brinks truck would be here to pick up two metal suitcases. Do you know what 'Brinks' translates to in French?"

"Translates?" Waddington decided Charlie had lost it.

"It translates to 'Frog Alert.' No. You are going to personally take this five million in one-hundred dollars bills to Greenwich and deliver each and every one to Popper." Charlie looked at his watch. " If you leave now, you can be in Greenwich by about six tonight. That's plenty of time. Popper told me they plan to meet with Slipwalker at about nine."

"Charlie, I don't think bagman is in my job description."

"Well, guess what? I've just made that your number one responsibility. This is not a subject for debate. I haven't asked you for one damn thing in exchange for having to sooth your goddamn ethics. You're the guy who wanted the recall. You got it. But part of our deal was for me to be able to settle this suit and get my hands on Slipwalker's copy of the *CEO*. We've had to delay the bastard twice. Popper says he's startin' to bitch. The last thing I want is for that asshole to get the idea that maybe he can hold us up for more. Or worse, tell us to screw ourselves and go ahead with the suit. I want this shyster off our backs, tonight!"

Waddington looked at the two suitcases. "But what if I get in an accident or what if the car is stolen?"

Charlie wasn't about to suffer an argument. "Do you know what my answer is to that?" he shot back.

"What?"

"Don't! Don't have an accident! Don't let the car get stolen!"

54
Pissing Off Petula

Among the many penalties meted out by Petula as punishment for Jack's unabated philandering was to banish her consort from the conjugal bed and ship him off to the guesthouse on the other side of the pool and tennis court. Jack welcomed his exile. He liked the imposed distance between himself and Petula's constant carping.

For several days, he had been gathering those possessions he intended to take with him into his new life in the Florida Keys. Carefully, so as not to draw the attention of one of the servants, he had removed his things from the house and taken them to the dealership. Once the money was in hand, all he would have left to do was to say goodbye to Petula.

Just after nine in the morning, Popper called to tell Jack that his son-in-law had left Detroit with the money and was on his way to Greenwich. The news that it was finally going to happen was like a shot of adrenalin. Jack was buoyed, energized; he'd never felt more alive in his last forty years. In less than twelve hours he would be free of Petula. The prospect of finally removing the shackles of his relationship made him slightly giddy and unable to repress an involuntary series of chuckles.

At ten, he was at his desk in the dealership creating his own version of a time bomb designed to blow a hole in Petula's and Bumper McCoy's checkbook. *Deny me my twenty percent, will you?* He called the <u>Greenwich Times</u> and <u>Westchester Chronicle</u> and ordered a full-page ad. All it was to say was:

Krazy Klearance
Jack Poor Must be Krazy!
Every one of the new cars he has in stock
will be sold for $1000 per car.
Every pre-owned car for just $500.
No ifs, ands, or buts.
Come in now! Pick a car.
Pay a grand and drive away.

Jack had more than sixty new cars in stock and about thirty used. He estimated the loss from his Krazy Klearance sale would amount to nearly two million dollars. He knew it would only make a minor dent in their checkbooks, but the irritation factor would be, as the ad says, *priceless*. He was almost sorry he wouldn't be around to see their reaction when they discovered what he'd done.

At two, Popper reported that Waddington was on I-84 in Western Pennsylvania. Estimated arrival in Greenwich, about 6:30.

Jack had chosen a white Cadence with its cavernous trunk and backseat area as his getaway car. The Cadence was anything but stylish. Forgettable was more descriptive. But it was functional in that there would be plenty of room for his belongings and–most importantly–the *money*. The plan was simple. After Slipwalker had been paid, he and Popper would drive into New York for the night. He had already made reservations for two suites at the Plaza. They would divide up the money and, the next day he would leave for the Keys. For a moment he thought about his Insurance Claims Adjuster. Maybe he should ask her if she'd like to come along. *No, God, no!* He admonished himself at the thought. *Are you out of your mind? She'd clean out my bank account in a month. Anyway, I'm tired of her. Besides, she dresses like a hooker.*

Popper arrived at the dealership just after six. "What time do you close tonight?"

"Eight," Jack said.

"Good, I told Slipwalker to be here by nine."

"Have you heard from Waddington?"

"Talked to him on his cell ten minutes ago. He was on the New York Thruway heading south toward the Tappan Zee Bridge. I give him thirty to forty minutes. He should be here by no later than seven."

"So, it's really gonna happen, right?" Jack needed one last reassurance before he made his announcement to Petula.

"It is really going to happen," Popper said with confidence. "In about three hours, we will be looking at a large pile of money."

"I have one more thing to do," Jack said. "I'll be back in less than an hour."

"Where you going?"

"I'm going to do something that I've wanted to do almost all my married life." With that, he got into his Cadence and drove home for the last time.

He found Petula in her room, relaxing regally on her chez lounge, hoping to find her picture in the Parties section of <u>Town & Country</u>. She glanced up, annoyed at the interruption. "What do you want?"

"As it turns out," he said, savoring the moment, "I want nothing from you. Absolutely nothing at all. I've got everything I need."

Petula looked at him suspiciously. "What are you talking about?"

"No, I was wrong. I do want something. I want just a minute of your precious time, Petula. That's about as long as it's going to take for me to say 'Sayonara, Baby.' I am outta here. Gone. I'm flyin' the coup. Starting in about one hour, you will be a thing of my past."

"What are you saying?"

"Petula, I am declaring my freedom from forty-odd years of indentured servitude. I am saying good-bye and leaving the most egoistical, self-centered, ugly, overweight lump of humanity that God ever created. I am finally free of you, your father, the dealership, and this town. Free. I don't need your money. I don't need you. I don't need anything."

"You're leaving me?"

"Well, I'm glad you finally got the message."

"Don't be ridiculous. Without me, you're nothing. Nothing! You haven't got lunch money without me. Where will you go? Or more to the point, where can you afford to go?"

"Well, for starters, once I leave here, I'm going to stop by the dealership, pick up my things, and then go driving off into the sunset. I'll send you an address so that your lawyer can send me the divorce papers. I had planned on asking for nothing. But, on second thought, maybe I'll ask for alimony. You're the one with the money, and it wouldn't be the first time a wife has had to pay the husband. I think I could make a very strong case for extreme mental cruelty. Wouldn't that make great reading in the <u>Greenwich Times</u>?"

"I can't believe you'd have the audacity to drag our name through the mud."

"No," he said to taunt her, "I'll just drag it though Greenwich society."

"You'd actually do that? You'd actually create a scandal? Do you know what people would say?"

"I hope the hell they say, 'good for Jack Poor. He's finally gotten rid of the old battle-ax.'"

If anger could be converted to heat, steam would have been billowing out the top of her head. "I know what this is all about. I know. It's about that woman. That insurance person you've been shacking up with. That low-class slut."

It wasn't about her, of course. But Jack saw an opportunity to inflict more punishment. "As a matter of fact, it is. Now that I think about it, why should we drive off into the sunset when we can just drive down the street and find a place to live here in Greenwich? That way, we could be very, *very* visible to all of your friends. With the way she dresses, most of her would *really* be visible. 'There goes Jack Poor,' they would say. 'Look what he got when he traded old Petula in.' Can't you just see all those old farts falling all over themselves when we have brunch at the club? And remember, the membership is in my name so you can't keep me out of there."

"You bastard! You sonofabitch. After all I've done for you. You'd do this to me after forty-three years of my putting up with your crass habits and low-class upbringing? Well, I will not let you embarrass and humiliate me. I will not be made the subject of gossip and snide comments. I will not have my reputation besmirched by a ... a ..." She seemed to be searching for a truly derisive epithet. Finally, she found one, "... car dealer!"

"God, you are pathetic. You really are. Look at you. You've had two face-lifts, and you still look like a dried chamois. Your boobs have fallen down around your knees. Your hips are so wide it would take two weeks of liposuction to reduce them. You've got legs that would look better on a piano. You are an ugly old woman, Petula. And all your money can't do a damn thing to change that. All you can do is surround yourself with a bunch of social sycophants who keep telling you how great you look, so that you won't cut them off from your invitation list. If you were a used car, Petula, I'd have to mark you salvage and send you to the dump."

Petula was beyond retort. Virtually struck dumb. She was teetering on the edge of violence.

"And so, my dear Petula, I bid you good-bye and good riddance." With that he turned and left. As he walked down the front staircase, she appeared at her bedroom door yelling.

"I will not let you humiliate me! I will not let you scandalize me in the Greenwich paper! I will not have you throwing that floozy in my face and embarrassing me in front of my friends! I will not have my reputation compromised! I will see you dead before I let you get away this!" Her voice rained down on him like hail stones. Only when he closed the front door did her rantings end. He was free; he'd inflicted heavy psychological damage. He'd hit her where it really hurt. Right in her social register. And when she found that he had advertised the entire inventory for one thousand dollars, he'd hit her in her pocketbook as well. Oh, how sweet. For forty years, he'd been living as a victim. Now, at last, he was walking away a victor.

55
The Payoff

It had taken Waddington eleven hours and forty-five minutes, including two gas stops and an hour wait for the police to clear an accident on the Tappan Zee Bridge. He was exhausted. As he drove into Jack Poor Motors' parking lot, both Popper and Jack came out to meet him. From what he could tell after a quick glance around, they were the only ones at the dealership.

"You were supposed to be here an hour ago," Jack said. "I about shit my pants when I found you hadn't shown up!"

"There was an accident on the Tappan Zee Bridge, and my cell phone battery went dead so I couldn't call. Sorry."

"Where's the money?" Popper asked.

"In the back." Waddington got out of the car, opened the trunk, and gestured toward the two silver suitcases. "There it is. Five million in hundred-dollar bills. That should make Slipwalker happy."

"I'm *sure* it will make him happy." Popper picked up both suitcases and began to lug them into the dealership.

"Are we meeting Slipwalker here or going to his office?" Waddington asked.

"We?" Popper stopped and looked at him with some concern. "Were you thinking of sitting in on this?"

"Are you saying I shouldn't?"

"Probably best if you didn't. Slipwalker is a very nervous cat. Too many people and he could change his mind."

"Whatever you say."

"You can take off and head back for Detroit, if you like," Popper said.

"I've got to get some sleep first. Jack, can I use a phone?"

"Sure, use Ivan's old office."

"Old?"

"He's no longer with us. There's lot of turnover in this business." Jack began to laugh and Waddington had no idea why and no inclination at that moment to ask. He followed Popper and Jack inside and watched them climb the stairs with the suitcases to Jack's office.

Waddington's first stop was the men's room. When he came out, he caught a glimpse of Slipwalker and Mrs. Swenson going upstairs and heard Jack's voice saying something to them which he could not make out. Waddington was tired. There was no way he was going to ask to stay at Petula's. The nearest motel would be just fine. He turned the light on in what had been Ivan's office, sat down behind the desk, and began to rummage through the drawers looking for the Yellow Pages.

When he pulled out the bottom drawer, he noticed that it still had the radio he'd seen the first time he was in Ivan's office. He remembered thinking it curious that the man would keep his radio in a drawer. *Wonder if I can get a weather report for tomorrow?* He reached down and turned it on. Where's the tune button? How do you find a station on this thing? He tried to pull it out of the drawer but found it attached. He pressed another button and heard voices.

Voices? But not just any voices. He recognized Jack's voice and then Popper's. Damn. Jack had mentioned to Waddington that he suspected his office was bugged. And it was. Ivan could hear everything that was going on, which meant he could report all of Jack's conversations to Petula. He turned up the volume.

"I have papers for you to sign, Mrs. Swenson. Here they are. And Abner, this is our agreement, the one between you and the company. It states that you'll notify the court of Mrs. Swenson's decision not to pursue the suit."

"Can I see the money first?" he heard Slipwalker ask.

"It's all there. Five hundred thousand. If you want to count it, be my guest.

"Five hundred thousand?" Waddington heard himself ask. "What's he talking about? Maybe that's the lawyer's share.

"And three hundred thousand is mine. Right?" It was Mrs. Swenson.

"As we agreed," Slipwalker replied. We can go back to my office and put it in my safe for the night, if you like."

"I don't trust your safety. I'll take my money home."

"Suit yourself."

What the hell is going on? Where's the five million? Waddington was leaning close to the speaker.

"There, I think we've signed everything," Slipwalker said.

"Yeah, looks good," Popper said. "And may I remind you, we've agreed that the amount of the settlement will not be made public."

"It's nobody's business but ours," Slipwalker said.

"Then I guess that's it. We're done." Popper said.

"We're done," Slipwalker echoed. "I must say, I like doing business with you guys."

"I don't think the people back in Detroit would say the same."

"If there's nothing else, Mrs. Swenson and I will be going."

Waddington heard movement and Jacks' office door open. The next voice was Jack's. "Mrs. Swenson. Just out of curiosity, what are you going to do with all the money?"

"First thing, I'm going to do is buy myself a Mercedes-Benz. I'm sure not going to buy one of your turds on wheels."

Waddington heard the office door close as she and Slipwalker left. He continued to listen on Ivan's bugging device.

"The woman does have a way with words," Popper said laughing.

"Now you know why Swenson was dickin' his secretary or whatever she was," Jack added.

"Well, Mr. Poor," Popper said, "I must say that you look a lot better than you did a couple hours ago. In fact, you look at least two point two-five million times better."

"And I feel better. I've got to hand it to you, Popper. You're a fucking genius," and then he added laughing, "and a hell of a con man. You missed your calling. I had my doubts that you'd be able to pull this off. But goddamn, you fucked old Charlie but good. Too bad he'll never know it."

"And let's not forget your son-in-law. If it hadn't been for his *CEO* report, I wouldn't have had the leverage to scare the shit, or more precisely the money, out of Charlie."

"Do you have the papers Slipwalker signed?"

"Yeah, I'll give them to Charlie."

"Won't he be looking for the copy of the *CEO* that Slipwalker was supposed to have?"

"It's in Detroit locked up nicely in my desk."

"By the way, where did you get it?"

"Took it off Waddington's secretary's computer," he said with an exuberant chuckle.

"Well, I have to say, it was a work of art. The whole thing."

"Oh, I need to make a quick call."

There was silence for a moment and then Waddington heard Popper say, " Deal done. We're off the hook. No more lawsuits." The phone clicked back on the cradle.

"Short conversation," Jack said.

"Short and sweet. Now, I think it's time you and I picked up those lovely suitcases and got out of here. You say you have reservations for us at the Plaza tonight?"

"I thought it only right we go first class."

Waddington was flabbergasted. He couldn't believe what he was hearing. It was a scam. A total scam that was netting Popper and Jack four and a half million dollars. *They're goddamn crooks. And I've been the bagman.* Then it occurred to him that maybe Charlie was in on this. But why? A third of the money would be chump change to him. *No,* he realized, *this is Popper's scam, front to back. And Jack's. But what the hell do I do?*

He heard the door in Jack's office open and Jack say something about having parked his car by the side door.

Waddington got up, turned off the light in Ivan's office and opened the door a crack. Jack and Popper were coming downstairs, each carrying one of the metal suitcases. At the bottom of the stairs, they turned and headed for the side door that led to the car lot.

Waddington was frozen. He had no idea what to do. Should he confront them? Should he tell them he'd heard everything? Then what? Was he supposed to wrestle the money away from them in the name of the company? Maybe he should just call the Greenwich police, tell them what happened and let them do whatever the police do in a situation like this. Bad idea. It was a sure way to have the scam make the evening news. Once that happened, it would be Katy-bar-the-door. Plus, with his luck, they'd probably accuse him of being an accomplice. After all, he *was* the bagman. No, best to call Charlie. Tell him everything and let him deal with it. They said they were going to stay at the Plaza. It would be easy for them to be picked up there. Yes, call Charlie. But where would Charlie be? Olivia had made him move out. When he talked to her that afternoon from his car, she mentioned that she had no idea where he was staying. Nichols. He could call Harvey Nichols. Waddington knew where he lived and it would be easy to get the number from information. He went back into Ivan's office and picked up the phone.

Wait, he said to himself. *Could Nichols be in on this?* After all, he was the guy who actually siphoned the money out of the company. To add to his concern, he remembered that Nichols and Popper played a lot of golf together. Damn! It could only be one of two things, he decided. This was either just a clever scam pulled off by Popper and Jack or it was a goddamn conspiracy.

He held the phone in his hand until he heard it begin a pulsing buzz demanding that he make a decision: Use the phone or hang it up. And then suddenly, the decision was made for him.

56
A Scorned Wife Can Kill You

Petula had parked her Bentley across from the dealership and about a block from the main driveway entrance. Her lights were off, but she left the engine running. She had no plan other than to find a way to initiate damage control before Jack could ruin her reputation. He was not going to get away with making her a laughingstock. She knew full well how the upper-class Greenwich tongues would slice and dice her behind her back. She would not, *could not* let that happen. No. Somehow, Jack had to be stopped. She had to take control of the situation. She had no idea how, but she had to take preventive action.

The clock on her dash said, nine-fifteen. There were a few lights on in the dealership, but the driveway area was dark. Movement. People. She could make out Jack by his pear shape, putting suitcases in the back of a white Cadence. There was movement on the other side of the car. It was too dark to make out who it was. It had to be the Insurance Claims Adjuster, she decided. That tart. Jack's whore. She could see Jack lower the trunk lid and get into the car on the driver's side. He was leaving. Getting away! He had to be stopped! *Do something!–Now!* her ego screamed.

There was only one thing she could do. Flushed with righteous vengeance, coupled with an overwhelming desire to punish the ungrateful and unfaithful bastard, Petula put the Bentley into gear, turned on the headlights, and floored the accelerator. The 6000-pound beast responded, gaining a remarkable amount of speed for so heavy a vehicle. With a snarl on her lips and animus beyond measure in her chest, she took dead aim at the side of the Cadence. The Bentley's light caught Jack's attention, and he looked up at the on-rushing car.

"Bitch!" He yelled recognizing the driver.

The Bentley's speedometer was passing fifty miles-an-hour when it hit the Cadence. "Take that, you bastard!" she bellowed just before her air bag exploded and whacked her in the face, obscuring, momentarily, the completeness of her revenge.

57
Hit and Run

It was an unmistakable sound. Metal impacting metal at high speed. Waddington had heard the same sound many times at the company's crash test facility. He dropped the phone, bolted toward the front of the dealership, and looked out the window. The Cadence looked like it had been the loser in a demolition derby. The car had been bent in the middle almost to the point where it appeared that both the front and rear end were making an effort to point in the same direction. The impact had driven Jack's car into one of two stone pillars that supported a protective portico over the front entrance to the building.

Waddington's first thought was to get Jack and Popper out of the car in case it caught fire. As he approached the front door of the showroom, he noticed a large car moving quickly through the car lot toward the exit near where the used car office was located. The driver had turned off the car's lights and all he could see was a partial silhouette, mostly hidden behind the doubled line of new cars that had been neatly lined up as if waiting for a military inspection. The vehicle pulled out of the dealership onto Putnam Avenue and disappeared into the night.

***

Waddington waited until the ambulance left with Popper, unconscious, but alive, and after the EMS people had confirmed officially what he already knew. Then he returned to Ivan's office and called Petula. The phone rang several times before it was answered. It was Petula, but her voice was hoarse, dry, sounding muffled like someone suffering the aftereffects of major periodontal surgery.

"Hello?"

"Petula?"

"Yes."

"It's Pres Waddington. I'm afraid I have some very bad news."

58
A Resplendent Funeral

It might have been Jack's funeral, but it was certainly Petula's party. It seemed that everyone she had ever known, or more appropriately, everyone who had known her, showed up at the church. The only thing missing was Jack. Petula had decided the day before to have him cremated. Her father had refused to let him be buried in the same cemetery as all the other McCoys. It was, Waddington decided, the final ignominy. As Waddington looked around the church, it occurred to him that there were probably more people at Jack Poor's funeral than had been inside his dealership in six months. Petula had come in last, parading down the aisle on her father's arm, like a bride for god's sake. She played the grieving widow well. Right down to the large dark sunglasses, which Waddington noticed she'd been wearing for the last two days. The poor woman doesn't want us to see that she has been crying her eyes out, was the general consensus. Once, yesterday, he had seen her without them for a moment. Both eyes were black. He wasn't sure if it was the aftermath of a recent eye job, a fight with Jack (which, knowing Jack seemed highly unlikely), or maybe she'd accidentally run into a door. Waddington didn't bother to ask.

The service was very short and what remembrances there were seemed more like homage to the forbearance of the widow than mourning for her husband's passing. Spud Korman, Jack's sales manager, had planned to say a few words as a representative of everyone who worked in the dealership, but was notified just before the service that his remarks would not be needed.

The reception was held at the country club. Waddington estimated that it took less than fifteen minutes for the wake to become a party. It took only that long for the mourners to relegate Jack Poor to the ranks of the immanently forgettable. Since it was Saturday, none of the guests apparently had anything better to do than drink and eat on Petula's tab. It seemed to surprise no one when, at seven, an eight-piece band showed up and invited everyone to conga.

He had seen Muffy only twice since his Thursday night call to Petula and then only in the presence of other family members. He was standing alone on the edge of the club's rear terrace, looking out at the last round of golfers approaching the eighteenth green. He turned to look back into the club and saw Muffy making her way through the dancing mourners. She was headed his way. The woman he saw approaching had the slightly detached look of a truly upper-crust Greenwich patrician. The smiles with which she returned the greetings of those who spoke to her were painted with an undercoating of false sincerity.

As she walked up to Waddington she said, "I don't know why you found it necessary to stay in a motel the last two nights. Mummy, as you well know, has more than enough beds and the house is big enough that we wouldn't have had to see each other all that much."

Waddington had no intention of defending his decision to stay away from the house. She might more appropriately have asked why he even stayed for the funeral. Jack didn't like him, Petula hated him, and Muffy was divorcing him. Even he was unsure why he stayed in Greenwich, other than out of some sense of distant obligation. For a moment, he thought he glimpsed the vestige of the girl with herbs in her hair. No, he was mistaken.

"A nice day," she said seeming to make an effort to lower the tension level.

"Too bad Jack missed it. Petula seems to be holding up well. Actually, very well. I was surprised to see you driving Jack's Road Warrior SUV. Was that some sort of tribute to Jack?"

"No. Normally Mummy wouldn't be caught dead in one of Daddy's cars. It couldn't be helped. Mummy sent the Bentley in for service yesterday. Something was wrong with it."

"What about the Mercedes?"

"The battery was dead and it was too late to call for a limo. So that left us with the Road Warrior. I can't tell you what a *truck* that thing is. How can your company sell those?"

"Good question. When you look at the sales figures, you'd have to say that we *don't* sell those, at least not very many."

There was an extended and uncomfortable gap in the conversation. Waddington watched the foursome hole out on the eighteenth while Muffy dug in her purse for whatever it was she was trying to find. Finally, she broke the void. "Have you heard anything from the police? Do they have any idea who did it?"

"I spent most of yesterday talking with them. I never saw enough of the other car to make even a guess at the make. It was big, that's all I can say."

"It must have been some drunk. Maybe he fell asleep at the wheel." She shrugged, "Who knows?"

"What about the other man with Daddy?"

"Poppenhaus?"

"He works for the company, right?"

"Our VP of Marketing?"

"What was he doing with my father?"

"It's a complicated story."

"Is he going to be all right?"

"In time. I went to the hospital yesterday, and he's in a full body cast including his head. Just holes for his eyes, nose, and mouth. The doctors say he's likely to recover, but it will take a while."

Muffy fumbled with her purse for a moment, as though buying time to prepare herself for what she wanted to say next. "Pres, this may not be the most appropriate time to bring this up, but you will be getting the divorce papers shortly. I do hope you're going to be civil about this and not drag us into a nasty legal battle."

"I intend to be compliant beyond belief. For me, our marriage is over. All I want is the right to visit the children, assuming either of them want me to visit."

"Naturally I would not deny you that. I'll have to work out some type of schedule, of course."

"Whatever works for you. The sooner we get this done, the sooner we can get on with our lives."

"I couldn't agree more," she responded defensively. Then, adopting a surprisingly conciliatory tone, she said, "On the other hand, for the sake of our children, I am willing to reconsider my decision to go through with the divorce if you, in turn, will reconsider your decision to stay in Detroit and move back here with me." Then in what seemed an afterthought, "With Daddy gone, maybe you could take over the dealership?"

Had he not immediately caught himself, he might well have responded with, *you've got to be kidding? You want me to be Jack Poor Redux? No, thank you!* Did she really think there was any chance he might accept? She must have, why else would she have asked? Out of the corner of his eye, he could see she was getting impatient for an answer.

"I asked you a question, in case you missed it," her voice had an icy edge.

"No, I didn't miss it. I was thinking how difficult it must have been for you to make the offer."

"Well, it wasn't all that difficult." Her tone seemed to suggest that she was having second thoughts. "I like to think I'm a big enough person to forgive and forget. I just felt, for the children's sake, that I owed you one last chance to change your mind."

Forgive and forget what? He wondered. *She's decided the divorce is all my fault. Well, what's new?* He shook his head, "This is where you belong, Muffy." Waddington turned and looked back at the ballroom. The room was jammed with revelers and the decibels had risen considerably. They looked to be anticipating a late night at the old County Club. "I belong in Detroit. I think it best we leave it that way … for everyone's sake." Apparently, that was not the answer she had hoped for, and he could see her jaw tighten. He decided the best antidote for the situation was to change the subject.

" Your mother throws a nice wake." It was meant to be a factious comment, but it sailed right by Muffy.

"He didn't deserve it."

"Deserve what?"

"A party like this. He was a bastard. Do you know what he did? He actually tried to place an ad in the local papers offering any car for $1000. Fortunately, my father seems to have forgotten that he was on a COD basis with the newspapers and the ads never ran. If they had, and people had taken us to court, it could have cost Mummy millions. Millions!"

Millions, he repeated to himself. Then almost reflexively he nearly shouted "Sonofabitch!"

"He was that and more," Muffy responded.

"I wasn't referring to your father. Something else."

"What?"

Waddington suddenly was a man in need of the nearest exit. "Excuse me, Muffy, but there is something incredibly important that I've got to attend right now." He started looking for the fastest way out of the club.

"More important than discussing our divorce?"

"Oh, about that: Let's get it over as soon as we can, okay?" He began to back away.

Muffy was not taking his sudden decision to depart well. She looked at him stiffly, raising her chin to show that she had been offended and turned away as if looking for solace among the throng of gyrating mourners who were snaking around the dance floor in what looked to Waddington like a Greenwichized version of a tribal dance.

"Take care of yourself," he called. With that Waddington turned and worked his way through the crowd, out the door, and into the parking lot. He showed his stub to the parking valet, gave him two dollars and said, "I see it over there. I'll get it myself."

59
Finder's Keepers?

Jack Poor Motors was closed and a long yellow tape with "Crime Scene" on it was stretched around the perimeter. Waddington parked by the curb and stepped onto the lot. It was just after six. If Jack's Cadence was still here, and why wouldn't it be, he reasoned, it would have been towed, or pushed, or carried on a forklift behind the service bays. He took a moment to look around. No one to be seen anywhere, but the car was right where he expected to find it. It looked even worse than he'd remembered. Remarkable that Popper had survived. The next stop for that car was the scrap yard.

Waddington walked around to the trunk and saw that it was closed. The keys were still in the ignition. When he used them to try and open the trunk, he discovered that the lid was so badly bent that the lock would not release. He looked around for something to use as a crowbar. A metal rod was sticking out of a trash barrel. *This will do it,* he decided. It took fully five minutes, but he finally was able to pop the lock and lift the trunk far enough to get his hands under the lid and lift. He looked inside and there they were. The two metal suitcases. He pulled one out and balanced it on what was left of the rear quarter panel. He popped the lock and opened the lid just a crack. The money was still there. He checked the other suitcase. Same result.

Waddington found himself looking at four-point-five million dollars. Charlie and Nichols would assume that it had been paid to Slipwalker. Popper would never ask about it, even after he recovered, because then he would have to admit his scam. Even if at some time in the future Popper decided to confess all, who was to say the money hadn't gone to the junkyard with the Cadence and been lost forever?

Temptation reared its alluring head and its voice said, "Hello, Mr. Waddington. Now this is what you might call an opportunity. You could put those cases in your car, drive off, and no one would ever know. Four point five million dollars would buy you a lot of suits, Mr. Waddington. You might even pass for a Grosse Pointer. And wouldn't you love to buy your very own Bosendorfer with the nine extra keys?"

He closed both suitcases and carried them across the car lot where all the new Cadences and Defiants and Verites waited for buyers that would not be coming until the police decided the dealership had been a crime scene long enough. Putnam Avenue was quiet. Barely a car within a quarter mile of where he stood. No one anywhere in sight to question, or even wonder about, the man putting two metal suitcases in the back of his car. What was there to wonder about? Nothing unusual about putting suitcases in the trunk of a car.

Waddington closed the trunk, looked around, then opened the door and slid in behind the steering wheel. He gave the dealership a slow one-eighty, left to right, final look. No more Sell-a-Thons for poor Jack Poor. He was mildly surprised to find himself feeling sorry for his father-in-law. Waddington's life with Muffy had been difficult, but Jack's life with Petula had been unbearable. Jack had been a virtual prisoner, bound to Petula and his dealership by her money. A life of frustration had ended in frustration. There was no escaping for him after all. Waddington let out a long sigh, then pulled out his cell phone and hit the automatic dial.

"Hello?"

"I'm on my way home. And guess what?"

"What?" Olivia asked.

"I'm bringing four-point-five million dollars with me. I think it's time I had a talk with your father."

60
The Whole Verite Truth

The return trip to Detroit felt like it was taking forever. Every mile seemed like ten. Every ten, a hundred. He called Olivia as he turned north off of I-80 at Toledo and headed north on I-75. He estimated he'd be at her house around six. She was waiting for him and immediately got into his car and drove five minutes up Lake Short Drive to Perkins' house. They turned in through the stone pillars and there, just across a heavily treed front lawn was an English Cotswold style house. The house Olivia had grown up in. It wasn't the Versailles that her Grandmother had left her, but it was a substantial house, nonetheless. And, as Olivia pointed out, her father had bought and paid for it himself.

As they pulled up to the front door, Waddington noticed two other cars already parked off to the side.

"Your father has company. Members of the inquisition?"

"Members of the board, I think."

"Could be one in the same."

"No. Not where you're concerned. You can trust my father. He's a good man, Pres. Tell him everything. You have nothing to hide. From where I sit, you may have just saved this company from a public relations disaster, to say nothing of a nasty investigation."

Waddington got out of the car, opened the trunk and removed the two suitcases, then joined Olivia at the front door. After a moment, Perkins opened the door, gave his daughter a welcome peck on the cheek, then held out his hand to Waddington.

"Thanks for coming," he said simply. Perkins ushered them into his library where Olivia immediately excused herself, as she had told Waddington she would, and left the room.

"I was hoping to have more members of the Executive Committee here this evening, but with such short notice, only Hardman Tuber and John VanFleet were available. This is something I'd like everyone to hear firsthand, so I may have to ask you to meet with the others one day next week."

Waddington did not know Lomeriello well, but understood that he, along with Perkins, had steered the company through the negotiations with the French. Tuber, on the other hand, was a relic from the distance past who, so it was said, had been Henry Ford II's hammer man. His large block of stock rather than any business acumen had earned him his place on the board.

"I think it would be best if you just started from the beginning and gave us as much detail as you can. I want to make it clear that you are to hold back nothing. You have no obligation to try and protect anyone who might have had a hand in this. There are no sacred cows; none whatsoever. Understand that I respect honesty and reward it. Do I make myself clear?"

"Very." Waddington nodded. Then he began. He recalled the meeting in which Perkins had asked him to call his father-in-law to learn what he knew about a possible suit from Mrs. Swenson. He recounted everything he knew from firsthand knowledge to that which he'd been able to deduce. He told them how Axel and he had discovered the problem with the Verite 300 suspension. How Axel had confronted Charlie and why and how he had let Charlie push him out of the company without protest. He told them how he had decided to force a recall with the publication of Axel's information in the *CEO*. He told them of his meeting with Charlie, his promotion to VP of Dealer and Customer Relations, and the scheme that Charlie, Nichols, and Brewster had concocted to slip five-million dollars out of the company. Waddington told them about being asked to drive the money to Greenwich and what he'd overheard via the bug Ivan had planted in Jack's office.

"I was actually about to call Nichols and ask him what I should do when I heard the crash. I knew immediately that somebody had hit something very hard. For a moment, I thought maybe Jack had smashed into one of the cars on the lot. When I got to the window, I saw it was Jack's car, a white Cadence, that had been hit broadside and driven into one of the pillars holding up the portico. By the time I got outside, the other car was leaving the lot. I didn't get a good enough look to identify the make. Frankly, by the looks of Jack's car, I'm surprised the other car was able to drive away. Its front end must be a mess. The

437

Greenwich police classified it as a hit-and-run, but as of yesterday, they still had no leads."

"No leads at all?" Tuber asked, sounding incredulous.

"None that I know of."

"Ummmm," was his response.

"The rest of the money is all in those two cases. I presume that if the money could be taken out of the company, there is some way to put it back, and the French auditors never need know."

"I'll take care of that," Perkins said, as he reflected on all that he had heard.

Waddington added, "I think you can safely assume that only the three of you and I know that there was never a five-million-dollar settlement and that the lawyer never had a copy of the *CEO*. It was all part of Popper's scam."

"You're sure the lawyer had no idea about the five million?" Tuber asked.

"Very sure. Otherwise, he would most certainly have demanded more. You won't be hearing from him again."

"If I understand correctly, you have not talked to either Charlie or Nichols since the accident," Perkins said.

"No, but I did hear Popper make a call after Slipwalker and Mrs. Swenson left. I think it was probably to Charlie. All he said was something like. 'It's done. We're off the hook.'"

"But you personally have not talked to either man?"

"No. I decided that it would be best to come to you first."

Perkins reflected for a moment and then said, "I want to thank you for your candor, Pres. I also appreciate the return of the money. Right now, I need some time to think. Thanks to you we may have dodged more than one bullet here. We could be in deep trouble about now. You've done well by us, Preston. I only wish we could thank you publicly, but as you can readily understand, our thanks never goes beyond this room."

Waddington stood up, shook hands with each man and left the room.

Olivia was waiting for him in the foyer. "How'd it go?"

"Okay, I guess. I told them everything."

They left the house, got back in the car, and drove to Olivia's house.

"Come on in. I want to show you something."

Waddington followed her into the house, through the enormous living room which was dark save for the light of several sconces on the wall. She took his hand and led him to the staircase. "It's up here," she said. She led him down the hall to her bedroom and opened the door. He was back in the room where it had all started. He followed her in and closed the door. This time, he would not leave until morning.

61
Charlie Finds Out

Charlie couldn't believe what he was seeing. Preston Waddington was pulling out of his driveway. It was eight in the morning and Preston Waddington was leaving his house. At 8 a.m. on a fucking Monday morning. What the hell was he doing at his house at 8 a.m.? He sure as hell wasn't there to talk about Olivia's petition brochure. That was history weeks ago. *No, Goddamn it, the sonofabitch has been here all night. With Olivia. With my wife! He's the one? She's having an affair with Waddington? He must have been the man Jeanette saw her kissing. Olivia kissing Waddington? What the hell has she been drinking?* Obviously, the woman was suffering something mental. *Waddington. Of all people. He's nobody!*

He found her in her bathrobe in the kitchen having coffee. He wasn't sure, but it looked to him as if she had nothing on underneath. There were two cups and saucers, two plates, two glasses with orange juice residue. They'd had breakfast together. How fuckin' cozy.

"What are you doing here?" she asked coldly.

"While I may not live here anymore, some of my clothes do, and I needed a couple of suits. Tell me something, Olivia. Did I or did I not see Preston Waddington just leave our driveway?"

"You did," she said making no effort to conceal the truth.

He continued the interrogation. "Am I or am I not to assume that he spent the night?"

"Assume whatever you want. But he did spend the night. Here. With me."

The woman was brazen, shameless. She was tossing her affair in his face. Daring him to object, to assume the role of the cuckold husband. The unmitigated temerity.

"And you slept with him?" It was more of a challenge than a question.

"Yes, I slept with him. All night." Her manner was irritatingly matter of fact.

"I hear what you're saying, but I don't believe it. If you were going to have an affair, you might have done a little better for yourself than Preston O. Waddington. He's not one of us."

"And by that you mean–?"

"You know what I mean. I mean he's not exactly, well … *Grosse Pointe*."

"And thank God."

"I don't get it. You're tossing me out for him?"

"Let's just say that I prefer his company to yours."

Oooh. That was a punch that landed in the old narcissus complex. Charlie recovered and countered, "Olivia, tell me the truth. Have you really taken a close look at him? I mean a really close look?"

"Are you asking if I have performed some dermatological inspection on him?"

"I don't think this is funny, Olivia. I'm wondering if you have really thought this through?"

"Oh, I do appreciate your concern, Charlie," she said facetiously.

"I'm just trying to understand what you see in the guy."

"Actually, I see a great deal. While it may come as a shock to you, I find him far more attractive and more appealing than present company."

"Olivia, come on!" He said in disbelief. "Open your eyes. The man is shorter than I am. He's nowhere as good looking. He isn't even a VP. Well, I made him one a couple weeks ago, but it's a bogus title. And one more thing; he's going to be out of a job real soon. He's nobody, from nowhere, and he brings nothing to your party, Olivia."

Charlie could barely contain himself. It was not so much that he minded losing Olivia. Hell, anything resembling marriage had been a distant memory for years. And one woman in his life at a time just wasn't enough. So, she'd finally had enough. Okay. He understood that. He didn't like it, but he understood. But to be replaced by that twerp. That–*training manager*, for God's sake. That did not sit at all well with him. That was, he decided, her way of trying to get even. It was time he defended himself. The gloves were off. He began with what he assumed would be a well-placed cut. "The more I think about your making it with Waddington, the more I find it hard not to laugh. In fact, I really am having a very hard time containing myself. Of all people. What can he possibly give you that I can't?" Other than some platitude about love and understanding, he knew she'd have a hard time finding an answer. He gave into a chortle that began well down in his chest. It said volumes about his contempt for the quality of her affair. At least the man could have been an executive or had a low handicap.

"Oh, you'd be surprised what he can give me that you can't."

He was laughing harder now. "Like what? Scintillating conversation?"

"Well, as a matter of fact, that *is* one thing he provides that you can't. But what really makes him different from you, what really makes him so very special, is what he gave me last night."

"Which was what, a poetry reading?" Oh, he was having fun now. Laughing at her expense.

"No, he didn't read poetry last night," she continued evenly, showing no sign that Charlie had aroused even the merest inclination to strike back.

"So, what then?"

"He gave me the most extraordinarily, satisfying, and romantic night in bed I've ever had."

Charlie stopped laughing.

62
Things Could Get Ugly

Annual dealer meetings are pivotal events in every car manufacturer's year. The purpose is to reveal the new model or models for the coming year and to build dealer confidence in the company, the management, and the value of their franchises. The company's meeting had the same objectives. However, considering the current rate of sales, the bloated inventories, and the Verite recall, building confidence looked to be a nearly impossible challenge.

Almost from the moment the first group of dealers checked into the Renaissance Center hotel on Thursday, Waddington realized that it was going to take a miracle to deal with them. The men looked like they had just joined a vigilante group and the women were grousing about having been dragged to Detroit. Detroit for god's sakes! Who the hell has a dealer meeting in Detroit? No one even builds cars in Detroit anymore. Every wife shared the same sentiment. All the other car companies take us to resorts or the islands or someplace where we can lie by the pool and visit a spa and be entertained. But Detroit? What's there to do in Detroit? The city that still, after all these years, looks like it's been firebombed. Nobody was happy. Plus, it was hot. Detroit's kind of hot. A mid-August hot that arrives like a steam bath and turns hairdos into something that look like wilted spinach. The message from the dealers was that they had no intention of making this a pleasant experience. Within hours, word was spreading through company management: If you can avoid the welcome dinner, avoid it. Because *you* will not be welcome. Let the zone managers take the heat.

***

By seven, most of the dealers had plundered the bars of most of their liquor and had formed into small groups, like militia, waiting for the word to "form up" and get ready for the attack. Harry Spar was generally unknown to the dealers. In fact, he could have passed for one of them. Maybe someone with a new franchise. Whatever, he was able to infiltrate by looking like someone wondering where his wife had wandered off to and eavesdrop on their conversations. Within minutes he'd learned enough to report back to Charlie.

"Bottom line? They are pissed and looking for someone to piss on. And I think that someone is you," Harry reported. "The hostility is as thick as sludge. The bastards are drinking everything in sight. If they're sober enough to make it to the meeting tomorrow, things could get ugly."

"The bastards," Charlie groused. "Those ungrateful bastards." He could feel the sweat pop out on his brow. His intestinal track felt like it had tied itself in a knot. "You have your cell phone, right?" Charlie asked.

"I'm on it now."

"Give me a minute to think. I'll get back to you."

What a fuckin' lousy week it had been for Charlie. It really hadn't helped matters to discover his wife was having an affair with Preston Waddington. That piece of shit was diddling his wife right under his nose. It had taken every bit of control not to walk into Waddington's office and deck him. Fortunately, he'd been able to contain himself. He would wait until after the dealer meeting. No way he was going to give Waddington an opportunity to screw that up. He was walking a tightrope with the dealers and he knew it. Waddington was in a perfect position to knock him off. All it would take was for Waddington to pull the plug on the Teleprompter in the middle of his speech or screw up the Le Vent reveal to assure a disaster. No, dealing with Waddington had to wait until after the meeting.

But now this report from Harry Spar: "Things could get ugly," he'd said. Those bastards were going to blame him for things that were beyond his control. It wasn't his fault that the cars weren't selling. And what control did he have over quality on the production line? That was manufacturing's responsibility. He didn't work on the assembly line. And the dealers? They were always whining. Always complaining. Yet, he'd made most of those bastards rich. They lived in big houses with wide-screen plasma TVs. So, what if they'd had a downturn in the last couple of years? Hell, if they'd not been so damn greedy and let him cut their profit margins, the company would have been fine.

But no, they had to feed their bloated bank accounts and their big boats, and their summer homes, and in more than a few cases, their mistresses. He was not going to stand up there tomorrow and let those bastards take shots at him. He was not going to put himself in the line of fire. Let someone else get drawn and quartered. Yeah, why don't I let someone else catch the shit? Charlie began to smile. He knew exactly who that someone else should be.

He dialed Spar. "Harry," he said, his voice raspy and almost inaudible. "I've developed laryngitis. I won't be giving my speech tomorrow. Someone will have to stand in for me."

"Who?"

63
Nothing to Lose

It was after nine when Waddington pulled up to Olivia's house.

"Can I get you anything? A drink? Coffee?"

"No, I just want to talk."

"Come out on the terrace. There's a breeze, and it's cooled off a bit."

After they'd sat down, she took his hand. "This is like Charlie. When the going gets rough, he gets going in the opposite direction. What are you going to do?"

"I'm going to give the speech," Waddington said with a touch of defiance. "But it won't the speech I pulled off the teleprompter. In Charlie's speech, he gives himself credit for the Verite sales numbers, the design of the Le Vent, and creation of the *Easy* campaign. The rest of it is designed to blame everyone but himself for the company's failures and every worldly event that might have conceivably influenced consumers to stay away from their showrooms. I think the only thing he didn't blame for our weak sales was mad cow disease. The dealers are not going to buy his same old song and dance. So, if I'm going to give the speech, it's going to be my speech."

"Are you sure you want to do this?"

"Absolutely. What have I got to lose? Nothing. I'm going to get up on that stage tomorrow and say all the things I believe should be said to the dealers. I'm not going to make excuses for our screw ups. Instead, I'm going to lay out a vision for the future. After tomorrow, I may not be part of that future, but I'm sure going to leave them with something to think about. At the same time, I'm going to do my best to give Charlie a bad case of indigestion as I stuff all this down his throat. If I get the ball rolling, he may not be able to stop it."

Olivia was beaming. She leaned over and kissed him. "I love it. And I love you. Sometimes it takes a tsunami or an earthquake to get people's attention. You can do that. I know you can."

"Only one thing concerns me."

"What's that?"

"I don't mind giving a speech that puts Charlie in a box, but I am concerned that by shaking things up too much, I might be creating problems for your father. If I'm presented as speaking for the president, and the dealers buy what I have to say and demand the company deliver, your father is going to have to deal with the fall out."

"He may surprise you."

"Right, by asking for my head to be delivered on a plate."

"I have more faith in him than that. I know he wants what's best for the company. He can't do it all himself. What he needs are people who believe we have a future, who want to turn things around. But no matter. You go out there tomorrow and give 'em something to believe in."

"I'll do my best." Waddington stood up. "And now, I'd better get back to my motel room. I need to write a speech."

"I have a feeling you're going to be fantastic. An automotive Marc Anthony," she said as she walked him to his car.

Waddington smiled and nodded. "Marc and I have a lot in common. His crowd was ready to kill him too. Unfortunately, I don't have Shakespeare ghost writing for me."

64
It Worked for Marc Anthony

The dealers began to arrive at the auditorium in Cobo Hall about 8:15 and were welcomed with Neil Diamond's "Coming to America" blasting over the sound system. While no such implication was intended, it appeared to some that the song was actually meant as a welcome to the French financial investment which was not only coming to America, but to the company. Most of the dealers and those wives who chose to attend showed the residual damage of the night before. Many of the men hadn't bothered shaving. A few looked like they'd slept in their clothes if they'd slept at all. The women looked as if they had done their best to paste together their faces and blot out bad memories with make-up. The animus that had begun to build during the welcoming buffet had not abated, only intensified. Tom Thomas suggested, at least partly in jest, that it might be a good idea to check the crowd for guns. They were an angry bunch of dealers with hangovers, which made them madder yet.

At 8:30, the lights went down and a spotlight came up on the podium that had been placed in front of the curtain on the right side of the stage. In the past, the president always opened the meeting with a state-of-the company speech. The music stopped. Everyone expected to see Charlie appear behind the podium. Had he missed his entrance cue? The rumble in the audience grew louder. The collective dealer attitude was not unlike zoo animals before feeding time. Finally, a voice came over the intercom.

"Ladies and Gentlemen, we regret to inform you that President Charles Fair is incapacitated and will not be able to deliver his speech to you this morning."

There was a perceptible increase in volume. One voice was heard above the roar, "He'd better be on his deathbed."

"He has been struck with a bad case of laryngitis. To deliver his speech, we would like to introduce the man you know as your Manager of Sales Training. A man who has recently been promoted to Vice President of Dealer and Customer Relations, Preston Waddington."

Preston walked out on the stage to a less than cordial welcome.

"We want that fukker, Fair!"

"Yeah, bring him out."

"If he can't talk, let him use sign language."

"Afraid to face us, Charlie?"

The announcement had served as the spark to set them off. For a moment, it looked like someone was going to have to call out the National Guard.

Waddington quickly stepped to the podium. He knew immediately that his only hope to get through to the dealers was to employ a form of shock and awe. He pulled the wireless microphone from its stand and stepped to the edge of the stage.

"Friends! Dealers! Ladies and Gentlemen!" he shouted into the mike and over the tumult in front of him. "Give me your attention for just a moment. And hear me! You have every right to be angry. You have every right to be mad. Our performance as a car company *sucks*! The fact that we have had to issue a recall on our best-selling car ever *sucks*. The way you've been treated *sucks*. And in case you missed my message, I'm saying that we **suck**!"

The room fell into stunned silence. No one had ever heard a car executive, *any* company executive, stand up before a dealer body and admit to something like that. We suck?

Someone in the back could be heard to ask, "Did he say what I think he said?"

"He said the company sucks."

"Sucks?"

"Shut up!"

"Let's hear what he has to say!"

"I come before you this morning, not to beg your pardon for our mistakes. I come not to offer excuses for our lack of quality. I come not to place the blame for our poor sales performance on events beyond our control. Rather, I come to admit to you a fundamental reality: We are what we are because we have failed to be the car company that I know we can be.

"But what *can* we be, you ask? Is there hope for us? With sales slow and inventories high, I know it will be difficult for me to convince you that the future for this company is far brighter than it appears. At times like these, the good things we have done, the changes we've made are easily forgotten. That's reality. We accept that reality."

Charlie and Harry Spar had crept into the wings and after a moment had positioned themselves, fully expecting to witness the carnage. "What the hell?" Charlie whispered to Harry. "That's not my goddamn speech. What's he up to?"

"Beats me."

"The media has told you that we are teetering on the edge of bankruptcy. They have said that our chances of survival against our U.S. competition and the flood of imports are between slim and none. They have fostered rumors that our French investors were having second thoughts about investing in us. That they have said those things about the company does us a grievous disservice. As of noon yesterday, the world, *our* automotive world, changed. Today, I speak to you as a representative of a financially healthy company. Today, I speak to you as a representative of a company that has taken the first steps to becoming a very different car company. As of noon yesterday, when we signed the final agreement with the French consortium, the winds of good fortune began to fill our sails. Immediately, we took a new tack and a new course."

There was a spontaneous burst of applause. It was not tumultuous applause. Rather, it had a guarded quality about it, as if the dealers were not all that sure they believed what they were hearing.

"Yesterday, I was shown a list of the proposed changes that your board of directors has approved for immediate implementation. Changes that will improve quality, reduce inventories, and create new products that you will be proud to display in your showrooms."

Charlie looked befuddled. "What list is he talking about? I never saw any list."

"If I were to read some of those changes, you would find yourselves saying things like, 'at last,' 'finally,' 'great idea.' Your frustration with this company and its lack of aggressive action would begin to ebb. You will begin to understand that today, we have a new vision of what this company can be. And because of our new partners, that vision is achievable."

There was a murmur of approval mixed with several calls from doubters.

"You'll have to prove it."

"I've heard this before."

"What's this new vision?"

"Why don't you tell us about it?"

"Ladies and Gentlemen, I would do so, happily. But knowing how you feel about the company, sensing your level of disappointment in us, I wonder if raising your hopes and expectations would be a good idea. Hearing them, you may expect too much from us too soon. You may become impatient and in so doing, become discouraged. Let me be honest with you. The changes I saw on that list will not produce a miracle. The company will not turn around in a month or a year. But then, who could reasonably expect anyone to achieve an instant reversal of fortunes? The changes and plans I saw might be implemented next week, but it will take time for them to impact our business. What I saw on that list was a roadmap. A roadmap for a journey. As with any journey to a worthwhile destination, it will take time, effort, and commitment. And so, I put the question to you: If I were to reveal to you our plans and changes, and if you found them to your liking, would you be willing to spend the time, expend the effort, and make a personal commitment to help us achieve success?"

"Try us!"

"Hell, yes!"

"If you've got a good plan, count us in."

"Hey, we're your partners in this."

"But no bullshit, okay?" came another voice.

"I see you leave me no choice but to tell you what your board is planning. The list of changes they have proposed is long, far too long to detail in what little time I have here with you this morning. So let me share with you those decisions and changes which we will implement first and whose impact will be felt almost immediately."

"First, the practice of shipping your cars that fail their final quality inspection and asking you to fix them in your repair shops is over. Done. Buried. From now on, only those cars that pass our new and rigorous ninety-six-point quality inspection process will be shipped to you."

There was a general murmur of cautious approval.

"Goddamn it, if you mean that–"

"It's about time."

"I'll believe it when I see it."

"Second, we will use some of our new funding to support a rebate program designed to help you reduce your inventories down to a forty-five-day level."

That met with instant and sustained applause.

"What's he talking about? What new ninety-six-point inspection process? What rebates? He has no right to tell us where we'll spend our money." Charlie growled. "He's out of control. He's got to be stopped before he destroys the company. For God's sake, Harry, have someone turn off his mike!"

Harry did not move.

"Third, we will continue to seek out the best automotive designers, wherever in the world they might be found, to design our new cars. The stodgy, bloated, unimaginative, upside-down bathtub-like designs that have been our trademarks will be history."

"At least he's got that part right," Charlie groused. "What the hell does he think I've been doing?"

"I know that all of you were greatly disappointed when Axel McPherson announced his retirement."

"The best sales manager you fukkers ever had," came a voice.

"Absolutely."

"The guy was tough, but he was always on our side."

"As of today, we are asking that Axel come back to us. Not just as a Vice President, but as our new Executive VP of Sales. I am happy to report that I talked with him last night, and he is more than ready to accept. By the way, if you will look in the back of the room, you will see the man I consider my mentor. The man each of you knows can provide the kind of sales leadership that is so necessary for our success." Waddington gestured toward the back of the room. "Axel McPherson, please stand up. My friends, let's show Axel how happy we are to have him back." Waddington started to applaud and it set off a resounding roar of clapping hands and shouts in the audience.

"He can't do that! I've fired the bastard." Charlie snapped at Harry Spar. "What the fuck! Get out there and drag him off the goddamn stage!" Charlie's voice was low, but angry and intense.

Suddenly a chant began to roll through the dealer body, "Axel, Axel, Axel." The volume rocked the hall.

"We pull Waddington off now, and they'll kill us," Harry warned.

As the chant died down, Waddington resumed, "I know many of you have expressed great dissatisfaction with our advertising over the last several years." Waddington looked down at the dozen or so agency people who had commandeered seats in the front row. "You have complained that our agency does a far better job of selling their own creativity than selling our cars. That will no longer be the case. Dealers, I would like you to say good-bye to these fine ladies and gentlemen, because as of today they are no longer our agency."

A whoop went up from the dealers. George 'Walrus' Walarus and his minions looked as if they'd just realized their mortgages had been called and their credit cards canceled. They were stunned, immobile.

Charlie's laryngitis disappeared. "I don't believe it. He just fired our advertising agency. He can't do that. Harry, if you don't get out there and pull him off the stage, you're going to be looking for work!"

"Hey! You're not sending me out there. If you want him off the stage, you get him off. But I'd advise against it. Let this play out. He's got the dealers loving him."

"But the promises he's making. How the hell can we keep those promises?"

"Let me ask you something? Has he really promised anything that in one form or another can't be delivered now that we have the French money?"

"Well, no. I mean, firing the agency wasn't in the plans."

"Screw the agency. Who needs 'em? They were charging us too much anyway."

"What's your point?"

"Think about it. As far as the dealers are concerned, Waddington is delivering *your* speech. That makes *you,* not him, the dealer's hero. I say, let him go. He's doing you a hell of a favor."

As the applause died down along with the shouts of, "Send them back to New York," a tall, dark-haired dealer with a large mustache stood up and shouted above the din. "But what about the recall?"

"Yeah, the recall," another voice echoed.

"Did you think we'd forget?"

The audience had momentarily forgotten one of the primary reasons for their displeasure. They remembered quickly and the buzz of voices rose dramatically.

"No, I did not think you'd forget. I purposely left the recall issue for last because I know it is of your most immediate concern. As we all well know, a recall is never a pleasant prospect for any car company, especially if they are struggling as we are. But what is the option? What alternative do we have to a recall? There was and is none. Dare we let ourselves be pilloried by the press as neglecting our responsibility to our customers? Dare we risk turning a blind eye to the need to modify our suspension? To do so, my friends, would have been unconscionable and courting a legal disaster. However, even a recall can offer an upside, an opportunity to prove that we are a responsible, ethical car company."

"Opportunity?"

"To do what? Take guff from our customers?"

"Like what kind of opportunity?"

"Like the kind I'm about to tell you about. As you are aware, of course, we will pay for all parts and labor. While that relieves you of the financial burden, we understand that you're the ones who have to take the heat. You're the ones who have to suffer the complaints firsthand. There would seem to be no way that a recall will make your customers feel more kindly toward you, unless," he paused dramatically, "unless we use the recall to our advantage. What we're proposing is to use the recall to offer our Verite customers a value-added bonus. This will become a positive public relations event. The recall gives us the opportunity to demonstrate our concern for the safety of our customers by making the changes to the suspension system. To compensate our customers for the inconvenience of having to bring their cars in, we are going to pay you to offer a free oil change, a free carwash, and a coupon worth two thousand dollars off on the purchase of any Cadence, Defiant, or Road Warrior. One more thing; next spring, we will send each of your recall customers a special invitation and a special incentive to test drive the new Spirit. Speaking of the Spirit, now that we have new financing, we will be able to accelerate the Spirit launch. As your dealer council will attest, this new mid-size sedan is truly one of the most innovative, imaginative, and great looking cars to come out of Detroit in many years."

The applause was genuine. The dealers were nodding. If not total believers in the changes Waddington was telling them about, they had at least been primed to become believers. All the company had to do was deliver on what he'd promised. He'd made it virtually impossible for them not to.

"A moment ago, I told you that I had come before you today, not to make excuses for our mistakes, but to present a vision of our future. It's no secret that the realization of that vision will require a close working relationship between you, our long-suffering dealers, and the factory. I have briefly outlined the first steps in our journey to making this car company a company of which we can all be proud. It's a long road. But as the Chinese say, the journey of a thousand miles begins with the first step. Today, we have taken the first step. Will you take the next step with me? Are you with us?"

The dealers rose to their feet. Clapping. Shouting. Whistling. Tom Thomas quickly told his soundman to play "Coming to America" again. The dealers were shouting and high-fiveing one another. Waddington caught a glimpse of Olivia. She was standing in the back near the door. She was giving him a thumbs-up.

"And now," Waddington yelled into the microphone. "I give you your new Le Vent."

That was Tom Thomas' cue to begin the reveal. No one sat down. No one stopped clapping. The music changed to "I Get So Excited" by the Pointer Sisters.

"This is incredible," Charlie said peering out at the audience from behind the curtain. "Look at 'em! They're going crazy. They're lovin' it."

"And in a few minutes, they're going to be loving you."

"But how?"

Harry cupped his hand between his mouth and Charlie's ear in order to be heard over the music.

Charlie listened and then brightened. He began to smile. "Harry, you are nothing short of a genius."

Waddington stood just out of sight in the wings to watch the Le Vent reveal. It was spectacular. Twenty leggy blonds were dancing in front of a large glass box. The box was big enough

462

to hold a car, but at the moment, it appeared to be empty. A magician appeared and one by one, as the music blared, he herded the girls into the box. When all twenty were inside, the magician made a sweeping gesture with his cane. Pyrotechnics lit up the stage and a drape from high up in the flies floated down over the box. More fireworks. More music. Trumpets. The magician began to count down "five, four, three, two, one. He yanked on the curtain which flew back into the flies. The girls were gone and in their place was the Le Vent. One side of the box folded down to create a ramp and the car rolled out to center stage.

The dealers let out another roar.

Waddington smiled. He'd loosed an avalanche and now someone was going to have to deal with it. That someone was either Perkins or Charlie or maybe both. Well, what's done is done, he decided. Charlie will be going nuts, but so what. As he turned to walk off the stage, he was surprised to pass Charlie and Harry walking onto it. Charlie spotted him and stopped. He walked over and smiled like something was up and only he knew what it was.

"You can have Olivia, but understand, I'm going to fight her for the house. And thanks for making me the man of the year." Nary a hint of laryngitis.

Waddington had no idea what he meant by his "man of the year" comment. He found out quickly. He watched as Charlie and Harry virtually ran out on the stage. Harry grabbed the wireless mike and walked to the edge of the stage. Charlie stayed back by the Le Vent, which sat gleaming in the spotlights.

"Ladies and Gentlemen," he heard Harry say into the microphone. "The man who just delivered the president's great speech was *not*, as you know, our President and CEO. He is still suffering from acute laryngitis. But let me assure you, the words you heard, those great and welcome words, belong to Charles Dunwood Fair. And now, I give you your president, your man of vision, Charlie Fair." A roar of approval went up from the dealers. The spotlight followed Charlie as walked slowly forward, like a king approaching his loving subjects, to acknowledge the standing ovation.

"Way to go, Charlie Fair!"

"Atta boy."

"Let's hear it for Charlie."

"We're with ya!"

Waddington was dumbfounded. *Charlie's taking credit for my speech. The sonofabitch. The man has no shame. They're applauding him for what I said. I should do something, say something. But what?* Waddington realized there was *nothing* he could do. There was no way he could expose Charlie. Who'd believe him? The announcer had identified him as giving *Charlie's* speech. Now it *was* Charlie's speech. At least as far as the dealers were concerned. A purloined triumph, but a triumph, nonetheless. Waddington heard Charlie whisper into the microphone. His laryngitis had suddenly returned. "Thank you. Thank you. Sorry about the voice, but I'm glad you got my message.

Welcome to the future. Together we'll make it great!"

The dealers were again on their feet. Like generals of old, Charlie had clearly taken the field of battle and won the day.

65

You Are Cordially Invited
to Fall Upon Your Sword

Other men who found themselves waiting in what the company euphemistically called their "corporate guest office" ended up having their heads handed to them. Waddington felt sure that they, unlike him, had arrived in this room confident, secure in their positions and considered by their subordinates to be pivotal cogs in the car-building enterprise. They had walked into the boardroom, trusting in their own importance, unaware that they had made grossly erroneous assumptions as to why they'd been called.

Surprise! Whack! Their heads rolled.

That bit of reality was not lost on Waddington. However, he had decided, after a fitful night's sleep, that his fate would not be so clean as a private beheading performed behind the closed doors of the boardroom. No, he was quite certain that he would be asked, *coerced* might be a better word, into making a very public sacrifice by impaling himself on his sword in front of the press and the dealers. It wasn't fair, of course. He deserved better. Far better. Hadn't he saved the company from a series of potentially disastrous lawsuits? Hadn't he retrieved most of the five-million-dollar extortion payment? Hadn't he pacified a rebellious dealer body? So much for gratitude.

Yesterday, several hours after the dealer meeting, Perkins Byrd had called and said, "Waddington, we'll need you in the boardroom tomorrow at 11:00, but I'd like to have you there a little earlier, say ten o'clock, just in case."

In case of what? he wondered. "What's on the agenda?" Waddington asked, hoping for some clue as to what awaited him, and at the same time fearing that Perkins might, in fact, tell him.

"Let's not worry about that right now,," Perkins Byrd replied in a tone that offered no hint as to the chairman's mood or intent.

While Waddington sensed that Perkins was purposely avoiding an explanation as to why he had been summoned, he decided there was little to lose by asking one more question. "So, there's nothing more you want to tell me?"

There was a long pause on Perkins' end of the line and then, "One thing."

"Yes?" he asked expectantly.

"Be sure your suit coat matches your pants."

"Right," Waddington said, shuddering at the memory of the embarrassment he'd suffered at the Fair's cocktail party. "I usually try not to make the same mistake twice." Waddington wasn't sure if he heard Perkins laugh or just clear his throat before he hung up. Whichever, he made a mental note to wear his dark charcoal-grey suit, the one he usually reserved for weddings and funerals.

That was yesterday. Now, eighteen hours later, here he was. He had arrived on the executive floor and was greeted by Perkins, who asked him to wait in the guest *office.* Waddington tried to read something in his expression, but it was a blank page.

Waddington found nothing in the decor of the guest office that invited an extended stay or suggested that it was to be inhabited on a full-time basis. The furnishings were sparse. All that distinguished it from a latter-day Tower of London waiting room was a tall tropical plant doing its best to survive in a large porcelain pot and two pictures of cars that had long since been expunged from the company's model line. Waddington stood up, walked over to the door, and looked out at the expansive executive reception foyer. The floor gleamed with white Italian marble that was partially covered by a lush, thick pile, custom-blue Stark carpet that had been embroidered with the company's logo. Across the way, he could see the two large mahogany doors that led to the boardroom. He found a spot where he could watch the doors, but remain mostly hidden. One by one, the board members arrived. Charlie stepped off the elevator in animated conversation with Hardman Tuber. At about 10:15, he saw Emma Rae close the doors and sit down at a desk just outside the boardroom. Apparently, she was to be on call if Perkins or Charlie needed anything, like Waddington for example.

In his mind, he sifted through the events of the last several months. There were a lot of reasons Perkins might have called him to the board meeting, and none of them were very good. Considering all that had happened, he wondered if maybe the French, now that they controlled fifty-one percent of the company, had decided that a public display of management blood was needed to cleanse the company of its sins. Certainly, the French, historically, had a penchant for spilling blood in public. *But why mine?* he wondered. *The speech? Of course.* It had certainly raised his profile. He'd made himself an obvious target and maybe an expendable one as well. *Well,* he thought, *even Marc Anthony was eventually deposed by Octavius.* In this case, he presumed Charlie was playing that role. Maybe this was the finale in Charlie Fair's nefarious plot to exact revenge for what had happened between Olivia and him.

Olivia. The mere thought of her sent a pleasant ripple through his body. He had never intended for it to happen, but it had happened and he had no regrets, no shame, only a longing to be with her as soon as this was over. Waddington had decided his affair (my God how preposterous the word *affair* sounded). He, Preston Waddington, Sales Training Manager, having an affair with the president's wife. Maybe Charlie had convinced Perkins he was one of the conspirators in the extortion plot. Considering that his name was on all those bogus invoices, Charlie could claim that Waddington had been part of Popper's scam. Maybe he was using that to mask the real reason for staging a formal corporate seppuku–he wanted *retribution.* That would explain why the call came from Perkins. Or would it? Knowing Charlie, it didn't make sense that he would go to all this trouble just to punish him for the affair. No, there had to be more to it than that. And then, it dawned *on* him. He suddenly understood the real reason for Charlie's animus. Waddington had become a rival, a corporate nemesis, an inadvertent usurper. *A threat!*

66
What No Parachute?

As Charlie entered the boardroom, he said good morning to Perkins and several of the board members. There was no sign of the laryngitis that, but twenty-four hours before, had forced him to whisper his thanks to the dealers.

"You sound a lot better, Charlie," Perkins said.

"Ahh, Harry Spar got me some pills."

"Isn't modern medicine amazing?"

"I only wish I'd had them when this came on."

Perkins nodded, but it was the kind of nod that bore no sympathy.

"If you'll take your seats, we'll get started. The first order of business is to discuss the change in our management."

Charlie had no idea what Perkins was talking about, and he hoped it didn't show. *What change in management?*

"As you all know, for some time the position of Vice Chairman of the Board has been open. Now that the French have come on board, it's important that we fill that position. It's my suggestion that Charlie Fair be given those responsibilities."

Charlie literally beamed. Vice Chairman, CEO, and President. *That confirms me as heir apparent to Perkins. He's not going to last as Chairman forever. The old bastard is ready to be put out to pasture any time now. If I play this right, in a year he'll just be Chairman of the Executive Committee, and I'll have control of everything else. I'll be able to stack the board with my people and, eventually, freeze old Perkins out completely. Or at least neutralize his power. What a day!*

"There's only one thing you need to know, Charlie," Perkins continued. "Now that the French own fifty-one percent of the company, they have made a request. They want to be sure their investment is protected. I think we can all understand that."

Charlie glanced around the table. Everyone was nodding, and he added his nod to the group.

"Therefore, they have asked that one of their people, Pierre Artier to be specific, be appointed CEO and President. Which means, Charlie, we are asking that you vacate those titles, and your office, for that matter, and serve only as Vice Chairman."

Charlie blanched and bolted upright in his chair. "Wait a minute. Are you telling me I'm out?"

"No," Perkins said with a measured calm that Charlie found unsettling. "You will be Vice Chairman. However, your role in the company will be markedly reduced. Under our agreement with the consortium, all decisions regarding the company's major operations will be in the hands of the new president. Of course, Pierre will depend on all of us to provide counsel and support. I'm sure you'll be happy to learn that they absolutely agree with the plans outlined in your speech. Your new job will be to act as a liaison with the dealers and customers and to help the new president in whatever capacity he feels will be most beneficial to him. You will probably want to take French lessons, as his English is about as good as my French, which is limited to 'Where's the toilet?' Now, Charlie, can we assume that you are prepared to accept this new position?"

Charlie felt like the man who had been told he won the lottery, but all his winnings and then some had to be donated to Ralph Nader for President. "I think we should discuss this. Are we really willing to turn over control of this company to some frog who doesn't even speak our language?"

"Well, I exaggerated a bit," Perkins said, apparently amused at his characterization of the new president. "He does speak English and rather well. His accent is a little heavy, I must admit. However, it would be useful if you could at least understand the language. Especially, when you're attending meetings that might involve members of the consortium who don't speak English well."

"Well, let me say that, while I accept your nomination to be Vice Chairman, I am absolutely opposed to giving up my titles as CEO and President. I see no reason why we can't give Pierre the title of Executive Vice President and COO. Make him a Vice Chairman as well. Hell, make him an Executive Vice Chairman for all I care. Give him whatever title makes him feel good. That would give the French all the assurance they need that their money is properly spent."

"But that's not what they're asking, Charlie."

"I don't care what they're asking. Whose company is this?"

"In terms of control, it's really theirs now. However, they made it very clear they want to regard our affiliation as a partnership and not an acquisition. But they do insist on having their man as CEO and President."

"I am against it. I think it's wrong. I do not think our dealers and stockholders ever envisioned that this deal would force their management to step aside."

"You're not stepping aside, Charlie, you're stepping up to Vice Chairman."

"To what? A public relations function? No. No. I do not and will not agree. I'm sure I don't have to remind you that after yesterday's reception to my speech, the dealers will not look favorably on having my position and influence in the company compromised by the French. Even they have to be impressed with the reception I got."

"Are you saying that you will not accept the position of Vice Chairman and relinquish your title and responsibilities as President and CEO?"

"That's sums up my position very well." Charlie bristled. He was adamant. He looked around the table. Most of these men belonged to the same country club he did. They played golf together. Sure, he beat them all the time, but hell, he had a three handicap. In addition, he felt sure none of them loved the frogs any more than he did.

"So, you're telling us that you intend to demand to keep your position as President and CEO."

Charlie was growing irritated, and it showed. What was it he didn't understand about *No*? "If I have to repeat myself, I will. I will not give up my current position in this company."

"Let me be sure I understand: Are you rejecting our offer, as I've outlined it, to become Vice Chairman of our Board?"

Had the man lost his hearing? Was he daft? "Again, and I feel that I'm beginning to sound like a broken record, I will accept Vice Chairman only if I remain President and CEO. I have worked very hard to make this company a success. I have given it my life's blood to keep it afloat through some very difficult times. I have made sacrifices for this company. I have given it my every waking hour. If you think I will give up control as we stand on the edge of the greatest opportunity in our history, an opportunity that will assure us of a profitable and growing company, you've got another think coming. I have no intention of stepping down from President and CEO. I have no intention of letting some fucking frog make decisions for an American car company. My answer is I am rejecting your offer."

"Well, I guess there's no mistaking how you feel."

"I'm glad I finally made my position clear." *What the hell is wrong with Perkins? Doesn't he understand that after yesterday, I have the dealers on my side? My God, they love me. Does he think they'll sit still and let some frog run their company? There would be a rebellion. No, I've got the dealers on my side, and that gives me all the clout I need to hold on to number one.*

"In that case," Perkins said with the look of a man who had finally drawn a Royal Flush, "you leave me no alternative. With the power vested in me as Chairman of the Board, it is my duty to inform you that we have accepted your resignation."

"What?"

"Under our bylaws, it clearly states that, should an officer of the company refuse a promotion or assignment, it is to be regarded as tantamount to an offer of his or her resignation. You have refused the promotion, and we therefore accept your resignation. It's as simple as that. May I have a show of hands to indicate that the board has accepted Charlie's resignation?"

Charlie looked around the table as each man met his eyes and slowly, some not so slowly, raised his hand. Even Hardman Tuber, who had lobbied Perkins seven years ago to appoint Charlie CEO, slowly raised his hand and added his vote. Et tu, Hardman. It was unanimous. Suddenly, it all became very clear. Perkins had set him up. There was no way he could gracefully fire him, so he let him fall on his sword all by himself. The bastard knew he would never agree to the Vice Chairman's title if it meant giving up everything else. It was all planned. Perkins had orchestrated this sham like a man who had read the end of the book before he began. Charlie wasn't sure, but he thought he detected the trace of a smile on Perkins' face.

"I will call security and ask them to assist you in cleaning out your desk and removing your personal belongings. And now, on behalf of the board, I want to thank you for your years of service to the company and wish you well in the years ahead." Perkins had just let Charlie buy his own bus ticket. For the second time in their association, albeit with a twenty-five-year interval, Perkins was sending Charlie packing.

Charlie could not move. It was as if he'd just been told by the mafia chieftain that he was to take a long car ride. He looked around the room, hoping for some sign of support, someone who might yet come to his rescue. He made a desperate grasp for survival, "Under the circumstances, I might want to reconsider your offer."

"A vote has been taken, Charlie. It's done. And so are you. Oh, I should tell you that since you have tendered your resignation by having refused the promotion, you have also forfeited your financial parachute. You will receive two weeks pay and that's all."

The man was not even waiting to put him in the car. He was hacking him to death right there and then.

"I have one question, Perkins."

"Yes," Perkins said, looking him straight in the eye.

"Is what you've just done to me personal or business?"

Perkins did his best to appear to be shocked by the question. "Business, of course. I never mix my personal feelings with business. I think you, of all people, should know that. Now, if you'd be so kind as to leave us, we have other personnel matters to attend to."

Charlie straightened himself up and pulled his shoulders back like a man who was determined to go to the firing squad maintaining his pride and dignity. As he reached the door, the meeting behind him resumed, and he heard Perkins say something, he was not sure what, but he did manage to hear him mention four names, Nichols, Brewster, Spar, and Waddington.

67
The Hour Is at Hand

Waddington glanced at his watch as the boardroom doors opened. Charlie came out, said something to Emma Rae, and then the two of them went into his office. It was 10:25. Five minutes later, Waddington noticed two men who he knew to be security guards get off the elevator and go into Charlie's office. *Shades of Felicity Turehart?* Waddington asked himself. *Are they for me? If so, it won't take long to remove my personal items.* Several more minutes passed and he saw Emma Rae leave Charlie's office and take up her post outside the boardroom.

He waited. No one came. Charlie did not reappear. The mahogany doors remained closed. Emma Rae was sitting with her back to him. She'd barely moved since she'd left Charlie's office. Finally, the door to Charlie's office opened. Charlie came out followed by one of the security men who punched the elevator button. *Where's Charlie going?* Waddington wondered. The elevator arrived and the two men got on.

Waddington continued to wait. He began to wonder if they'd forgotten about him. Maybe he should ask Emma Rae. No, bad idea. She'd tell him nothing. He looked at his watch. It was almost eleven. That was the time Perkins had set. The appointed hour. The moment of truth. The defining moment between what was past and what was yet to be. Had he let his overactive, well-honed sense of corporate reality get the best of him? Had he worried himself into a state of near mental anorexia for no reason, or had he read the tea leaves of uncertainty correctly? In a few moments, he would walk across the foyer, pass through the double doors, and take a seat at the foot of the teak conference table. There he would look across the polished expanse at the solemn faces of the executive committee. Would their expressions be stern, sympathetic, resolute? Waddington was betting on the latter. After some perfunctory explanation, he would be asked if he would be so kind as to fall on his sword, in front of the press, please. At this point, he had no idea how he would respond or what action he might take. He'd have to play it by ear.

Waddington heard a sound coming from across the foyer. One of the double doors opened and a board member leaned out and said something to Emma Rae. She nodded , reached for a box of Kleenex, and stood up. He could write the script: Emma Rae would come into his office, greet him with a malevolent smile, and say something flip and nasty like, "You drew the short straw, asshole! So, you're it!" Or "Times up, shithead!" Or maybe she would decide to say something really ugly, like, "I hope they start by smashing your nuts in a vice." Emma Rae was capable of extraordinary verbal cruelty.

Waddington turned and stared out the window, as if by turning his back on the approaching Emma Rae, he would prolong the inevitable. He heard her knock on the doorframe. Waddington turned. There were tears in her eyes. Now he understood the Kleenex stop. *For me?* he wondered. Good heavens. Could she, at this eleventh hour, have developed a sense of compassion? It was hard to believe.

Emma Rae dabbed at her eyes, "Allergies," she mumbled and then looked at him with the same disdain she might have shown had she caught him relieving himself in the potted plant.

What's with her? Waddington wondered. *What have they been saying about me in there?* He searched her face for some clue, but all she did was give him a contemptuous follow me, shit-for-brains flip of her head.

They trod over the lush, blue Stark carpet with its corporate logo. The heavy, mahogany floor-to-ceiling boardroom doors loomed large in front of him. Emma Rae veered off toward her desk, leaving him standing alone before the portals. Before she turned her back to him, he could see her start to dab her eyes again. *Those tears don't look like allergy tears to me*, he thought. Waddington considered saying something, but what? Should he ask her what was wrong? No. She wouldn't tell him. In fact, she was probably hoping he'd trip over the doorsill and fall on his face in front of the executive committee. Emma Rae glanced back at him and gestured with her left hand toward the door, as if to say, "There's the door handle, schmuck; use it."

Waddington extended his hand toward the large, polished, brass handle with the ornate grape vine motif on the faceplate. The metal felt cold to the touch. His fingers rested for a moment before they began to tighten. Slowly, they complied with his command, though they seemed reluctant to fully affix themselves with any degree of firmness. Finally, he had the handle full in his grasp.

Waddington opened the door and saw before him the Board of Directors. *What's this?* They were smiling. They stood up and held out their hands offering congratulations.

"Preston," Perkins Byrd began, "I want to first congratulate you on that speech yesterday. A bit unorthodox maybe. Your 'we suck' approach had me worried for a few minutes. But I understand it was probably the only way you were going to get their attention. Frankly, I found the whole thing brilliant."

"You knew?" he asked.

"Oh, yes. I learned from a very reliable source whose speech that was."

Olivia. She'd told him.

"It said everything that every one of us would like to have said, had we the opportunity. More importantly, you helped us avoid what had all the earmarks of a revolution in the dealer ranks. Instead of excuses and finger pointing, you gave them hope that we have a future. You can be sure the dealer body will be told who was, in fact, the author of those remarks. I also learned that you were the creator of the *Easy* campaign. The dealers love it, and so do we. Finally, for what it's worth, I have received great feedback from the ride-and-drive you and your staff staged for the dealers out at the proving grounds. I must apologize to you, Preston. I'm afraid much of what you've done for this company has gone unrecognized. Judging from your salary, it's also gone unrewarded. You sir, have proven to be indispensable to this company."

Waddington was speechless.

"Please take a seat." Perkins gestured toward the chair that Charlie had occupied only a half hour before. "It may interest you to know that earlier today, Charlie Fair gave up that seat and resigned from the company. He will, I imagine, be seeking a position somewhere else. The French want their man to be CEO and President, and we, of course, have acquiesced. Charlie chose not to. Now, in addition to thanking you for the speech and your efforts on behalf of the company, I want to tell you why we've asked you here. Our new CEO and President, Pierre Artier, is a very bright car man. We like him a lot. But he's going to need our help, particularly when it comes to communicating his messages and plans to our dealers. Therein lays a problem. Pierre speaks English well, but his accent is very ... well, shall we say, very French. Add that to the current attitude many Americans have toward the French, and his message could be colored by both factors. He needs a voice. He needs someone who can carry his message to the dealers and to the public. We want you to be that man. We want you to be as convincing and persuasive as you were today. You will be the bridge to our dealers. As such, you will also be our pipeline to market reality. Now, to be effective, to convince the dealers that you speak with authority, you'll need an impressive title. VP doesn't do it. For that reason, we would like to offer you the position of Vice Chairman and Executive Vice President for Dealer and Customer Relations. The position, I might add, also comes with that chair." He nodded to where Waddington was sitting. "You will be a member of this board. If you accept, of course."

Waddington was overwhelmed. Ten minutes ago, he expected to have his head on the block. Now he was being asked to become Vice Chairman. "Mr. Byrd …"

"Perkins, please. We're all very informal here."

"Well, Perkins, I would be honored."

And that was that. No ax. No sword to fall on. Just a much larger office on a higher floor and a bigger paycheck.

***

That afternoon, after the board had agreed to fire Nichols, Brewster, and Spar for cause, Waddington was shown into his new office. He was being given the guest office. The very same room where he had waited and fretted about his fate across the white, monogrammed Stark carpet. Pierre Artier was to inhabit Charlie's old office.

The guest office, now the office of Vice Chairman and Executive Vice President for Dealer and Customer Relations, was still, or course, mostly barren and devoid of decoration other than the potted plant and two pictures of long-forgotten models. Soon he would make it his, leaving no sign that it had ever doubled as the Tower waiting room holding the company's nobility prior to their execution.

Waddington had to admit: It felt good to be Vice Chairman. But at the same time, he began to worry. *What if the company doesn't turn around? If I'm the guy building bridges to the dealers, they may decide one day to blow up my bridge.* And everyone was well aware of the potential perfidy of the French. The guillotine was, after all, their gift to humanity.

He looked around at his office as through searching for some divine guidance and heard himself ask the walls, "What do I do now?"

He really did not expect an answer, so he was surprised when the walls answered him back. Their voice was that of his father, repeating his credo, his singular truth, the mantra of a survivor: "Keep a low profile, son."

Epilogue
Louis XVI–Redux
One Year Later

But Waddington did not keep a low profile. He became very visible to the dealers and, in fact, to everyone in the company. The company's turnaround became his private mission. He developed ideas for new marketing programs. He helped pick the new advertising agency and insisted they focus as much on helping their dealers with local advertising as with the national ads. He expanded the training staff and increased the number of sales seminars, earning high marks from the dealers. Most importantly, he could strategize with Pierre Artier in near perfect French. Slowly, the company showed signs of progress. Everyone, even Wall Street, began to have hope.

He and Olivia were married soon after their divorces were final. For the first time in years, Waddington found there were no eggs to walk on.

Charlie, of course, did not get the house. He moved to New York and took an apartment on the Upper East Side with Emma Rae who, one day, disappeared with the building's super and never returned. After six months working with headhunters, his efforts were rewarded with the top job at Xerox. It took less than two months for him to drive the stock down twenty-five percent.

Muffy refused to speak to Waddington after she learned that he was going to marry Olivia. Her only communication was passed through her lawyers. Adrift and at a loss, having no idea of what to do with herself, Muffy took over the management of her father's dealership. It proved to be her calling. She immediately fired all the sales*men* and replaced them with attractive, aggressive, retail-wise sales*women*. The dealership immediately showed the best monthly sales increases in twenty years.

Hildy developed a real affection for Olivia and, over Muffy and Petula's objections, made increasingly frequent visits to Grosse Pointe.

It took some time, but eventually the police identified Petula's Bentley as the hit-and-run vehicle. Petula hired a Johnnie Cochran wannabe who worked hard to convince the jury that, in part, Jack's death was the Bentley's fault. A clear case of unintended acceleration redux. As far as Petula's culpability, the wannabe called several psychiatrists to the stand whose expert testimony was that Jack Poor's infidelity and sudden departure had result in temporary insanity, making it impossible for her to be responsible for her actions. The jury bought the part about the Bentley and took the temporary insanity claim under consideration. Petula spent one year in the cell recently vacated by Martha Stewart.

Popper was terminated from the company, of course, but the board decided not to press charges to avoid the publicity. Within three months after his release from the hospital, Popper had reinvented himself again and turned up in San

Diego as the marketing VP for an Amway-like MLM sales company.

At first, Waddington was uncomfortable moving into what he had regarded as Charlie's Grosse Pointe Versailles. But Olivia reminded him–more than once–that it was her house and that she would carefully remove every last vestige of anything that reminded either of them of Charlie– with the exception of the wine collection. Out went Monique, the last of the French truffles. Flaubert, who was known to dislike Charlie immensely, was kept on. Other than his clothes and some personal effects, there was little that Charlie had contributed to the house.

It was shortly after they returned from their brief honeymoon at the Villa d'Este at Lake Como, that Waddington became aware that people in Grosse Pointe had begun to look upon him as the heir apparent to Perkins. People who had totally ignored the man in the mud-brown suit but a year earlier now came to the Grosse Pointe Versailles to drink his wine, eat his canapés, and pay homage.

But unlike Charlie, who had made every party an opportunity to hold court and bestow supplicants with his opinions, wisdom, and bad jokes, Waddington was far more reserved. He shed compliments like water off a duck. He refused to take the overly zealous compliments seriously. Often, he was seen fetching drinks for his guests and acting more like a middle-class host than the consort of a Grosse Pointe scion. In private, he played Chopin on her Bosendorfer and remained what he had always been. For that, Olivia loved him.

Only once, just before their first anniversary, did Olivia find it necessary to put chocks on the wheels of Waddington's ego. They had hosted a party at their house, and Waddington had drunk too much champagne on a near empty stomach. It had gone to his head and given him a great sense of omnipotence. He, Preston Olivier Waddington, had fulfilled his mother's dream. At last, his weighty name mirrored his position in life. He felt an almost giddy sense of superiority as he and Olivia bid their last guest good night. Olivia immediately recognized this aberrant behavior as having leaped from a bottle and muddled her pragmatic, down-to-earth husband's mind.

"You know," he said to Olivia as they walked into the grand salon, gilded with fine art and resplendent in its reflection of Olivia's taste, "sometimes when I'm in this room I feel just like King Louis."

Olivia looked at him in askance. She was not about to let the opulence of their surroundings or the servility of would-be petitioners infect him with the haughtiness that had pervaded the ego of her former husband. His bubble needed deflating. "Which Louis?" she asked. "Fourteen, Fifteen, or Sixteen?"

Without consulting his knowledge of French history, he let the champagne answer for him, "I don't know. Maybe Louis the Sixteenth."

"You might want to rethink that. Sixteen is not a good choice," she said, taking his arm and pointing him toward the staircase.

Waddington remembered why before she told him.

"They chopped off his head."